THE
HOUNDS
OF
ROME

Mystery of a Fugitive Priest

To Caroline

◆

With Love,

TOM
CLANCY

Grandpa Tom

"The Hounds of Rome — Mystery of a Fugitive Priest," by Tom Clancy. ISBN 978-1-62137-396-4 (softcover); 978-1-62137-397-1 (electronic copy).

Cover art by Rex Poole

To LaRee

ACKNOWLEDGEMENTS

I firmly believe that no book can be produced in a vacuum. Not only does it take the ability of the writer to outline a plot and set down the words, but the life experiences of others to provide valuable inputs, suggestions and corrections.

LaRee Simon, a Diplomate clinical social worker, read the draft manuscript several times and reviewed the psycho-social behaviors appropriate for the characters in the situations they encountered in the story.

Barbara Rule, fellow author, proofed the manuscript and offered wise counsel and encouragement.

Three of my daughters provided invaluable contributions to the project:

Carolyn Clancy, a poet and author in her own right, edited the manuscript and helped develop a critical aspect of the plot.

Susan Clancy, President of Rex Media, working with the publisher, produced the final camera-ready copy.

Madelyn Rygg, associate editor of a national publication, reviewed the manuscript in detail and by means of questions, comments and suggestions, greatly improved the manuscript.

My thanks and gratitude go to all who participated in this undertaking.

PROLOGUE

This is a work of fiction. The setting is at a time in the near future. The persons and events depicted are fictitious. The only exceptions are principally historic religious figures, such as the fairly recent popes: John XIII, Paul VI, John Paul I, John Paul II, Benedict XVI and Francis. The pope who appears in this story is an unnamed future pontiff.

The Second Vatican Council (Vatican II) was instituted by Pope John XXIII, who, in the early 1960s, said he wanted to open the windows of the church and let in some fresh air. A major change in the liturgy resulted: the virtual elimination of the Latin Mass, referred to as the Tridentine Mass, that had been the worldwide standard for millennia. The revised liturgy was then performed in local languages, on occasion with guitar rather than organ music, and a decidedly more social atmosphere. Lay men and women were permitted to serve on the altar and some were even permitted to distribute the Holy Eucharist. Later popes, however, by encyclical letters, pressed for a return to the more traditional aspects of the church. Pope Benedict XVI has encouraged bishops to return to the traditional Tridentine Mass.

The Passion Brothers Monastery in Arizona is fictional as are the Knights of Carthage in Rome. Both represent dogged religious zealots referred to in the story as the '*Hounds of Rome*'.

The San Callisto Catacombs (in English – the Saint Callistus Catacombs) are located south of Rome on the Via Appia Antica – the ancient Roman Appian Way.

Some of the action in the story takes place in the catacombs involving a fictional pack of marauding wild dogs. The San Callisto are the largest of the catacombs, stretching almost fifteen miles under Rome. In some areas the catacombs are five levels deep; they have not been completely explored; therefore, it may be possible to fall unexpectedly into deep crevasses. Although in actuality packs of marauding animals have never been discovered, it is possible that some have gained entry seeking shelter and food.

Visitors to the catacombs will find the environment completely safe as long as they closely follow a guide as they proceed along well-trodden passageways.

The *'Hounds of Rome'* plays out against some of the ethical and moral issues that are likely to become important to religious organizations in the twenty-first century. The issues may in particular affect highly organized churches like the Roman Catholic Church as well as other Christian churches and non-Christian religions that have evolved longstanding traditional theology and doctrine. These serious issues and their resulting complications arise from the revolutionary biological technology under development that raises questions about the fundamental nature of humanity and its relationship to God.

Across the horizons of the world I fled

Pursued by The Hounds of Rome

Reverend Steve Murphy, Diocesan Catholic Priest

1

His eminence, John Cardinal Wollman, Archbishop of Washington, a prince of the Roman Catholic Church, was angry. Seated at a large ornate desk in his spacious office in the Washington chancery, he tried in vain to suppress an anger that he knew was killing him. The cardinal, florid of face, heavyset, balding with the remains of a white fringe ringing the back of his head, suffered from a host of health problems not the least of which was failing short-term memory. As time passed, it made reliance on his principal auxiliary bishop, Phillip Rhinehart, more and more necessary.

A full ten minutes had elapsed since Phillip Rhinehart had been summoned. The cardinal suspected that, as usual, Bishop Rhinehart was taking his sweet time before coming in from his adjoining office. The cardinal knew it would be the same worn excuse: tied up on the phone in an important matter. One might think that meeting with his superior wasn't important. It was another example of Rhinehart's tactics to remind the cardinal who was nearing seventy-nine that he had an excellent chance of either being forcibly retired to one of the church's assisted living facilities or of dropping dead—whichever came first.

Cardinal Wollman was well aware that the end of his exalted position as a luminary of the church, was drawing near. Knowing this to be the will of God, he tried to accept it. But late at night, sitting at his desk in the dark, he was despondent and frightened. In fact, he remembered one night when he was so depressed he actually saw the Angel of the Lord seated cross-legged on the corner of the desk...waiting. It was all just a matter of time.

The cardinal reminded himself that Rhinehart had not been of his choosing. When his hand-picked principal auxiliary had retired five years before, of the four auxiliary bishops in the archdiocese he had found himself presented—saddled? with Bishop Rhinehart by those in Rome who believed that the American Catholic Church had become too liberal. Even the pontiff himself had spoken with admiration of "...our beloved brother, Phillip Rhinehart, who has struggled mightily to keep alive the church's traditional moral values in an America that sometimes seemed to forget... to go astray." But although he had found it onerous much of the time, the cardinal had tried to make the best of it. Unlike himself, Rhinehart acted more like the dictator of a small suppressed country rather than a good shepherd tending the flock of the archdiocese.

Over five long years with almost daily pacing back and forth in front of the cardinal's desk by his restless auxiliary bishop, Cardinal Wollman had come to know every facet of Phillip Rhinehart's opinionated thinking. To stop the pacing, he often had to say, "For heaven's sake, Phillip, you're making me nervous. Sit down, or if you must pace, do it in your own office."

The cardinal had heard it so many times before. Each of the pronouncements was as worn as the beads on his rosary. His auxiliary bishop made no secret of the fact that he was a strict doctrinaire, convinced that the Second Vatican Council—Vatican II, had been an unmitigated disaster by opening the floodgates to all manner of dissent. He deplored the Catholic Church's departure from the Latin Mass, abhorred the presence of women on the altar even in the minor role of altar girls, and denounced parishioners who, after Vatican II, thought erroneously that pre-marital sex and birth control were only venial sins—minor disorders too trivial to bother confessing. Auxiliary Bishop Rhinehart held that Vatican II set the stage for immense difficulties for the popes who followed John XXIII, not only because of the rules it loosened but also because of the rules people thought it had loosened when in fact, that was not the case. The first pope who was destined to live with the backlash against Vatican II was Pope John Paul I who died only 33 days after he was elected pontiff. Apparently the Holy Spirit took the poor soul to spare him the anguish of dealing with the turmoil in the church—turmoil the sick man was ill-equipped to handle.

Yes, the cardinal had heard it all; so many times in fact that it was like a ringing in his ears. He could quote Bishop Rhinehart from memory. According to his auxiliary who often said bitterly: "Wasn't it within one year after Vatican II that priests began clamoring for the right to marry and then began wholesale defections when they found they could not? Didn't an astonishing ten-thousand priests request of the Holy See permission to renounce their vows and leave the priesthood? And what of the laity who, in the years following Vatican II, misperceived that the church's firm stand against divorce and remarriage would soon be relaxed? Would all of these, laity and clergy, remain practicing Catholics or join the millions who would be Catholics in name only?"

Cardinal Wollman, having heard these diatribes over and over from his auxiliary, learned after a time to listen quietly without saying anything. He knew that if he raised counter-arguments—reflecting a somewhat more liberal approach, the debate could go on forever. Arguments with Rhinehart always brought a flush of scarlet to the sagging jowls of the cardinal's face, a quickened heartbeat, the flatiron pain of angina, and most certainly a surge in his already high blood pressure. As the years had gone by and his memory had begun to fail, he found arguments increasingly difficult to win. In an attempt to maintain some semblance of control, he made some decisions in an impromptu fashion—some right and some perhaps wrong, avoiding argument by simply exercising his authority—all to the utter disgust of his subordinate. But perhaps more important to the cardinal than his ebbing competence, was his subordinate's increasing arrogance directed towards the lower clergy and the laity of the archdiocese. Administering at the auxiliary bishop level, Bishop Rhinehart displayed a supercilious cold-heartedness that terrorized those beneath him.

As he leaned back in his reclining chair and fingered the crucifix perched on his ample stomach, waiting for his auxiliary to appear, the cardinal said a silent prayer to subdue his irritation.

A figure appeared at the open door—tall, thin, ramrod straight, iron gray hair cut flat brush-like short and pressed down on the tonsure by a small skullcap.

Deep-set eyes and a beaklike nose gave the impression of a bird of prey. Bishop Rhinehart used the bent knuckle of his index finger for a formal, polite tap on the cardinal's door to gain the attention of his superior who was seated head down, presumably concentrating on the papers on his desk. "Come in, Phillip."

"Good morning, Your Eminence."

"Phillip, I wanted to talk to you about this reverend... aah, yes, Reverend Murphy business. Are you familiar with the details?"

"Yes, I've been following the case very closely, and if you recall, I was the one who originally brought it to your attention."

Another example of the cardinal's failing memory, Rhinehart thought as he took a seat facing the cardinal's desk. "The Murphy case presents a dangerous situation, potentially a huge embarrassment to the archdiocese and Holy Mother Church."

"I'm aware of that," the cardinal snapped. "The question is what do we do about it?"

"Why, transfer him of course."

"Where?"

"The Passion Brothers Monastery in the Sonora Desert outside of Tucson comes to mind. After he gets a taste of it, Murphy will likely resign the priesthood and request a dispensation of his vows. It could all be handled quietly. We might actually avoid a massive revolt in the archdiocese."

"Aren't you exaggerating?"

"I think not."

"The Passion Monastery? That godforsaken place? One of the priests we sent to the monastery died there last year."

"The year before last."

"I understand it was under suspicious circumstances."

"That is only a rumor. My understanding was that it was an accident."

"But regarding Reverend Murphy, you may recall that he has been in the diocese for many years and pastor of Holy Rosary Church for...aah...how long has it been?"

"Eight years."

"Oh yes, eight years. He has only to put the finishing touches on a grand new church for his parish. You may not be aware of it, but he single-handedly raised all the funding for the new church. The archdiocese wasn't asked to contribute so much as a dollar. In fact, until this new information, I was getting ready to elevate him to Monsignor."

"Murphy, a Monsignor? Your Eminence, permit me to remind you of a few things you may have forgotten. The archdiocese contributed forty percent of the funding for Holy Rosary's new church. You are confusing Holy Rosary with Holy Comforter Church, and you may recall, I raised stringent objections to the architecture Murphy decided on for the new church. Catholic churches should be designed in traditional fashion: a long nave symbolizing the upright shaft of Christ's Cross; a nave that also offers a main aisle suitable for solemn processions at High Mass; in addition, a transept symbolizing the outstretched arms of Christ on the Cross...not these modern multi-colored ornate round glass bubbles that have no religious significance. Think of it. In such churches, you have to pray the Stations of the Cross in the round. Ridiculous! When Jesus walked the Via Dolorosa to his crucifixion on Mount Calvary, he walked in a straight line, not round and round like a carousel in an amusement park. He walked straight to his death. And I know I've mentioned this before but a Catholic Church should be built of solid stone designed to last thousands of years—following the tradition of the medieval Gothic churches and cathedrals. You are close to God in such a building, immersed in a dark interior lighted only by stained glass windows depicting events in the life of the Lord, the Blessed Virgin and the saints."

The cardinal uttered a weary sigh. He was being treated again to an all-too familiar lecture on the architecture of ancient and modern churches.

"And as to the elevation of Father Murphy, although it might have seemed appropriate based on his long tenure, now of course, I think it is out of the question."

"Yes, I suppose so," the cardinal said with resignation. "It is unfortunate based on his background. You may remember that he spent several years at the Pontifical Gregorian University in Rome. In fact, he was later offered a prestigious position in Vatican service but decided to return to America to perform diocesan work in a parish in our diocese."

"What you tell me about the offer of Vatican service makes it all the worse," Bishop Rhinehart commented.

"Phillip, based on the latest information, I am forced to agree with you."

The cardinal was embarrassed about his ill-fated plan to elevate Murphy. "We might of course ask Murphy to resign the priesthood."

"He won't do that," Bishop Rhinehart said with an air of finality. "I know the type. He won't request to be released from his vows. We might defrock him if it could be done quietly, but Your Eminence well knows that the first thing a defrocked priest does is seek a lawyer and redress through the courts."

"Naturally. They are deprived of a chosen career, not to mention the income and a comfortable retirement."

"I believe we should get Murphy out of the way and the isolated Passion Monastery is the place. After a few months there, he'll resign willingly." The auxiliary bishop shifted uncomfortably in his chair. He was growing tired of the discussion about this one priest when he had a million other things to attend to. In making decisions, the principal auxiliary bishop of Washington never permitted himself to be swayed by emotions. The good of the church had to rise above any other consideration. And characteristically, in this case he had no feelings for the individual involved and deplored the soft-hearted stance the cardinal seemed to be taking despite the risk of tremendous embarrassment to the church. "Without prompt and appropriate action, the church will be harmed," Bishop Rhinehart said finally in a determined whisper that had more force than a shout as he leaned forward in his chair to press home his point. "Your Eminence, information like that on Stephen Murphy always has a way of leaking out."

"The church has survived supposedly great harm in the past and has lived through what you refer to as embarrassment," Cardinal Wollman said in rebuttal, leaning back in his leather swivel chair and folding his arms as he realized he was on the doorstep of another disagreement with his auxiliary. "Look at the business of the Austrian cardinal who sided with Hitler in the early days of World War II. The church survived that. And that whole Galileo business. It took the church four hundred years to admit that Galileo was right. Many people laughed, of course, but the church has overcome it and moved on. Phillip, I don't think you fully appreciate the resiliency of the church."

"Perhaps not, but the Galileo thing is ancient history as is the story of that Austrian cardinal. Who really cares about the position taken by a churchman years ago in the time of Hitler and since repudiated? And with all due respect, let me remind you that Pope John Paul II did not say Galileo was correct. He simply said that there had been a miscommunication between Galileo and the church."

"Well, Phillip, I feel I must disagree with you again concerning the danger of Murphy's case coming to light," the cardinal said. Then standing up with a great deal of effort he slowly walked towards the door intending to usher his auxiliary out of his office. "We must take action, but we must also act with Christian charity. And we must give some consideration to the long service Murphy has provided to the church. My decision then is to move Murphy to Catholic University in a temporary teaching position."

"But you would be removing him from a ministry only to assign him to a position where he would be expounding church doctrine and theology to students? It doesn't make sense."

"I recognize your objection. But we can see to it that he is assigned to teaching duties of a secular nature. I believe we should tackle this problem in easy stages. And before I take any further action, I would want to contact the Vatican for an opinion."

"Your Eminence, please consider for a moment a worst case scenario. The old woman talked. Eventually, Murphy will find this out, and it may be that he knows it already, but in his obstinacy he would refuse to resign. Defrocking him would raise questions and the entire situation would become known. We can't let that happen. Thus, if it were my decision, I would transfer him faraway. Besides, there are other issues."

"Such as...."

"There have been allegations of misconduct. The sexton of Holy Rosary Church for one."

"Phillip, in my many years in the church I have heard numerous allegations and complaints. Some have been substantiated and in those cases I have taken appropriate action, but in the Murphy case, the sexton you mentioned was dismissed for embezzlement."

The cardinal, pleased with himself for remembering the details of the case, went on. "And you must admit that some complaints are ridiculous. I remember the case of the father who complained because Murphy called three strikes against the man's son while acting as umpire in a softball game. He said Murphy was biased against his son. However half-a-dozen other witnesses agreed that the calls were correct."

With his usual dogged persistence, the auxiliary said, "But you surely see that in this case, if Murphy was transferred to the isolated Passion Monastery, it would preclude any further action on our part? Problem solved. We'd simply hand him over to the Tucson diocese, with proper funding of course, and then be rid of him."

"My dear Bishop," the cardinal said, with growing impatience, addressing his subordinate with an attempt at formality, "at this point we are not sending him to that godforsaken outpost."

"What if he requests a hearing when he is transferred from Holy Rosary to Catholic University? Do we grant him one? Being right here in Washington, he could become a pest."

"I think not. He will do as he is told without question. Need I remind you, Bishop Rhinehart," the cardinal said formally, "that Murphy has taken a vow of obedience and hasn't to my knowledge ever broken that vow?"

"One never knows that the vow of obedience will be observed until it is tested."

"Then this transfer without explanation will serve as the test. I will assume any risk. Bishop Rhinehart, will you for once, just once, follow my instructions? You might think of it as observing your own vow of obedience."

"It will be carried out just as you wish, Your Eminence."

2

Father Steve Murphy hurried down the long corridor of the rectory with a sidelong glance at the line of photographs of former pastors of Holy Rosary Church that lined the wall. He gazed momentarily at the empty space reserved for his picture. He had only been pastor for eight years, so it might be a long time before his black-framed face hung on the wall with the rest. The priest turned left into his office and slipped into the big comfortable leather chair behind his desk. He wheeled around to the PC at his workstation and signed in. He usually smiled when he put in his password—priest. Not very creative he thought, but after all, he wasn't protecting state secrets. Twenty-two e-mails. He read the one from his brother, Jonathon, in Wayland a suburb of Boston. It was not a cheerful message. Jonathon had been having difficulty swallowing with a tentative diagnosis of early-stage Lou Gehrig's disease.

The priest sat back in his chair, softly felt his throat with his fingertips and tried swallowing nervously a few times. Still OK. Their father had died of the disease and Father Murphy was beginning to believe it was hereditary. He knew there was no cure. Jonathon was sixty-six, eighteen years older than him. It went without saying that he felt badly for his brother, but in his gut he had a more primordial fear for himself. Maybe prayers would help. But Father Steve Murphy didn't think prayers worked that way. He was a fatalist and although he loved God deeply, he didn't believe in modern-day miracles. He doubted that God interceded in cases like this.

Ignoring the rest of the e-mails, he turned to face the stack of mail arranged neatly on his desk by the church secretary. He saw it on top of the pile—the letter from the archdiocese. He nervously sliced open the envelope.

Hearing a slight rustling sound, he glanced up and saw Father Davis standing in the doorway. "That could be it, Steve," Father Davis said as he glanced at the envelope with a congratulatory smile. "The archdiocese has finally recognized your talents. Looks like you'll soon have the title of Right Reverend Monsignor."

Steve smiled back. "Maybe," he said, "but with Bishop Rhinehart, as second in command, you never know."

He opened the letter. He glanced at the opening paragraph. At the bottom he saw that the letter was signed by Bishop Rhinehart. A sudden stabbing pain ran through his gut. He dropped the letter on the desk. Then he picked it up again and held it out. "Here, John, read it." He reached into his lower desk drawer for a cigarette. "Forgive me for lighting up in a smokeless rectory. But since it looks like I'll be leaving, let's just say I'm having one for the road."

"Leaving? Incredible. But you're right. The letter says you're being transferred with only three days to pack up and go. You're being transferred to a house of studies...the Dominican House? It doesn't make sense. You're not in an order, you're a diocesan priest. On top of that, your record here has been excellent.

I don't want to seem nosy, but have there been any complaints?"

"If there were, I've never heard them."

"Why would the cardinal let Rhinehart do this?"

"Everyone knows the cardinal is aging and in poor health. He lets Rhinehart make almost all of the decisions."

"But Steve, the cardinal must know the parish is in the final phase of the building program. You raised the money, worked with the architects and builders. Who could jump in at this point?"

Father Murphy looked over at the figure in the black cassock with the starched white Roman collar, who had just slumped into a chair near his desk. "You, John," he said, nervously tapping cigarette ash into an empty styrofoam coffee cup. "I suppose you'll have to take over. You've been assistant pastor, so who else?"

"Maybe they'll assign another priest here."

"Perhaps, but didn't you see Bishop Rhinehart's attempt at an explanation at the end of the letter about the archdiocese having to cut back? Frankly, what the devil does 'cut back' mean?"

Father Davis used the letter to wave away some of the cigarette smoke that had drifted in his direction. "Could it be finances?" he asked. "Parish finances are in pretty good shape, and with the great influx of middle class Hispanics into the Washington area, the coffers of the archdiocese must be overflowing."

"I doubt that it's money and I'll bet it has nothing to do with the shortage of priests, because if it were, he'd be transferring one of us to a parish that was badly understaffed...not to a house of studies. There must be something else going on. The thought crosses my mind that he might be punishing the parish, and me, in particular, for building a modern church rather than a traditional Gothic monstrosity."

"But I still don't get it, Steve. I just don't get it. Out of the blue. No warning. No real explanation. I might believe it if the parish finances were in bad shape, but they aren't. And look at the school—just about on budget; top marks on standardized tests! I knew Rhinehart was a pain in the butt. I never thought he was this callous. Can't you appeal it?"

"Oh come on John, that pompous ass sits down there at the right hand of the cardinal like Jesus at the right hand of God the Father. Only it's terribly sacrilegious of me to compare him to Jesus. More like the serpent under the Virgin's foot. And if I did appeal directly to the cardinal, it would bounce right down to Rhinehart. I don't think the cardinal gets involved at that level. On top of that, we both know that an appeal borders on breaking the vow of obedience."

"What do we tell the congregation? They've been making plans to celebrate your elevation for months."

"I know this sounds sour, but I didn't see any mention of becoming Right Reverend in the letter. It's a transfer, that's all. And I don't know how we'll explain it to the parishioners. I can't explain it to myself. As Rhinehart said in the letter, I'm being sent to the Dominican House of Studies—it's right across the street from Catholic University. The letter says 'temporarily'. One puzzling aspect," Steve added with a smirk, "is how the archdiocese convinced the prior of the Dominican House to agree to take me in when I'm not a Dominican."

"What will you do there? It's a retreat house isn't it?"

"It's run by the Order of Saint Dominic. Ancient order. Mendicant friars, vows of poverty and God knows what else. Frankly, I don't know what I'll do there. But I do know I'm not spending the rest of my life wearing sackcloth and ashes. I did hear once that some of the orders located at the university provide teachers. Who knows, I may become a professor—pro-temp, that is."

"Steve, that's an idea. Why don't we tell the parishioners you've had a long-range goal to be on the faculty at C.U. and the opportunity finally came along? Of course, they're still going to feel you're abandoning them."

Father Murphy shrugged his shoulders at the suggestion. "Why not?" he said. "Not a bad idea. It avoids having to explain something that can't be explained." He nervously lit another cigarette from the lit end of the first one.

As Father Davis left, Steve Murphy got up and went to the window. He could see the new church nearing completion. He felt sick as he realized he would never participate in the dedication. He might be invited back for the ceremony, but someone else would assist the cardinal in the dedication.

It was growing late in the day. The new church loomed as a large round dark blue glass silhouette against the setting sun. Here and there a few weak rays of sunlight filtered through the glass. He glanced to the side. He could dimly see his reflection in the partially open side casement window. If the story of his happily going off to fulfill the dream of university teaching was to be believed, he would have to brighten up that glum look. He ran his hand under his chin. He needed a shave. As he studied his image in the side window, he bent his head and examined the tousled black hair on top. He turned his face to check out the slightly graying sideburns at the temples. Dark emerging stubble below. He always shaved twice a day. He had no choice. Maybe as a college professor he could grow a beard, if in fact, the transfer to the Dominican House turned out to be a teaching job. He wasn't happy that the transfer letter made no mention of his new duties, but considering the way Bishop Rhinehart usually operated, it wasn't a surprise.

As he looked at his reflection in the window, the priest stroked an imaginary beard. He hadn't been on a campus in years. Did today's professors wear beards? He saw a twisted grin reflected in the glass. He uttered a mirthless laugh. With his tendency to heavy hair growth, with a full beard, he'd soon look more like an Orthodox Jew than a Catholic priest.

A thought came to him—one born of years of absolute trust in God and the church. Maybe things would turn out OK. Maybe a new assignment could provide relief from the heavy stress he had been under for a long time. It could turn out to be a spiritual renewal after years spent running a parish church and school, and building a new church on top of that. His latest year had consisted of a continuous round of fund-raising, studying blueprints, arguing with architects and builders, and paying bills. There had been little time for reflection, meditation, prayer.

But as Steve Murphy stood at the window, suddenly the shock came back. He winced at the sickening pain in the pit of his stomach. There was something he could only describe as sinister going on. Temporary transfer. What does that mean? After all the years of his service to the church, why should he settle for that? But he knew he had poor choices—he could follow orders and go or he could resign. It was that simple. He wondered for the first time in his life what place there really was for him in the church. Had God forgotten him?

Nothing could compensate for the double blow of being passed over for Monsignor and losing his parish at the same time. He thought of all the unfinished work. Someone else would finish it. Someone else would get the credit. He resented that. He didn't hunger for credit, but he didn't like it stolen from him either.

Another glance in the glass at the narrowed eyes and tight-drawn lips told him his initial shock at the transfer was slowly being supplanted by new emotions: rising anger and a feeling of hopelessness.

*****

Gym bag in hand, Father Murphy crossed the courtyard and entered the school. Saturday afternoon. Pickup basketball game going on as usual. "Hiya, Father." "Hiya, Father."

"Keep on with your game, boys. I just came over to lift some weights." In the locker room he changed into gym clothes in a small separate room reserved for the priests of the parish.

Over in a corner of the gym, he slid weights onto a

barbell. He was tall. Rugged build. Thought of himself as wiry. Strong, but certainly not a muscle man. Not a body builder. He knew cigarettes and exercise were a contradictory mix and he was usually able to keep it down to an occasional cigarette—unless he was under stress.

He worked out because it made him feel good. He liked the heft of the weights. He liked pulling against something and having it resist. He found he could always work off some stress. Today he had a lot to work off. He locked the weights onto the barbell, but as he lifted it on his fifth rep he carelessly let the weighted bar down too hard. A loud clank echoed through the gym. Embarrassed, he waved at the boys who had stopped their game in surprise.

"Just a slip, boys. Just a bit careless."

After his workout, the priest noticed that the basketball game was one-sided. "Need another player?" he asked.

"Sure, Father. You can be on the side of Timmy and the other altar boys."

An hour later, the priest sat on one of the benches surrounded by the group of boys. "There's something I have to tell you guys. I'm leaving Holy Rosary. I'm being transferred to Catholic U. to do some teaching."

This announcement was followed by groans. "Don't you like it here?" Timmy asked.

"Yes, of course I do. But being a priest is like being in the army. You get an order and you have to follow it."

"Will the new pastor take us to baseball and football games?"

"When I find out who it is, I'll speak to him about it.

Until then, Father Davis will take over. As you know, he tagged along wherever we went, so I'm sure he'll keep taking you."

"We'll miss you Father," the boys said almost in unison.

"And I'll miss you," Father Murphy said with glistening eyes that he covered up by wiping a handkerchief over the sweat on his brow.

*****

As Father Murphy walked back to the rectory, he thought of a day several months before. He had been in the sacristy, ready to begin morning Mass. He had been following the usual preparation. He had slipped on and smoothed down the long white alb. Tightened the cincture around his waist. Kissed the stole, slipped it on. Kissed the chasuble, slipped it over his head. Then suddenly, Timmy, his regular altar boy, had rushed into the sacristy crying with a bloody nose. The boy had fallen on his face rushing to the church. In the sacristy, holding the boy's head back, and pressing his nostril closed, he had managed to stem the flow of blood. Then to console the boy, he put his arm around him, pressed him close. He remembered it was at that precise moment that the sexton had walked into the sacristy. The sexton had a surprised look on his face.

"Oh, did I come in at the wrong time?" he had asked with a sly grin.

Father Murphy had tried to explain but he knew it sounded lame. It was really nothing. Just a friendly gesture to comfort the boy. Why make anything of it? But he and the sexton had never gotten along. Several run-ins over church supplies had never been resolved. He thought the sexton might have been skimming off the top. He eventually had to remove the sexton and explain the situation to Bishop Rhinehart when an audit of parish finances concluded that the sexton was a thief. He wondered whether the abrupt transfer had anything to do with the earlier incident with the altar boy. To get even, had the sexton made a complaint to the archdiocese? The church was so beleaguered by reports of pedophile priests, Steve Murphy didn't kid himself—even a spurious complaint could cause trouble.

3

Father Murphy pulled his car up in front of the Dominican House on Michigan Avenue, directly across from the Catholic University campus. The House had no reserved street parking and no parking lot. The Dominicans took a vow of poverty. No private autos, hence no parking lot. He finally parked on a side street two blocks away, and trudged with some of his belongings to the front entrance. Inside, it was dark, musty smelling. He blessed himself at the holy water font just inside the door. The only sound came from the floorboards that creaked as he walked through the hallway of the ancient building. Cracked oil paintings of what he assumed were dead former Dominican Priors in yellowed ivory robes stared down at him. They had oil paintings, he noticed, unlike Holy Rosary where they were content with simple photos in cheap black frames. The vow of poverty doesn't extend to the paintings, he thought wryly. With a twinge, he recalled the empty space back at the parish that would soon hold his own photograph. "I may be gone," he muttered with a set jaw, "but at least I'm not dead."

"Welcome, Father. I assume you are Father Murphy. Has someone died? I thought I heard you say something about the dead."

"No, I was just thinking out loud."

"I am Friar Joseph, prior of the Dominican House." The speaker, in a light cream-colored habit, elderly, thinning gray hair, had come out of a side office. "I'll show you to your room. You have a cheerful room overlooking the campus. Nothing fancy, however. Sorry, no elevator, you'll have to walk up three flights." Every step creaked as the old friar, breathing heavily, reached the third floor, followed by the priest. Bending over to peer out of the window of the small, sparsely furnished room, the friar said, "You can just barely see the bell tower of the Shrine from here. You'll be able to hear the bells from the Shrine. They ring every fifteen minutes. Around here, you don't need a watch which is helpful because we have a vow of poverty. We have no adornments."

"You mean you don't even wear wristwatches?"

"No."

"And of course, no cell phones."

"No."

"Tell me," Murphy asked, "where can I park my car? I brought my car. I want to keep it somewhere around here. I didn't take any vows involving watches, cell phones or automobiles," he added with a smirk.

Friar Joseph gave him a quick uncertain glance. "I believe that as a member of the university teaching staff, you'll be able to park in the faculty lot on the campus. Of course, you'll have to pay for it, and I understand it's quite expensive."

The comment by Friar Joseph about being a member of the teaching staff was the first real indication Father Murphy received of any plans his superiors had for his future.

"We have laundry tubs in the basement. We each do our own. Our off-white habits are difficult to keep clean but are washable. We do it all by hand. We offer up the chore as a furtherance of an eternal reward."

"Very commendable," Father Murphy said, all the while thinking there were better ways priests could help mankind and please God than by doing laundry.

"Your starched Roman collar and your other raiment will need professional cleaning from time to time. It's just a short walk up to Brookland where I am sure you can find a cleaning establishment. We take meals at 7 A.M., Noon and 6 P.M. In order to be served, you must arrive promptly. Of course, since you receive a monthly stipend, you'll be able to take some or all of your meals elsewhere if you like. The Shrine has a good cafeteria, so I have heard. And a well-stocked religious articles store."

"That's something I never quite understood," Father Murphy said, seemingly itching for an argument—suspicious that this friar was either trying too hard to please Bishop Rhinehart, or perhaps intimidated by the bishop. "Maybe you can explain it. The National Shrine has a gift shop and cafeteria. I thought Christ chased the money changers from the temple." A slight forced smile crossed his face.

"I'm surprised you do not know the situation," the friar said, parrying the priest's thrust. "There's something you obviously are not aware of, Father. The Shrine church itself begins at the front door. The gift shop and cafeteria are under the long flight of stone steps in front—thus not part of the church."

*****

Later that day, Father Murphy sat in the prior's

office. Friar Joseph leaned back in his chair trying to get the measure of the priest. "No, I do not know why you were sent here. All I know is that I received a call from Bishop Rhinehart. He asked if you could be housed here temporarily. Since you are a diocesan priest and not a member of the Order of St. Dominic, you understand I am doing this solely as a favor to the bishop."

"I noted the mention of temporary in his letter to me. What do you think it means?"

"I really don't know and when I put the same question to the bishop, he did not give me an answer. Perhaps he doesn't know himself. The only clue I have came when I told him the university has a few positions of Lecturer open."

"You said that gave you a clue. I don't understand. What conclusion can you draw from that?"

"Since Lecturer appointments are made by semester, if appointed, I conclude you would be here for at least four to five months. After that, you might even be reappointed."

Father Murphy's expression began to soften. It wasn't much to go on but at least he would be able to see some months down the road. "Am I to have a faculty position?" he asked.

"Not as a Lecturer. It's tantamount to a part-time teaching position. Without a PhD it's difficult to attain official faculty status. My understanding is the Language Department needs someone to teach a course in Latin and there is a course opening in the Department of Religious Studies. The latter has to do with world religions with some emphasis on the

Ecumenical Movement. These are on a fill-in basis. You appear to be well qualified, so I would think you would be offered an appointment, especially since you come on Bishop Rhinehart's recommendation."

"Forgive me," Father Murphy said, straightening up in his chair, a grimace on his face. "I would have thought that with my pastoral background I would be teaching something like Catholic marriage, or the church's guidance for raising a Catholic family. Something along those lines. The courses you mention have no pastoral content. They're secular courses."

"Kindly remember that I am only providing housing for you. Your appointment will be made by the university departments involved. But I do understand that Bishop Rhinehart informed the university he wanted you to be assigned to teach only secular courses."

"Did the bishop tell anyone that I spent four years studying at the Gregorian University in Rome?"

"I suppose he did. And that's why you will probably wind up teaching Latin. Since I understand that many of the programs you had were conducted in Latin, you are obviously proficient in the language."

"True, but from a practical standpoint it is a dead language. The principal reason for teaching in Latin in some Roman universities attached to the Vatican is that it provides a common language for the clerics who come from all over the world. It's obvious that the Vatican colleges can't be expected to teach courses in every language from Dutch to Swahili." Father Murphy shifted uneasily in his chair. "I wonder if there are really any students interested in learning Latin these days? Even from a religious standpoint, the worldwide church liturgy has almost completely changed to local languages. Since Vatican II, the Latin Mass has become as extinct as the dinosaurs."

"What you say is not completely true. I'm sure you are aware that a few parishes right here in Washington still offer the Latin Mass because some people want it. The Latin Mass has not been completely discontinued by the Vatican. And you are probably aware that with the Vatican's approval, Bishop Rhinehart has recently encouraged pastors to return to the traditional Tridentine—Latin Mass."

"Yes, I've heard that. And along with his other objections to any attempts to modernize the church, he appears to be trying to turn the clock back a thousand years."

With growing restlessness, the priest felt in his pocket for a cigarette then changed his mind.

The friar narrowed his eyes as he leaned forward in his chair, elbows propped on the desk, hands clasped under his chin. "Father Murphy, I can tell you're upset. Let me give you a word of advice. Two meetings have been set up for you at the university. The first is with Sister Francine, Chair of Foreign Languages; the second is with Doctor Stanton, Chair of the Department of Religious Studies. Things will go much better for you here in the Dominican House and at the university if you will take the chip off your shoulder and do the best you can to follow Bishop Rhinehart's plan for you. Now, if you will excuse me, I have other matters to attend to."

As Father Murphy rose to leave, he began to regret getting off to a bad start with the prior—someone who might not be in collusion with Bishop Rhinehart—perhaps just an innocent party. "I'm sorry I've been disagreeable," he said apologetically, "but this whole business, my parish taken away and the sudden transfer here is difficult to accept. I haven't done anything that would warrant this kind of treatment. And I'll tell you honestly, I object to being sent here as a fill-in teacher. I'm just obeying the bishop's orders. Anyway, for what it's worth, thanks for letting me stay here."

*****

Father Murphy felt himself wobbling slightly as he walked behind the altar boy from the sacristy to the altar. He was also disturbed because this was not one of his regular altar boys. He had never seen this altar boy before and he prided himself on knowing the boys and something about their families. Was this boy new in the parish? Did he know the Latin responses? But now it was too late to question him.

The huge altar that loomed above the priest seemed unreal. Sanctuaries typically have one or a few steps leading up to the main altar. This one had eight steep steps. But covered as it was with garlands of flowers set between six tall golden candlesticks, together with the brilliant white tabernacle in the center, the altar struck him as a beautiful sight, one that glorified God.

His slight unsteadiness was a problem, but hadn't he been able to say Mass many times before when he felt this way? He genuflected to begin the prayers at the foot of the altar, and made the Sign of the Cross as he said aloud, "In Nomine Patris, et Filii, et Spiritus Sancti. Amen." Then he began the opening prayers. "Introibo ad altare Dei." I will go in unto the Altar of God. The new altar boy stood mute. He looked down at the boy at his side. No response. He found he had to prompt the boy with every Latin response. Surprised and somewhat irritated, the priest then climbed the steps, genuflected and bent over to kiss the altar as he began the Mass. He was saying a Latin Mass the way Mass was said before the Second Vatican Council and the way it had been said for centuries. The priest faced the tabernacle and God, his back to the congregation, placing himself between God and the people, as intercessor for them. This day was the feast of the Assumption of Mary into Heaven and the church was full.

Father Murphy was dismayed as the Mass proceeded because he felt increasingly weak and unsteady. He slurred some Latin words as he struggled through the reading of the gospel. His brother Jonathon came to mind. Was this the onset of the family's genetic inheritance—Lou Gehrig's disease?

He was standing in the pulpit. Suddenly his mind was blank. He could not remember the sermon he had prepared. As he began speaking, his sermon was a blur, a simplistic exhortation on the subject of moderation in all things— somehow twisting itself into a discordant plea for moderation in the use of alcohol. He banged his clenched fist repeatedly on the rim of the pulpit surrounding him, making a hammering noise that reverberated through the church. Some of the congregation put their hands to their ears to block the noise. Shocked and disgusted faces stared up at him. He could see heads turned whispering into neighbors' ears. He knew what they were saying—a priest who most certainly was drunk swayed in the pulpit speaking incoherently about moderation, moderation, moderation, as he looked down through a mental fog at the congregation.

During the consecration of the Mass, he raised the host: "Hoc est enim corpus meum." This is my body. Repeating Christ's words at the Last Supper. Next, the chalice containing the wine, arms raised high overhead, head thrown back, eyes staring up through the glass roof of the sanctuary, up through the clouds, up to where God lived. "Hic est enim calix sanguinis mei." This is the chalice of my blood. While speaking the words of the miracle when the wine is transformed into the blood of Christ, he fell dizzily backwards, tumbling down the altar steps, his vestments twisted around him, pinning him like a straitjacket as he fell heavily onto the cold, grooved ceramic tile floor at the foot of the altar.

The congregation rose as one in horror. The priest's left temple struck the tiles as the chalice flew out of his hands spewing the newly transformed wine-red blood of Christ across the blue tiles, spilling over the edges of the tiles in miniature waterfalls, and running in thin streamlets along the beads between. Then the blood from the side of his head spurted across the tiles as if to mix his blood with that of Christ. Lying on his side, his head pressed against the floor, nearby tiles grotesquely enlarged, he noted curiously that Christ's blood flowed away from his blood, rushing to separate like waves retreating from a shoreline in the strong undertow of an outgoing tide. As he lay on the sanctuary floor, he suddenly knew why he had been transferred so abruptly. He was an alcoholic. The Church wanted to be rid of him. Even Christ abandoned him. "My God, my God, why hast thou forsaken me?"

He sat upright on the floor next to his bed. His chest heaved as he broke down sobbing. Sweat covered his face and trickled down his neck into his pajama tops. He must have twisted violently and fallen out of bed. He felt the side of his head for a sign of blood. He looked at his hand. There was no blood. The same dream—over and over, night after night, growing ever more vivid.

*****

"Friar Joseph, how can I help you?" The speaker was Bishop Rhinehart in his office at the chancery, answering the call from the Dominican.

"It concerns Reverend Murphy," the friar said. "He has us worried. He seems terribly sick."

"What makes you think he's sick?"

"In the very short time he has been with us, late at night he thrashes around in bed like a person in the grip of a demon; then, he wakes up shouting and sobbing. His behavior is as one possessed. Further, in our discussions, he comes across as terribly angry."

"Come now, Friar Joseph. He isn't possessed. And I would take his anger in stride. I hope you didn't call seeking permission for exorcism," the bishop said, trying to pass the whole thing off with a chuckle.

"But, Your Grace, I must tell you, through the night, apparently while he is dreaming, he sobs Jesus' words on the Cross: 'My God, my God, why hast thou forsaken me?' He thinks God has abandoned him and

Satan has him in his grip."

"Tell me this, Friar, have you seen his head twist around in full circles?" the bishop asked sarcastically. "Does he spew green vomit or speak in strange tongues?"

"No."

"Well, until you see such phenomena, let's stop talking about 'possession'. This is not the church of the Middle Ages. There may be a few exceptions, but I believe in general that cases of possession can be handled by good psychologists. However, if Father Murphy continues to be a problem, I'll talk to the cardinal and see if we can have him moved somewhere else. Goodbye, Friar Joseph."

*****

Sister Francine was genuinely happy to meet Father Murphy. Gray haired, a matronly figure partly hidden behind a desk piled high with paper, she had the look of a person who might have been someone's sweet grandmother. She wore no habit and, appearances to the contrary, she had a reputation as a tough administrator. Sitting in her cluttered office that resembled a town after a tornado, she smiled broadly at the tall handsome priest and motioned him to a chair. Father Murphy found he couldn't sit down until he moved the half-dozen books on the chair. "Just toss them on the floor," she said lightheartedly, laughing.

Do I address her as Sister or Doctor? he wondered, noticing the Ph.D. next to her name on the desk nameplate.

"I'm so happy you're here. You can help me out of an

awful jam. I have no one to teach Latin and I understand you are fluent. The good Lord has delivered."

"I believe you mean that Bishop Rhinehart has delivered. Can you tell me if there are any students for the first course in Latin?"

"Yes, a goodly number—ten so far."

"Why so many students interested in a dead language? Only the church has kept it from oblivion. What possible use could it be to the laity?"

Sister Francine did not miss the negative tone in the priest's questions. "They're not interested in Latin, per se; they want the language because it is the foundation for the romance languages—French, Spanish and Italian. Their interest is in tracing the roots of the romance languages."

"I know Latin; that is, Church Latin and I speak Italian fairly well, but I know nothing about the process that one goes through when tracing roots."

"The students are expected to trace roots on their own," Sister Francine explained, her smile disappearing. It was obvious that the priest sitting in front of her wasn't enthusiastic about the job. "Father," she said, glancing at the clock on the wall, her pleasant demeanor disappearing, "I don't have all day. Let's settle this here and now. It's take it or leave it time. Which will it be?"

He bristled at being spoken to in that tone by a nun, but he recognized that he was boxed in. The vow of obedience to the bishop came to mind. "I'll take it," he said grudgingly as he got up, and giving the nun a forced smile, turned and left the office.

*****

Father Murphy walked across the campus in the direction of the National Shrine of the Immaculate Conception. On earlier visits, he had gawked like the tourists and prayed in the huge basilica. He stopped in front of the wide stone steps leading up to the entrance and gazed up at the eighth largest church in the world. Byzantine architecture. Brilliant blue and gold dome squatting beside the tall bell tower topped with a slender blue pyramid and golden cap. Structure of solid granite. He had learned there was no steel supporting structure to rust over time. Just granite blocks keyed snugly on top of other blocks. Like the pyramids, it was built to last. The architect had talked in terms of thousands of years.

Once inside, he was overawed as always by the vast interior of the nave of the church and the sparkling brilliant colors of the mosaics in the side chapels. He saw no paintings or frescoes. Mosaics, he knew, like the granite structure, could last through millennia. Overhead, high up behind the main altar in the apse a huge round concave mosaic of an angry Christ poised hovering over the world as if He were about to rain fire and pestilence down on the earth. It clearly was anger in the expression. He wondered why Christ was depicted as angry. From the Christian point of view, Christ was seen in a supernatural role voluntarily submitting to punishment and death to atone for mankind's sins. But none of this divine altruism was evident in the mosaic. Then it occurred to him... why not? From another standpoint, if someone had been betrayed, vilified, scourged and put to death without committing any crime and came awake in an afterlife, anger would be an appropriate reaction, especially so if most of the world just went on sinning.

The mosaic mirrored Steve Murphy's own feelings. As he knelt in one of the pews, he realized he was angry, more upset than he had ever been in the past. Over and over again, he asked himself why this was being done to him. What had he done wrong, if anything? Didn't he deserve an explanation? Ordained at twenty-six, and now forty-eight, he had given over twenty years to the priesthood. He thought of them as good years, productive years, but now his life and his chosen vocation seemed to be crumbling into ashes at his feet. His life was going down the drain. As he knelt in the church, he tried to pray, but the sickening depression he felt about the actions of the archdiocese kept bubbling up to the surface of his brain with a constant stream of questions that crowded out everything else. And he was helpless to do anything about it.

*****

"Now, about the religion course, do you know much about world religions?"

"Nothing except Catholicism," Father Murphy said as he sat in Dr. Stanton's cubbyhole office in McMahon Hall. "But," he added sarcastically, "I know that the word 'Catholic' means universal—essentially worldwide. Are there any other legitimate religions?"

The Religion Department Chair, an elderly, patient oblate priest, ignored the comment. "Fall classes begin in two weeks," he said. "If you are not well-versed in the precepts of the world's other religions, I expect you will be quite busy for a time researching material for the course. Father Murphy, let me give you a bit of background. The university's doors are open to students of all faiths. All students are required to take a minimum number of religion courses. The Catholics, of course, take courses in Catholic subjects, the non-Catholics take World Religion. You will be teaching a first semester course to Protestants, Jews, Muslims, Buddhists, and perhaps even atheists. The course is taught along the lines of comparative religion. And I am sure these students know a lot more about their own religions than you do. So you can expect to have some lively debates."

"Sounds more like chicken fights than debates. You know the old saying: If you want to avoid arguments and hard feelings, avoid topics like religion and politics with people of diverse faiths and differing political philosophies. The reason is simple: you're going to create endless controversy and you aren't going to change any minds."

"Well that may be, but the university feels it has an obligation to offer this course. An area to stress among your Christian students is the Ecumenical Movement. Are you familiar with that?"

"Yes, to some extent. It's supposed to bring together the Christian Churches in sort of a unifying and healing process. In the sense that these churches band together to improve the human condition, I agree that the cause is worthwhile but as to real unification, despite the best efforts of the pontiff, I believe that goal is unattainable."

"Why do you say that?"

"Well, I heard somewhere there are at least several

thousand versions of the Christian religion—many with widely divergent views. When you add the further fact that each one, including the Catholic Church, and especially the Catholic Church, claims to be the one true faith, you hardly have a chance at unification. The sticking point, of course, is not so much different beliefs as the fear of many that their religion would presumably wind up under the jurisdiction of the pope."

"Father Murphy, let me be frank," the chairman said standing up behind his desk with growing annoyance in his voice. "The course is only expository. We are not attempting to solve the problem of unification and we are not trying to convert anyone. As the instructor, you will merely be encouraging the students to tell about their religions and to note differences in belief systems. You will avoid being judgmental. Is that understood? Do you want to teach the subject or not?"

Steve Murphy knew the game was up. The bishop always wins. "I'll take the job," he said quietly as he left the office.

*****

As he walked back to the Dominican House—his new home, Steve Murphy thought about the courses he would teach. The Latin course. Baby stuff. No point spending any prep time on it. But the other course could be a bitch. He realized he would be spending days and evenings in the university library researching other religions. How many major ones were there— twenty? A hundred? From the Catholic viewpoint it struck him as a colossal waste of time. As he entered the Dominican House, he was slightly amused as he thought back to the nuns he had had in elementary school. Hadn't the good sisters preached over and over again there was only one true religion? Wasn't all the rest of it baloney? Of course, they never used the word 'baloney' but didn't they continually press home the point that the only sure way to heaven was through the Catholic faith?

Another thought occurred to him: Since I have only secular courses I won't need any religious zeal. I don't see anything relating to my lifelong vocation to strengthen the faith in Catholics or convert atheists. There's one nice thing about atheists. They are like empty vessels waiting to be filled. Since they have no religion, you can offer them something to add to their lives—not like trying to transplant those who since early childhood have had their feet stuck in the cement of their parents' chosen religion. He recalled that some pundit had said that religion is strongly related to geography. If you are born in Israel you are Jewish; if you are born in Saudi Arabia, you are Muslim; if you are born in Boston, you are very likely Catholic. On and on....

As he walked up the stairs to his room, he could smell dinner in preparation. The aroma was not appetizing. It hadn't taken him more than a few days to realize that the food served in the Dominican House gave strong evidence of the vow of poverty—part of the sacrifice one makes when becoming a mendicant friar. He decided to eat most of his meals out.

4

She was probably one of the most beautiful women he had ever seen. Soft waves of silken chestnut hair tumbled down lightly touching her shoulders. When she glanced up at him and their eyes met, he had a nervous momentary reflex to look away lest he get lost in the wonderland of her deep blue-eyed gaze. He was never completely comfortable in the presence of women and beautiful women almost made him tongue-tied. When he looked at this woman, he realized that for a moment he had stopped breathing.

She was sitting in the Shrine cafeteria eating lunch with another young woman, Maria, one of the students in his Latin class. He noticed that every man who passed by the table looked at Maria's friend somewhat wide-eyed and admiringly; the women who passed had a look of envy mixed with discomfiture.

"Mind if I join you, Maria?" he asked, holding his lunch tray.

"Certainly, Father, as long as I don't have to respond in Latin. Only joking. Please sit down, Father. By the way, let me introduce you to my friend Janet. She's a graduate student in the School of Social Work."

"Grocery bags to indigents?" he asked the beautiful young woman sitting across from him who seemed to be staring at his face. He wondered if he had shaved well enough. He ran his hand over his chin wondering if there was a bit of stubble he had missed. "They teach that in graduate school?"

He was instantly sorry for the comment.

"No," Janet replied, briefly flashing a smirk at his comment. "Clinical Social Work—psychotherapy, specifically Family Systems Therapy." Janet had a confident attitude that spoke contentment with herself. Unlike a good many others, Catholics especially, she was not shy in front of a priest. "I've heard a lot about you, Father," she said with a curious smile. The sun came out. But was she really smiling?

"Good, I hope."

Maria wondered where this conversation was headed.

"Not really," she said, her smile vanishing. To him it was if the sun had gone down. "In fact, just the opposite," she said. "They tell me you have the makings of a tyrant in class. Your zeal runneth over."

His student, Maria, shrank down in her chair. She was taken aback at Janet's frankness, yet she couldn't disagree with what her friend was saying. It occurred to her that the priest probably knew that Janet had heard some of the complaints directly from her.

"I am heavy handed," he admitted, as he took a bite out of his sandwich, "but I didn't think it showed so much."

"They tell me it shows," Janet answered. "The word is you act as if you'd rather be someplace else."

"*I'd* rather be someplace else," Maria said softly.

"You're right," he admitted, but immediately regretted saying it in front of one of his students.

"If you'll excuse me," Janet said, getting up. "I have a class coming up."

As Janet and his Latin class student walked away, Steve Murphy found himself unnerved by the brief meeting. Was it the brusque accusatory manner of the beautiful young woman who had stared at him with her penetrating blue eyes as she was calling him a tyrant or was it something more? Was he embarrassed? If so, why? It was certainly no secret that he was feared and disliked by his students. In the past, he had had other confrontations that were easily dismissed. Why did it bother him that this young woman knew about his reputation and openly confronted him? In his years as a parish priest, he had worked with many women in handling church affairs. It was always in the context of pastoral work. During all these years, he never let himself entertain thoughts of a personal nature about any of the women. He was a priest, dedicated to God and the celibate life. He was above all that. But this young woman intrigued him, challenged him in a way he had never before experienced.

After the brief meeting, Steve Murphy began to take the first really introspective look at himself since the day he had opened the transfer letter from Bishop Rhinehart. He knew the young lady was right. Absolutely everything he had done since his transfer sprang from his disappointment. It was consuming him. He was cool and cynical with others and when alone, he studied or marked papers with gritted teeth, but he was at a loss to know how to lift his feelings of depression and loneliness.

He was directed to say early morning Mass in a side chapel in the crypt church of the Shrine, side-by-side with a dozen other priests at an array of small altars.

A production line of Masses. Here in the Shrine he was alone without an altar boy or a congregation. How unlike his morning Masses as pastor at Holy Rosary in the large, comfortable, well-lighted church, before an altar bedecked with flowers, assisted by one of his regular altar boys and giving communion to parishioners he had come to know and love. Here, alone at the small altar in the dim basement church, it was a struggle to keep focused on the mystery of the Mass. It was depressing that his life had all come down to this. Still, he knew that before God, he had to suppress his feelings and had to keep faith that an unfair move made by the archdiocese, might soon be corrected.

*****

Steve Murphy stood in the open doorway.

"Come in, Father Murphy. Please take a seat."

The priest took a seat and glanced around Dr. Stanton's cubbyhole office. He remembered his first visit to the office and concluded that it still smelled of a pungent mixture of leather, after-shave lotion and mold. The chairman did not have a pleasant look on his face. "Father Murphy," he said slowly, as if measuring his words, "I had a delegation of your World Religion students in here earlier today. Frankly, they were here to complain. Their specific complaint was your all too obvious bias against any religion other than Catholicism."

"I'm a Catholic priest," he said. "If I weren't strongly biased towards Catholicism, I would make a hell of a priest."

"Yes, I understand that, Father. But it would be extremely helpful if you could approach the subject with more of an open mind. This is a university. Our mission is academic. Your students say you engage in arguments with them as if you're trying to dissuade them from their own religions and convert to Catholicism. You were expected to conduct classes that are understanding of other viewpoints, intellectual, academic—not pastoral."

Steve Murphy crossed his legs, folded his arms. "I find that hard to do," he said. "I have tried, but my mental transition from pastoral to academic thinking is slow in coming. What do you suggest I do?"

"I don't know, but I do know that if I keep getting large delegations of your students trying to crowd in here with complaints, I'll have to remove you and bring in a substitute. And this is hard to do now that the semester is well underway. But I will do it if I have to."

"Is that all?" Father Murphy said crisply as he got up to leave.

"Yes, that's all."

*****

Steve Murphy's next stop was no better. Another delegation of complaining students—this time about his method of teaching Latin by 'total immersion'.

The Chair of Foreign Languages leveled a steely gaze at him over the reading glasses perched on her nose. "This is not Berlitz," Sister Francine said. "Our students do not have to learn to speak a new language in five days. I understand you permit not a word of English to be spoken in your classes."

"How many complained?"

"The entire class."

"Well, that's not so bad," he said jocularly. "It means only ten students complained."

"Reverend, I am Chair of the Foreign Language Department. I am not some timid novice nun teaching in a parish elementary school under your thumb. You will follow the outline for the course or I will drop you in a heartbeat. Have I made myself clear?"

*****

He was sitting alone in the Shrine cafeteria. He played with the food on his plate. Why had he ordered anything when he wasn't hungry? He was thoroughly miserable. Crowding the front of his brain was the loss of his parish and his expected promotion to Monsignor. He had been suddenly dumped in a job he didn't like, and, from the looks of it, one he was performing poorly. He had made no friends at the university. There was no one he could really confide in except in the confessional and kneeling at the altar—reminding God, who certainly already knew. But these refuges for a lonely priest were not now uplifting or comforting—certainly not as they had been through the years. God and his confessor did not now seem terribly interested in his problems.

He was part way through his lunch in the Shrine cafeteria when she walked past him with a lunch tray and a book. He barely had time to acknowledge her presence with a nod of his head as she brushed by his table on her way to a far corner to study while she ate. It happened so quickly, he wasn't really sure whether she had recognized him or whether he was being snubbed. He suddenly felt undesirable, unworthy. Perhaps he was merely too old to attract the interest of a younger woman. But more likely, she had been turned off by the student gossip about him. He berated himself for feeling hurt. What did it matter whether she noticed him, whether she liked him or not? What difference did it make? He was a priest. He was at the university only because he had been dumped there.

As he left the cafeteria the thought crossed his mind that he might pass near her table, say hello, and strike up a conversation. He knew his loneliness made him vulnerable to needing a friendly smile, but an approach could also lead to rejection.

As he approached, she did not look up. She was engrossed in her book.

He decided not to bother her. He walked out. He went to class to do battle with the world's other religions.

*****

Another week passed without seeing her. Her lunches in the cafeteria seemed to be sporadic. She probably lunched occasionally at the Pryzbyla Student Center. The next time he saw her she was with a young man. They appeared to be good friends, perhaps more. She laughed merrily at some of the things he said. At one point, the young man leaned over, put his arm around her shoulder and gave her a kiss on the cheek. So that was it. They were more than friends. He was disappointed. But wondered why he cared. He certainly could never have seen any possibility of establishing a relationship with her. As she and the young man left the cafeteria, they passed very near his table. She brushed by without so much as looking over at him. He glanced up momentarily but seeing no glance in his direction, no trace of recognition in her face, resumed staring down at his plate as he played with his food.

After all he had gone through, all he had lost in recent months, whatever feelings of self-worth he had left, ebbed like an outgoing tide. His anger began to fade. He started a long slide down a slippery slope to bottom out in depression. Of the two conditions, he felt depression was far worse because it trapped him in a helpless state. He had always been able to use his anger to stimulate action. It had helped him crawl out of some tight spots. Depression, on the other hand, was a trap—a deep pit lined with slimy walls.

*****

He was at an evening faculty cocktail party. She was standing on the other side of the room a few feet from the bar with a drink in her hand. Three men, probably professors, surrounded her. Each seemed to be vying for her full attention.

Her shimmering blue silk cocktail dress matched the blue of her eyes. She wore high heels. He had to restrain himself from ogling her trim figure and her legs. He smiled to himself as he remembered what the guys in high school used to call a beautiful woman—'drop dead gorgeous'.

He walked over in her direction. She slowly eased her way past the other men. She smiled. Was she smiling at someone coming up behind him? He twisted around, looking over his shoulder. But he quickly realized there was no one directly behind him. She was smiling at him. Heaven only knows how much he appreciated that smile.

"I saw you in the Shrine cafeteria the other day," he said, "but I don't think you recognized me."

"I recognized you. I was punishing you for being so hard on your students."

"But now you're smiling."

"I forgive easily. The forlorn look on your face told me you were contrite."

"Will three Hail Mary's suffice for my penance?"

"Only if you start giving your students a better break."

He decided to chance teasing her a little, but hopefully not to the point of making her angry. The spiked punch emboldened him. He arched an eyebrow. "And what may I ask are you doing at a faculty party? You're a student, aren't you?"

"I do some teaching as a grad assistant," she said. She smiled and sipped her drink. She looked at him over the edge of her glass. "May I ask what you're doing here? I understand you're a Lecturer, a part-timer. That doesn't really qualify as faculty either."

He thought the comment was illuminating. She had been checking up on his official status.

"Can we go somewhere for coffee after the party?" he asked, completely surprised at hearing himself say it. He tried to cover up. "I'd like to learn more of what the students are saying about me." He already knew what the students were saying about him, but it might serve as an excuse to spend some time alone with her.

"Why? I know little more than I've told you before.

In a word, they think you're too uptight. One of them says quite openly that you are a hard-ass, Father."

"Perhaps if you'll come have coffee with me, you can give me some pointers on how to soften up. You are a therapist, after all."

The room was crowded. She was standing very close to him. Her soft chestnut brown hair reflected golden highlights. He detected a slight trace of springtime perfume. It made him feel he was outside under a blue sky instead of in a crowded party room. As she sipped her drink, her questioning eyes searched his face. He knew she was trying to make up her mind, wondering why this priest really wanted to see her alone. He waited an eternity for her answer.

"All right," she said almost in a whisper. "After I circulate a bit. I'll see you at the front door in about half an hour."

*****

They decided to have dinner together. He drove her across town to a restaurant in Chevy Chase to avoid prying eyes at places near the university. Even so, there were stares from people who wondered about a clergyman, middle-aged, Roman collar, probably a priest, having dinner with a young woman. The people who were of a charitable turn of mind ignored them thinking she could be a niece or a cousin. The busybodies whispered.

She agreed to call him Steve, although being Catholic, it made her uncomfortable calling a priest by his given name. She had never called a priest by his first name.

"We're in an academic environment," he argued. "It's not like being home in a parish church. Besides," he laughed, "calling me Steve is a lot better than the names some of my students call me. I'd settle for Steve any day."

Taking a sip from his wine glass, he told her his story. He began way back. Back to his days in the seminary. He spoke of the wonderful days he had spent in Rome at the Vatican. "Ever been to Rome?"

"Some day," she said. "Of course, I've read about it, but I'd like to hear more first-hand about it."

"It has breathtaking wonders...and I mean more than St. Peter's, the Vatican Museum and the Sistine Chapel. Rome has the remnants of a great civilization that flourished almost two thousand years ago, albeit a cruel and conquering one. One of my favorite pastimes in Rome was to walk or jog along the Via Appia Antica— the old Roman Appian Way just south of the city, and imagine Caesar's legions returning from a far-off war, my iPod playing Resphigi's *Pines of the Appian Way*. The music portrays the return of the conquering army."

"You sound intrigued by the old Roman army. Did you ever have a desire to join the army?"

"Not really, but I admit to being intrigued by power and majesty. That's one reason why I became a priest. What more power could a person have than to be a spokesperson, to intercede for others with God? In a church with ten people or a thousand people, the priest is the focal point."

"Sounds like a bit of ego there, Father Steve," she said grinning.

"OK, back to the Appian Way. You know, it stretches

500 miles from Brindisi on the southern coast of Italy all the way to the gates of Rome. Of course, Italy now has a new Appian Way—a modern highway to the south; that's why the Roman road is referred to as the ancient Appian Way. It's a cobblestone road in surprisingly good shape even after two thousand years. I was also fascinated by the tombs of famous Romans that line the road and the catacombs with entrances along the way. The catacombs have been played up in Hollywood movies as Christian hiding places during the Roman persecutions, and perhaps they were, but there's no real evidence of that. They may have been simply underground cemeteries, and not only Christian—there are also some Jewish catacombs."

"The Hollywood version is more intriguing," she said grinning.

"If you're ever in Rome, I'll have my friend Angelo take you on a tour of the catacombs."

"Who's Angelo?"

"He's the Italian priest in charge of the San Callisto Catacomb. We've been friends since our days at the Vatican. In fact, we were university roommates for a couple of years. I've visited Rome a few times since and have seen my old friend. He lives in the priest-house built on top of the catacomb. If you ever visit the catacombs, let me warn you—it's pitch black down there and if you let the guide with the flashlight get too far ahead and he turns a corner leaving you in the dark, I can assure you, you'll get the cold shivers."

"I understand there are quite a few catacombs under Rome."

"Yes, about fifty of them. But, including San

Callisto, only about five are open to the public. The entrances were sealed for almost a thousand years, and the catacombs were really discovered by accident in the sixteenth century. Many have never been fully explored. San Callisto, for example, has numerous passageways that reach out almost fifteen miles under Rome."

When dinner was served, Steve Murphy went on to talk about his early days as a curate and his eventual rise to pastor. After some hesitation, he finally told her about the recent, abrupt, unexplained action of the archdiocese. He hoped that by telling her, it would explain his behavior. Perhaps explain why he was considered such a tyrant in class. She was sympathetic. She understood anger and depression—they could be serious conditions encountered in psychotherapy. It was clear to her that his anger, which should have been directed against the archdiocese, was misdirected towards his students and almost everyone else. She leaned closer to him. She studied his face across the table. She sensed that his anger was giving way to depression.

"But why, oh why," she asked puzzled, "would the archdiocese do a thing like that to you? It doesn't add up. Is there something you're not telling me?"

"Whoa," he said abruptly. "This is a turnabout—you sound like you're inviting me into the confessional."

"Sorry, but I just can't understand why they've done this to you. It begs for more explanation."

"Who in God's name knows what's going on?" he said softly, miserably. "I don't. It could be anything: an anonymous complaint about the new church I was building? Was it atrociously expensive? Or was I guilty of drinking too much? You realize, of course that when you say three Masses in a morning, that's six partial chalices of wine. Who wouldn't smell that on your breath? Especially heavy red church wine. There's something else. A sexton saw me not long ago with an arm around a young altar boy, I was simply comforting him after he took a bad fall. I may have a hard shell, but inside, a soft core. I believed, and still do, that some of these kids needed a friendly arm around their shoulders."

"An arm, that's all?"

"That's all. What I'm saying is that virtually anything can be taken the wrong way. False accusations are nothing new."

"But if there was a formal complaint, wouldn't the archdiocese have consulted you about it? Aren't you considered innocent until proven guilty in the eyes of the church? And even if they thought you were guilty, wouldn't the first offense result in a warning?"

"I would have thought so," he answered, shrugging his shoulders and taking another sip of wine, "but I'm sure you know—the church's first reaction is to transfer the priest to someplace else. Let's talk about something else. Let's talk about you."

"I don't have a long history like you do." She hesitated. "Sorry. I guess that sounded like a comment about your age. It wasn't meant to be. I was born outside of Boston, actually about twenty miles west of the city, in Concord."

"I grew up in Wayland," he said surprised. "Just a few miles away."

She thought a moment, then brightened. "You're one of the Murphy's of Wayland. I'm impressed. Your father was a congressman. Wayland is where the swells live, old money," she said laughing. "Are any of your family still up there?"

"My mother and father are both dead; however, I have a brother, Jonathon who still lives in Wayland. No other siblings. Jonathon's in real estate. He doesn't need the money—only does it to keep busy. He's eighteen years older than me. I keep telling him it's time he retired."

Janet was curious. She thought the age spread between two brothers seemed unusual. "Was either of you adopted? Or is Jonathon your stepbrother?"

"No, not that I'm aware of. And by the way, it isn't just the action of the archdiocese that has me upset. I found out not long ago that my brother has a medical problem—he's in an early stage of Lou Gehrig's disease. My father died of it. The scary part is that it seems to run in our family."

"That's a tough one. I understand it sometimes settles in the throat in the early stages. Difficulty talking and swallowing. Then, trouble breathing and loss of coordination."

"How did we get back to talking about me and my family? But while we're discussing me, I suppose I should tell you I had a serious run-in with the chairs of both departments I work for. They say I'm a terrible teacher. Too tough...expect miracles from the students. I could actually be dropped."

"Have you ever thought of leaving the priesthood, especially after the way the archdiocese has been treating you?"

"No. I'll just stay and take whatever lumps are coming to me." Pushing his dinner plate away, he grew silent as he propped an elbow on the table and rested his cheek in the palm of his hand. He stared down into his coffee cup. Then he dropped one hand flat on the table.

"Now you sound like you're feeling sorry for yourself. All your world has been giving you a hard time hasn't it, Steve Murphy?" she said, lightly chiding him, trying to cajole him out of his funk. Then reaching over, she put her hand on his. The gesture was meant to soften her comment. She did it impulsively because he looked so crestfallen.

The touch of her hand electrified him. No woman had ever held his hand in that way before. Nor did he draw his hand back. Her hand was soft, warm and spoke of caring. Although he was middle-aged, he was childlike emotionally, continually making new discoveries and discovering new needs. At this point in his life, in this restaurant, at this table, the attraction of this beautiful woman was one of the discoveries.

5

The seaplane taxied out through the narrow inlet into the bay. It was one of those rare fall days when the Chesapeake Bay was flat calm. Not a ripple ahead of the pontoons as Steve pushed the throttle forward. As the plane gained speed, the smooth gray water surface almost looked like a concrete runway spread out in front. Two large rooster tails fanned high behind the pontoons of the plane as the engine roared for takeoff. Easing back on the wheel, Steve smiled over at Janet sitting in the copilot seat as the plane rose into the cool clear morning air. The little plane climbed up into the blue, the towering spans of the Chesapeake Bay Bridge looming before it.

"Go under the bridge," Janet said excitedly.

"Hey, I'm crazy but I'm not that crazy," Steve said over the noise of the engine. "I know you can fly under the Golden Gate Bridge but here in Maryland it's against the law. Take a good look. You see that most of the bridge is supported by columns. There's just a short suspension span in the middle for ships. Another thing, it's really two bridges side by side. Interested in some sightseeing information about the Bay?" he asked as the plane soared over the bridges.

"Of course, that's what I came for."

He was disappointed. He had hoped she was there mostly to be with him.

"Who owns the plane?" she asked.

"It's a one-day rental."

"I didn't know you were a pilot. A flying priest. And on pontoons. You could be a missionary. You could bring religion to snowbound Eskimos in Alaska or natives in southseas backwaters."

"It could happen, I suppose."

"Do you fly a lot?"

"When I have time."

"Can you fly a bigger plane with more than one motor?"

"I've had quite a bit of multi-engine experience. I have a commercial pilot's license—instrument rating and all. My family owned a pontoon plane when my father was alive. When I was a kid he took me up occasionally and let me hold the stick. That's what gave me the incentive to take lessons and get qualified. My family had.... in fact, we still have a house on a small lake in New Hampshire. My brother, Jonathon goes up to the house in the summer, but I haven't been there for years. I believe the plane is still there although considering Jonathon's condition, he may be leery of flying it off the lake."

"You mean the pond," she laughed. "Have you forgotten that we New Englanders refer to them as ponds? Walden Pond, for example."

"Yes, of course," he replied, with a quick look over at his passenger. He smiled. "You mean like Pond Winnepesaukee."

"There are exceptions for really big ponds," she said as she playfully poked an elbow into the side of his rib cage.

"Careful," he warned, smiling, as the plane dipped

slightly to the left. "The FAA says there should be no physical contact with the pilot—especially when you're up in the air. But about Wayland and New Hampshire," he continued, "I haven't been home in a long time. When I was a kid, I was very close to my father. Are you sure you want to hear this?"

"Of course. I can understand you better if I learn about your family. That's what Family Systems Therapy is all about."

Steve glanced over at her. "Good grief," he laughed, "I'm being analyzed by a shrink. The rest of the story is not very pretty and I have to say I have never quite figured it out."

"Maybe I can help," she said smiling.

"Actually, it's kind of weird. Maybe I shouldn't tell you this, but my mother was a lush. And it galled me the way she fawned all over my brother. The old saying, he could do no wrong; I could do no right. When my father wasn't around, and my older brother did something wrong, mom would get angry and I'd get slapped around."

"It's a common thing in dysfunctional families."

"Dysfunctional? I never thought of it that way."

"With an alcoholic parent, it sure wasn't a normal family."

"I thought that by becoming a priest, she'd see some good qualities in me. But, although she was a Catholic, or at least called herself a Catholic, she thought it was stupid. I was wasting my life. Anyway, enough of that."

Steve banked the plane to the left. "We're passing over Greenbury Point and just off to the right is the Severn River, and on the opposite shore the Naval

Academy. If there aren't too many sailboats out there I might try landing on the river later on. If not, I can taxi in from the Bay."

"Why?"

"Because the Shrine cafeteria where I've been having most of my lunches is OK but it certainly isn't gourmet and I occasionally have a strong urge for fresh seafood. See that small building and attached dock on the north side of the river? That's where we'll have lunch after we do some sightseeing."

Steve banked the airplane to fly south. The dome of the Annapolis State House was visible in the distance. "Recognize Annapolis?" he asked.

"Yes, I've walked around there a few times. Kind of touristy, I find. Crowded in warm weather, but fun."

"Now we're south of Annapolis. Look down below. That's the Thomas Point Lighthouse. The hex-shaped building on stilts. Time was when there were lots of them on the Bay, but they aren't around anymore except for a couple on shore used as tourist attractions. They became obsolete first by radio navigation, later by satellite navigation."

"What's that big island across the bay?"

"That's Tilghman's Island. That's where Michener lived when he wrote the book *Chesapeake*. I suppose he wanted to be immersed in the local culture."

"Speaking of immersion," Janet asked, arching an eyebrow, "how is your total immersion Latin class doing?"

"Not good. In fact, I'm going to drop that approach. If the class ran night and day continuously for a whole week the way Berlitz does it, fine, but it doesn't seem to work when you see students in class only three times a week for fifty minutes. When they come back on Wednesday, they've forgotten everything they learned on Monday."

"They'll thank you for dropping it. And they might just drop calling you a hardass."

"Janet, do you see that dark narrow jagged band that runs down the middle of the Bay?"

"Yes, what is it pollution?"

"No, it's deep water. Thousands of years ago during the last ice age, the Chesapeake Bay didn't exist. There was only a narrow one-hundred-foot deep trench from the Susquehanna River up north in Pennsylvania that ran down through the middle of this area all the way south to the ocean at Norfolk, Virginia. Then, when the ice age ended, the river overflowed its banks and formed the Chesapeake Bay."

"Steve, what's that huge shadow down there under the water? Sunken ship?"

"No, that's an island that has sunk out of sight. Through the years some low-lying islands have actually disappeared."

"Were they developed? You know, houses and stuff?"

"Yeah. A lot of people want to be right near the water's edge. But they often lose land during storms, so it's rocks, steel mesh jetties, anything to hang on. You can buy a half-acre and wind up with a quarter-acre," Steve said shaking his head. "And in some cases, like that dark patch there, you lose everything."

"It sounds like a tragedy."

"It may be a tragedy but it's certainly not a surprise. The Bay is an estuary—a mix of salt water that comes in from the ocean down at the southern end and fresh water from rivers flowing into it mostly from the north. As a result, the shoreline is tidal, active like an ocean front. These people all know it but they keep buying shoreline lots anyway. They wind up paying a big price to have the Bay on their doorstep."

A half-hour later, Steve brought the plane down for a smooth landing in an area north of the Bay Bridge that had no small boats. He taxied down the Bay, passing under the Bay Bridge spans and turned into the Severn River.

"I thought you weren't supposed to go under the bridges."

"When I'm on the water, dear heart, I'm a boat just like the rest of the boats." He pulled up to the dock of the Severn Inn.

From her vantage point, Janet could see the Naval Academy across the river and the church spires of Annapolis as she sat at a table under an umbrella on the dock. She could feel a light warm breeze as rippling waves came in from the Bay. After double-checking the moorings on the plane, Steve slipped into a seat beside her. It was almost noon. Janet ordered a cocktail.

"None for me, thanks. I'll just have a coke."

"Going on the wagon?" Janet asked.

"Not really. My rule is 'no alcohol when in the cockpit'."

"Oh, I never thought of that."

"Janet, every time we talk, it always narrows down to me telling my long-winded tales. Never about you. Don't ask me any questions about myself. You talk. I'll listen."

"There isn't a lot to tell. I haven't been educated in Rome like you have; in fact, I've never even been to Europe. OK, from the beginning—I was raised in Concord right near where you lived in Wayland."

"About you. Only about you. By the way, I've been meaning to ask you about your name, Tarentino, sounds Italian. Are you Italian?"

"No, I'm not. My parents live in Concord. I have two brothers, one in New York, one in Boston. Both married with children. I went to Catholic elementary and Catholic high school in Concord. Then to Harvard where I earned my B.A.; then down to Catholic U. for graduate studies in Social Work."

"Do you mind my asking about your love life? Got a steady boyfriend?"

"No boyfriend."

"Come on now, you can tell old Father Steve. Haven't I seen you in the Shrine cafeteria with a young man? And didn't I see him kiss you a few times?"

"Is this merely general interest in my morals, Father Steve, or do I detect a note of jealousy?"

"I'm jealous."

"He and I are just friends. Nothing more. He's gay. The pecks on the cheek are just the way he is. In fact, if you were having lunch with him he'd probably give you a peck on the cheek. I'm sure he'd rather kiss you than me." Steve Murphy leaned back in his chair. A sense of ease came over him as he stared into her blue eyes. Her loose flowing hair was tousled from the sea breeze. He wanted to run his hands through it. He wanted to....

"No boyfriend," she repeated. "I'm married. That's

where the Italian name came from. Actually, I'm mostly Irish. My maiden name is O'Brien."

Steve didn't know why he grew red in the face. It was spontaneous. He couldn't control it. Somehow the shock of her revelation embarrassed him. His feelings about her began to wane as if a pall had slowly lowered over a lovely statue...gradually concealing it from view. He stared far away, across the river.

"There's more to the story," she said. "We were teenagers. It lasted all of three months. No children. We found out early it was a mistake. We're officially separated and may have to get a divorce. Looks like the church is going to refuse an annulment."

"But you're Catholic. You can't get divorced. In the eyes of the church, if the marriage is not annulled, you'll always be married to him." Steve heard himself saying this while at the same time he was asking himself why part of him felt better when she said she might be getting divorced. How could a Catholic priest be relieved, almost happy to hear of a couple divorcing? He realized that this train of thought was dangerous. Was he beginning to doubt one of the basic precepts of the church concerning Catholic marriage? "Janet, why didn't you tell me all this before?"

"I knew you had a reputation as a hardliner. I thought what friendship we had would turn into one long sermon." She knew it was a lie. He wasn't the type to harangue her about it. What she feared deep down was that it would drive him away.

He suspected she was not being quite truthful. She surely knew him well enough by then to know that he might comment on something he thought was wrong, while at the same time not abandon his staunch belief in one of the pillars of the Church—free will. He found it curious why she hadn't mentioned before that she was married. Did she try to cover it up because she was embarrassed? Perhaps she was afraid it might drive him away. He did have thoughts that it might create a distance between them, but he also knew that no matter what, he wanted to go on seeing her. In what had been the vacuum of his life, he realized they had developed a friendship, a kind of bond, perhaps with some early awakening feelings of affection. He could tell by the way she had begun to smile and brighten whenever she saw him, by the lighthearted peck on the cheek she gave him when they met and when they parted. She would furtively glance over her left and right shoulder to make sure no one was watching, then stand on tiptoe and kiss him on the cheek. "Sure 'n begorrah, and wipe the lipstick off, Father Murphy," she would say laughing with an imitation brogue.

As the weeks went by, she continued to brighten his life like no one before. Maybe it wasn't love, but considering the circumstances, their friendship was the next best thing. It was all they dared to give one another.

6

Despite her revelation about being married, they began having lunch together several times a week in the Shrine cafeteria. He slowly became aware that days when he didn't see her were empty, melancholy. During lunches, they always sat at a table in a corner, deep in conversation. At times, they both burst out laughing then looked around concerned they might have disturbed people near them. No one paid any real attention to them with the exception of an occasional student who knew Janet and sometimes a student in one of his classes. Since the faculty dining room was considered the only socially acceptable place for faculty to lunch, none of the professors or deans saw them.

His daily solitary Mass in the Crypt Church of the Shrine became a joy, especially on days when he knew he and Janet would be lunching together. It was a thanksgiving, a celebration of life. In his uplifted state of mind, even his nightmares had begun to taper off and lose some of their sting.

After morning Mass, he frequently visited the Lourdes Grotto in the Crypt Church—a replica of the original grotto where the Virgin appeared to Bernadette. As he knelt in the dark candlelit interior of the grotto his feelings for Janet gradually became entwined with a renewed devotion to Mary, the Blessed Virgin.

On the walk back to the Dominican House, he often

recalled a statement attributed to Norman Vincent Peale, the advocate of positive thinking. Wasn't it Peale who said that when one door closes, another opens?

But he couldn't always shake the melancholy days… days when Steve Murphy was actually frightened that the church door was closing on him. There were times when he was devastated by this feeling. Ever since he had been transferred out of his parish, he had gone over the possible reasons hundreds of times in his mind without ever coming up with an answer. Was the case against him—he knew there must be some kind of case hidden behind it all—based on supposed excessive alcohol use, or a false accusation of pedophilia, or misuse of church funds, or even some preposterous claim like insubordination? Whatever it was, it was being kept a mystery.

Whenever these thoughts came, he grew weary and disgusted. His brain ached from reasoning pro and con. It resembled a tense and depressing courtroom drama playing out in his head. He imagined himself on the stand. His hands were clammy. The jury looked somber. The prosecutor shot an arrow: "Are you telling me, Father, that you never abused alcohol?"

"I'm innocent."

"What about church funds? How could so much money just disappear?"

"I'm innocent."

"You were seen fondling an altar boy. You've probably done it dozens of times when no one was looking."

"I've told you a hundred times, I'm innocent."

Then an apparition would appear. The courtroom

would disappear, thank God. Janet, a lovely, beckoning apparition leaning against an open door in the distance. The door was far away. Could he ever reach it? Did he really want to reach it? He knew if he passed through that door there would be no way back.

As the days went by, he asked himself if he could be falling in love with her. The question was a new one for him because at age forty-eight, he had never been in love with a woman. Not even puppy love in grade school. What was love like? Was this really it? Was it love that made him want to skip instead of walk whenever he thought of Janet? Why did the sky seem bluer, the clouds whiter, people friendlier? But this thing called love had a dark side. In all his adult life, he had always maintained strict discipline. Now he was concerned about losing control. Strange things seemed to be happening in his head. Strange things were happening to his body. When he saw her, his heart beat a bit faster; he noticed a tingling in his loins; something down there that had been dormant now seemed to be coming alive.

Janet, on the other hand seemed friendly, affectionate in a humorous, companionable way, but always managed to keep him at arm's length. He wondered if she was more concerned with the risk to his vocation than he was. He wondered if her marriage breakup was her husband's doing or hers.

At times, when he thought of the women with whom he had worked in various parish functions and fund drives, he became acutely aware of their selfless devotion to the church. As a result of his feelings for Janet, and his renewed devotion to the Virgin, the legions of downtrodden in the Catholic Church—the women, aroused a new interest, a new significance for him. How poorly they were treated. They were left to clean the priestly vestments, but never to wear them. He had to acknowledge to himself however, that until he met Janet, he had never given it a moment's thought. Women were destined to play a minor role in the liturgy of the church. It was a matter of church doctrine. The exclusively male clergy was accepted without question; that is, until Vatican II. But In the years following Vatican II, the issue of women priests was pounded into oblivion in the papal encyclicals. At one point, the clergy were even forbidden to discuss it. The best that women could hope for was a role in managing parish affairs, and although the pope was known to disapprove, girls could now serve on the altar during Mass. It was a small concession from the Vatican to the American cardinals and bishops in particular.

Steve was also well aware of the striking similarities between many practices of the Catholic Church and the ancient Jewish faith from which it had evolved. Some parallels he thought comical, some troubling. One small example always made him laugh: didn't the pope and the bishops wear yarmulkes just like the Jews? The only difference seemed to be that some were red, some white, some embroidered, while others were simply black. He also wondered about how the Catholic Church evolved the ceremony of the Mass which had its origins in the Last Supper. Wasn't that meal actually a Jewish Seder commemorating the exodus of the Israelites from Egypt? And when Christ gave his first public sermon at Capharnum, wasn't it in a synagogue?

Steve Murphy was well aware that Christianity grew out of the ancient Hebrew faith into what is called 'The New Testament', but the parallels nevertheless amazed him. Haven't the Catholic Church and Jewish orthodoxy both been male dominated from early times? His chosen church seemed to be only one step better than the ancient orthodox synagogues where women were not even permitted on the main floor. Their lot was to watch discreetly from tiny windows high up on the walls that overlooked the bent sea of yarmulke'd praying men far below. The women were relegated to the role of silent observers, never participants. But he recognized that times were changing in the Jewish faith—women rabbis and bas mitzvahs for girls. And he had to admit that the Catholic Church was making a few changes concerning women, although they were minor.

As Father Murphy crossed Michigan Avenue in front of the Dominican House and entered the front door, he suddenly wondered whether the Catholic Church, his church, was really as superior and unique as he had been taught. But the thought was fleeting and quickly dismissed. He was reminded of the scolding given by the nuns in elementary school who repeatedly told their classes they must accept everything the church teaches without question. The process of lapsing from the one true faith begins with questioning and doubting. He remembered one nun saying: "The road to hell is paved with Catholics who began questioning the tenets of the faith."

*****

Friar Joseph, standing in the doorway to his office, watched Steve as he climbed the stairs to his room. In the past weeks he had seen a distinct change in the priest but was at a loss to know the real reason. He smiled as he heard Father Murphy whistling as he climbed the stairs. Further, he had not for weeks heard Murphy thrashing around in bed calling out in a loud anguished voice that God had deserted him.

The friar concluded that the Dominican residents had heeded his call to unite in prayer for Murphy, and apparently the combined prayers had produced a wonderful change.

7

The Washington Post ran the story on the front page. Beloved Cardinal Wollman, Archbishop of Washington, was dead of a heart attack. The Washington area's Roman Catholics numbering in the hundreds of thousands were in mourning. Auxiliary Bishop Phillip Rhinehart had been appointed pro-temp by the Vatican to assume the duties as Archbishop of Washington amid strong rumors that he would soon be elevated to the Papal College of Cardinals.

It had happened suddenly although not unexpectedly. The cardinal was seated at his desk in the chancery. Cardinal Wollman and his auxiliary, Bishop Rhinehart, were in a heated discussion that bordered on a full-blown argument. Red faced, breathing heavily, blood pressure soaring, in the middle of a sentence, the cardinal's head suddenly snapped back leaving his jaw agape. Slumped in his chair, he spoke no more.

As he leaned over the prelate, Bishop Rhinehart felt a weak erratic pulse and instantly notified the secretary to call for medical assistance. Instinctively, the bishop reached into a side pocket where he always carried the viaticum—a custom that dated back to the year of his ordination. Dipping his fingers in the sacred oil, he made a Sign of the Cross on the dying cardinal's forehead to begin the sacrament of Extreme Unction. Then, after stripping off the cardinal's shoes and socks, he anointed each of the senses in succession: eyes, ears, nose and mouth, as well as the limp hands and feet, repeating the prayer, "Through this holy unction and through His most tender mercy, may the Lord pardon thee whatever sins thou has committed...".

As the final breath left the cardinal's body, the bishop stood over the figure slumped in the chair. The cardinal's dead glassy eyes stared up at the ceiling as if searching for a land somewhere above, a land where the cardinal's long journey would end—up with God and the angels.

After the funeral, Bishop Rhinehart found he had little time to waste since as the cardinal's successor, he was inundated with the task of running the archdiocese. However, there was one lingering matter that deserved priority attention.

"Your call is ready, Your Grace," the secretary said on the bishop's intercom.

"Bishop Hernandez, I have a favor to ask. I would like to send another priest to the Passion Brothers Monastery, one who has been giving us a great deal of difficulty. Yes, I know you have limited facilities, but I'm sure Brother Berard can find room for one more. Be assured that I will forward funding to cover. Oh yes, everything is under control here in Washington. The cardinal's sudden death saddened us. I leave for Rome next week. The American cardinals are meeting with the pontiff to discuss matters pertaining to the church here in America. When I return, I look forward to seeing you at the upcoming Synod of Bishops in Washington. Do I have your approval to discuss arrangements for this latest priest directly with Brother Berard? Thank you, and my prayers are with you too."

"Brother Berard, this is Bishop Rhinehart calling from the Archdiocese of Washington. Can you hear me? This is a terrible connection. All I hear are squeaks and squawks."

"Yes, I can hear you, Your Grace. It's our telephone. We only have one telephone here at the monastery and it is quite ancient, I'm afraid."

"I have spoken to Bishop Hernandez about sending you a priest. Your bishop has given his approval. This priest has been giving us considerable difficulty and we would like to send him to spend some time at the monastery. His name is Stephen Murphy. I'm not at liberty to discuss details of his case at this time. I will forward his file later. For the time being, simply consider him an open-ended resident. No, do not assign him to any therapy group. We are still in the process of finalizing a determination of his aah...condition. Yes, you will receive further instructions by mail. Is this arrangement satisfactory? Good. Many thanks. I would appreciate your having someone meet Father Murphy at the Tucson airport. My secretary will call you with all the details. Thanks again. Yes...remember the Crucified Christ. Yes, of course, I will. We all must."

Bishop Rhinehart hung up the phone and leaned back in his swivel chair. He fingered his crucifix. The Passion Brothers, he mused. Strange bunch. Strongly focused on the crucified Christ. Perhaps too focused on the Crucified Christ. Not much was known about the place far out in the Arizona desert run by the Passion Brothers. They had a reputation for being contemplative, ascetic, hard on themselves as well as the priests assigned there—somewhat on the outer fringe of the mainstream church. But he had to admit they perform an important service for the church. They take in the derelicts—the unreformed alcoholics, the pedophile priests, the embezzlers, the end-of-the-line cases, the three-time losers. He wondered what really happened to one of the priests the archdiocese had sent there two years before. The monastery reported the death as an accident. But who really knew? There was no next of kin, no one to claim the body, so the monks had buried him there at the monastery. It was similar to the ancient practice of burying paupers in 'potters fields'. No paperwork was forthcoming and it wasn't even clear that a coroner had gone out to that distant desert outpost.

Considering their task, Bishop Rhinehart knew the monks had to be tough. He did not like the fact that they exercised a strong degree of independence from the mainstream church. It went against the grain with him. It reminded him of the Jesuits, although the Passion Brothers seemed to be immensely more independent. But he had to admit that he admired the way this group of monks had gone out into the desert many years before and rebuilt an abandoned mission with attached monastery. He had heard stories, of course. There had even been a few hints of brutality, but to his way of thinking the motivation and usefulness exhibited by the monks under Brother Berard justified their purportedly unorthodox ways of serving God.

Bishop Rhinehart, now vested with the powers of the cardinal's office, called in his secretary to make the travel arrangements for Murphy. He dictated a transfer letter addressed to Reverend Stephen Murphy in care of the Dominican House, Michigan Avenue, NE Washington, DC. The letter offered no explanation for the abrupt transfer and did not use the word temporary. Two other letters were addressed to the university departments where Murphy had been assigned. The letters expressed the bishop's confidence that the university would be able to find a suitable substitute to take over Murphy's classes.

Satisfied that these actions would rid him of Stephen Murphy, the bishop next turned to pressing matters affecting the Roman Catholic Church in the Archdiocese of Washington.

8

Steve Murphy was sitting on the sofa in Janet's small apartment. He fidgeted, unable to relax. After serving him a cup of coffee, she sat in a chair across from him as she read the letter. "It says here you're being transferred to Arizona. It doesn't say for how long. How long will it be?"

"Beats me," Steve replied. "I can't figure it out. The only conclusion I can draw is that Bishop Rhinehart is after me again. He seems determined to get me out of the way. This time, far out of the way."

"What happens to your classes?"

"Somebody else's problem now."

"What's in Tucson?" she asked puzzled.

"Well, I've heard that the church has a monastery attached to a mission in the desert outside of Tucson. Far out of Tucson. Although I don't know exactly where it is. It's a place the church sends priests who are repeat offenders."

"Repeat offenders of what?"

"Things like pedophilia, alcoholism, gross disobedience... transgressions along those lines."

"You're not a repeat offender, are you?"

"Not even a first time offender, as far as I know."

Janet walked over and sat on the sofa next to him. "What about priests who break the vow of chastity?" she asked as she took his hand.

"Those too, I suppose, if it's repetitive, and especially

if there are complaints. From the little I know, the place we're talking about is intended for priests who have persisted in their sins. The ones the church has not been able to reform in the confessional or by retreats or by conventional psychotherapy. I'm embarrassed even to admit to you that I'm being sent there. And speaking of the vow of chastity, I haven't broken the vow, except perhaps in my dreams," Steve added with a sly grin as he searched her eyes wondering if she *was* tempting him. And with a fleeting thought, hoping she was tempting him.

"I wonder if the bishop knows about us," she said tentatively. "Maybe he thinks we've been having an affair. Maybe he's trying to separate us. You know I think an awful lot of you Steve, but I've put on restraints."

"Janet my dear, this business of the transfers started before I met you. It began with the sudden transfer from my parish, although our friendship may have added fuel to the bishop's case against me, whatever it is. And I suppose people saw us having lunch together a lot, and some may have seen me visiting your apartment. In the eyes of the church it gives cause for scandal and it's an occasion of sin. Even if nothing really happened, the church doesn't favor that kind of conduct. But I'm convinced Bishop Rhinehart has something bigger on his mind than our relationship."

He looked into her eyes and managed a smile. "There's some truth to rumors that may be floating around," he continued, "because I do care for you very much. I suppose I'm really in love with you, although you've done a masterful job of keeping me at arm's length."

"You know the reasons."

"Tell me again."

"I love you, Steve, although I try to keep telling myself I only love you as a friend. I could easily fall head over heels in love with you, but I've struggled hard to keep from doing so. And even if my husband and I can't get an annulment and wind up getting divorced, you wouldn't be in the picture because you're a priest and I will not get between you and your God...our God. Frankly, I'm carrying enough Catholic guilt without having that added on top."

"If I quit the priesthood?"

"Maybe a long time after that, but I don't see you ever leaving the priesthood. There's one thing I realized when we got to know each other: you have always been a priest. Yes, even as a boy serving on the altar I'm sure you had a mindset about the priesthood, and you still do. It's your whole life."

"The tricky part," Steve said, "is that it's not a decision process. We learn that we are called to the priesthood. We do not choose, we are chosen. We answer the call."

"I don't understand. It sounds as if you're denying free will. I thought you were a great believer in free will."

"If it will help, let me cite an example. You've heard of the Dalai Lama— the spiritual leader of the Tibetans. As a very young boy, he is told that he is the reincarnation of Buddha and as such, he must forgo a normal childhood and grow spiritually in order to care for the souls of his people. The boy can refuse, of course, just as a boy can who is called to the priesthood, but they rarely do. Anyway, let's leave it at that," Steve said finally as he walked over to the dinette counter to leave his coffee cup. He glanced at his watch. Almost time to go.

He walked back and sat close to Janet on the sofa. She smiled at him while she almost imperceptibly leaned away. This, the point of leaving, she knew, could be a dangerous moment.

He noticed her concerned look and realizing she needed more space, shifted away from her. "Janet, speaking as a friend, there are a couple of things I'd like you to do for me while I'm away."

"Anything, anything at all."

"I can't take my car and don't have time to sell it. I left it out front. Will you take care of it until I get back? I know you don't have a car so feel free to use mine. The papers are in the glove compartment. And, since I'm only allowed to take one suitcase, can I leave some things here with you? They're in the car trunk."

"I'll store them in the spare closet."

"You may object, but I added your name to one of my credit cards. Keep this card. Use it for maintenance on the car or for repairs. Use it to keep the tags and insurance in force. It has a big limit so if you need anything at all, feel free to use the card."

"You sound as if I'm becoming a member of your family."

"There's no one else."

"What about your brother in Wayland?"

"I don't want him involved in any of my affairs. I have my reasons. One other thing—I've added your name to my bank account. You have to have a way to payoff credit card charges. It has a one-hundred-thousand dollar limit so you won't have to worry about it going over the limit."

"Steve, are you sure you want to handle things this way? Good grief. Where did the money come from?"

"No, I'm not an embezzler in case that crossed your mind," he said with a laugh. "Remember, we Murphy's of Wayland are 'old money.'"

"Is there any way I can get in touch with you?"

"My guess is no. And I don't know when I'll get back. I may be able to get in touch with you. I'll try to write. Here's the address of my brother Jonathon in Wayland. Somewhere down the road if you don't hear from me you might get in touch with him. If I'm gone a long time you may get tired of taking care of my stuff."

"How can you say that? When I leave the university, wherever I go, your things will go with me," she said, fighting a sudden strong temptation to wrap her arms around him and press her body against his. But she knew that if she did, they would cross a threshold that would forever change their lives. A brief happiness bought at a price—guilt, confusion, perhaps the loss of mutual respect, and ultimately, unhappiness.

He thought he knew what she was thinking as he stood up, gently pulled her to her feet, and stared into her eyes for a long time. He ran his fingers lightly through her tousled hair. She closed her eyes as he held her face softly in his hands and brushed each of her smooth white cheeks with a kiss.

When she opened her eyes, he was gone.

9

As the jet circled for a landing at Tucson International Airport, Steve Murphy marveled at the sight of a modern city glistening on a broad flat plateau completely ringed by high snowcapped mountains. It was his first trip to the city which he had always imagined as a movie-land cowtown—complete with clapboard buildings, cattle pens and dusty streets. "So much for fantasy", he said to himself.

At the gate, the card simply read, "Murphy." The young man holding it was an unlikely representative of a monastery. Long dirty blonde hair, scraggily blonde beard, T-shirt cut off at the shoulders, tattoo on each upper arm, blue jeans and loafers. He introduced himself as Jeremy, shook Steve Murphy's hand and led him outside the terminal to a vehicle the likes of which Steve had never seen before. It must have been homemade, at least in part, Steve thought. The car was a topless modified Chevy convertible perched high off the ground on a chassis that held four huge tires.

"Off-road capability. You need it where we're going," the young man said smiling as Steve stood beside the vehicle trying to figure out how the devil to climb into it.

"How do I get up there?" Steve asked. "Got a rope ladder?"

"Let me climb in first," Jeremy said. "Then I'll lower the body some so's you can get in."

"You can lower the body?" Steve asked incredulously.

"Yeah, watch this. It's hydraulic. I rigged it up myself."

Jeremy started the engine with a roar and a blast of exhaust that startled Steve. Then yanking on a lever, the young man lurched in his seat as the body ground haltingly down with a squealing noise that sounded like a wounded animal and a solid thump on bottoming out. Steve found the climb to the seat difficult. His knees had stiffened up during the long flight to Arizona. He threw his suitcase into the back seat. "Seatbelts?" he asked.

"Nope, you'd best just hang on," Jeremy said as he roared out of the parking lot and swung onto the road leading to Interstate 10 West in the direction of Phoenix.

"How long is the ride?" Steve shouted, his hair flying, right hand gripping a bar on the side, left hand groping unsuccessfully for a handhold.

"About four and a half; maybe five hours."

The car flew up I-10 at what must have been 85 miles an hour as Steve asked in a shout, "Why so fast?"

"Speed limit's 75 miles an hour. Why not take advantage of it and let it all hang out? You scared or something?"

After 45 minutes of weaving in and out of a line of cars, SUVs, RVs towing family cars, and tractor-trailers, Steve pointed to a peak that lay ahead. "What's that strange peak up there that looks like a hand with a raised forefinger?" he shouted above the noise of the engine and the wind.

"That's Picacho Peak. Some priests I take out this

way say it looks like a finger pointing up to heaven. I say it looks like a mountain giving God the finger."

"You're not very religious are you?"

"No. I think that crap is something people thought up because they're scared shitless about dying and what comes after...if anything."

Passing reddish brown hills that lined the highway, Jeremy began slowing down. As they approached a turnoff, Steve noticed a sign beside the road that read 'Picacho State Prison. Do not stop for hitchhikers'. "I stopped for a guy here once," Jeremy shouted, "and he like to beat the shit out of me before I kicked him back out on the road. After that, I sure'n hell do what that sign says."

"Are we going to the prison?"

"No, we're heading south, southwest...in the opposite direction, but the place we're going ain't much better."

Jeremy turned the car left onto a side road. Steve relaxed as the going became slower. "What they sending you here for? You a drunk, or something?"

"No, I'm not."

"Fall in love with an altar boy?" Jeremy asked with a sidelong glance at the priest.

"No," Steve said bristling at the accusation. But he held his tongue.

"Well, you must'a done something pretty bad otherwise the church wouldn't be sendin' you to the monastery. That's where they send the bad-asses."

"I don't know why they're sending me and I don't think I've done anything bad."

"Yeah," the young man replied, "all you priests bein' sent here say the same thing. Ever been in this part of the country before?"

"No," Steve replied, growing increasingly angry at the young man. But his attitude softened as he said to himself what difference does it make what this kid thinks? He decided to change the subject. "Tell me," he asked, "have you lived here a long time?"

"All my life. In Tucson, oldest city in Arizona, after Tombstone, that is."

"How did you get a job at the monastery?"

"I don't work for the monastery. I work for an outfit in Tucson. I'm hired to pick you guys up and get you out there. Once in awhile I get calls to take one of the priests back to civilization. O'course, on the way back from the monastery, I guess they ain't priests anymore."

"Just where is out there?" Steve asked as the young man turned the car off the paved road onto a winding dirt road and began careening around potholes and rocks. "Is there a town near the monastery?"

"Nope, nothin' but an old mission church that was abandoned years ago and rebuilt by the brothers, plus the monastery. It's on the other side of those mountains." Slowing down, Jeremy pointed to a line of jagged peaks on the horizon.

"How far on the other side?"

"Couple hours. That's if I step on it."

"Do any tourists visit the mission? Any visitors?"

"Nope. That place has fallen off the map. It ain't rundown, you understand, but it's off limits to visitors. Only a few delivery people and someone like me can get on the property. They got it walled like some kinda jail or something. Weird bunch out there." He resumed whipping the steering wheel to left and right to avoid potholes that could have swallowed a small elephant. "Ever been in these parts? Guess I asked you that before. Have you?"

"Can't say that I have. The countryside is beautiful."

"This ain't countryside you're looking at. It's desert. Bet you thought deserts were just hot sand, hot sun and no water—like the Sahara. This is a different kind of desert. We're in the Sonora Desert. Runs all through southern Arizona and down aways into Mexico. Gotta watch where you walk here. Shitcan fulla life. Diamond back rattlesnakes—some up to six feet long, scorpions, giant desert centipedes, lizards, black bears, some mountain lions, bobcats and Gila monsters, to name a few. Gila monster get his teeth into your ass, he'll never let go. They're not like snakes. When a snake bites, the venom comes out automatically, so he right away lets go. But with the Gila monster, he has to grind his jaws while he's got you in his grip so's the venom can mix with the saliva and wind up in your leg or your ass, case may be. I knew a guy had one stuck to his face. Damn thing didn't let go 'til the sun went down."

"Sounds wonderful," Steve commented sarcastically. "Where is all this teeming life. I don't see it."

"Oh, it's there all right, but it's almost all nocturnal because of the heat. In summer this place can get up to 120 degrees, then, turn around and you freeze your ass off at night."

"All those green telephone poles on the hillside are cactus, right?"

"That's saguaro cactus. Takes forever to grow. It takes a hundred years for it to get up to twelve, maybe fifteen feet high. No one can figure out why every one is different—some have one arm poking out here, some have an arm poking there. Some have two arms, some have a dozen. Some of the arms are twisted like a corkscrew. Beats figuring."

"I notice a lot of them have holes," Steve said.

"Saguaro is like an apartment house. The Gila woodpeckers make the holes and build nests inside, then they shove off and in come screech owls, purple martins and other birds. They move right into ready-made apartments. Despite all those heads peeking out, the holes don't seem to hurt the cactus. See those fuzzy clumps by the side of the road? That's Teddy-Bear cholla. Looks soft and furry to the touch but watch out, the spines can jump right into your skin. People goin' in the hills around Tucson carry a pair of pliers when they walk their dogs because that's the only way to pull some of them spines out when the dog gets nailed. I heard of a male dog once, lifted his leg on a cholla and got a spine in his prick. Howled something awful. Woman that owned him grabbed his dong with one hand, pliers in the other, and yanked with all her might. She got it out, but you can bet that dog didn't do no fucking for a long time."

"Glad I didn't bring my dog," Steve said.

Jeremy gave his passenger a quick puzzled look. He never heard priests were allowed to have dogs. Then he resumed whipping the steering wheel to left and right to avoid potholes, sudden dropoffs and rocks.

"Is this the only road in? This is a disaster, not a road."

"That's the way the brothers want it, I suppose. Keeps people away. You know what we're actually drivin' through right now?"

"You told me—the Sonora Desert."

"Yeah, but now we're actually driving through a humongous extinct volcano. This region was jumping with volcanoes at one time. In fact, you can see the chopped up outlines on the horizon. Those cutoff mountains are volcanoes that blew their tops off some time back. Shit's all dead now."

"Gosh, that's good news," Steve said as he hung onto the door frame, hair flying and rear end beginning to get numb from the bumps in the road. "With all those scary things alive out here, I'm glad at least the volcanoes are dead."

Hours later, as they came over a high pass between two snow-capped peaks, in a distant valley Steve thought he could dimly make out the shape of a mission church and outbuildings. "Is that it?"

"Yeah. It ain't far off, but considerin' this road it'll take us a coupla hours to get there. When I leave you off, I gotta head back to Tucson pretty damn quick. I don't like bein' way out here after dark. By the way, do you have a flashlight?"

"No," Steve answered wonderingly.

"Let me explain. The monastery generates its own electric power—has to, there ain't any city or county utilities way out here. So they turn the power off at night. I think about nine or ten o'clock. And if you want to get up and take a pee, you have to go in the dark to the john."

"No private toilets I guess. Why do I need a flashlight; can't I feel my way along in the dark?"

"Sure, but you gotta watch out for scorpions.

The monastery is loaded with them. The large hairy scorpions ain't so dangerous, but a sting from one of the small ones—they're called 'bark scorpions', can kill you."

"Well I'll have to buy a flashlight at the monastery store."

"There ain't no monastery store. I'll sell you a flashlight if you want."

"How much?"

"I carry the small six inch flashlight. Let you have one for fifty dollars."

"Good grief! They usually only cost six or seven dollars."

"Well then, forget it."

"No, I'll take one."

"Good. Just put the money in the can on the dashboard. I usually use it for tips and stuff."

"Is that a hint?"

"Tip only if you like the service, as they say."

"What about spare batteries? The small flashlights take double A's."

"Sell you them too. Ten dollars each."

"I'm glad I brought my bankroll with me because I assume you don't take credit cards. Okay. Money in the can too?"

"Yeah. Next question: do you smoke?"

"Once in awhile. I brought a couple of packs with me."

"No smoking allowed at the monastery. If the monks find them they'll take 'em away. Keep 'em hidden."

"Are they health conscious?"

"Nope. If they catch any priests with smokes, the

monks take 'em and smoke 'em out behind the chapter house. If you're gonna be here a long time like most priests, you're gonna run out of cigs. I can sell you a carton or two. And what you do to hide 'em is put the packs in a plastic bag which I include free of charge and bury it somewhere in the compound. Don't put 'em under your mattress. They search your room."

"How do you know all this stuff?"

"When I take a guy out, he fills me in."

"Okay, how much for a carton?"

"Let you have one for two hundred."

"You must be on the way to becoming a millionaire."

"Father Murphy, yes or no."

"I'll take a carton. Cash in the tin can?"

"You catch on fast, Father Murphy."

"And here's a twenty dollar tip for the can. And, I'd appreciate it if you don't let on what I'm doing," Steve said as he opened his suitcase, took out his chalice case and hid the carton of cigarettes in a false bottom of the case.

"Like the monkey said, 'See no evil, talk no evil,' " Jeremy said with a conspiratorial grin.

*****

It was late in the day as they approached the large wooden gates of the walled compound. Jeremy honked the horn. After a few minutes the gates were swung open by two monks on the inside. Jeremy gave them a wave as he drove through. They drove past the mission church—whitewashed adobe with large oak front doors in the center and a pair of four-story bell towers fronting either side, standing like brilliant white sentinels against a deep blue sky.

As Jeremy's strange vehicle roared off into the dust leaving the priest standing in the compound with his suitcase, Steve looked around at a cluster of single level adobe buildings. He decided to enter a small white, one-story building that looked like it might have an office. Inside, it was cool and musty smelling, the floor hard-packed earth. He put his suitcase down inside the entrance as a very tall thin monk in a gray robe with hood—he presumed one of the Passion Brothers, limped across the courtyard to the building.

"Good afternoon," the brother said. "I am the abbot here. I am Brother Berard. Your archdiocese told me to expect you. Let's go into the office."

Steve followed the monk into the small dark office that had a few tiny windows. A coarse wooden desk stood in the center, surrounded by a few rickety chairs. Steve noted the monk's severe limp.

"Accident?" Steve asked.

"Yes, many years ago. I lost the big toe on one foot. In those days, not much could be done about it. Even though it's only a toe, when you lose it, you can't avoid the limp. Perhaps with today's medicine some kind of prosthesis could be made, but I long ago decided to live with it this way. The phantom pain from the missing toe is a constant reminder of the Crucified Christ. I think of a wounded, weakened Christ limping up to Calvary. We here at the mission, have a special devotion to the Crucified Christ."

As Steve gingerly sat down on one of the wobbly chairs in front of the desk, wondering whether he'd wind up on the dirt floor, the brother seated himself behind the desk. He stared at Steve with deep narrow-set eyes. His long hair and beard were streaked with gray. Here and there were places on his robes that seemed to be covered with dust. "I am the abbot." Then abruptly, the monk asked, "Do you know why you are here?"

"No. I have no idea."

"Nor do I. Do you know of any transgressions you may have committed? Anything at all. Excessive alcohol, insubordination, heresy, embezzling, sex with minors, anything along those lines?"

"No, absolutely not. I know of nothing I've done wrong. I have committed no serious sin."

Brother Berard's mouth drew up in an almost unnoticeable tight-lipped smile, but Steve noticed it. He didn't pretend not to be irritated by it.

"I am frankly puzzled, Father Murphy. Every priest who is sent here has been a repeat...how shall I say it...a repeat offender with a long history of earlier attempts to reclaim his soul at other institutions. Each had repeatedly broken one or more of God's commandments or a religious vow. In some cases, criminal laws had also been broken. Some of our priests are ex-convicts. We have the difficult task of trying to reclaim these priests, and I must say our success rate is not high. Although you are not willing to admit it, I have to believe that you are one of these; however, until the archdiocese—your archdiocese in Washington that is, gives the Tucson diocese more information, I don't know what category to place you in."

"So where do we go from here?" Steve asked, completely puzzled. "And by the way, I've never before heard of your Order of Passion Brothers. Are you newly organized?"

"Yes, we formed about twenty years ago. We are a monastic order devoted to the passion of Christ on the Cross. We think of ourselves as deeply religious and hardworking. We pattern ourselves after the Trappist Monks—an offshoot of the Cistercian Order that dates back almost a thousand years to its origin in France. But we have a far more serious mission than merely running a monastery. In recent years we have been assigned the difficult task of providing therapy to reclaim the errant priests sent here by the bishops."

"Do you have psychologists or licensed therapists on the staff?"

"We have no need of them. Our monks provide the therapy."

Steve shook his head. "That's ridiculous," he said.

Brother Berard leaned forward in his chair menacingly. "Father Murphy you are not likely to be happy here, but you will certainly be less miserable if you avoid ridiculing us. As I said earlier, our driving force is deep devotion to the Crucified Christ. You'll see that much of what we do is related to atoning for the Crucifixion."

Steve thought it best not to respond, but it crossed his mind that the abbot's attitude seemed more directed towards avenging Christ's death rather than accepting it as God's effort to redeem mankind.

"I sense that you are disturbed, perhaps somewhat angry," Brother Berard said. "I would caution you that we have a long history of dealing with angry priests. We much prefer them to be submissive and anxious to be cured and absolved of past offenses so they can return to pastoral work."

"And if they aren't?" Steve asked challengingly, thinking all the while: This monk has the damned nerve to ignore the hierarchy of the Catholic Church. He doesn't seem to be aware that brothers and their counterparts, nuns, serve on a level below that of priests. "Need I remind you that I was pastor of a large metropolitan church? I was about to be elevated to Monsignor."

"But you weren't elevated. You were sent here instead. For your information, we have some Monsignori here. We even have a bishop. In addition to other virtues, they have learned humility here."

On hearing this, Steve caved in. He realized that arguing with this monk was pointless. "Where do we go from here?" he asked.

"For the time being, you will be assigned to a private cell in Row A. You will find a copy of the Monastic Rule in your cell. It will explain when you are to say daily Mass, hear confessions, attend vespers, have meals, and so forth. You will be assigned work in the fields as the season approaches."

"And therapy?"

"Until we get further instructions, you are not assigned to any therapy group."

"Let me ask you a question, Brother Berard. Am I free to leave?"

"No, I'm afraid you are not. I say this for several reasons. First, you have been assigned here by your bishop. This is where you must remain or risk being defrocked and perhaps excommunicated from the church for gross disobedience. Second, transportation back to Tucson is not available to you and it would be foolhardy for you to attempt crossing the mountains and desert on foot. Some peaks around Tucson for example, reach up to nine thousand feet. They are formidable considering that they are snowcapped in winter. Then there is the desert to consider. Dangers abound for the unprepared in the Sonora Desert. You may not know this, but most illegal immigrants from Mexico attempt to cross at cities like Nogales; however, some try to negotiate the Sonora Desert. Many of these die."

"That's terrible," Steve replied, fully conscious of the fact that he had no intention of leaving, not at least, until he got to the bottom of his present situation and could make the right decision about his future. "But tell me this— the driver who brought me out here said he occasionally returns a man to...civilization, as he put it. What about that?"

"Some priests decide to resign the priesthood. Subject to dispensation of their vows from their diocese, they are permitted to leave."

"You're saying they're defrocked."

"Not exactly. Defrocking is levied on a priest. These men are simply permitted to resign and, of course, they relinquish all benefits from the church. There are also various categories of administrative action; for example, some priests are permitted to remain as priests with curtailed duties. They are no longer allowed to say Mass or perform any of the other sacraments. Others reacquire these benefits after a period of good behavior."

The shadow of a huge monk in gray habit that Steve

thought must have been made from ten yards of cloth, appeared in the doorway. To Steve, the monk could have been a former professional wrestler or boxer who had decided he had broken enough bodies and wanted to atone by entering the religious life.

"I have asked Brother John to escort you to our supply building. After that, he will show you to your quarters and tell you about some of our regulations. Good-day, Father Murphy."

10

Steve stood at the counter in the supply building. Brother John, without saying a word, had escorted him to the building and disappeared, leaving him at the counter. A tall rugged-looking monk in a gray hooded robe stood behind the counter. He introduced himself as Brother Michael. He made a point of saying that he had been a professional football player before entering the religious life.

"Here's a robe that will probably fit you and sandals that seem to be too small, but they're all we have right now. There may be more available soon but whether they'll fit you or not, I don't know."

"Does everyone wear gray around here?"

"Passion brothers and resident priests both wear the same type of robe here, the difference being that those worn by the priests have a code embroidered on the breast."

"What are you talking about? What kind of code?"

"The code, simply, is a number."

"Steve was astonished. "This sounds like a prison rather than a monastery."

"You miss the point, Father. We have priests here who have committed some grave offenses in both the religious and legal sense. We use no names. This protects their privacy. I'm sure you understand the need for this."

Steve nodded that he understood. He had a sudden

pain in the pit of his stomach, as if a clawed hand had reached inside his gut and tried to tear him apart. What kind of isolated outpost of civilization had he been sent to? Could this Devil's Island actually be a legitimate monastery of the Catholic Church? Was the pontiff aware that such places existed under his supposedly beneficent rule? While he was ruminating about his situation, Steve failed to heed Brother Michael's command to empty his pockets onto the counter.

"I said, Father, empty your pockets! And I don't have all day," the brother demanded in a surly tone as he glared at the priest.

"I would caution you not to speak to me that way, Brother Michael," Steve said, bristling. "I'm a priest. I'm not accustomed to this kind of treatment especially from one who serves in the lower religious orders."

"Maybe so," Brother Michael challenged, "but who are you going to complain to? We brothers are the only authority in your life from here on in, and we intend to exercise it."

"I beg to differ. Bishop Rhinehart in my archdiocese in Washington is the anointed authority." Steve thought mention of the archdiocese would carry some weight with the brother, although he knew full well that Rhinehart would never support him in a dispute.

Brother Michael had had enough backtalk. "Let me explain something, Father, and I want you to listen closely. The bishops send priests here because they are trying to get rid of them. Very, very few are 'reclaimable' here. Some of them resign and then go back into society and do whatever the hell they did before—drink, do drugs, molest children—whatever.

In almost every case, we are the chosen exit door. We don't kick them out of course. I suppose you would call that 'defrocking'. Instead, we make it easy for them to leave. We make them want to leave the priesthood. Do you get the picture?"

Steve quietly put his wallet on the counter together with a few keys he carried, his cell phone, cell phone charger, wristwatch and some coins. He laid two unopened packs of cigarettes next to his other belongings. "I'm glad you surrendered the cigarettes, we don't allow smoking here."

The monk opened the wallet. "Hmm... you must be here for embezzlement—you've got about eight hundred bucks in your wallet and four credit cards."

"What happens to my personal belongings?" Steve asked. "When do I get my wallet and stuff back?"

"We keep them locked up in a safe place that has your number on it. None of the cells have locks and we wouldn't want you to complain that some of your valuables were stolen. Do you have anything else on your person? I assume for the moment that you only have clothing, your chalice case and other religious articles in your suitcase."

"No, I don't have anything else," Steve lied. He thought of the cigarettes he had bought from Jeremy hidden in a false bottom of his chalice case, as well as a stash of sixs hundred dollars. "But if you doubt it, you can frisk me, and go through my suitcase," he replied caustically.

"That won't be necessary. After all, if you can't trust a Catholic priest, who can you trust?"

*****

Brother John showed him to his cell. The cell was exactly that—one of thirty or more small rooms that opened off a long portico with a roof that slanted down to catch rainwater from downspouts hovering over large barrels. He was located in Row A. Across the wide dusty courtyard he could see an array of other cells labeled Row B. And in the distance, Rows C, D and E. "Cellblocks without visible bars, but cellblocks nonetheless," he mumbled to himself.

"Did you say something?" Brother John asked gruffly.

"No."

His new home contained a cot, a makeshift table in the corner holding a gooseneck lamp, a chair, and a grisly, bloody picture depicting the Crucifixion on the wall over the cot. The table had a few drawers for storing underwear and small items. There was no closet. Steve shivered slightly as he thought he caught a glimpse of a scorpion that scuttled under the bed. It unnerved him. He was a city type—one who had never encountered anything in his bedroom larger than a cockroach. "I think I saw a scorpion," he said. "They're poisonous, aren't they?"

"Yes," Brother John replied with a broad grin. "We just try to stay away from them, although I should warn you it is difficult when we are literally overrun with them. Before you put anything on, shake it out thoroughly first. There is one more very important piece of information I need to tell you. We have a vow of silence here. This goes for the priests as well as the brothers. We eat in silence, work in the fields and do other chores in silence. No priest is permitted to speak to another priest. Meals are consumed in silence in the refectory after Brother Berard says the blessing. Silence is enforced with stringent disciplinary action. Nor can any of you speak to one of the brothers unless it is absolutely necessary. Breaking this rule is a serious infraction. There are a few exceptions: you can pray aloud in church and you are free to speak in therapy sessions."

"I haven't been invited to any therapy sessions. What about speaking in the confessional?"

"Are you trying to be sarcastic? The confessional is, of course, sacrosanct. It is another exception. However, the confessional, as you know, is not a place for idle communication. We expect that sessions be restricted to confession of sins, contrition, absolution and penance, nothing more. No chitchat among you priests. The Monastic Rule and a few other instructions in the top drawer of your table describe the schedule of services in the main chapel. The instructions also tell when, and in which of the small chapels, you are to say Mass each morning, work assignments, meal times and everything else you need to know. There is also a map of the monastery—please use it instead of asking directions."

"You took my watch and I don't see any clocks so how am I supposed to know when to do anything?"

"We have a system of bells. The schedule is with your instructions. When the bells ring, hop to it. There are penalties for being late."

"Just like being in the army," Steve said dourly.

"Not quite. In the army there is a payday. Priests

here have no payday. Any money that a diocese thinks a priest should have is put away with his stuff. After all, there's nothing here to buy."

Steve visibly jumped as a scorpion suddenly scuttled out from under the cot. With a quick movement, Brother John slipped off his sandal and killed the pest with one blow. The crushed remains were pushed over into a corner. "Now, if you do not have any questions, we will speak no more," he said calmly as if the incident with the scorpion had never happened.

Steve thought for a moment. The only real question that popped into his head was: How in hell did I get myself into this place? Then he remembered Bishop Rhinehart.

"No questions?" Brother John asked. "Fine. Then the silence rule begins as of now." With that, Brother John backed his hulking frame out of the cell leaving Steve to unpack his suitcase. Steve closed the heavy oaken door noting with satisfaction that it could be barred from the inside. "I may want to keep those guys from poking their heads in here unannounced," he said to himself, although he was aware that when he left the cell, there was no lock on the out-side of the door. I most certainly want to keep the door closed to keep the scorpions out, he thought. He was unaware that a partially opened door together with a small window high on the back wall of his cell, created a draft that kept the room from becoming a furnace in the summertime.

Steve placed his underwear and socks in one of the drawers in the table. He removed the case that held his chalice from the suitcase. Taking off his black suit and Roman collar, once starched white, but now brown resembling the color of sand mixed with dirt from the dusty ride in the desert, he placed them on a hangar and the hangar onto a hook mounted on the wall. He placed a spare suit that he had brought with him on the hook. He placed his stole in the bottom drawer. Next, he slipped into the gray habit. It was coarse, homemade and musty smelling. The cuffs were frayed. Obviously a hand-me-down, but from whom? What happened to the priest or the succession of priests who had worn it? The number 1203 was embroidered in yellow on the breast. He wondered whether the number had any significance. Did it mean twelve hundred and three priests had gone through this place? Or was it a code for a specific priestly transgression? Or did it identify his diocese? Maybe he would never know.

There was no way he could tell how he looked in the garb of a monk because there was no mirror in the room, nor even glass that he might see his reflection in. Then he remembered the shiny gold paten in his chalice case. Pulling the cowl up over his head, he looked at his reflection in the gold plate. It occurred to him that with the hood up almost covering his face, and by bending slightly forward with hands clasped in prayer, he could probably pass for one of the brothers. A beard would help. It was a resemblance he might need one day. Then he remembered the number embroidered on the chest of his garment—the very visible number that distinguished between the prisoners and the guards.

He sat on the cot and slipped into the worn leather sandals. Out of the corner of his eye he saw a centipede that must have been six inches long feeding on the remains of the scorpion that Brother John had killed and kicked into the corner of the cell. "Hope he gets enough to eat so he leaves me alone," Steve muttered to himself.

He opened the top drawer of the table. In it he found a Catholic Bible, a copy of the priest's daily office, a map and a copy of the Monastic Rules. Riffing through the pages of the Rules, he decided he would read the document some other time. He picked up a card that contained the daily schedule. He was pleased to note that Lauds—which some monasteries held at two-thirty A.M. was missing. This was probably because the monastery operated on self-generated electric power and the monks didn't want to turn on the generators in the middle of the night.

The canonical day began with Mass in the church at six A.M., although some priests were permitted to say a private Mass in one of the small chapels. He assumed he was one of these. As the monk had said, he noted that all events were announced by the tolling of bells. According to the schedule, breakfast was served at seven, lunch at noon, followed by one hour of meditation in the church. Dinner was served at six; followed by Compline; lights out at nine o'clock. All of the non-canonical hours were apparently spent working in the fields, the kitchens, or in therapy. He knew that monasteries usually rang the Angelus at noon at which time, everyone stopped activities and said three Hail Mary's, but the schedule here said nothing about prayers to the Blessed Mother. Strange.

What really puzzled Steve was that there were no clocks so the listed times were meaningless. Every event began with the ringing of electric bells that had been installed for each compound. It reminded Steve of bells at a high school. The loud bell announcements could even be heard when out in the field. While the church bells were tolled for the start of religious services, the electric bells were sounded for everything else.

The electric bell schedule seemed to have been designed by an idiot. There was no discernible order: five bells for breakfast, three for lunch, six for dinner, four to start therapy classes, one to end classes. Eight bells signaled the start of work in the fields, etc. It would take awhile, he thought dourly, until he learned whether it was time to take a shower or to go to the refectory for a meal. But he figured he could rely on his stomach for the time to go for meals. The map showed the route to the shower room. He sorely needed to stand for a long time in a warm shower. It could help him relax and think of how he could adjust himself to life in a monastery. An austere one at that. The wash room and shower room were empty. He wondered where everyone was. He remembered hearing a bell ringing but had ignored it. "Maybe it's afternoon tea," he chuckled to himself. "Fat chance." Maybe he was missing a meal but he wasn't hungry, so no matter.

The water in the shower was like ice. He remembered it was January, and he had learned that in Arizona, winter days were somewhat warm, the nights chilly. The water, he thought, may have come from a well. An oasis in the desert. Or, perhaps, runoff from some snowcapped peaks he had seen in the distance. Threadbare towels and gritty soap were provided in the shower room. It adjoined the washroom where the priests brushed their teeth and shaved in the morning. With the single exception of the toothbrush, toilet articles were not taken back to the cells. He looked at the line of sinks. He examined a shelf of obviously shared combs and brushes. The brushes were clogged with white, brown and black hair—usually all three in a single brush. He tried a dull safety razor and winced. No wonder there are so many beards in a monastery, he thought. The washroom did have a small mirror over each sink. He noted that his stubble was already becoming a beard. Something under the sink caught his eye. It was another scorpion standing erect with its curved tail in the air. They stared at one another for a few seconds, then the scorpion scuttled away into the shower room.

Later, map in hand, he took a walk around the compound. He noted that the map showed the adobe wall around the perimeter of the compound and the heavy wooden gate. At a distance behind the lines of adobe priests' cells, stood the brothers' chapter house. The map also indicated a barber shop. "I'll bet," he said to himself, "haircuts simply consist of inverting a soup bowl on your head and trimming around the edge of the bowl." The brothers and priests he had seen up to that point looked every bit like they had orbital haircuts. The monastery also had a small library, but nothing else. No post office, no store where he might buy an occasional snack, some sundries, or cup of coffee. Besides, they had taken all his money except for that he had hidden in his chalice case.

About a quarter mile behind the church he came across the cemetery.

It was surrounded by a grove of strange-looking trees. He was surprised at the large number of cross-covered graves spread over half an acre. Some grave markers had identification, but for the others, only God knew who they were. There were also a few mounds of fresh earth that hadn't yet received their crosses, and a few empty graves that hadn't yet received their bodies. It occurred to him that the abbot had talked about priests resigning, but the driver, Jeremy, seemed to imply that he took few priests back to civilization. This somber place accounted for the discrepancy.

He noticed what looked like a telephone line that ran from Brother Berard's office out over the back wall of the monastery. But there were no power lines. He wondered where the phone line went. He was pretty sure there was no cell phone service way out here, so the only way to communicate with the outside world was by means of Berard's phone or by message through Jeremy.

*****

Walking back, Steve peeked into the small library. Next door, he looked into a large room filled with decrepit hospital-style beds. As he walked in the stench of death was almost overpowering. He had to cover his nose and mouth with his handkerchief. A dozen men lying in the beds raised their heads inquiringly as he appeared at the door, but then with blank looks, fell back into a confined world of disease, pain, and vanishing hope of recovery.

One man suddenly sat up and motioned to Steve. As Steve went to the man's bedside, the man twisted to one side and whispered, "I'm a priest. My name is Bill. All of us in here are priests. I can tell by the number on your robe that you're not one of them. When one of the brothers gets sick they put him in their facility behind the chapter house. I don't know what kind of care they get but we get very little here. They throw the food at us even though some are too sick to feed themselves. Many in here are in pain, but the brothers just ignore it and tell us to offer it up to the Crucified Christ."

"Don't you follow the rule of silence?" Steve whispered.

"Why bother. The monks seldom come in here. The only one who really comes is that young guy—the nurse."

"You mean there's no doctor here to attend to you men?"

"There's no doctor as such at the monastery. The only monk with any knowledge of medicine was a former Navy nurse and he can't handle anything that requires more than a bandaid. The story goes that he was drummed out of the Navy due to misconduct. Even so, no one can help me… I'm dying of cancer. I'm sure it's spread. I don't have much time left."

"How do you know?" Steve asked.

"The nurse examined me. He pushed and prodded and shook his head. He told me they've already got the hole dug in the cemetery for me. Will you look in on me every few days and when the end comes will you give me Extreme Unction?"

"Of course," Steve said, "and is there anyone on the outside who should be notified? Any relatives?"

"Not really. I have a few distant relatives but we

parted company years ago."

As the two priests talked, a man hobbled in with what appeared to be a cruelly twisted leg. He introduced himself to Steve as Father George. No last name, just Father George.

"Do you mind my asking, what happened to your leg? Have an accident?"

"I got into a disagreement with a monk and he kicked me so hard he broke my leg. Later, the nurse tried to set it but he did a lousy job as you can see."

As the priest talked, Steve had a foreboding that he had been sent to a monastery that was a prison without any rules—one that operated on the idea that suffering and pain were tickets to heaven in the hereafter—as long as it was the priests who suffered. He doubted that the monks underwent any real suffering.

Turning back to the bedridden priest, Steve said, "Bill, is Brother Berard aware of all this? Doesn't he try to do anything about it?"

"Not much he can do," Bill replied. "Berard is only abbot because he has been elected to the post by the other monks. If he isn't careful, he gets dumped back into the ranks."

Before Steve left, he said a prayer for the dying priest and blessed him with the Sign of the Cross.

*****

Dinner in the refectory was a dismal affair. Brother Berard stood at the head table flanked by what were probably his most trusted lieutenants. Steve recognized the hulking figures of Brothers Michael and John plus a number of other monks. They looked like a lineup of pro football players or wrestlers waiting to be interviewed by the press. The only monk in the lineup who didn't look like a gorilla was tall, thin Brother Berard in the center.

"Hear us, O Crucified Christ," Brother Berard said in a hoarse ringing voice. "We thank thee for the food thou hast provided us this day. It is simple fare in keeping with our penitent and contemplative life here, but through thy tender mercy, it will give us the strength to persevere in thy work on the morrow. Amen."

"Amen," echoed from the mouths of almost two hundred priests and thirty-some brothers as they clambered over the picnic benches to take their seats.

Steve glanced around cautiously at the rough-surfaced picnic tables and benches. Food was served on a plastic plate accompanied by a skimpy paper napkin and plastic cutlery. He noticed his spoon was not very clean. He deduced from this that the plastic-ware was not throwaway—some haphazard attempt was made to clean it after use. Like eating out of a fast food garbage can, he thought. The food was deplorable. It was so tasteless he wasn't sure what he was eating. He was forty-eight, and doubted he would make it to fifty on meals like this. Although he had seen what appeared to be a sizeable farm on the monastery grounds, it was winter and the land lay barren. The food, poorly preserved, was apparently left over from a previous growing season. Despite this, the priests across from him and on each side, ate hungrily. They seemed to attack their food with animal eagerness. The voiceless gaunt faces opposite him, eating hunched over their meals, told him the story.

Almost all the priests in the refectory were bareheaded. Many were bearded and bald older men, but a few scattered here and there had their cowls pulled over their heads He wondered what that was all about. A few priests had to be helped over the picnic benches by their seatmates. Was it arthritis or had they been kicked by one of the brothers like the priest he had met in the clinic?

Immediately after dinner, he followed a gray, shuffling, undulating side-to-side crowd to the mission church for Compline, the evening service. It was the first opportunity he had to see the interior of the mission church which had been partly destroyed and later abandoned many years before but rebuilt by the Passion Brothers. In rebuilding, the brothers had devoted the church completely to remembrance of the Crucifixion of Christ. Inside the front door, a large wooden cross leaned up against a side wall. Easily ten to twelve feet tall, it could have been the actual size of Christ's cross. Its purpose was a mystery to him— not like the thin gold cross he used to carry when he led processions as an altar boy. This cross seemed far too heavy and cumbersome to carry upright in the vanguard of a procession.

High up on the walls surrounding the nave were a dozen large crucifixes holding figures of the bleeding Christ. As he knelt in the last pew, Steve studied the church. He did not see a single statue or image of the Virgin Mary. The Passion Brothers seemed to have no room for display of a statue or painting of a female in their single-minded devotion to the Crucified Christ. The Stations of the Cross omitted all female figures.

Even the station for Veronica's veil showed the veil but not Veronica.

Over two hundred priests and monks knelt in prayer in their coarse gray monastic robes. The men were so tightly packed together the scene resembled a congealed mass of gray rounded lumps like egg cartons turned upside down. The service was conducted by one of the priests in the dark church that was lighted only by candles. The aroma of incense filled the air. Steve imagined the priests probably performed the evening service on a rotating basis.

After the service, as he left the church, Steve managed to glance through the open door of an adjoining building that held a bank of small altars arranged in the form of a cross. This, apparently, was where the resident priests said morning Mass, perhaps as many as or fifteen or twenty at a time. Another production line, he thought, remembering the basement of the Shrine church.

After some prodding, Steve again followed the shuffling crowd of gray-robed figures as they silently moved back to their respective areas and disappeared one-by-one into the cell-like rooms lined up along the adobe buildings. On entering his cell, he was surprised to find the clothes he had hung on the wall hook were gone. Even his suitcase and shoes were missing. The suitcase had been opened and his chalice case had been removed. It was left standing on the table. His worldly possessions now consisted simply of the gray monastic robe, ill-fitting sandals, his stole, his chalice case, silver crucifix, breviary, his small flashlight, a few sets of underwear and around his neck, a scapular in which he had hidden a tiny picture of Janet.

He rummaged around in the hidden compartment in the bottom of his chalice case. The cigarettes and money were still there. He pulled out a sheet of writing paper and a pen. He sat at his table to write a note to Janet, although he had no idea how he would get it to her. But at least, the act of writing would calm him, remind him of the good times they had enjoyed together. Halfway through the note, the table lamp suddenly went out. He first thought it had blown a bulb, then he remembered from the instruction sheet that the power was turned off promptly at nine P.M. Since he had no watch and no bell sounded, he had to assume it was actually nine P.M. Electric power, supplied by diesel generator, would remain off until 5 A.M.

He stretched out on the cot. He lay on his back in the blackness with his arms folded behind his head. In former times, he had always knelt by his bedside to say nighttime prayers but he dispensed with them because the thought of kneeling on a scorpion in the dark made his spine tingle. He satisfied himself that the evening service in the church and a few prayers said while lying in bed sufficed for his nighttime prayers.

Janet was close to him. She was leaning over to kiss him. He felt her warm sweet breath on his face as she smiled at him. He peered into her blue eyes as he imagined their lips meeting. They had never before kissed on the lips. Never before had there been anything more than her kiss on his cheek and a friendly embrace. He wondered if he would ever see her again. As he relived their few brief months together he knew that eventually the memories would, by constant repetition in his brain, lose their sharpness, their pleasurable excitement like a scratched and worn video of an old movie that has been played too often. His only hope then would be to fantasize new memories—things they hadn't done but for his part, wished they had. The reality however, was that she might, after a time, wind up falling in love with someone else.

As he lay in bed, he wondered about the problem of human love as related to the love of God. He remembered that Thomas Merton, the famous Trappist monk, author of the bestselling, *Seven Story Mountain*, told of the same paradoxes when he admitted that as an ordained priest, he had fallen head over heels in love with a student nurse named Maria. Steve wasn't sure if the Merton-Maria incident ever developed into a full-blown affair, but eventually Maria went on to marry a doctor and raise a family. Steve, partly to assuage his guilt over thinking of Janet, recalled that Thomas Merton, in his early years, had been a hell-raiser surrounded by girlfriends, whereas he, Steve, studious and dedicated to his faith from the beginning, had never even dated a girl, and only found love when he met Janet. As he drifted off to sleep he knew that despite what might happen to him or to her in the future, he would always be in love with her. His love would stay alive if nourished only through his memories and fantasies.

11

"Bless me Father for I have sinned. My last confession was three weeks ago. I took the Lord's name in vain four times. I have been angry."

"How many times?"

"Almost all the time, Father. Anger mixed with fear. I don't understand why I was sent here to this monastery. I'm scared, and don't understand what the church's future plans are for me."

"You must understand, this is a confessional, not a place for discussion of the motives of Holy Mother Church. I ask you again, how many times have you been angry since your last confession?"

Steve had a feeling the priest who was hearing his confession had been either scared or brainwashed by the brothers into keeping it simple, short and to the point. It was two or three minutes and out. In a way it was a blessing because the uneven boards he was kneeling on had begun to cut into his knees. Steve had received counseling and emotional support in the confessional before, but it would not be an ingredient in confession here at the monastery. "Good grief," he said to himself, "he wants a number. It's only a venial sin, so make up a number." At several times a day, it would make well over a hundred times. "One hundred and five times," he said almost sarcastically into the darkened screen between him and his confessor. The ridiculous assumption that he could count the exact number of times he had been angry almost made him walk out. But he stayed because he wanted absolution.

"Anything else? Any impure thoughts?"

He thought of Janet. Was love impure? Certainly not. "No, he answered, that's all."

"For your penance say twenty 'Our Fathers' and make a good act of contrition."

The priest closed the rickety door between them as Steve, knees aching, stood up and pushed his way through the curtain of the confessional. Outside, a long line of priests and monks waited for their turn to rapidly blurt out their sins and receive absolution.

*****

On his fourth day at the monastery, Steve returned to his cell after saying morning Mass and eating breakfast to find that someone had been in his cell again. The few things he had on his desk had been moved slightly. One drawer of the table was slightly ajar. It irritated him that he had no privacy. Everything was subject to inspection. Luckily, he had been carrying his letter to Janet tucked inside his robe. His hope was that he might persuade Jeremy—the driver who had brought him to the monastery, to mail it in Tucson. But, there had been no sign of Jeremy and that strange vehicle since Steve's arrival on the first day.

Walking out onto the portico near the door to his cell, Steve saw that the posted therapy sheets still had blanks after his number, so there would be another morning spent walking in the compound and praying in the mission church. On another list he did see his number listed for afternoon field work. He was pleased with the assignment to field work. It would give him a chance to exercise his muscles.

On one visit to the church, as he knelt alone in the first pew, he was puzzled by a piece of plywood covering a hole in the floor in front of the altar rail. Why hadn't someone repaired the hole? He also noted a few reddish brown stains on the floor. Could they be blood?

As he set foot on a morning walk, his first stop was at the clinic where he spent a few minutes praying with the dying priest. As he continued to explore his new home he found he could pick up some of the rhythm of the monastery—noting particularly where the monks went in the morning and where the priests went after Mass and breakfast. He strolled to the far end of the compound where a dozen large rooms filled with folding chairs were set up for meetings. Groups of fifteen to twenty priests were meeting in each room. A few glimpses through open doors seemed to indicate that the moderator in each case was one of the Passion Brothers. As Steve passed by the open door to one room, holding his breviary up close to his face so that observers would think he was concentrating on his daily office, he distinctly heard one of the priests say something about being an alcoholic. From what little he heard as he walked by the rooms, the tone of the speakers sounded as if they were making open confessions, along the lines of Alcoholics Anonymous meetings.

*****

It must have been around midnight when Steve

heard a faint tapping on the door to his cell. He sat up in bed. A few thin threads of moonlight spread down from the small window high up in the wall of his cell. On opening the door, as the bright moonlight flooded into the room, he recognized the face of a priest who occupied the cell next door to his.

"What do you want?" Steve whispered, shocked at having a visitor.

"Let me in. I want to talk to you," the priest whispered back as Steve ushered him into the room, quietly closing the door behind his visitor.

They sat on the cot in the dark. For a moment, Steve was worried. Was his nocturnal visitor responding to some dark homosexual urge?

"My name's Elmer," he said. "I saw you arrive a few days ago, and I've seen you here and there around the compound. How are things going?"

"OK, I suppose. My name's Steve. Don't you adhere to the rule of silence?"

"Only when the monks are within earshot. It's just another one of those oppressive rules laid down by the monks here. These guys are not priests, by the way. They call themselves 'brothers' like some of the orders of teaching brothers. Remember, from our standpoint, their rules are strictly that—rules not vows, there is no sin for us in breaking them."

"This is a weird place," Steve said. "One for the book. What's going on here?"

"I'll explain. One of the priests helped me when I arrived about a year ago, and you look like you could use some help. I'm an alcoholic. Surprised? It's no secret, I tell it to my therapy group every other day.

I saw you pass by the door of our meeting room this morning. You've probably figured out we have a therapy session each morning, after which we go to assigned work in the afternoon. By the way, why were you sent here?"

"I don't know," Steve replied.

"Now that's a bit hard to believe! Don't be reticent about it, we're all sinners here."

"I really don't know. What else can I say?"

"Absolutely everyone here that I know of has been accused, diagnosed, initially sent to other places and failing elsewhere, finally got assigned here. What's different about you?"

"I know it's hard to believe, but I can't remember doing anything that would cause me to be kicked out of my parish and eventually sent here. Unless someone has made a false accusation."

"Well, let's suppose someone did, wouldn't your bishop have confronted you with the accusation? Allowed you to defend yourself? Or maybe just quietly transferred you to another parish?"

"I was transferred to a temporary teaching job at Catholic U. But it didn't last long. Elmer, you may not believe this, but I've been wracking my brains over this for months. I did ask for a hearing in my archdiocese in Washington. It was turned down. I was at Catholic U. for less than one semester and then sent here. So, now I drift along day after day, thinking something will happen to clear this up. What else can I do? Can't we just drop it?"

"Whatever you say. Do you smoke?"

"Occasionally."

"You know, I'm dying for a cigarette but I don't suppose you have any. They must have taken away any packs you had when you checked in here."

Steve laughed. "Well, they did and they didn't." He showed Elmer the compartment in his chalice case. "I bought a carton from that kid Jeremy on the way here. He charged an arm and a leg. I can let you have a couple of packs but where would you hide them?"

"It's not too difficult. I can double wrap them in plastic and hide them in the dirt out back."

As they both lit up, Elmer took a deep inhale. "Steve," he said, "I know you're not happy you were sent here, but, believe me, I am. I can use a friend—especially one who has cigarettes," he said with a chuckle. "But a word of caution—when you finish a cigarette, hide the butt and flush it down the john later."

"But these packs won't hold out long. How do you get more around here?"

"If you have some money, which I don't, it turns out that there is a hole in the wall out back where you can leave some dough and a note, and when Jeremy comes by, about a week later, Voila, your number is on a carton. But it's expensive."

"Will Jeremy take a letter?"

"Yes, but in the confusion of bouncing around on the desert some letters just get blown away. I've sent out a few letters but since I never got a response I assumed they never reached a post office."

"Elmer, you have found a friend. I have a lot of money hidden in my chalice case. Just tell me when the time is right to order us some more cigarettes or anything else. Now, tell me more about this place. This morning, as I passed the doors to the meeting rooms, it seemed as if the brothers were moderating meetings of the priests. Some of the things I heard sounded like the stuff you'd hear at an AA meeting."

"We have meetings of recovering alcoholics. Three meeting rooms on that. I'm in one of those. Also two meeting rooms with pedophile priests grouped with homosexuals, and one for embezzlers. Oh yes, and rooms for priests who are guilty of disobedience, heretical writings, and so forth."

"Tell me about these Passion Brothers and this monastery. I never knew places like this existed in the church."

"I'm sure you've heard of the ancient monastic order of Cistercians, dating back a thousand years. Organized by St. Benedict. These brothers are a recent off-shoot of the Cistercians. The whole nine yards—contemplative, penitent, vows of poverty and silence, living in the desert to get away from the evils of everyday life."

"Yes I heard that from Brother Berard when I arrived. But what do they live on? I saw a farm and a cowshed. How do they feed and house a couple of hundred priests and also the monks?"

"If you've seen the meals, and I know you have, you can see they don't spend much on food. And they skimp on electricity, water and everything else."

"But still it costs something to run this place."

"From what I understand," Elmer continued, "when your bishop sent you here from your diocese, he also began providing a monthly amount for your support."

Steve thought a moment. "So Rhinehart," he said to himself, "is paying the hotel bill."

"By the way, you mentioned Washington and Catholic U. Where was your parish?"

"In Maryland… Rockville, Maryland."

"I've been to Maryland. In fact, my sister lives in Brunswick—not far from Harpers Ferry."

"Are you still in touch with her? Does she know you're here?"

"No. She got fed up with my drinking. And it was embarrassing in front of her kids. My parish was in York, Pennsylvania; that is, until the bishop started moving me around. After two other parishes and a stint in a rehab center, I got sent here."

"Elmer, are these Passion Brothers qualified to do therapy? I find it hard to believe because every one I've come across seemed either like a former pro boxer or football player. Some could pass for thugs. But having said that, I'm not against lay people realizing they have vocations and embracing the religious life. But these guys don't seem like the type."

"As I understand it," Elmer replied, "a lot of Catholic colleges have schools of Social Work where they educate therapists. Maybe these guys have had some training. But from what I've seen, it couldn't have been much. About the therapy—the sessions are conducted in groups. The group you get assigned to depends on your particular problem. The sessions run along the lines of open confessions. No Seal of the Confessional in the meetings, I might add. The other priests try to offer helpful suggestions. The brothers don't do a damn thing but sit up there and listen, then report back to Brother Berard. The sad fact is they're not trying to help us recover from our problems. The way I see it, we were sent here because the church has given up on us, and all they want us to do is quit the priesthood. They want us to get lost. The therapy is a sham."

"Once a priest, always a priest," Steve said in disagreement. "Ordination is a sacrament that can't be revoked. Brothers and nuns can renounce their vows, but priests can't."

"That's not quite true. The Second Vatican Council brought about some changes as I'm sure you know. There are ex-priests who admittedly can't perform priestly functions, but are still in the church as lay Catholics without any ecclesiastic penalties. In fact, some are married with children."

"Receiving the sacraments?"

"Yes. Where have you been? In Timbuktu?"

"I spent night and day raising money and supervising the building of a new church. I never had cause to get involved in any of the problems you're talking about."

"Well, a lot has to do with the diocese you're in and your particular bishop and I expect you know, or maybe you don't know, the American bishops have become a lot looser about some of the rules, especially when they see the whopping shortage of priests. The dropouts typically become very active lay people. They still have the stamp of the vocation on their souls. Many parishes out in the boondocks don't have priests or not enough priests and the bishops are aware that ex-priests can fill in on some of the non-eucharistic pastoral chores. God knows, they'd rather have that than women on the altar. In fact, in some parishes, former priests—now deacons, can distribute communion"

"But what about the priests here? I've heard them called three-time losers. Don't take offense— it's just something I've heard."

"You heard right. The church wants them out. Wants us out."

"Why doesn't the church defrock? Isn't that the most direct way to get rid of priests?"

"Problem is," Elmer answered, as he stood up, getting ready to leave, "when a priest is defrocked, there can be retaliation—bad publicity, even lawsuits. Although the priesthood is a vocation, we both know it's also a job, a career. If you found yourself forced onto the street in your fifties or sixties, even if you knew the church was justified in getting you out, and let's say you were desperate or angry enough, you might want to talk to the media or write a book. What would you have to lose? After all, your job is gone, your retirement's gone. No more health care. On and on. You'd probably feel you were screwed. What kind of job can a priest get who's forced out? He's even too old to flip hamburgers."

Elmer cautiously opened the door and peered down the length of the building. Seeing no one, he looked back at Steve. "By the way," he warned, "only smoke late at night."

Steve was puzzled. "Why all this cloak and dagger stuff, Elmer? So what if I break some of their rules, what can they do to me?"

"Other than cutting off some of the things they loosely regard as privileges like showers and food, my friend, they can find some pretext to pick a fight and beat the hell out of you. Right after I got here, I gave one of the monks some backtalk. You see this hole in the inside of my mouth. That's where a tooth used to be. After he knocked it out, the monk was kind enough to pick it up and let me have it as a 'keepsake.'"

"Elmer, that's absurd. Catholic brothers beating Catholic priests? I don't believe it. Isn't there any Christian charity in this place? Does the church hierarchy condone this?"

"My friend, church authorities don't know what goes on here and frankly, they don't care to know. If anything, the bishops are frustrated and angry at the priests they send here, and the brothers, knowing this, believe they have a free hand."

"Are you serious?" Steve asked, surprised.

"Come on, don't act so surprised. The bishops are human too. They can put up with only so much crap. Remember Christ's anger at the money changers in the temple? Hasn't the behavior of some of these priests been worse than money changers?"

As Steve shrugged his shoulders, Elmer whispered, "Good night my friend and God be with you."

"And also with you," Steve replied.

*****

After his visitor left, Steve sat on his cot for a long time thinking. Although some of the Passion Brothers looked and talked like street thugs, he was upset to find they would actually do violence against a priest—an ordained minister of God regardless of how low the priest might have sunk in adherence to his vows. Of course, the crippled priest he had met in the clinic gave confirmation of the situation that prevailed. He also began to realize there was a way of thinking that the Passion Brothers, for all their crudity and narrow-minded devotion to one aspect of Christianity—the Crucifixion, performed a service for the church. By quietly pressuring unworthy priests to resign, they were able to circumvent a lot of cost and scandal that might plague the church hierarchy. But then he thought of Elmer, a short, skinny, harmless guy who made the mistake of opening his mouth. As he drifted off to sleep, now more aware of the control exercised by the monks, Steve began feeling a deep-down chill about his own prospects at the monastery and, more importantly, his future role in the church.

*****

Three weeks went by. If it weren't for the icy showers, bad food and constantly clanging bells, the place would have been almost tolerable. Steve walked a lot, prayed a lot and was even able to get a few books from the library. His field work assignments were sporadic. There were some days when he realized his anger had almost faded away. But he knew that boredom would set in before long. He was still troubled by the fact that some of the priests eating in the refectory had cowls drawn closely over their faces while others were openly bareheaded. Had some of them been beaten? Were they trying to conceal black eyes and cut lips? He made a point to ask Elmer about it on his friend's next nocturnal visit.

*****

One morning when Steve returned to his cell after Mass and breakfast, he noticed a flyer that had been slipped under his door. It was an invitation to play in the following Saturday football game between the priests and brothers. It took him completely by surprise. The guards and the prisoners playing together? Was the purpose to have an afternoon of entertainment or to beat up on the priests under the guise of a football game?

Just about midnight that night, Elmer visited again. Steve liked the idea of the visits—thank god there was someone to talk to, but he also thought it could be risky if Elmer intended to drop in every night.

"Ever play touch football?" Elmer asked. "And another question: are you under fifty?"

"Yes to both. But I haven't played in a long time."

"The under-fifty question is important because it gets rough out there and they don't want some elderly priest who thinks he's a jock, dropping dead during the game. Although we greatly outnumber the brothers, like six to one, there's a lot of gray hair among the priests. By the way, if you volunteer to play, you'll find an extra ration of potatoes and probably even a slice of meat on your plate at dinner. They want the priests who play football to be at least strong enough to put up some kind of show against the brothers. The brothers want to win and they always do. It's important to them, but they don't want it to look too easy. The negative side of this comes from the other priests at your table watching you eat a decent meal. You can expect some scowling."

"Elmer, tell me why some of the priests have their

heads covered in the refectory. What's that all about?"

"Sorry, friend. Some other time," Elmer replied as he walked to the door, glanced both ways along the portico and left, quietly closing the door behind him.

12

Saturday afternoon was bright and warm under a cloudless blue Arizona sky. Steve was in a small locker room with a group of priests getting ready for the game. He fished for a T-shirt, jockstrap and shorts from a large barrel. Another barrel held tennis shoes. He selected a pair that gave him a tight fit. They would play on the grass in a large side area near the compound wall. It was two-hand touch, played without helmets or other gear. The priests wore white T-shirts, the brothers, red. Steve thought wryly that the red probably was meant by the brothers to represent the blood of Christ. When he saw the lineup of brothers—all bruisers, stomping like bulls, getting ready to run roughshod over the priests, he thought dourly that the priests' white T-shirts might also be red from blood by the game's end.

The game would have been a rout except for Steve's pinpoint passing and a couple of priests who as pass receivers could break fast and almost never miss a catch. Steve himself was surprised that his old throwing arm was still intact. As the game progressed, the brothers, fearing they might lose their only game in many seasons, began to put the pressure on. Steve was sacked several times, the brothers in their enthusiasm apparently forgetting that the game was supposed to be touch football. During the game, one of the priests was roughed up so badly he had to be carried off the field. Another had a bad limp from a twisted knee.

There was more than one bloody nose. After awhile, it looked as if the brothers' plan was to win by attrition. As the day wore on, the game became more brutal. In all, five priests were injured, nevertheless, spectators and players all thought it was an exciting game. At one point, finding that both of his best pass receivers were on the sidelines due to injuries, Steve faked a pass and surprised a close-in pack of brothers by running right through them. It even surprised him. Almost fifty years old and he could still run like the wind.

The game ended 36 to 24. As he walked off the field, a few of his team members whispered to him that although they had lost, it had been the best showing by the losing priests as far back as anyone could remember. Everyone was so up, there were actually silent 'high fives' between the priests and the brothers after the game. Standing on the sidelines, Brother Berard was visibly displeased by the display of fraternization. He began to think seriously of canceling future football games but he changed his mind when he recalled that his monks needed some diversion and football was a wonderful way of burning off their pent up hostility. Besides, there would only be a few more Sundays left before the beginning of Lent at which time all such activities would cease.

That evening, Steve was so stiff he could hardly walk to the refectory. Once inside, he swung his legs painfully over the bench of the picnic table to take his seat. As he did so, he saw furtive admiring glances from the priests sitting opposite. There was an extra ration of potatoes and some meat on his plate. And, in fact, as he glanced at the other plates, he saw that every table that had one or more football players had extra rations. One or two priests openly smiled in his direction. With the exception of his clandestine meetings with Elmer, the day of the football game gave him the first signs of recognition, not to mention approval, he had received from any of the other priests in the refectory.

*****

Steve slid the small rickety wooden door back. The speaker's voice was familiar. It sounded like one of the brothers but Steve couldn't put a face to it.

"I killed a man, Father."

Steve was stunned. "What do you mean? How did it happen?"

"Well, it wasn't murder, if that's what you're thinking. It happened this afternoon. He was giving me a hard time...a very hard time, and I invited him out back of one of the buildings. I don't think anybody saw us go back there. When we got there, he was mad and tried to get the jump on me, but two punches and he was down. I told him to get up but he just laid there. I went over and saw his face was white like the blood was gone. I couldn't feel no pulse."

"Don't you think the authorities should be notified? Does Brother Berard know of this?"

"Brother Berard saw the body. It's up to him. But look, I'm only here to make a confession and get absolution. I did what I had to do."

"It doesn't sound to me as if you're filled with remorse. Part of the forgiveness of the confessional is to be sorry for your sins."

"I'm sorry it happened, that's all."

Steve thought a moment about the Seal of the Confessional. The penitent said he was sorry. Even if Steve didn't believe it, there wasn't much he could do. "For your penance," he said, "I want you to say the Rosary one hundred times."

"That's pretty stiff. Too stiff if you ask me. Besides, we don't say the Rosary here."

"Why not?"

"It's filled with Hail Mary's."

"Well now's your chance to begin a long overdue devotion to the Blessed Virgin. Let me ask you something. Are you one of the Passion Brothers?"

"Yes, but what's that got to do with anything? I'm a Catholic and I need absolution."

"Look a man is dead. You did it. You could have resolved the affair without killing him. Accept this penance or get out without absolution."

As the brother made an act of contrition, Steve gave him absolution. He closed the small rickety door. A moment later, in a rustle of monastic robes, the brother was gone.

*****

Around midnight that same night, Steve heard Elmer's familiar tap on the door. Steve let him in. They sat on the cot. Elmer held the match as they lit up.

"Big happenings here today, Steve. One of the priests was killed. None of us knows how. His body was found behind one of the buildings after he didn't turn up for dinner. But I'll bet one of the brothers did him in. Don't know for sure."

Under the Seal of the Confessional, Steve felt he

had to act surprised—as if he had not even heard of the incident. "Are they going to notify anyone? The coroner or the police? What about his family?"

"Don't know. The word is he had no living relatives. He was kind of a derelict. Boozing for years. If he had relatives, they must have abandoned him along the way."

"What if someone does inquire about him?"

"If anyone asks, not that anyone outside is likely to, they'll just say he was bitten by a scorpion or a rattlesnake, or maybe fell down and hit his head on a rock. If someone tries to investigate, it'll come out that he had been an alcoholic. And the claim would be that his brain was shot. He didn't know what he was doing. And there's some truth to that because in therapy sessions, all he did was mumble. He never shut up—just constant angry muttering."

Steve shook his head. "I guess all we can do is pray for his soul. When is the funeral?"

"He's already buried. It was done right after dark tonight."

Steve sat in stunned silence. Just like that, a life is snuffed out. And a priest at that. No funeral Mass, no eulogy. But far more serious, no repercussions. No punishment. He thought back to what had happened in the confessional. He should have thrown that monk out. He suspected the contrition was not genuine. The brother had even balked at was a trivial penance compared to the killing.

"Elmer, I'd like to see where they buried the priest."

"What's the point? It's a freshly dug grave. They haven't even put a cross on it yet. And maybe they never will."

"I want to see it anyway," Steve insisted.

"Well come on," Elmer said, "I'll take you to it. It's in the cemetery behind the mission church. It's getting late… we'll have to step on it."

A yellow moon was dipping down to the horizon on one of its erratic night swings as the two priests walked through the graveyard to the fresh mound of earth covering the grave. In the moonlight, Steve could see that it had been a quick sloppy job. He shuddered in the chilly air as a rattler slithered across the mound and disappeared into the night.

As the two priests stood looking down at the dirt mound on the unmarked grave that held the body of a priest whose name would be forgotten, Steve made the Sign of the Cross over the grave. "Eternal rest grant unto him O Lord and let perpetual light shine upon him. Requiescat in Pace…" Rest in Peace.

Before they left the small cemetery, Steve noticed two other freshly dug graves. "Who are they, I wonder?"

"They're two priests who died a few days ago. No foul play. They both had AIDS. They must have been homosexuals. You probably never saw them because they were moved to the clinic before you came."

"I saw the clinic and frankly I wasn't impressed with it. It just looks like a place where the sick go to die. Let's go back," Steve whispered, as the pair inched along the portico past closed doors to Steve's cell. They sat on the cot in the dark.

"Tell me more about how to get in contact with that kid Jeremy. How often does he show up?"

"Every couple of weeks. If you want cigarettes or

want to send a letter, I can leave a note and money in the hole in the back wall. We can't get much at one time because we'd have no place to hide it. But, Steve, let me read your mind. If you're thinking of running away and having Jeremy take you out, there's two problems. First of all, his runs are erratic. You could sit out there for three or four days never knowing when he'd show up and they'd be sure to catch you. On top of that, I doubt that he'd take you."

"Why not?"

"He doesn't mind making some money on the side and breaking the rules a bit by sneaking in contraband, but helping someone get out is a completely different ballgame. Way out here in the desert, Berard knows you don't just walk away from this place. You need someone to supply transportation. Berard and the bishop in Tucson would come down hard on him if some priest just disappeared."

"I wasn't thinking so much of getting out of here right now, but what about him delivering a letter for me?" Steve asked, thinking of the letter he had written to Janet.

"You can try, but like I said, it could lie in the dirt on the other side of the wall for days, and as you know, we do get some rain once in awhile or some animal could pee or poop on it and it would just be a hunk of paper in the crud."

Steve got up and paced the floor. He lit a cigarette. He lit one for Elmer. "There's something that has me puzzled," he said. "What about the priests who decide to resign? How do they get out?"

"That's a different situation. After a priest makes a

request to dispense with his vows and if it's approved by his bishop, Brother Berard makes the priest sign papers saying he's not just leaving the monastery, he's leaving the priesthood. It's a formal document—you know with clauses renouncing any claims against the monastery and the Catholic Church, including an agreement never to file suit or get a book agent to produce a best seller. In return for that, the priest's bishop agrees to let him remain in the faith, get married, whatever, sacraments and all. Then Brother Berard gives the man a grubstake of a few hundred bucks, a pat on the back and calls Jeremy to take him away. Case closed nice and clean. No scandal. If the priest later reneges on the deal, he is excommunicated. Few, if any priests want that. By the way, if this place gets to be too much for you, you can always get out that way. Of course, Berard first has to get permission from your bishop and probably also his bishop in Tucson."

"Not interested," Steve replied, shaking his head. He threw the remains of his cigarette on the floor and stepped on it."

"That's a no-no," Elmer reminded him. "You're gonna get your priestly little ass in trouble,"

"What are you talking about? What else can they do to me after sending me to this place?"

"Let me enumerate just a few things," Elmer said, "although I believe I went through all this with you before. How's about half-size portions at meals for openers? After all, the supplies come courtesy of Brother Berard. And there's other things like no hosts for your Mass. Or maybe they just ran short of wine— only for your Mass, that is."

"But that's harassment. It's probably sacrilegious," Steve contended.

"You're dealing with strange types here. The whole damn place has the makings of a sacrilege. There's another little form of punishment I've seen them impose for rule breakers—no access to the washroom or the showers."

"That's ridiculous, Elmer. I'd force my way in."

"A nice thought, my friend, but as the saying goes, 'you haven't got near enough force.'"

As Elmer got up to leave and walked towards the door, Steve stopped him. "Hold on a minute. There's one thing I asked you about before, but you never gave me an answer. What about those priests in the refectory who have their cowls pulled over their heads? And, I can tell by the seating, it's not always the same ones. Have they been in fights?"

"Not that I know of."

"Then, what for heaven's sake?"

"Forgive me, Steve, but as I said before, I just don't want to talk about it."

13

Janet walked up to the Colonial Inn which faced Monument Square in the heart of the historic district of Concord. She loved the picturesque inn that dated back to revolutionary times. Old North Bridge where the Minutemen routed the British with the 'shot heard round the world', was just a short walk from the inn. The town of Concord lay at the western end of Battle Road, the bloody road stretching twenty miles west out of Boston along which the revolutionaries fought the British redcoats.

Whenever she returned to Concord, her mind flooded with memories. As a schoolgirl, she had visited the graves of the great literary figures of early America and their families buried on Authors' Ridge in Concord's Sleepy Hollow Cemetery. On her walks around the town, she had often visited Orchard House, the former home of the Alcott family, built by Bronson Alcott— father of Louisa May Alcott, author of *Little Women*. The house was now a museum. She never ceased to be enraptured as she paused in front of the former homes of Ralph Waldo Emerson, Nathaniel Hawthorne and Henry David Thoreau. Unbelievably, all right here in her hometown.

The scent of aged wood permeated the air as Janet entered the inn and snaked her way through the narrow corridors to the tavern in the rear. A hostess showed her to a table in front of a large open fireplace in the dark paneled tavern. With the exception of a couple lunching in a dark corner, the tavern was empty. The only light came from a few soft orange sconces mounted on the walls, and the fireplace with its crackling logs that every now and then catapulted bits of glowing chips up through the yellow flames.

She ordered a drink, took a sip when it came and cradling the glass in both hands, waited staring into the dancing flames. She reminisced about past summers at home in Concord with pleasant afternoons sunbathing and swimming in nearby Walden Pond. In winter there was ice skating, and later after dark, hot chocolate and roasted marshmallows beside bright roaring fires that cast their flickering light on the branches of the tall pines surrounding the pond. Sitting on logs around the fires, she and her friends would laugh at silly jokes and preposterous tales. But her fondest memories were of Christmas eve nights when she and her brothers in warm woolens and holding lighted candles, would gather with hundreds of other carolers in Monument Square, the heart of Concord, their voices rising in joyous harmony on the frosty night air.

Now she felt very close to Steve in Concord even though they had been brought up a generation apart. A man appeared in the doorway. In the dim light of the tavern, she was startled to see Father Steve Murphy. He was casually dressed, not wearing the black suit and Roman collar. She was taken by surprise because she had expected only to meet with his brother, Jonathon. Smiling, she jumped up ready to throw her arms around the priest in an enthusiastic, friendly hug, but as the figure drew closer, she hesitated, puzzled. Was this Steve? Had he aged that much in a few months at a monastery? This man was tall, ruggedly built like Steve, but as he approached, she could see from the reflected light of the fire that he was quite a bit older than Steve. Realization dawned. It was not Steve. It couldn't be. It must be Jonathon. But the resemblance was remarkable—almost eerie. She knew that if the brothers had been closer in age they could easily have passed for identical twins.

Jonathon walked up to her. "Janet?" he asked in a voice that sounded like he had a bad cold. "Janet Tarentino?"

"Yes, that's me," she said, nervously holding her hand out to grip a hand that looked and felt uncannily like Steve's. As she took her seat again, she realized it was more than the resemblance in face and stature that unnerved her. The sound of Steve's voice coming from this older look-alike, simultaneously attracted and puzzled her. But after a few seconds she noticed differences. She remembered what Steve had told her about his brother. This voice had traces of a tremor and hoarseness that she knew was due to the early onset of Lou Gehrig's disease.

Jonathon slipped into a chair at the small table and waved to the waitress to order a drink. "I recognized you as soon as I saw you," she said, trying to cover up her mistake. "You look so much like Steve."

"Only older."

"Yes, I suppose so," she replied honestly.

"Janet, when we talked on the phone, you said you were born and raised in Concord. Steve and I were raised near here."

"Steve told me about you and the famous Murphy family of Wayland," she said, settling back in her chair and trying to regain her composure. "I'm impressed. Your father was Congressman Murphy. That was somewhat before my time. But I haven't heard or read anything about the Murphy family in a long time."

"My father died some years ago" Jonathon explained, "and since neither Steve nor I were interested in politics, the Murphy family fell into a kind of obscurity. And quite frankly, it was OK with me when we were no longer fodder for the media. Of course, we still had several of the family businesses to run, handed down by an uncle. But tell me, how is Steve? And how did you come to know him? Did you meet here in Concord?"

"Steve and I met at Catholic U. while he was teaching there. We became good friends."

Jonathon arched an eyebrow, wondering how a man could manage a simple friendship with such a stunningly beautiful woman without falling in love.

"Just friends," Janet said, trying to appear casual, but from his facial expression, she knew he suspected it was more than a simple friendship.

"Forgive me," Jonathon said, "but for a moment I was hoping Steve had found someone to love and to love him. I mean, in addition to God, the pope and the saints. You see, I never could fathom why he wanted to become a Catholic priest. It seemed to me a waste of a potentially happy and productive human being."

"I'm a Catholic," Janet said, growing slightly vexed at Jonathon's comments. "Even if *you* don't, I think I understand why he chose the church as a way of life. You asked me how Steve is—that's what I want to find out. I agreed to meet you hoping you could give me some information about him. The last time I saw him he told me he was assigned to a monastery in Arizona. Since then, I've heard nothing. Do you know anything about this and when he might be coming back?"

"I haven't the faintest," Jonathon said, holding up the empty peanut dish to attract the waitress for a refill. "I thought he was still in that parish in Maryland he was pastor of. It's news to me that he was teaching at Catholic U., and now you say he's gone from there. Maybe Steve never told you, but he and I have tended to drift apart through the years. I don't make much of an effort to stay in touch. He doesn't either. No great falling out, it's just that our lifestyles and interests go in different directions. I did see him briefly last year when our mother died. At the time, he was still head of his parish church. After that, nothing."

"I'm worried about him. He left months ago. He turned his car over to me and left some of his other things with me. There's been no word. I contacted the Archdiocese of Washington, a Bishop Rhinehart's office, but all I learned was something that confirmed what I already knew: Steve was in Arizona. When I pressed for more information the secretary or whoever it was, refused. And, I hate to admit unpleasant treatment from the Catholic archdiocese, especially to a skeptic like you, but I was then abruptly cut off. What's going on?"

"You're asking me?" said Jonathon with an incredulous look on his face. "How would I know what goes on in the secret chambers of the Catholic Church? I was a Catholic long ago, but those days are gone forever. For a long time, I used to refer to myself as a lapsed Catholic, but eventually, lapsed became 'ex' and ultimately, 'ex' became 'non.'"

"What kind of brother are you not to inquire or care about Steve's whereabouts?"

Janet had touched a nerve. It was Jonathon's turn to be annoyed. "Do you mind if I ask you a personal question?"

"Go ahead."

"You're attending a university. Are you studying to become a trial lawyer or something?"

"I'm in graduate school, training as a psychiatric social worker. In other words, a psychotherapist."

"Well forgive me, young lady, but I always thought psychotherapists did a lot of sympathetic listening rather than hurling blunt accusations."

"I was hoping to come across as anxious rather than accusatory."

The waitress approached and asked if they would like refills of their drinks. "Yes, I'd like another," Jonathon said managing a laugh, "but none for her. I'm cutting her off."

Janet hung her head embarrassed that the meeting had turned into an argument. "I'm terribly worried, that's all," she said.

"Since you're interested in Steve, let me tell you a few things about him that you may not know. Yes, I do care about him, but I haven't heard from him since last year. Steve was never very good at keeping the family informed as to his whereabouts. And this goes way back. Years ago, after he left home for the seminary, he pretty much turned his back on the family. When

Steve was sent to Rome years ago, the first we learned about it was by a postcard. The only one he had contact with was our dad, and even that was sporadic at best. Then, after dad died, nothing. He turned his back on the family."

As Jonathon talked, Janet remembered Steve had told her he came from a dysfunctional family—the mother was a lush, one who lavished all her affection on her older son. The father was a politician, away in Washington much of the time. "Jonathon," she said, "my interest at the moment is in finding out how Steve is and when he's coming back. And since you're family, I thought you'd be in a much better position to do it than I."

"I'll let you in on a little secret," Jonathon said. You're not the only one who contacted the Archdiocese of Washington and learned absolutely nothing. And they didn't even tell me anything when I called Steve's parish. I left a message and never got an answer. I hit a dead end just like you did. So what was I to do after that—report my missing brother to the police? Let's face it, Steve is buried somewhere in that huge ancient mystery known as the Catholic Church, and although I'm inclined to think this whole business is worrying, maybe even suspicious, all I can do is trust that since he's in the church he loves, he's in good hands."

Janet sat back in her chair. She turned partly away from Jonathon as she stared disconsolately into the fire. "My intuition tells me he's not all right. He's in some kind of trouble."

Jonathon pulled his chair up closer to the table. He tilted his head and leaned closer, smiling, attempting to make eye contact with her. He regretted having sounded off, especially to someone he hardly knew and who obviously was so upset about his missing brother. He studied her delicate face, her captivating blue eyes. In silhouette, a body that Aphrodite herself would envy. He wondered if he hadn't suddenly become jealous of Steve as flames from the fireplace highlighted wisps of her chestnut hair. As she glanced over at him, then quickly looked away, he saw a glint of tears in her eyes reflected from the fireplace.

Jonathon took a sip of his drink. He sat back wondering. He studied the leaping flames and the red sparks that flew when a log crunched down in the fireplace. She can say she's just a friend of Steve's, he said to himself, but I think I just discovered something. This beautiful young lady is head over heels in love with my brother.

14

Ash Wednesday. The first day of Lent, and the beginning of the Lenten fast. In the Passion Monastery Church, the crucifixes were covered in a coarse brown burlap wrap to be removed on Easter Sunday. The only exception was the large wooden cross leaning against the wall just inside the door of the church. A large white Paschal candle, taller than a man, was set up near the altar. The small red pieces of wax imbedded in the candle signified the wounds of Christ. In the refectory, throughout Lent only one meal a day would be served—dinner. Breakfast would comprise little more than a few tiny morsels—hardly worth eating. The bell would not ring for lunch. No meat would be served.

On the first Friday of Lent, as the priests were shuffling out of the church following the evening service, two of the brothers suddenly grabbed Steve, one on each arm, and pulled him out of line. As soon as the last priest left the church, one of the brothers quickly bolted the doors shut. Steve, wondering what was happening, started to protest. He received a backhand slap on the face. Before he could move to defend himself, four of the brothers stripped off his robe and tied his hands behind his back. His head was wrapped in a ring of thorns which were forced in to penetrate his head. As the blood trickled down his face and the back of his neck, he remembered some of the priests he had seen in the refectory. He now knew why they wore their cowls pulled over their heads. Now it was his turn.

Two of the brothers stepped out of the shadows holding short leather whips. Steve was surprised to see they were wearing knee-length tunics and shiny metal helmets. The other brothers formed a ring around him shouting at him, spitting on him. As the reincarnated 'Roman soldiers' began to beat him the way the Romans flagellated Christ, Steve was scared. It was clear they intended to reenact Christ's Crucifixion. He was the sacrificial lamb. How far he wondered did they intend to take this reenactment? Had some of the elderly priests been put through this torture? Had any of them died? Maybe the brothers only picked priests they thought could come out alive, but perhaps not all did, and maybe the priests with the cowls over their heads in the refectory were the lucky ones. As the beating proceeded, Steve noted that although the thorn wounds were real, the beating was painful but relatively superficial. He suspected that if the victims were beaten to the point where they passed out, the show would come to an abrupt end.

The beating over, his hands were untied. They loaded the huge wooden cross on his back. An edge of the wood pressed a groove into his bare shoulder. He had always wondered about the big cross that leaned against the wall just inside the front entrance to the church. What was it used for? Now he knew. The weight of it pushed him down on one knee. They prodded him with poles until he stood up and clumsily adjusted the cross on his back. He was pushed in the

direction of the altar. Stumbling under the massive
weight, and whipped by the brothers imitating Roman
guards, Steve inched toward the altar surrounded by
a small group of following brothers. The remainder
of the brothers—perhaps 30 in all, hurried up the side
aisles and slipped into the front pews of the church.
There was no sign of Bother Berard.

There were moments during the staggering walk
through the nave of the church when Steve was not
sure he was going to make it all the way to the altar.

As the bleeding stand-in for Christ approached the
altar, the 'soldiers' lifted the cross from his shoulder
and laid it slanting down on the altar steps. Next, they
pushed him down on his back spreading his arms on
the crossbar. They tied his wrists and ankles to the
cross with strands of rope. He thanked God that he was
tied rather than nailed to the cross. It took six brothers
to elevate the cross, sliding it into the hole in the floor
in front of the altar rail. He realized then why the hole
he had seen before had never been repaired. As the
base of the upright hit the bottom of the hole, Steve felt
his body slump under its own weight. The wrist ropes
grew taut, rope burns reddening his skin. His arms were
almost wrenched from their shoulder sockets. Small
pools of blood collected on the floor beneath the cross.
Blood streamed down over his face and chest from the
crown of thorns on his head. As he hung on the cross, it
became clear to Steve why Elmer never wanted to talk
about this ritual whenever Steve had asked about why
some priests had their cowls pulled over their heads in
the refectory. Elmer must have known that his friend
might be a candidate for crucifixion, and Steve might

have been so disgusted he would risk death by trying to escape from the monastery.

From high on the cross, Steve looked down at the congregation of brothers kneeling in awe—each of whom seemed almost overcome by the sight of Christ, their Christ on the Holy Cross. They believed that by being crucified he was atoning for their sins.

Steve, looking down, realized he was the only priest left in the church. He recognized at once that the grisly ceremony was not only intended as a reenactment of the Crucifixion but also as a punishment for the priest selected that it was truly their Christ hanging above them—and by his suffering, as the stand-in for Christ. But why was he being punished? Was it to restore humility after his popular performance in the football games? Did they think he had committed the sin of pride?

As Steve hung on the cross, his head lolled to right and left in pain as the brothers in the congregation looked up at him in a growing fanatical religious fervor. Then in a loud voice, a brother standing at the foot of the cross shouted the words of Christ during the agony: "Father, forgive them for they know not what they do.... My God, my God, why hast thou forsaken me?...I thirst...today thou shalt be with me in paradise... Father, into thy hands I commend my spirit...".

Although he was in a fog of pain, Steve knew that the brother had left out the words that Christ spoke from the cross as he looked down at John: "John behold thy mother." Then Looking at Mary, "Mother behold thy son." Steve was not surprised. The brothers did not include anything in their services that made reference to women—not even the Blessed Virgin, Mary the Mother of God who the Bible says stood at the foot of her son's cross.

As Steve hung, struggling for air, he knew that although he had lost a lot of blood, the death of the cross was not due to loss of blood, but rather to asphyxiation. The body hung in such a stretched position that getting air into the lungs was difficult and when the arms and supporting feet grew tired, the body slumped and asphyxiation began to set in. His breath came in short gasps. After two hours, he knew he was fading. He drifted in and out of consciousness. How long would this go on? If it did not end soon, he would die. He prayed. "Am I the priest that thou, O Lord has forgotten? My God, my God, why hast thou forsaken me?"

By the time Steve was taken down from the cross, he was unconscious. He woke up hours later in his cell. This had been no dream—he knew it because his pillow was covered with blood.

Later that night Elmer came into the dark cell. He brought a glass of water and a wet towel. He gently wrapped it around Steve's head.

"Elmer, is that you?"

"Yes. I brought some water."

Steve tried to sit up to drink but couldn't. Elmer dripped the water into his mouth. Then Elmer tried to lightly rub an anesthetic into the thorn words on Steve's head, but the pain was so great, Steve pushed his hand away.

"Did you know about this?" asked Steve.

"I knew someone was going to be grabbed for the

ceremony but I didn't know they'd pick you. You'll be excused from your duties for a few days while you recover. In the refectory, they'll expect you to wear the cowl over your head. Everyone knows about these passion plays of course, but the brothers don't want to go overboard advertising them."

Elmer lit a cigarette and put it between Steve's lips. Steve took a deep pull then slowly blew the smoke up into the darkness.

"This grisly ritual should be banned," Steve groaned in disgust.

"Yeah, but who'll come from the outside to this isolated outpost to abolish it? And remember, my friend, when you play the Passion reenactment against the long history of the church, it's not terribly unusual. Canon Law never said the saints shouldn't suffer; you know many were canonized after they allowed themselves to be tortured to death."

"I didn't see Brother Berard there. Is he part of this ritual?"

"No. My understanding is that Berard doesn't approve of this."

"Then why in hell doesn't he put a stop to it?"

"Remember Steve, Brother Berard is elected to be abbot; as such, his power is limited. He could be voted out at any one of the monthly meetings the brothers hold in the chapter house."

Reluctantly, Elmer left Steve's cell and returned to his own. There was nothing more he could do for his friend.

*****

At about three in the morning of Steve's crucifixion, Steve was roughly shaken by the shoulders and when he sat up was slapped in the face. In the darkness, he couldn't see who it was but it was very likely one of the brothers. He was confused, angry. Was this another part of the ritual?

"Look here, priest," the brother said, "you were yelling and screaming in your sleep. You were waking up half the monastery. If you keep this up we're gonna move you to a solitary cell way out behind the church cemetery. Out there you can scream all you want and nobody will hear you. If I were you, I 'd try to think of nice stuff before you go to sleep."

"You mean nice stuff like the crucifixion," Steve said disgustedly.

"No I was thinking more along the lines of some teenagers you probably screwed before they sent you here, or maybe some dough you stole from the church that you have hidden somewhere. Think of how you're gonna be able to live it up after you get out of here… if you get out of here."

The next day, although still wobbly, Steve hobbled to the clinic because the nurse told him that the priest, Bill, was dying.

*****

Steve showed up in the refectory for dinner two days later. He sat at the picnic table in his accustomed place. He did not wear the cowl over his head. He wanted everyone to see his thorn wounds. But before he could lift the first forkful to his mouth, a hand reached from behind and took away his plate. Glancing over his shoulder, he saw the surly face of Brother Michael. "No cowl, no food," was all the brother said.

*****

As the days of Lent proceeded, the fasting began to take its toll on brothers and priests, but mostly on the priests, all of whom were middle-aged or older and not in very good health. And even though everyone was served only one meal a day, the meal served to the brothers was decidedly more substantial than that received by the priests. In the shower room, Steve saw that some of the thinner priests began to look like prisoners in a Russian gulag. His nocturnal visitor, Elmer, who was a head shorter than he and lightly built, had grown shockingly thin. His clean shaven, sunken-cheeked face had a cadaverous look. Steve knew he was losing weight as well. At first he wasn't too concerned at slimming down, but after a time, he knew he was losing muscle. As he stood in the shower—warmer now that spring had come, he entertained his first real thoughts of making an escape from the monastery. Not quitting the priesthood— he would never do that, but just leaving and taking his chances outside. It would make him a renegade since he would be leaving a formal assignment of his archdiocese. Bishop Rhinehart would be furious and would certainly label it gross insubordination. There might be a move to defrock him. But there was always a chance of appeal to higher authority, perhaps even to the Vatican through a few friends he had made when he studied in Rome.

*****

The Lenten season was over. It was now after Easter and Steve had still not been assigned to a therapy group. His assignment sheet only specified work on the farm. A therapy assignment could have been an advantage because at the very least, he would have learned the type of transgression he had been accused of.

He found work in the field, new to him, exhausting, but it could have been much worse—it could have been hot. It was still spring and many days were warm but pleasant. He worked in cutoff jeans and the boots Brother Berard had given him. He wondered whether the gift of the boots stemmed from a weak moment of kindness or could it have been that Berard recognized that he was a strong worker who could produce twice as much if his feet were protected. As he picked tomatoes and other vegetables, he managed to eat when no one was looking. "One for them, one for me," he said chuckling.

As the long strenuous days of field work dragged on with clearing brush, digging up roots and hand plowing, his hands, once soft and white, unused to physical labor—delicate instruments preordained to hold the host and chalice, became hard, browned and callused. In his first week working on the farm, his hands had blistered and bled from scrapes and tiny cuts. He had asked for gloves but none were available. As he worked, he had tried hard to spare the tips of his thumbs and index fingers—so important for holding the sacred host reverently in these fingertips during the Consecration of the Mass. For a few weeks he said Mass with bandaged hands. Eventually, the problem resolved itself as he became hardened to the work. The outdoor work, the sun, marvelously fragrant pure desert air and improved nutrition in the meals—augmented by produce from the farm, all produced a feeling of well-being in him. His love of God was as deep as ever but doubts kept surfacing about the hierarchy of the church. Since he had no recollection of any wrongdoing, inevitably, resentment set in. He struggled to conceal a deep-seated bitterness towards the Passion Brothers. Their medieval cruelty was allowed to flourish without diocesan supervision.

As the days in the sun wore on, Steve began feeling trim and strong as he dried his tanned body after his daily shower. He had given up smoking once again, partly because of the risk and inconvenience of smoking only in secret in his room at night. There was another reason he was just beginning to be conscious of: a feeling that he must stay as fit and strong as possible for whatever lay ahead. He gave the rest of his hidden cigarette packs to Elmer. He also removed the money and his stole that had been hidden in the false bottom of his chalice case. He hid them in the folds of his robe. He was taking no chances. He had an idea that a day might come when his chalice case would be removed.

During morning Mass, and during the readings of his Holy Office, followed by the remainder of the day working in the fields, Steve almost thought he could adjust to living a long full life at a monastery, but then at night in bed, it would all fall apart again. Anxiety would creep up on him and submerge him in doubt and unresolved questions. He was determined to find out what had gone wrong in his former life as pastor. Then, lying on his cot in the dark cell, after giving vent to his worries, he was always able to calm himself down with thoughts of Janet. When he thought long and hard about his days with Janet, he found that his dreams were not penetrated with violence. He would drift off to sleep with prayers and an image of Janet leaning over to kiss him goodnight.

*****

Steve sat up in bed. It was the middle of the night. He had been dreaming of men involved in a fistfight. But as he sat listening in the dark, he knew the thuds and groans of pain that were coming from outside behind the building were no dream. It sounded like someone getting a beating. He quickly slipped on his work clothes and hurried over to tap on Elmer's door. He could hear Elmer getting out of the creaky cot and shuffling to the door. "What's going on back there?" Steve asked in a whisper.

"What else?" Elmer replied softly. "Some poor priest is getting the stuffing kicked out of him by a couple of Brother Berard's thugs."

"Let's go help him out. Come on," Steve said as he ran back to his cell and slipped on his work boots.

"Sorry," Elmer replied. "I'm no good at that. I'd just get in the way." He stepped back into his cell, and slumped on his cot, burying his face in his hands.

Steve dashed around to the rear of the building and came face to face with two brothers standing over a priest. The priest was lying in a fetal position, bleeding from nose and mouth. In an instant, catching them by surprise, Steve lunged at the brothers. He felt an adrenalin rush, followed by almost superhuman strength as he angrily grabbed one brother and swung him around ramming him full against the other. Two heads cracked together. While Steve had full mobility in shorts and a T-shirt, the brothers were hampered by long gray robes twisted heavily about their arms. After the head butt, the brothers dizzily wavered trying to regain their footing as Steve followed through with lightning body punches that doubled both of them over gasping. As he kicked one of them under the chin with his work boot, the brother's head snapped back. His body rose in the air then fell flat backwards winding up trapped in the folds of a tangled robe that looked like a pile of dirty laundry lying on the ground. The other brother, on his knees, raised a hand in a kind of surrender. In the dim light, Steve recognized the face of Brother Michael. He assumed the one on the ground was Brother John.

Elmer arrived as Steve was helping the beaten priest to his feet. Ignoring the defeated brothers, Steve and Elmer half-dragged, half-carried the limp priest back to his cell in the same compound as theirs. Elmer ran to the shower room for wet towels and then to the clinic for bandages. The two priests then spent the better part of the remainder of the night cleaning and dressing the man's wounds and trying to comfort him. When Steve asked the priest what had happened, he received no answer. The man just turned his head away. As they left him resting on his cot, he gave them a barely audible thanks. On the way back to their cells, they realized they didn't even know the priest's name.

"What do you think happened?" Steve asked.

"Who the hell knows? Around here, it could be anything. He probably made a remark the brothers didn't like and they decided to give him a bit of religious suffering—something he could offer up for his sins."

"Do you think they recognized us? After all, it was pretty dark."

"Me, no," Elmer replied. "You, yes, and if I were you, I'd watch my step around here. Berard's thugs have long memories."

*****

A few days later, as he returned to his cell, Steve was startled to see that his chalice case was gone. He was happy that he had emptied the money and cigarettes from the false bottom. If the case had been taken by a thief why didn't he take the silver crucifix lying on the table? How could it have been overlooked? Recalling the beating incident, he wondered if the brothers were trying to even the score. He went immediately to see Brother Berard to report the theft. Brother Berard seemed unperturbed. "Father Murphy," he said, "there has been no theft. I had your chalice removed. It has been stored with your personal effects."

"But how am I to say Mass without it?" Steve demanded. "Does this have anything to do with the beating I gave two of your brothers the other night? Don't you realize what they were doing to that priest?"

"No, that's not the reason. Let me explain. We have received correspondence from your bishop to the effect that you are no longer required to say Mass, nor do you need to carry out any of the normal priestly duties like hearing confessions, conducting other services, and so forth. Since you are still a Catholic, you are free of course, to attend Mass, receive the Eucharist and attend the services, but that's all."

Steve was outraged. "I'm a priest," he roared, pounding on Brother Berard's desk. "It is my duty to say daily Mass. It is a sacred obligation. No one can take this from me. I refuse to believe it until I see the letter you speak of from my bishop."

"No, I am not permitted to show it to you. You simply have to take my word for it. The letter also states that Bishop Rhinehart wants you to return to the Archdiocese of Washington where you will be asked to sign papers resigning from the priesthood."

"That's absurd. That's one thing I will not do."

"Don't you realize this is an order from your bishop?"

"Yes, I do. But I don't follow orders like that without knowing why and without being allowed to file an appeal."

"Then, if you refuse, and apparently your refusal is definite, your bishop goes on to say that you will then consider yourself transferred to the authority of the Bishop of Tucson. Our bishop has concurred in this matter, and now on the local level, you are again asked to resign. Remember, you will remain a Catholic. Our bishop will give you a dispensation to receive the sacraments. Think of it, you can find someone, get married, have children, raise a family. Is that so terrible?"

"It is for a priest who has given his whole life to the church. I would like to have a hearing before your bishop. I need to know what's really going on here.

Why is the church doing this to me?"

"Father Murphy, you've asked me that before and I really do not know. All I can tell you is that Bishop Rhinehart's latest letter speaks to some serious problems in your past—not necessarily transgressions, mind you, but things that make you unfit to remain a priest. I have been in touch with our Bishop Hernandez of Tucson. He says that if you do not resign, the process will begin to have you defrocked. Do you still refuse? Yes? Then, please excuse me, I have a number of things to attend to."

With that, Brother Berard stood up, and holding Steve's arm at the elbow, escorted him to the door.

Steve left Brother Berard's office and went to his cell where he spent a full hour pacing the floor. "This is preposterous," he said aloud, as he paced. "I have been threatened with defrocking, unless I cooperate and resign. And again, it seems Bishop Rhinehart is behind it all. And to top it off, no reason has been given. They speak of serious problems in my past. Am I an amnesia victim? What could I have forgotten? Could there have been a deluge of false accusations?" At that point, he was so confused and angry that if a scorpion had appeared in his cell, he would have crushed it without hesitation. Finally, after much thought and indecision, he came to the conclusion that he had to get into Brother Berard's files. He simply had to know whether he had been told the truth. And if so, he might find clues in his file that would help him better understand his so-called past problems. He was aware of the embarrassing risk of getting caught breaking into Berard's office, but since he was about to be defrocked anyway, he had nothing to lose.

That night he said his prayers kneeling by his bedside for the first time since he had come to the monastery. The thought of a possible sting from a scorpion hidden in the dark under his cot, did not bother him in the least. In his depression, he felt so miserably helpless, he almost wished it would happen. After his prayers, he threw himself onto the cot and lay on his back with arms folded behind his head. It was the posture he always took when he thought of Janet while falling asleep. In his mind he brought to life and caressed his memories and fantasies of Janet. After what had happened that day, he realized that the love of God and his relationship with Janet were all he really had left— because everything else had been taken away from him.

15

Steve slowly opened the door to his cell. It was a moonless night. He glanced carefully down the length of the open passageway. He thought it was about two in the morning. They were all asleep. The only sound came from a mournful coyote somewhere outside of the monastery wall. He slipped noiselessly across the compound to Brother Berard's office. Although the door to the office was locked, he was able to slip the tongue of the lock with a plastic knife he had taken from the dining hall. Inside the office, he found the rickety old file cabinet unlocked. Not very tight security he thought, wondering whether the gate to the walled compound around the monastery was really locked and barred as he had been told.

He fished through Brother Berard's desk looking for his file with his small flashlight. He wondered whether his file would be listed under his name or his assigned number. Finally, under the 'M', in the file cabinet, he found the file labeled: Murphy, Stephen, Archdiocese of Washington. He saw that a line had been drawn through the word 'Washington' and 'Tucson' had been added in pencil. He read Rhinehart's letters addressed to Bishop Hernandez of the Tucson diocese. They were copies forwarded to the monastery from the diocese. The contents were exactly as described by Brother Berard. And, as Berard had said, in the final letter there was no explanation other than the statement about

Murphy's not being fit for the priesthood 'because of serious past problems'. At least Berard had been telling him the truth. Looking further, he came across photocopies of his birth and baptismal certificates from Wayland, Mass, plus photocopies of his diplomas, a copy of the certificate from the Pontifical Academy in Rome and a resume of his years in the priesthood including comments about his performance. He was heartened to read the comments, all of which were favorable. There were no notes or annotations containing accusations against him. Then he saw a copy of the letter he knew by heart— the one he had received from Bishop Rhinehart abruptly transferring him to Catholic University. Next, a letter dated some months later transferring him to the monastery. None of the letters contained any explanations. Then, a recent letter contained the order that he should be returned to Washington to resign. And, presumably after he refused, next came the handoff to the Tucson diocese. Rhinehart, he thought, as he read the letters must be trying to drive me crazy. In going through his file he also found a terse note from Bishop Hernandez of Tucson to Brother Berard saying that Father Murphy must be convinced he should resign the priesthood; failing that, pressured to resign. Ultimately, if all else failed he would be defrocked.

He wracked his brain. None of it made any sense. He felt lead in his stomach as he realized that these few pieces of paper spelled the doom of his vocation and his life. Then, as he continued rummaging through the papers, he came across a record of a telephone conversation between Brother Berard and Bishop Hernandez. As recorded in the notes, Berard had written to his bishop for clarification of the reason for defrocking Murphy. The bishop's reply stated that Bishop Rhinehart in Washington had additional confidential information on Murphy that was being retained in Washington. If divulged, the information could cause grave scandal to the Church. Bishop Hernandez said he did not need to know the details—Bishop Rhinehart's word was good enough for him. Since Murphy was now under his authority, he would take appropriate action to remove him from the priesthood. However, he wrote that he was somewhat curious about the unusual case and on his next trip to Washington, would look further into the matter.

After looking over the file, Steve decided he had no choice but to leave the monastery. He would leave quickly. He had to stay one step ahead of formal notification that the process of defrocking him was about to begin. He was slightly comforted by the fact that the levels of approval required in the church's bureaucracy took considerable time—ultimately requiring even Vatican approval. He decided to steal the file. If they searched for him after he left the monastery, he reasoned, why should he make it easy for them by leaving a lot of identifying material behind?

*****

It was almost three A.M. when he tapped lightly on Elmer's door. Elmer opened it groggily as Steve slipped into the cell. "I'm leaving," he said. "Tonight." He told the story to Elmer who sat on his cot shaking his head in disbelief. Elmer offered him a cigarette.

"No thanks, I quit."

"But where will you go? What on earth will you do?"

"I haven't thought out the details but I know I have several stops to make. I'm going to see my brother. He lives near Boston. And I want to do some snooping around to find out what in hell is behind all this."

"What can I do to help?"

"Thanks, but I have to do this alone. By the way, do you need money?" Steve asked. "I can give you a couple of hundred from the stash I had hidden in my chalice case. You may need it if you ever think of leaving this place. And when I find where my other stuff is stored—my wallet and credit cards—I'll be in pretty good shape financially."

"Some dough would be a big help," Elmer said. "I doubt that I will ever leave here, but the money will keep me in cigarettes."

"Elmer, if you ever want to get in touch, you can reach me through my brother Jonathon in Wayland, Mass., Murphy Real Estate. By the way, realizing they go only by numbers and first names here, you probably don't know my last name. It's Murphy. Stephen Murphy."

"I'm Elmer Gustafson. I have a sister, Anna. She's divorced so she goes by her maiden name. You may be able to get in touch with me through her. She lives in the family homestead—a little town called Brunswick, Maryland. Everybody knows the Gustafsons in Brunswick. But tell me, Steve, how are you going to find your way without getting lost in the desert?"

"I plan to follow that decrepit old phone line."

"I don't think that's a good idea. The line goes west,

maybe all the way to Yuma… I'm not really sure. You could spend a week traveling and God knows where you'd wind up. If you get into that hot part of the desert you could fry in the sun and if you travel at night that's when the animals are on the prowl. I think you'd be better off heading east to Tucson. Try to go northeast towards Interstate 10. Follow the rising sun, and before long you'll see the mountains in the distance. You'll have some mountain passes to get through, but it will be cool at the higher elevations. Although frankly, Steve, going on foot, and trying to get to civilization from here will be difficult no matter which direction you choose. That's why the brothers rebuilt this mission out here to begin with."

"Thanks for the advice. I guess I'll take a chance on Tucson. Jeremy brought me out here from Tucson on I-10. I might be able to spot some recognizable landmarks."

The two priests then said goodbye in a friendly embrace, then, making a Sign of the Cross, gave each other a blessing: "In nomine patris, in filii, in spiritu sancti."

"God be with you, Steve."

"And also with you, Elmer."

*****

Steve slipped back into his room. There was almost nothing there worth taking with him except his silver crucifix, rosary beads and some underclothes. Next he went to the supply room. It was locked. As he fiddled with the lock, a tall figure in a gray habit came out of the darkness. It limped towards him looming over his shoulder as he crouched pulling on the lock with all his might. Looking back over his shoulder startled, Steve thought he would have to fight his way out.

"Here's the key," a voice said. It was Brother Berard. "You can take all of your possessions with the exception of your chalice and the file you took from my office. I can't permit you to take the chalice because you are to be defrocked. It would be too much of a temptation for you to simply continue pastoral duties. Permit me to do the charitable thing and donate it to a priest who has to borrow one to say Mass."

Reluctantly, Steve agreed, knowing it would be difficult to lug the chalice case and his other stuff through the desert.

"And you really should leave the file with me. It contains letters addressed to me. The correspondence and the photocopies of your certificates belong to me. You may take whatever else belongs to you. I won't stop you. You may be interested to know, I left the front gate unlocked. Who's coming to get you? Jeremy?"

"No. I've had no contact with Jeremy."

"Then how do you propose to cross the desert?"

"On foot."

"That's impossible," Brother Berard said. "Only an Indian could make it and even he would be lucky to make it to Phoenix. If on the other hand, you're going to Tucson, it is even more absurd because you have first the desert to cross, then the mountains, and then more desert. But it's your decision. I leave it up to you."

"Why," Steve asked, "aren't you trying to stop me from leaving? Aren't you disobeying orders?"

"Perhaps I am. But I am abbot here and must act

according to the best interests of the monastery. You refuse to resign and I am concerned about your remaining here. You have beaten some of my brothers. There will be less trouble with you gone."

"You mean there may not be anyone to fight back when the brothers strong-arm the priests."

"Murphy, let's be frank with one another. I admire the way you have pitched in to help other priests in need, and when it came to work on the farm, you were an outstanding worker. I also don't object to the way you interceded when some of my brothers got out of hand. They are a tough bunch. We all know that. But you should understand, we are dealing with a number of recalcitrant derelicts who call themselves priests."

"Do you harbor some deep resentment against the priesthood?" Steve asked acidly.

"No, I do not. Years ago, I wanted to become a priest. I felt that I had a strong vocation, but I was turned down."

"Why?"

"The hierarchy did not want a priest limping on the altar. I suppose it didn't project the right image of the priesthood. Then, after being assigned here, I came into contact with hundreds of priests who were willingly accepted into the priesthood as having all of the qualifications. And here they reside— drunkards, pedophiles, homosexuals, thieves, heretics...."

"But they represent just a tiny percent of all priests. Remember, Christ had one bad apostle out of a total of twelve."

"That is true. I certainly don't condemn all priests, but I nevertheless deeply resent the way the priests sent here have repeatedly violated the sacrament of Holy Orders. They are all Judas's. They deserve to be treated accordingly. All they merit is pressure to resign."

"I disagree. They deserve God's mercy. They deserve some realistic effort to rehabilitate them. As a minimum, they deserve to be treated as human beings."

Brother Berard sat down on a stool next to Steve. "If you will only follow Bishop Hernandez' request that you resign, things would go much better for you. We would arrange transportation, money, whatever you need. The bishop is not an unreasonable man. He would give you dispensation of your vows. You would remain Catholic. You would be able to get married, have children and serve God's church as the head of a family and still retain some lay duties in the church. If you refuse the offer, you go in disgrace from the church. You become a renegade. Carrying on priestly duties would be a sacrilege."

"Next time you see Bishop Hernandez, thank him for the offer, but my mind is made up. I took a vow for life and will not renounce it."

Brother Berard stood up. "Well, let's leave it at that," he said. "I will have to apprise Bishop Hernandez of your decision. You understand the bishop will set in motion the process to have you defrocked."

Without replying, Steve continued rummaging through shelves of boxes in the supply room. He finally found a small box containing his wallet and his watch. He looked through the wallet. It still contained his passport, credit cards, checkbook and over six hundred dollars in cash. After wading through several racks, he found one of his black suits, Roman collar and shoes.

"You may not approve of us, but we are not thieves," Brother Berard said watching him from his position at the door.

Steve stuffed his small items and his suit and shoes into an unused backpack he found lying in the corner. He kept his stole hidden. "Mind if I keep these work clothes I've got on, and may I take this backpack?" he asked. "They're practically throwaways anyway."

But as he turned around for an answer, he realized Brother Berard had silently left him without saying goodbye. The file and the chalice case were also gone.

Steve had planned to force his way into the kitchen, but he found the door had been left unlocked—apparently a little extra assist by Brother Berard. He packed a few sandwiches and two flasks of water in his backpack. Then he walked across the compound and found the front gate unlocked as Brother Berard said it would be. He closed the gate quietly behind him and set out on a chilly, pitch black night along the rutted dirt road in the direction of the dark shadowy mountains that rose toward the heavens in front of him.

16

Steve picked his way along the bumpy, uneven road in the dark, occasionally drifting off to the side and stumbling on a rock. It startled him whenever he put his foot out thinking it would hit solid ground only to find it descending into a hole. Losing his balance, he would fall, pick himself up and continue on until he hit another rock or another hole. In his mind there was no plan, no thought of what he would do after he reached Tucson. He wasn't even sure he was still heading in the direction of Tucson, although he had started out from the monastery in that direction.

One step at a time. His mind was filled with the dangers that lurked on all sides. He walked in fear of a sudden strike on the leg from an unseen rattlesnake. Unlike the area around Tucson where mesquite trees and saguaro cactus often live symbiotically, in this part of the desert there were no saguaro cactus and therefore no chance of finding a long stick from a mesquite that he could tap to the left and right in front of him to scare away snakes. Failing that, he could only hope he would hear the rattle in time to freeze in his tracks. He knew there were jaguars and mountain lions in the desert that prowled at night looking for a meal. If *he* was the meal they were looking for, he would have to submit, having no defense. He thought of the Christians facing the lions in the Colosseum. They could huddle in groups on the ground transfixed in prayer—heroically proclaiming their faith before stands filled with bloodthirsty spectators, and die martyrs—soon to be followed by an everlasting heavenly reward. They would be honored as heroes of early Christendom, with whatever remained of their bones or half-eaten bodies secretly buried in crypts in the catacombs. Some would be canonized. He, a renegade, would face the same torture, but would die alone in the Sonora Desert without the glory of martyrdom.

Months or years later someone might find the skeletal remains of a desiccated corpse if the vultures left anything behind. As a renegade priest, he wasn't even sure of salvation despite his lifelong devotion to Jesus and the Virgin Mary, and how in the imitation of Christ he had tried to conduct his life. When these feelings came over him, he refused to believe they stemmed from self-pity. They were facts driven home by months of harsh and sometimes cruel treatment by his church.

He stopped suddenly, startled by a rustle of brush and a dark shape that moved silently across his path. Although he couldn't see it, he felt a slight movement of air as the thing passed. He also detected a pungent odor. He waited, standing perfectly still, trying to identify a shape in the blackness. Then another went by and still another. A line of some type of animal he couldn't identify. When one bumped into him, he stumbled backwards. The animal did not attack, it moved on, seemingly ignoring him. After a few minutes, he was satisfied that whatever line of animals had crossed his path, they were now gone. But he found he had fallen into a furry cholla bush which jabbed sharp spines into the side of his thigh. What seemed like fur was in reality a cluster of needle-sharp thorns. He was beginning to panic. He tried to recover by repeating a short prayer to himself: "Jesus, Mary and Joseph help me. Jesus, Mary and Joseph...". He crawled backwards, then settled down in a squat and began the painful process of pulling a dozen spines out of his leg as he repeated the prayer over and over. The prayer took his mind off the pain. When he had regained his composure, he pushed on towards the dark craggy shapes high in the sky in the far distance that seemed to stand out against the starlit background. With no stars glinting in front of shapes that rose like massive inkblots into the sky, he knew they must be the mountains. What he did not know was how far away they were—two days? three days?

Almost every bush he bumped into in the dark seemed to be covered with sharp thorns. He was scratched on arms and legs through his work clothes which began to hang torn in places.

Somewhere in the hours since he had left the monastery, he had strayed from the road and was crossing open country heading towards those high ominous shapes that he knew he would eventually have to cross. The going was made tougher by the fact that the land was not flat—he always seemed to be climbing small hillocks or stumbling down into ravines. He began to berate himself over the stupidity of thinking he could traverse this kind of terrain in the dark. Maybe the whole idea of escaping on foot was a mistake. Yet he knew that if he had stayed in the monastery he would have faced the ultimate calamity— his priesthood taken away from him. Regardless of what Elmer had said about the church preferring resignations to defrocking, Steve somehow knew his case was different. They were already trying to defrock him. But the multiple approval levels of the church bureaucracy in cases of defrocking worked in his favor. His plan was to stay ahead of any formal notice.

As the hours went by, the stars grew fainter. The mountains faded from black to gray. He was buoyed up by the first light of dawn in the eastern sky and finally, sunrise. The sun came up in front of him confirming that he was heading east or northeast to Tucson. As morning came, he realized he had been walking for over three hours. The breathtaking desert sunrise produced an exhilarating euphoria almost overcoming the tiredness he felt from a night without sleep. In the far distance he could see rows of tall saguaro cactus some with crazy twisted arms, silhouetted against the pink-orange light in the eastern sky.

Walking now with renewed energy, he suddenly came upon a swarm of large hairy, iron-gray animals that looked like wild boars. He shrank back wondering if they might attack him with their small sharp upturned tusks. He remembered they were called javelinas. They frequented the Sonora Desert munching mainly on prickly pear cactus. As he studied the animals who completely ignored him, he was surprised to see them devouring the prickly pear—thorns and all! He realized that the line of animals that had passed him in the dark the previous night must have been javelinas.

Later, his confidence grew as the warm morning

sun began to shine down on him. With lighter step, he trudged on, circling the arroyos and hillocks that dotted the great mesa. He could now clearly see the ground in front of him as he steadily made his way. Maybe things would be all right, he thought. Maybe he would make it.

*****

Brother Berard limped across the compound in the direction of his office. He had arisen early as usual to attend Mass, receive the Holy Eucharist and have breakfast in the refectory. As he crossed the compound, he glanced up at a parade of sparse white clouds drifting from the southwest across Arizona's pale blue sky. In the distance to the north, mixed white and gray layers of clouds scraped over the craggy mountain peaks. It was late spring; the rains were long gone and the Sonora Desert had become warm and dry in the daytime, cold at night. "Today will be in the upper eighties," he mumbled to himself, happy at the thought that the phantom pain he felt constantly in his foot near the missing toe, had let up considerably in the dry weather, although it would not disappear completely. He was more tired than usual this morning having slept only four hours instead of his usual five because of the late night incident with Father Murphy. As he approached his office, stirring up dusty brown gravel with every footstep of his dragging left foot, he heard the telephone ringing. Hurrying in, he picked up the receiver and stiffened himself for the annoying squeal he would hear due to the aging telephone, or neglected phone line coming into the monastery, he never knew which.

"Good morning," Bishop Hernandez said, with an unintentionally harsh squawk that sounded like an angry bird of prey fighting over a carcass. "May I speak to Brother Berard?"

"Good morning, Your Grace. This is Brother Berard speaking."

"How are things going at the monastery? Are you getting all the supplies you need?"

Brother Berard could have launched into a series of complaints about the poor provisioning provided by the diocese, but he had learned it would do no good. When payments, and in some cases, supplies intended for the Passion Monastery came in from dioceses around the country, addressed to the Diocese of Tucson—a region always engulfed in a tidal wave of dirt-poor Mexicans who had slipped across the border and needed his help, the Most Reverend Luis Hernandez in the goodness of his heart almost invariably found higher priority spending needs than an outlying monastery which adhered to a religious order rather than diocesan rule.

"I'm calling about a priest who has been staying with you," the bishop said, his voice barely penetrating the annoying squeal. "His name is Stephen Murphy. He is the diocesan priest who was transferred here from Washington. I sent you a letter stating that I wanted him to resign from the priesthood. Has he done that?"

"No, Your Grace. I told him about your wishes, but he refused to resign."

"Did you explain that he would leave the priesthood with the blessing of the church and thus be permitted to lead a full Catholic life?"

"Yes, Your Grace. I did, at length, but he was adamant."

"Well, in that case, we must take steps to defrock him because for a reason I have yet to determine, Bishop Rhinehart of Washington says we must remove him from the priesthood by any means possible. I really do not like doing this. It harms the man's soul and it hurts Holy Mother Church, but I must."

"I understand," Brother Berard answered.

"You must keep him at the compound until I've drawn up the necessary paperwork."

Brother Berard grew concerned. He visualized the bishop coming to a rapid boil as he was forced to admit, "I can't do that, you see he has already left us."

"Do you mean you just let him leave?" The squeal was louder now and more irritating as it moved into a higher pitch. "You didn't try to stop him?"

"No I didn't. He left last night. I tried to talk him out of it, Your Grace. I explained that he would be a renegade if he left."

"Well, you simply must get him back. Since he has refused to resign, he will very likely try to continue his role as a priest. We can't have that."

Brother Berard was growing tired of listening to the squeal. "I tried to take care of that. I gave his chalice to another priest to prevent him from saying Mass."

"Not good enough! He can easily get another. Brother Berard, I want you to send some of your monks out to find him and bring him back. Then hold him by force if necessary."

"I'll do what I can, Your Grace. But he has about a five hour head start. Frankly, I'm confused about this situation. Father Murphy was sent here with none of the abuses in his record that bring other priests to us. When he was assigned here, no therapy group was recommended, which I found unusual. Can you tell me why he was sent here? In the months he has been a resident, he has appeared to be a devout priest."

"I can't tell you any more than you have already been told. In fact, I do not know his particular problem myself. As I said before, Bishop Rhinehart has taken the lead on this. He writes that it is a serious matter and now that Cardinal Wollman is dead, Bishop Rhinehart will almost certainly be elevated to cardinal by the holy father. I am assuming there has been a serious past violation that is too sensitive to document in Murphy's file. Now if Bishop Rhinehart wants Murphy to resign or defrocked, that is all I need to know. However, you do arouse my curiosity and when I'm in Washington next week, I will take it up with his eminence."

"Yes, Your Grace. Is that all?" Brother Berard asked, impatient to end the call. The squeal had produced a ringing in his ear and possibly the beginnings of a migraine.

"See that you find this priest. Do whatever you have to. Just bring him back."

"I will do what I can Your Grace, and without meaning to sound impertinent, may I ask you to remember the Crucified Christ?"

"Yes, Brother Berard, I can assure you I always remember the Crucified Christ."

After hanging up, Brother Berard summoned two of the brothers, Michael and John, to his office. On entering, the hulking monks stood silently on the earthen floor in front of his desk. He had selected these two brothers in particular because he knew they harbored a grudge against Murphy which would make them well-suited to capturing him and dragging him back. Added to that, they were both tall, strong and through the years had exhibited a simple-minded obedience of which he was at times contemptuous but nevertheless always found useful. As the Principal Brother impatiently drummed his fingers on his desk, it was obvious to the pair that their leader was very disturbed. It made them anxious to do whatever was necessary to calm him. "Are both of you aware that Father Steve Murphy left the monastery last night?"

"We heard of it," Brother Michael answered.

"Bishop Hernandez says we have to find him and bring him back. I'd like you two to go out together to find him. Use the Ford pickup and take whatever supplies you need. Make sure you have plenty of gas. We don't need to be sending out a search party to find both of you as well. There is a problem: I don't know whether he was heading north to Phoenix or going east to Tucson. So it may take you several days to track him down."

"When we find him what if he refuses to come back?" asked Brother Michael with a leer that betrayed his relish for the upcoming task.

"Then use force," Brother Berard said. Noticing the look on Brother Michael's face, he decided to tease the brothers into action. "Murphy must be returned. And, after the beating both of you took the night when you were, shall we say, punishing that other priest, do I detect that you might enjoy this little trip?"

Brother Michael, with downcast eyes, ground the ball of one sandal-shod foot into the earthen floor. He was angry and embarrassed that his leader seemed to be fully knowledgeable about the incident. He decided to cover his embarrassment with tough talk: "If we bring him back with a few broken ribs to make up for when he almost broke my jaw, will that be all right?"

"Why do you think that if he beat you once, he can't do it again? Just do whatever is necessary to bring him back."

"May I ask a question?" Brother John chimed in. The Principal Brother gave a silent nod. "What should we wear on this task?"

"My thought," Brother Berard said, stroking his beard, "is that you are better off wearing your monastic habits. If by any chance Murphy has reached either of the cities and you need to apply pressure to bring him back, it would seem less like a kidnapping if you were dressed as monks. Added to that, the Border Patrol hiding on the back roads would be more likely to leave you alone. And remember, you must act quickly— once Murphy reaches a city, he could be very difficult to find. My thinking is he might try to get to Tucson because he came here originally through Tucson and would be more familiar with it. He would have to cross the mountains of course, which is probably impossible. If so, you may find yourselves looking for a corpse. But use your own judgment about where to look. One other thing, your vow of silence and other religious duties are suspended until this matter is finished."

17

Steve stopped his trek momentarily, wiped his brow with his torn sleeve, slipped off his backpack and fished around in it for his breviary. Slinging the pack over his shoulder again, he read his daily priestly office as he resumed walking. He felt he needed to keep moving. He read with only one eye on the book because he had to be careful about running into the spines of cactus that in places grew so thick they almost blocked his way. When he nearly stepped into a hole filled with crawling pit vipers, he decided to put away the breviary and focus on the ground in front. He ate a sandwich he had taken from the kitchen in the monastery and drank a mouthful from a flask of water. The nourishment lifted his spirits. Happily, when late morning came, the sun became comfortably warm.

He had a sudden uneasy feeling. Glancing over his shoulder, he saw a dust cloud rising from a vehicle in the distance. His first thought was that someone from the monastery might be pursuing him. On the other hand, he thought it might be Jeremy returning from the monastery after dropping off someone or something. If so, he could hitch a ride. But as the vehicle came nearer Steve saw it was not Jeremy's high off-road vehicle. As he studied the surrounding area, he estimated that he had strayed about a quarter-mile from the road. He crouched down hiding behind a cactus as the vehicle bumped along the road approaching him. It was a pickup truck with driver and passenger both in the gray habits of the monastery. It was hard to tell from the dust kicked up by the truck, but he thought he caught a glimpse of Brothers Michael and John. He remained hidden, hoping they hadn't seen him.

The vehicle passed, apparently heading in the direction of Tucson, but after bouncing a mile or so up the road it turned to the left on a dusty road as if the driver had decided to head in the direction of Phoenix. It crossed Steve's mind that they might be searching for him, that Brother Berard might have changed his mind about letting him go. If that were true, the monks' futile search for him in Phoenix would buy him some time in Tucson, if he ever got to Tucson.

The long tedious day wore on, the sun becoming hotter. He remembered in the old Hollywood movies how the rule in the desert was to sleep by day and travel by night. But he had no time to waste and although it was getting hot, this desert was certainly not as forbidding as the endless sands of the scorching Sahara or Death Valley in California. So he pushed on and although uncomfortable, he found his situation bearable. Sighting on the afternoon sun, he tried to head in the direction that would take him back to Interstate 10—the main thruway between Phoenix and Tucson.

Evening came. "Sunset and Evening Star and one clear call for me...." His hollow voice sounded almost unearthly in the silent desert as snatches of a poem came to him from the distant past. "Twilight and evening bell and after that the dark, and may there be no sadness of farewell when I embark...." He tried to remember the remainder of the poem, but gave up. Soon it would be night. Grimly, he knew the cold would come with it.

In the distance, across the flat tableland he saw the dark misty peaks of the high mountains, their jagged fingers pointing upwards toward the heavens. Lofty, black craggy shapes were outlined against the fading light of the sky. He had no idea what mountain range it was, but he knew he had to get over it to get back to Tucson and civilization. As daylight waned, so did the warmth. As soon as the sun set, the cloudless sky radiated the heat back into space. He began to shiver as he walked. He knew he would need shelter to last the night. Finally, he came upon a low-lying ridge bordering an arroyo. He climbed down, happy that the streambed was dry. He crumpled down in the sand with his back propped against a large rock that still held some of the heat of the day. Dinner consisted of a half-sandwich and a mouthful of water. It grew dark. As he drifted off to sleep he realized he had been walking for probably eighteen hours. He couldn't really keep track of time because although Brother Berard had given him his watch back the battery was dead.

*****

It was first light. Sleepily, Steve felt a slight tingling on his leg. As he moved his hand down to scratch, the scorpion struck. He was instantly aware of his mistake. He should have lain motionless until he knew what was pressing on his leg. After the attack, the insect quickly disappeared. It disappeared so quickly he couldn't tell if it was one of the small deadly scorpions. The searing pain of the venom spread through Steve's lower leg. In a panic, he knew that some scorpion stings were fatal. He knew that if he didn't calm himself down, he could have a heart attack whether or not the sting itself was fatal. He remembered reading that men in the southwest stung by pit vipers sometimes survived the fatal bites by lying absolutely motionless. With eyes closed against the pain, he prayed as he lay as motionless as possible. His only hope was that the venom would be absorbed in the tissues of his leg and not travel to his heart.

Three hours later, with the sun rising higher in the sky, Steve was able to get to his feet although he felt wobbly. Convinced now that he would survive, he decided to push on. He limped all day, his second day in the desert, and as twilight came on, he began to shiver again. Now in the foothills of the mountains, the extra effort in climbing the steepened grade tended to warm him, but it was never enough to make him feel comfortable.

In the night, it grew much colder as he climbed to a narrow pass that appeared to thread between two of the lesser peaks. Here and there in hollowed-out areas were patches of snow. He was freezing, his teeth chattering as he unsteadily labored to put one foot in front of the other. How could it be like summer in the daytime and winter at night? As his body temperature dropped, more than once he thought of lying down and letting the sleep of hypothermia end his misery, but he knew that as a priest it would be a sleep with an angry Christ waiting on the other side of the vale. Knowing that Christ expected, nay demanded, that despite pain and suffering, he and other Catholics like him fight to stay alive, he struggled on.

After a few hours in the dark, deep hypothermia began setting in as his brain clouded over. He decided he had to test himself by trying to remember simple things—it would give him a clue about how low his body temperature had fallen. But try as he might, he could barely remember his own name, a few simple prayers and little else. When he tried to pray out loud, his teeth chattered so badly, the words sounded like gibberish.

As he came through the pass and began the descent, a distant glow in the dark sky told him there was civilization ahead. How many miles away was it? With his slow progress the more important question was: How many days away was it? He began to hallucinate. Phantasms appeared before his eyes. In the moonless night, lit only by dim starlight, he thought he saw bats circling above him. They swooped down near his head as he flailed his arms to keep them away. He placed his hands flat on top of his head hoping to keep them out of his hair as he started to trot to get away. A little later in what he thought was a lucid moment, he wondered whether the bats had been real—or might he have imagined them? Were they simply the tricks played on the mind by deep hypothermia?

Steve came onto a level plain where the ground was smooth and loamy with no rocks or holes. He began feeling a little warmer. As he dragged himself across the mesa in the blackness, cut and bleeding from tumbling on rocks and scraping against cactus spines, he saw a large dark shape looming in front of him. It was a black ball seemingly suspended four feet off the ground. It looked like an oversized, almost giant, fuzzy bowling ball. He was certain he was hallucinating until it moved towards him. Then he wasn't so sure. Suddenly he was surrounded by other large suspended black balls. They rushed inward, scrambling and pushing to get at him. He fell to the ground. They nipped at his face, hands and torn feet. They kicked him with sharp clawed feet. He knew the Sonora Desert had several dozen species of birds of prey known as raptors. His mind raced. Weren't the Jurassic raptors ancestors of modern birds? Was this some throwback to the dinosaur age? Didn't they inhabit this desert at one time? What were these monsters? The oversized birdlike animals pecked at him in the dark with sharp pointed beaks on long twisted snakelike necks. They crowded around pushing to get at him. His screams rang across the open space but were unheard. He was on his back, covering his face with his hands as the animals nipped tiny bits of flesh from the backs of his hands and feet. The kicks opened bleeding cuts on his legs. His knapsack, which had fallen to his side was now being torn. If it kept up there wouldn't be much left of his black suit.

Suddenly, the animals stopped attacking him. He wondered why. Maybe they discovered they didn't like the taste of grimy, blood-soaked human tissue. His last sandwich disappeared in a struggle between the animals. There was now a crescent moon rising giving enough light so he could barely make out the cluster of birdlike faces with owl-shaped eyes that seemed to stare back at him in wonder, It suddenly occurred to him that these were emus—relatives of ostriches. He first thought he had stumbled onto an ostrich farm, but since he had come upon no fences, these birds must have been roaming wild. They had probably escaped from a farm. He knew that emus, although not generally considered dangerous, scavenged for food constantly, night and day.

Steve rolled over kneeling on all fours and scooped up a handful of sand mixed with dirt. He threw one handful after another at the birds. Finally, flapping their body feathers, they ran away on their toes like ballet dancers to look for food elsewhere.

He saw the headlights of a car in the distance and started to trot. He tripped on a small cactus and fell headlong into a ditch striking his temple on a rock. When he came to, he knew he hadn't been unconscious long because it was still dark, unless, that is, he had been out an entire day and now it was the next night. He wearily got to his feet and walked on.

At last, he came on a highway. He figured it was the interstate. He sat shivering by the side of the road with his back against a roadside sign for what seemed like an eternity. The light jacket he wore was now so badly shredded, it provided little warmth. He remembered his crumpled suit in the knapsack and pulling it open, slipped the black, now almost ragged, suit-coat over his shoulders. He was dismayed when he saw the trousers—long tears in the legs. The headlights of an approaching car slowed but sped away when the occupants had a closer look at the hunched and torn, bloody specter in the headlights. Then another car passed and another. As the night went by, dozens, maybe hundreds of cars and trucks passed but no one would stop. No good Samaritans in Arizona?

He stood up, turned around and looked at the sign. It

read: DO NOT PICK UP HITCHHIKERS. PICACHO PRISON TWO MILES.

After he read the sign, he knew he had to walk some distance back up the highway towards Phoenix, hoping someone heading to Tucson would stop to pick him up before the car reached the sign. If a driver saw the sign first, he would never be picked up.

A Border Patrol van came down the road. "Thank God," Steve said as he saw the white van grind to a halt by the side of the road. "I need help."

The uniformed guards looked at him through the windshield of the van and decided he did not look like a Mexican who had sneaked across the border. He was obviously a derelict, probably drunk or stoned.

The guard on the passenger side rolled the window down. Steve saw him stick his head out. He heard the man say, "Maybe we oughta pick him up anyway. He looks like he needs a hand. You know, a doctor or something."

The driver of the van wouldn't hear of it. "For Chrissake, we both know the border is goin' wild and I say we're too goddamn busy to screw around collecting homeless or drunks on the highway. The way they're comin' across the desert west of Nogales, you'd think there was a gold strike up in Tucson."

As an emergency call came in, the driver shouted, to Steve, "Sorry, but we gotta go. Good luck."

A half-hour later, a pickup truck stopped and pulled off to the shoulder. The lights of the pickup played on the ragged figure in front of the truck. Steve couldn't tell who was in the darkened interior of the vehicle. He limped up to the passenger side window. The driver, a young man, kept the door locked but lowered the window a bit. He was startled at the appearance of the hitchhiker when he saw the dirt, the blood and the torn clothes that hung on Steve like a scarecrow. "You look like you need help, buddy," he said, wincing at the sight.

"Yes, I do. Please take me to a doctor or a hospital. I can give you some money."

The driver knew the hitchhiker wasn't a Mexican but he might have been a prisoner from Picacho. "You on the run or something?"

"In a way, yes, but not from the police. I'm not from the prison."

"Then what are you doing out here? Where did you come from?"

"The Passion Monastery back beyond the mountains."

"I've heard rumors about that place but never heard of anyone walking out and getting this far alive."

"I guess I'm the first although I'm not sure I'm still alive."

"OK, hop in. Sit on this old blanket so's you don't get blood and shit on the seat. What in hell happened to you, anyway? You a drunk?"

"No. Just say I was mugged but got away."

A quarter mile down the road, they came to the DO NOT PICK UP HITCHHIKERS sign. The driver got nervous. He had forgotten about the sign. He kept glancing over at Steve. He pulled the truck over to the side of the road. "Sorry, but I gotta let you out," he said.

"But you don't understand," Steve argued. "I'm not

from the prison. I escaped from the monastery. I'm a priest." Steve rustled through the shredded knapsack and came out with a roman collar. He showed the crucifix to the driver. He pulled out his wallet and showed the driver his I.D. and credit cards. "I'm a priest," he said. "I was at the Passion Brothers Monastery in the desert, but I had to leave. Please believe me. I need to be taken to a doctor or a hospital. I need to have these cuts treated."

The driver stared at Steve long and hard. Behind the dirt and the blood and a face with a stubbly beard, he saw what was probably a halfway decent guy. For the first time, he noticed the gash on his passenger's head. He doubted the man he had picked up was an escaped prisoner. Probably some kind of religious kook— maybe a priest, maybe not.

Steve slumped in the seat. The driver shook him. "Shit, he's out cold. Why does this have to happen to me?" He started to drive as the thought occurred to him that his passenger might be dead rather than unconscious. "Jesus," he said to himself, "I could be driving a goddamn corpse!" He thought of pulling off the road and dumping the body, but Steve stirred in the seat. He began breathing with short rapid breaths followed by hard exhales as if he were in pain but was reluctant to admit it.

"You probably haven't eaten much. I've got some crackers and a beer in the cooler on the floor. Help yourself."

Forty-five minutes later, the driver pulled the pickup in front of the Emergency Room of Tucson General Hospital. Hurrying inside, he told them about his passenger and stood aside as two attendants ran out. Then gently, very gently they lifted Steve out of the pickup and onto a gurney. As soon as Steve was wheeled into the hospital, the driver took off. There was nothing more he could do and he certainly did not want his name on some piece of paper. The hospital people would call the cops and he might be accused of having beaten the man, or he could be sued. I got enough problems without all that bullshit, he thought as he sped away from the hospital.

In the emergency room, after checking his pulse, temperature and blood pressure, lifting his eyelids, feeling for broken bones, examining his legs and the wound on Steve's head, the ER doctor came to a conclusion: "He's pretty bunged up and the skin on his legs is cut up, but he'll live. Also looks like he's been bitten by a scorpion. "Let's get these rags off him, clean him up, and begin warming him to bring him out of hypothermia. The hypothermia's potentially a lot riskier than his other injuries. Then, get some X-rays. Let's look for a concussion. One of you check his pockets for an I.D. Call the police, although I see no sign of drugs. But his breath smells like he must have had a beer. He's most likely a homeless. He doesn't look old enough for Medicare, and I'll bet he doesn't have ten cents worth of insurance."

*****

Steve was slowly warmed out of his hypothermia. His injuries turned out not to be serious. There were no broken bones. The tests showed he had had a mild concussion but even that was dismissed by the doctors with a few words of caution that he should take it easy for awhile. The scorpion venom had been absorbed by his body without any noticeable harm. He was admitted to the hospital overnight. When they learned he was a priest, he was given a private room but happily, from Steve's standpoint, no one thought to contact the Catholic diocese. On the following afternoon, a police officer stopped by his room as Steve sat on the edge of the bed wondering what happened to his clothes. His legs were covered with some kind of ointment. He lightly touched the cuts and scratches from his trek through the desert. They weren't as bad as he might have thought. He could probably slip on a pair of pants, if he had a pair of pants.

"How're you feeling, Father?"

"Groggy," Steve replied as he struggled to his feet and began to brush his hair in the mirror. In the reflection he saw the police officer seated in a chair behind him.

"I want to get out of here," Steve said.

"I came by here last night but you were unconscious. Are you sure you feel well enough to leave?"

"Yes, I want to get a taxi out of here right away."

"That's not necessary. We contacted the Tucson Diocesan office. They're sending a couple of monks from the Passion Monastery. The diocese wants you to wait here for them."

"When was the call made to the diocese?"

"A little while ago. But the monks won't be here for another hour or so— seems they were looking for you in Phoenix. They're on the way down here now."

"By the way," the officer said with a hint of a smile,

"they discarded the clothes you came in here with. The nurse said she didn't think you'd mind because they were little more than a bunch of rags. They were covered with blood. The only thing worth saving was a long piece of purple cloth. It was rolled up tight."

"My stole."

"And your prayer book and crucifix. And they found your wallet."

"My black shoes?"

"No sign of them. Must've fallen out of the knapsack."

"Oh great," Steve said with a grimace. "Now what do I wear when I leave here?"

"The hospital is going to donate an outfit of sorts to you. You know, underwear, slacks, shirt, shoes and some kind of jacket. Nothing fancy, just what they had on hand. A hospital orderly took a few measurements while you were sleeping."

"But where do they get the stuff?" Steve asked, then quickly added with a slight grin, "Never mind. I guess I don't want to know."

None of the clothes brought by the nurse fit properly but Steve didn't really care. He had one thought—to get out of the hospital before the brothers arrived. He dressed in front of the cop who politely stared out the window. Steve tried to look calm as he packed his few belongings into a small plastic carry-all bag the nurse gave him. Then, leaving the officer behind in the room with the donated jacket and bag, he went to check out of the hospital. When asked if he was covered by the Tucson Diocesan health plan, it crossed his mind that he would be justified in sticking the diocese with the bill, but he didn't want to lose time with the paperwork. He paid the hospital bill with a credit card that he was pleased to find was still active after months of non-use.

Returning to his room to retrieve his things, he was surprised to find the police officer still seated in a chair in the corner. He had a sudden fear the officer might feel it his duty to restrain him and turn him over to the monks.

"Well, I'm about to leave," Steve said as he narrowly eyed the police officer, slipped into the jacket, and started to leave the room.

"Father, hold on a moment. Aren't you going to wait for the monks?"

"No, I'm kind of in a hurry."

"But hold on, please. I'd like to talk to you. By the way, my name is Greg. I wanted to talk to you about confession."

Steve raised his eyebrows. Although he was anxious to get out of the hospital, instinctively based on years of pastoral ministry, he resignedly put down his bag and drew up a chair near the officer. "What did you want to know?"

"I'm a lapsed Catholic," the officer replied. Haven't been to confession or Holy Communion in years. My wife thinks I should start going to Mass again and receive the sacraments...because of our kids."

"Can't argue with that," Steve said. "Why don't you?"

"This may sound silly, Father, but you know how when someone hasn't been to confession in a long time, how it takes a long time to get it all out? Added to that, I'm not sure I can give a complete reckoning of all my sins."

"God understands we are not perfect. All He asks is that we do our best."

"Father, I'm so well-known in my church and the other parishes around here, I'd be embarrassed to see a long line of friends waiting for me to get finished. I also don't think our parish priest is very understanding. He'd recognize my voice. He's impatient and frankly, kind of sarcastic. I don't think I want to go through all of that."

"So?"

"So, since you're here and I'm here, I wondered if you'd hear my confession."

"Right here? Right now?"

"Yes, if you don't mind."

Steve caught his breath. He glanced at the wall clock. He had a vision of the Passion Brothers speeding down the highway to Tucson. He figured he knew which monks Berard would have sent. It would be Michael and John, the strong-arm thugs. What a scandal if a scuffle broke out at the hospital between a priest and two monks. And there might well be a scuffle because he did not intend to go peacefully. But no matter what, here was a sinner who needed absolution. Reaching into the bag, Steve pulled out the purple stole. He unrolled it, kissed it and slipped over his head.

"All right Greg, he said softly. "Why don't I sit here in the chair? You kneel beside me."

"Bless me Father," Greg said in throaty whisper. "My last confession was eight years ago...."

Steve's mind raced. Good grief, he thought. I have less than forty-five minutes remaining to cover eight years.

The confession and absolution took fifty-two minutes.

"Greg, I've got to leave here right now," Steve said, hurriedly grabbing his bag. "Those monks are coming to take me back to the Passion Monastery and I don't want to go with them. I don't intend to go back to that place."

The pair walked down the long corridor to the elevator. "I've heard stories about that place, Father. They say it's run more like a prison than a rehab center. And, if you don't mind my asking, how did you come to leave that monastery, by the way? And before you answer that, how come you went there in the first place? I hear tell it's for bad priests...alcoholics, drug users. Guys like that. You don't strike me as being in those categories. But there's also pedophile priests," he added, glancing suspiciously at Steve out of the corner of his eye as they walked.

"Pedophile priests are a lot less obvious, I realize, and maybe you never really know, do you," Steve replied testily. "Why try to explain," he said to himself. "I don't know why I was sent there so how can I explain it to this guy?"

"No, I guess they don't brag about crimes like that do they," the officer said sourly, shaking his head as he thought of his own young children.

Steve relented. "You may not believe me," he said as they stepped into the elevator, "but I'm not a pedophile priest, and I'm not an alcoholic and I don't do drugs and I never embezzled a dime of church funds. To tell you the plain truth, I have no idea why I was sent there. They never gave me a reason and there were no clues.

For openers, they assign priests to therapy groups at the monastery. You know—one for substance abusers, another for sex deviants, and so forth. When I was there, if I had been accused of something, I really had no way of knowing what it might be because I never was assigned to a group. I was just left hanging."

"Doesn't speak well for the church I'm about to re-enter, does it, Father," the officer said as the two walked through the lobby of the hospital towards the front door.

"Don't judge the church too harshly. There may be a very good reason— one that I haven't found out yet."

"You angry about this, Father?"

"To say the least, and worried. That's why I ran away. I knew I could never solve the problem from inside that monastery."

There was something about this priest that led the officer to believe he was telling the truth. It was most likely the caring, gentle way the priest led him from a long sinful background into a present, which, through absolution, filled him with Sanctifying Grace. Sanctifying Grace—like a bright white light shining inside the body. A simple but powerful and uplifting purity that must surely resemble the state of the glorified body after death.

Steve smiled as he looked over at the officer. He could tell from the look on the officer's face exactly the emotions the officer was feeling at being suddenly elevated from the realm of sinful flesh into a state that presaged immortality in the awesome brilliance of the beatific vision—in Steve's mind, the unique gift of the Catholic Church.

"So where are you off to, Father, if you don't mind me asking?"

"Do you promise not to tell?" Steve asked with a sly smile. "By the way, do you have to file a report on all of this?"

"No report. I was just curious. You've got a trace of a New England accent."

"I'm heading to Boston to see my brother. He lives on the outskirts of the city, a small town near Concord. I may be able to work through him to find out what's going on concerning me and the church."

As the pair approached the front exit of the hospital, they shook hands and said goodbye. The officer turned and walked back along a side corridor to see if anything was going on in the emergency room.

Steve went out of the front entrance to a taxi stand. As he was entering a cab, brothers Michael and John came up behind him. They pinned his arms and began dragging him to their pickup parked in the side lot of the hospital. The few people who witnessed the abduction wondered about it, but did nothing. A woman passerby said, "What is this world coming to when you have monks beating up a man and no one to stop it. And is there ever a cop around when you need one?" A scuffle began as the three men reached the pickup. Brother Michael punched Steve in the stomach doubling the priest over as Brother John grabbed a tire iron.

Suddenly, Greg appeared at the side door. He confronted the monks. "What's going on?"

"We have orders to take him back to the monastery."

"What if he doesn't want to go?"

"We have orders to take him anyway."

"Put that tire iron down. He doesn't want to go with you."

"How do you know?" Brother Michael asked as he and Brother John began loosening their grip on Steve.

"Isn't it obvious?" Greg said, looking at Steve who was still slightly bent over and struggling to free himself.

"He's drunk, that's all. We got a lot of them up at the monastery," Brother Michael replied. "This one got loose and went on a drinking spree."

Waving the monks back, the police officer put his hand under Steve's elbow to help him straighten up. "You OK?" he asked.

"I think so," Steve replied. He whispered thanks to the officer and walked back around to the front of the hospital to the taxi stand as the officer ordered the brothers into their pickup. "Now I want the two of you to sit in there and don't make a move. If you leave, I'll catch up with you and have both of you arrested."

"That's ridiculous," Brother Michael said with a sneer. "You haven't got anything to charge us with."

"I wouldn't be too sure about that," Greg replied. "For instance, you were brandishing that tire iron like a weapon. Added to that, the vehicle you're driving doesn't look roadworthy to me. Bald tires, broken door, no environmental inspection sticker...if you get my drift. Just sit here for a few minutes until I get back." The officer then walked around to the front of the hospital to join the priest.

"Well so long, Greg. I'm off to the airport," Steve said as he shook hands and climbed into a cab. "And thanks for your help."

Greg looked worried. He shook his head. "Now, Father, let me tell you something. If you go to the Tucson International Airport, by the time you get a flight out, they'll be back on you. I can detain them for a little while, but they'll be after you soon enough."

Steve turned to the taxi driver. "Do you know of a small airport nearby where I can charter a plane to Phoenix?"

"I can take you to the Avra Valley Airport," the driver offered. "It's about twenty minutes up I-10. You can get a charter there to take you direct to the Phoenix airport. What do you think?"

"Fine," Steve said.

The police officer agreed. "But I suggest," he said to the driver, leaning into the taxi window, "you start out driving south down Silverbell Road as if you're heading for Tucson International Airport, then cut over to I-10 and head back up north to Avra Valley. I'll keep those guys occupied for a few minutes but I can't hold them very long. I don't intend to arrest them. My sergeant's a Catholic and there's no way I'm gonna walk into the station with a couple of monks under arrest."

Saying goodbyes once again, Steve shook the officer's hand and climbed into the cab. As the cab pulled away Greg walked around to the side lot where he would detain the monks with a brief inspection of the pickup. A few minutes later, he released the monks with a strong warning to make repairs to their vehicle and told them if he caught them speeding down Silverbell they would be arrested. He also said he was calling ahead to make sure there would be no incident at Tucson International Airport.

As he walked back to the police car, the officer thought: I'm no more than 15 minutes out of the confessional and already I've told a lie!

*****

At the counter in the small Avra Valley Airport, Steve made arrangements for a charter to Phoenix. Having a few minutes to spare, he placed a call to his brother Jonathon in Wayland and left a message on his recorder.

Several minutes later, Jonathon's return call came through. "Steve, I gather you're in Arizona. What's happening?"

"I've run away from the monastery, Jonathon, and I suppose the church now considers me a renegade priest. I'm flying up to see you. If anyone calls and asks about me, don't tell them anything."

"What about Janet? What if she calls?"

"Oh, you know about her. If she calls, tell her I'll meet her at our summer place on Pine River Pond next weekend. Better give her directions on how to get up to New Hampshire to the pond. But don't tell anyone else about me."

"Sure thing. Look forward to seeing you. How are you fixed for money?"

"I've got quite a bit of cash seeing as how there wasn't anything to spend it on at the monastery. And my credit cards are still active."

Steve walked out to the windy flight line where he boarded a Cessna charter aircraft to Phoenix, and from there a commercial flight to Boston.

18

Most Reverend Luis Hernandez, Bishop of Tucson, stepped into a waiting taxi at Dulles Airport. "Where to, Padre?"

"Please take me to the Chancery of the Archdiocese of Washington. Do you know where that is?"

"Been there many times. Have you there in about thirty minutes. Where you in from, if you don't mind my asking?"

"Tucson, Arizona."

"Never been there but I hear it's nice country."

"Yes it is."

"Hear it's hot in summer."

"Yes, hot, very hot," the Bishop replied distractedly as he gazed out the window of the taxi at the passing Virginia countryside. As the taxi droned on, Bishop Hernandez became lost in thought. He knew he had to take a stand with Bishop Rhinehart. His diocese and the Archdiocese of Washington were jointly facing a sixty million dollar lawsuit brought by five former altar boys against a pedophile priest. The priest and both dioceses had been named in the suit. The priest was one of those he customarily accepted without question when requested by an American cardinal. In this case, Cardinal Wollman, when he was alive, with Bishop Rhinehart acting as his executive assistant, had shuttled the priest around to various parishes in the Washington diocese for years. Then, after the cardinal died, Bishop Rhinehart finally hoped to get the priest out of the way by transferring him to Tucson to the Passion Brothers monastery. He naively thought the authorities might not find the errant priest at a lonely monastery deep in the desert. But someone had talked and the lawyers located the priest at the monastery.

Bishop Hernandez had convinced himself that at the very least, the Archdiocese of Washington should share in the responsibility and pay a significant portion of any court settlement. In fact, he found it not difficult to conclude that the Washington archdiocese was almost completely at fault in the matter and on top of that certainly wealthy enough to pay all of the final settlement in the case. But, although he had never met Rhinehart, he knew of his reputation, and knew that Rhinehart would fight like a wounded tiger to avoid paying even a dime. And now that Rhinehart, rumored to be a favorite of the pontiff, was likely to be elevated to the red hat, it would be an uphill battle.

As the taxi droned on, Bishop Hernandez had a depressing thought: What if his diocese was forced to raise an amount that could run into the millions? How could he manage it? He recalled that a few years before, short of ready cash, he had instituted the rule of three collections at Sunday Masses in his parish churches. But he soon learned the congregation gave little more in total. They simply stretched out the offerings of the first and second collections to allow for the third. And there were angry complaints from many parishioners. Unhappily, it was the more devout who complained that it was impossible to concentrate on the mystery of the Mass when the jingle of coins and rustle of collection baskets became almost continuous. And so, this attempt at raising money came to naught. He was left with the unnerving thought that although the church's lawyers would appeal the amount of any settlement and would very likely get it reduced, the amount could still be sizeable—probably in the millions.

Arriving at the chancery, Bishop Hernandez, a man well into middle-age, portly, with traces of neckline red showing through his olive complexion, perspired as he labored up two flights of stairs and was ushered into the anteroom of Bishop Rhinehart's office. After a few moments, the door opened and the prelate, rigidly erect, his usually stern visage softened by a slight smile, waved his visitor to a seat in his office. Bishop Hernandez, momentarily anticipating a pastoral embrace, but receiving none, shrugged very slightly, nodded and took a seat.

"I trust you had a pleasant flight from Tucson," Bishop Rhinehart said, to which Bishop Hernandez gave a slight nod. "This is our first face-to-face meeting is it not? You were elevated to the bishopric somewhat recently."

"That's correct, Your Grace."

"No need for such formality, my dear Bishop. The pontiff has not yet made any announcement concerning me. Tell me, how are you making out in your second year in the Tucson diocese?"

"Reasonably well," Bishop Hernandez replied guardedly, realizing that if he said he was doing very well, it could cost him money in the ongoing litigation, and if poorly, it could be reported negatively to the American College of Cardinals.

"The Conference of Bishops will convene tomorrow morning here at the chancery. I assume you are familiar with the agenda topics sent through the mail. I understand you wanted to meet with me before the conference."

"Yes, that's correct," Hernandez said, shifting nervously in his chair. "There is something I need to discuss with you. It concerns one of the priests who was transferred to my diocese from the Archdiocese of Washington. The sixty-million dollar lawsuit naming my diocese and the Archdiocese of Washington is a matter of great concern to me. My diocese is one of the poorer in the country. We have a large population of Mexican Americans who are plagued by high unemployment and low wages when employed. Thus, the coffers of the churches are depleted. In order to raise a large sum of money I would have to mortgage a number of my church properties."

"That sounds very sensible, Bishop. Why don't you do that? I can offer you this good news: I agree to contribute half of any court settlement."

"But that might still leave me to pay thirty million. Has it ever occurred to Your Grace that even if we mortgaged some diocesan properties, we might not have the resources even to make the mortgage payments?"

"God will find a way," Bishop Rhinehart said. "Besides, these lawsuits are always settled for a much smaller amount." Rhinehart found himself growing increasingly irritated that Hernandez was attempting to pass the problem back to Washington when Tucson had happily accepted the priest and the accompanying payments from Washington and without doubt intended to make money on the deal. He was aware that Hernandez and his predecessors had willingly accepted priests from all over the country together with somewhat exorbitant payments for their keep, and presumably for therapy at the monastery. Rhinehart had little sympathy at being asked to contribute any more money when it had been Hernandez' responsibility to accept this latest errant priest on a permanent, supposedly irrevocable transfer. "I'll take it up with my accountants, but I have grave doubts that we can do more than offer to pay half."

Bishop Hernandez realized that further protest was futile. He might appeal to the Conference of Bishops, but doubted they would do any more than offer their condolences. He had a sinking feeling he would have to raise a substantial amount in his own diocese.

Bishop Rhinehart's supercilious attitude began to grate on Hernandez who decided to change the subject. His tone grew firmer as he took up a matter concerning another priest in which he felt he had a stronger hand. "I would like to know more about another priest you sent me named Stephen Murphy. Brother Berard and I are frankly puzzled by your sending him to us without the benefit of any explanation of his aah...background. Most recently you asked that Murphy return to Washington presumably to pressure him to resign or to be defrocked. He has refused. Since he has been transferred to me, I at the very least should be made privy to his background and made aware of whatever errant behavior he may be guilty of. When we accepted Murphy, Your Grace, you said a complete personnel file would be forwarded to us. We have the file, but it is not complete."

"My dear Bishop, I have decided this matter needs the utmost secrecy because of potential grave scandal to the Church. I decided to enter nothing in Murphy's personnel file; however, by word of mouth, I can tell you what this is all about." Bishop Rhinehart got up from his desk and walked over taking a seat close to Bishop Hernandez. He leaned over close to his fellow prelate and lowered his voice, mainly to impress the other with the need for delicate handling of the information.

"What I am about to tell you must remain in this room. Even Brother Berard must not be privy to what I am about to say. At the present time, only a priest in Boston who reported the information and I know the story—as well as Murphy's brother. We are not sure whether Murphy himself is aware of this, although his brother in Boston certainly is."

"About a year ago, an elderly woman made a deathbed confession. She said that Stephen Murphy was born out of an incestuous relationship between the mother and her older son, Murphy's brother."

"So? Why should that impugn Murphy? He is no more than an innocent product of the sinful event. Is that the only reason why you are trying to remove him?"

"When it is fully understood, you will see that it is reason enough. You see the union we are aware of was not sexual incest. It was conducted in a laboratory thereby making Murphy the product of a lab process."

"Are you referring to in-vitro fertilization? Although

the church condemns this manner of procreation, why should this affect Murphy's life as a priest? Once again, he is an innocent party."

"My dear Bishop, I suppose I am not making myself clear. Since I am not a biologist I know none of the details. All I can tell you is that Murphy was...how shall I describe it?...produced, manufactured, if you will, in a laboratory. By the way, since he did not return to Washington after my order to do so, I assume you are holding him at the monastery until he either resigns the priesthood or you take further action against him. And if you don't, I certainly will."

"I do not like to admit this, Your Grace, but Murphy escaped from the monastery. At the moment, we do not know where he is; however, I have ordered that a few of Brother Berard's monks track him down and return him to the monastery."

"How could you have let this happen?" Bishop Rhinehart fumed. "You must have understood that Murphy represents a threat to the church? A threat of scandal?"

"As I recall," Bishop Hernandez said almost in a growl, "it wasn't until just a few minutes ago that you offered an explanation. And even that is sketchy at best."

Recovering his composure with some difficulty, and getting up from his chair to usher Bishop Hernandez to the door, Bishop Rhinehart said, "Now, if you will excuse me, I have important things to take care of that cannot wait. Rest assured this matter will become clearer at tomorrow's conference. I have put it on the agenda as the opening issue for tomorrow morning.

Try not to be late."

Bishop Hernandez, who had never been late for a meeting in his life, bristled at the comment but decided to say nothing.

Bishop Rhinehart, cupping a hand under the elbow of his fellow prelate, gently but firmly guided him to the door and snapped the door shut behind him.

19

The old woman lay in bed dying. The priest was at her bedside administering Extreme Unction—the church's sacrament for preparing a soul to face Christ and eternity. After dipping his fingers into the holy unguent, he touched each of her senses—her eyes, nose, ears, lips and hands, blessing them with the Sign of the Cross. He leaned over a body that had become wasted from alcohol and age—now in the clutches of death but soon it was believed, to be cradled in the arms of a forgiving Christ. The pungent odor of holy oil and smoke from the bedside candle permeated the air around the bed, mixing with the smell of death. The woman's frail hands, wrinkled skin covering porous bones attached with bulbous knuckles, groped spastically for her rosary beads like a drowning victim trying with frantic movements to grab onto anything that floated.

Jonathon stood in the dim light near the wall, a nurse at his side, stethoscope in her hand. It would confirm the cessation of heartbeats. She would announce death's arrival.

As the priest stepped back from the bed, the old lady's halting, grating voice called out to her son: "Jonathon...come closer...I need to talk to you...". Then rasping, "Get that nurse out of here, she doesn't need to hear this." The nurse glanced at Jonathon who whispered, "Just for a few minutes, please." The nurse left the room, but unknown to the dying woman, the priest who had conducted Last Rites, remained sitting in a dim corner, unobserved, reading from a prayer book.

Jonathon leaned close to his mother. He held one of her hands. Her dry shriveled lips were trembling as she spoke: "Jonathon, maybe I was wrong, but I always favored you. As the years went by I realized I loved you even more than I ever loved your father. He never had time for me. He was always tied up in his only love, politics...goddamn politics."

"Mother, you will soon be with God. Careful what you say."

"Goldarn politics. How's that?" she croaked, showing a trace of the fiery spirit he remembered from years back.

"Better, Dear. Now what did you want to tell me?"

"I want you to tell Steve that you and I produced him. He is the product of our flesh—yours and mine."

On hearing these words, the priest in the corner looked up from his prayer book stunned. Since the old lady had never mentioned it when he heard her last confession, he could only hope she had confessed the incest many years before and received absolution.

"Mother, what are you talking about? How could you have a child without father? I don't understand."

"Don't you remember when you and I were vacationing in upper Maine near the Canadian border? And don't you remember when I had to go into that small hospital? I lied when I said I had caught a bug and you were put in that hospital for a day of tests to make sure you didn't have it."

"Yes, I remember the incident, Mother, but I never really knew what was going on. They did a few tests and took a few tissue samples as I recall and then released me."

"Months later, my pregnancy was obvious. Your father jumped to the conclusion that I had had an affair because our marriage had become a kind of sham. That's when he left us for six months, although he came back later, after Steve was born."

"I do remember that! He threw me out of the house without so much as an explanation and said he'd kill me if he ever saw me again."

"Why do you think he threw you out of the house?"

"I never really understood. I thought he was out of his head."

"Frankly, he was suspicious of you because we were very close. He thought we were too close. He also noticed a remarkable resemblance between you and Steve. Although you were born many years apart, he said you looked like twins. Don't be too harsh on your father's memory, Jonathon. He had a lot to put up with. You were invited back home when I told him the whole story."

"I still don't understand. What story?"

"Let me put it this way—how did you think I became pregnant?"

"From Dad. Isn't that what everybody thought?"

"Because of your dad's position, that's what we wanted everyone to think, Dear. Jonathon, the tissue sample taken from you by the doctor in Maine had a single cell extracted which was then used to impregnate an egg from me that had its nucleus removed. After some sort of electrical treatment, the egg was implanted in me. The idea was to make an exact copy of you. In other words a clone."

On hearing this, Jonathon was stunned. He glanced over at the priest in the corner who, listening to the story, sat up transfixed.

"Now that you know, you must tell your brother he was born because, my Darling, I wanted another son like you. Steve is only a clone. But he has a right to know. He was cloned from your tissue. You've got to tell him. I never could bring myself to tell the story to either of you. And the whole thing was a mistake because although he looked exactly like you, he was different. His mind was different. He didn't think the way you did. You were always practical and loving. He was cold, distant. Always had his sight set on something far away. Instead of spending time with us, he was usually down at the church...altar boy, singing in the choir, helping with the collections...."

The dying woman's cracking voice was interrupted by a fit of coughing. Jonathon saw a thin trickle of blood on her lips running from the corner of her mouth. He wiped it with his pocket handkerchief as it ran down beside her chin.

"Mother, take it easy. Try to rest."

"I have an eternity to rest. Right now I want to make sure you understand what happened and agree to tell Steve. I want you to swear!"

"I will, Dear. I swear."

"What's the name of that church he's pastor of?"

"It's called Holy Rosary."

"Yes, down there outside of Washington. It has a nice

name," she said, nervously fingering her rosary beads.

"That's right, Dear."

On hearing that the clone was a Catholic priest, a pastor at that, the priest in the corner closed his eyes. He felt a mild tremor go through him.

The old woman struggled to sit up. "Where is Steve? Why isn't he here? If he was here, I could tell him myself...." As she spoke, the dying lady settled back in the bed, her voice trailed off into a whisper. She rolled her head to the side and seemed to fall asleep. For ten minutes her breath came in violent snorts as her pitifully thin chest rose and fell, struggling for air. Her skeletal fingers gripped the rosary beads with feeble, convulsive movements. The priest prayed as the nurse came back into the room and stepped forward readying the stethoscope. Jonathon leaned over the bed with his hands pressed flat on top of his mother's. His eyes were filled with tears. Then suddenly, her chest rose, her back arched up and with a rattle in her throat, she was gone.

Later, in the hall, after the nurse had left, Jonathon walked over to talk to the priest: "I suppose you heard what she said. About the cloning, I mean."

"Yes, I did. It's very strange and you surely know, immoral in the eyes of the church. The church only approves of conception as a result of the marital act."

"Yes, I understand, but the important thing is that this be kept a secret. You heard her confession before she died. You are bound by the Seal of the Confessional."

"Yes, I am. However, the confession was ended by the time she began talking to you."

"So what do you intend to do with this information?"

"I'm not sure. Maybe nothing. Then again, the person we are talking about—your brother, is a Catholic priest. And the church is strongly opposed to human cloning, if in fact, clones can be called human. It is an affront to the teachings of the church. While artificial conception is a mortal sin, in the eyes of the church, cloning may be much worse."

"Why? I don't understand," Jonathon said. "The people—the doctor and my mother, who performed or agreed to the...what can I call it...the 'union', may be guilty of serious sin, but surely the newborn infant has only Original Sin on its soul which is removed through Baptism. Isn't that what the Catholic Church teaches? My brother, Steve was Baptized, I know, I was there."

"Perhaps. But there is a troubling aspect to all of this. Let me put it this way. The Catholic Church recognizes that the person born of the union of man and woman in the marital act is a valid human being. The church teaches that God is present at the instant of conception and breathes an immortal soul into the fertilized egg."

"What about in-vitro fertilization?"

"There too," the priest said, anticipating the question, "the product of a man's sperm impregnated into a woman's egg in say, a laboratory setting is also valid although certainly not approved of. The important thing is that in either of these cases, living sperm impregnates a living egg and God is present at this instant of conception as he breathes an immortal soul into the embryo. Without ensoulment, there can be no human being. If Holy Mother Church determines that a clone—the result of a man-made laboratory process, that produces an unnatural twin twenty or so years later, does not have a soul, the newborn is no more than a sub-human, akin to an animal."

"That's an ultra-conservative way to look at it. Uncharitable, I would say. Certainly in the eyes of the law, a human clone is as valid as anyone else. My brother, for example, has a valid birth certificate, a baptismal certificate, a social security number, two arms and two legs; in short, no one can say he's anything less than a human being."

"Aside from the fact that human cloning is illegal, what you say about the cloned individual is true in the eyes of the law, but now we are talking about the eyes of God. Look, Mr. Murphy, I'm not saying I know the position Holy Mother Church will ultimately take on the validity of a human clone. The Pope's Curia in Rome will undoubtedly study the issue at length. But there is serious cause for concern, especially since your brother is a Catholic priest. Even if he is found to have validity as a human being, can you imagine the confusion and the scandal of having a clone as a minister of God? Who would want to go to confession, receive holy communion, or be married by what some people would perceive as a laboratory robot in the guise of a human being?"

"Wait a minute," Jonathon argued, growing angry, "there's a big difference between a robot and a clone."

"Is there really?" the priest countered, very conscious of the fact that the dialog had broken down into an argument. It prodded him to a decision. Walking abruptly back into the death room, he collected up his things, nodded as he brushed by Jonathon on the way out and went straight to a telephone to call Bishop

Rhinehart in the Archdiocese of Washington. It was this call that set in motion Bishop Rhinehart's investigation into the cloning of Reverend Stephen Murphy and his subsequent decision to remove Murphy from his parish.

20

At Boston's Logan Airport Steve rented a car and drove to a nearby religious haberdashery where he was fitted with a black suit complete with Roman collar. Since he was a perfect 44 long, the only tailoring required was to cuff the trousers. While waiting, he decided to walk down the block to a shoe store where he bought a pair of black shoes. On a lark, he stopped in a sports store for a short-sleeved Boston Celtics T-shirt.

Finally, suited up, he looked at himself in the haberdashery shop's full length mirror. Seeing a gauntness in his face, "not good," he muttered under his breath, "but not too bad considering I just got out of the hospital and also considering I spent a couple of days hiking through the Sonora desert."

Steve drove to a nearby Catholic Church where he sat in the back row during the noon Mass. Feeling buoyed up, he happily succumbed to the nostalgic urge to drive out to Boston's western suburbs via the scenic route: first through historic Lexington, then Concord and on past Walden Pond into Wayland. As he drove into Wayland, the town where he had been raised, his mood changed abruptly. He stopped briefly at the side of the road to peer through the sycamore trees at the palatial home of the Murphy family. He had little desire to enter the property. His memories of growing up there were not pleasant. As his mother's alcoholism had become more pronounced she became increasingly reclusive. He remembered how the family had lived in near total darkness in the house because the shades were pulled down and drapes closed almost all the time. She said the light bothered her eyes. The only bright periods came when his father returned from Washington after the legislative sessions ended. In later years, after his father died, the situation grew much worse. Steve was never able to decide whether the physical or verbal abuse was more difficult to bear. Visitors to the house were few. Social life non-existent. There were no other relatives he could appeal to. Although his brother Jonathon was sympathetic, he was careful to avoid getting into their mother's line of fire. As soon as he was of age, Steve left to prepare for the priesthood while Jonathon remained at home, doing what he could to care for their mother.

Despite the unpleasant memories, Steve found himself looking forward to seeing his brother again. Their only meeting in years had occurred in the brief encounter at their mother's funeral. Afterwards, Jonathon had gone on to assume the duties as executor of the estate and Steve had returned to Washington convinced that he was not in line to inherit anything substantial of the estate's assets. Nor was he troubled by this since he was reasonably comfortable in a financial sense. His wants were few and the acquisition of wealth had never interested him. He regretted not being able to get a timely flight from Washington to be at his mother's bedside before she died. Later, back in Washington after the funeral, he had offered up a Mass and made a special novena at Holy Rosary parish church for the repose of his mother's soul. It was only a few days after his trip to Boston to attend the funeral when he had received the letter transferring him to Catholic University. Then, a few months later, the transfer to the Passion Brothers Monastery in Arizona.

*****

Steve sat at a desk across from Jonathon in the Murphy Real Estate office. It was Sunday afternoon and the sign on the office door was turned to 'CLOSED'. The two saleswomen who worked for Jonathon were out of the office for the day sitting on open houses. Jonathon's long-time office manager, Marge, probably had the day off. Steve got up and walked over to the big picture window in the office. He saw that the white steepled church across the street, the library, the Wayland National Bank, the small red brick post office, and the drug store were exactly as he remembered them. This was the heart of Wayland, the place he rode to on his bike when he went 'downtown'.

Jonathon walked up to the window and stood beside his brother. "Just think, I've been here all my life," he said, motioning with one hand at the buildings across the street that made up the heart of the town. "Never went anywhere except into Boston. Although I did take a weekend trip to New York once. Nobody's ever had any trouble finding me, Steve. I've been here up to my ears running the family businesses. Spend half my week here in the real estate office, the other half running the tax office."

The same tiresome old complaint, Steve thought. I've left him holding the bag. I notice he doesn't complain about having all the property and most of the money.

"Do you ever get the feeling you'd like to pitch in? I could bring you up to speed in no time and I really could use some help. I don't know the time frame for this damn medical problem I've got and I don't want to know, but somewhere down the road I won't be able to handle all this stuff."

"I'm sympathetic Jonathon, really I am, but when the time comes some other arrangement will have to be made. I've got a lifetime job."

"Get real, Steve, your church doesn't want you. They ship you all over the place and now you're a renegade—on the run."

"Who told you that?"

"I learned it from Bishop Rhinehart. Yes, I called his office. I was worried. Find that hard to believe? After you left Catholic U, nobody knew where you were. All I could learn was that you were somewhere in Arizona. Even your friend Janet came up here to inquire about you. She was worried too."

"Janet actually came to see you?"

"Yes. And by God, Steve she's a beauty. And I'll let you in on a little secret, although you probably know already."

"Know what? That she's married?"

"That she's head over heels in love with you."

"Perhaps, but maybe she just thinks she is."

Jonathon put his arm around his brother's shoulder. He believed he meant it as a friendly gesture but Steve saw it as an opening gesture in attempting to exercise control. Whenever Jonathon had tried to bring his younger brother around to his way of thinking in the past, it was always with the arm around the shoulder. "Come on, Steve, give it up. Marry the girl and live happily ever after. Have kids, settle here in Wayland. Concord's her hometown, she's a New England gal, you wouldn't have any trouble getting her to agree to settle down here."

"There are just a couple of hitches," Steve said. "First of all she's married. And although they were separated, they may be back together. The other problem, and I know I sound like a broken record, but I'm a priest and plan to remain a priest."

"Well whatever happens Steve, one thing you don't have to worry about is money. You may not be aware of the fact that after Dad died, mother remembered you in her will. I guess toward the end she started feeling guilty. If you hadn't disappeared, you would have learned about it."

"I didn't disappear, I was transferred. When I got to the monastery there was no way to write or call out."

"The account is in your name in the Wayland National Bank. It's sitting right there across the street. It's a sizeable amount. Of course, I hold all the family real estate and titles to both businesses, but that could be remedied if you decided to settle here and pitch in. Frankly, I have far more in the way of assets than I will ever need. Why don't you think about it? I'll be here in Wayland... whatever you decide."

Steve walked to a desk and sank into a chair. Although the day was cool, he found the office uncomfortably warm. He removed his suitcoat and Roman collar with black dickey as Jonathon went to the rear of the office and brought out a couple of soft drinks from a refrigerator.

"Celtics fan?" Jonathon asked with a smile.

Looking down at the Celtics T-shirt front, Steve laughed. "Used to be, but it's hard to keep up on the team when you're in a desert monastery with no television sets."

As the brothers sat talking, Steve noticed something odd, something he had either never noticed before or never paid any attention to. Somehow, it gave him a strange, uneasy feeling, although he would have been at a loss to explain why. He sat examining two moles on his brother's right wrist and a small bony lump a few inches away. He realized all three body markings were the same size and in the same location as his own. He also observed something the average person probably would not notice—a slightly misshapen ear lobe on the right side. It looked like a v-shaped indentation. Steve realized his own right ear had an identical imperfection. Then as he studied the features of his brother's craggy, lined face, he had an eerie feeling he was looking at a twin of himself— but a twin almost twenty years older. How could it be? It was like looking into a demonic mirror and seeing himself twenty years in the future. My God, he thought, is this the aged face on the painting of Dorian Gray? Only this isn't a painting. This is real. He was confused. His mind raced.

"What are you thinking?" Jonathon asked, studying Steve's contorted face.

"Something peculiar just struck me. I never really noticed it before, but I see that you and I have some extremely similar physical characteristics."

"Does that bother you?"

"Frankly, I never paid any attention to our resemblance, even when people years ago were always saying how much alike we looked and how we had the same mannerisms. I guess I thought that's how brothers tend to look, but now I wonder. This seems to be more than that."

"You're right, Steve, it is more than that. We are more than brothers. We're identical twins."

"Utterly ridiculous," Steve said with a smirk. "You're almost twenty years older than I am." He thought his brother must be making a sick joke. But his skepticism soon changed as a thought occurred to him. He felt a slow burn coming on as he grew red in the face. It was anger not embarrassment stemming from a sudden, sinister suspicion. He leaned forward, glaring at his brother. "I remember that Mom and Dad had grown apart. You remember they had separate bedrooms. Did Mom have an affair?"

"Not really. I have to tell you that I was involved, although it was inadvertent."

"That's ridiculous. How could you not know?" Slowly, Steve's mouth drew up tight. He felt his fists clenching. "If I actually thought I was the product of an incestuous relationship, I'd beat the hell out of you."

"Funny thing for a priest to say," Jonathon replied.

"Well, tell me, straight out. You seem to know who I am. So, tell me— who am I?"

"It's not incest, Steve. At least, not the type you're thinking of. Don't get mad at me about it, I wasn't aware of it when it was happening. I went into the hospital for some kind of tests and a doctor took some blood and tissue samples. Mother was in the hospital at the same time getting some kind of treatment. They said she had contracted an infection from a bug. They said they were testing me for the same infection."

"Where did all this happen?"

"It was a hospital way up in northern Maine, out in the boondocks, close to the Canadian border. I think it was more of a medical research center than a hospital."

"What are you really talking about? What kind of treatment? Is 'tissue sample' a cute way of saying sperm?"

"It couldn't have been sperm. That's one thing I know for sure, I never donated any sperm. Steve, I had hoped I'd never have to tell you this, but I suppose now is the time. Steve, you've heard of cloning, haven't you?"

"Yes, but I don't know anything much about it. What has it got to do with me?" Steve angrily folded his arms waiting for an answer.

"Please calm down while I try to explain. I'm not a biologist. I can only tell you the little I know. You were not the product of a normal conception. You were cloned from me. The treatment was Mother's way of producing another version of me. I tell you I didn't know about it. Mother must have cooked it up with that doctor. Dad was undoubtedly told about it after the fact."

"How could you not have known about it?"

"For Chrissake, I was a teenager. Gimme a break. How in hell was I supposed to know what the adults were up to? I only went to that hospital once. After that, Mother must have gone up there a dozen times. The way I see it, the doctor probably froze some of my tissue, did some DNA manipulations and then re-implanted one of mother's eggs with the new DNA. These things are tricky, however. That's why I think it took a number of tries until a satisfactory fetus formed and later, you were born."

"What about this so-called doctor? Who is he? Where is he?"

"I have no idea. For all I know he may be dead, and since Mother's dead and Dad's dead the trail is cold, although I suppose it's all documented—if you were able to find the documents. As I said, they did it because Mother insisted on having another child. One, you might say, 'just like me.' I know it's sick, but I suppose she was afraid that if anything happened to me, she'd have nothing."

"Except Dad."

"Yes, Dad, but you know how she felt about him."

"So I was supposed to be another you," Steve said in disgust. "Exactly like you. A twin, but a twin who was a little tardy in arriving—in fact, almost twenty years late. Well, it didn't turn out that way, did it, because we're not really alike even though we look alike. Interesting that they couldn't clone my brain to make it exactly like yours."

"But they did, Steve. The differences in cloned twins and, in fact, in any twins, come during early brain development. I've read up on some of that stuff. At birth, the brain is not really completely formed. It develops in response to early stimulation. Even though we both started out with what you might call identical equipment, our experiences were different, we were treated differently and our brains developed differently, so now we are actually different people."

"Thank God for that because I'd hate to be sitting where you are selling real estate," Steve said sarcastically.

"You can't imagine how much I'd hate being a Catholic priest!" Jonathon said forcing a smile, trying to lighten up the conversation.

Steve stood up, lips pursed, head down, shoulders sagging. He started slowly pacing the floor. He was humiliated by the knowledge that his birth wasn't intended to produce a new person: him—it was only to produce a carbon copy of his brother. If the miserable treatment he had suffered at the hands of his church over the past months was difficult to bear, this new knowledge could, if he let it, throw him into the depths of confusion and despair. He felt cheap and cheated. He had been manufactured not created. "So now I know why I was abruptly transferred from my parish and finally sent to that hellhole in the desert," he said angrily. "Rhinehart must have found out about it. By the way, how do you think he found out?" Steve asked, as he abruptly stopped pacing the floor and stood over his brother glaring down at him.

"Must have been from the priest who attended Mother's bedside." Jonathon shrugged his shoulders, trying to explain. "The one who gave her last rites. He overheard her tell me about it."

"You mean, up until then you never knew?"

"No, I really didn't. It hit me like a ton of bricks too. And when I found out while Mother was dying, I certainly had no intention of telling you. What was the point of clouding your life? But Mother insisted that you would eventually have to be told."

"The priest in Mother's room must have called Rhinehart."

"Yes, he must have. When he and I met in the hall outside Mother's room we talked it over and I saw he was visibly disturbed. You know Steve, years ago, when I was in that hospital, or laboratory—whatever you want to call it, it crossed my mind that something unusual was going on there. The only thing I could think of was maybe they were testing me to see if I might be a suitable donor of an organ for Mother like a kidney or something, or maybe a bone marrow match. I figured it was something embarrassing they didn't want to talk about. In those days, you may remember, the adults only whispered about serious problems like TB and cancer and only when the younger generation wasn't around. And years ago, who in hell ever heard of cloning? They never told me the story. But nothing ever came of it that affected me, so I figured why sweat it? Eventually, when you were born and Mother seemed all right, I stopped even wondering about it. That's not so terrible, is it?"

"No, I suppose not," Steve said softening.

"You know Steve, if you had gotten up here pronto when I called you and told you Mother was dying, you would have been the only priest in the room. You could have performed the last rites instead of that priest who was brought in. When she kept insisting I tell you the story, it came out that the clone she was talking about was a priest. From then on, it escalated. And when that priest who gave her last rites and I had a discussion outside the room about cloning and the attitude of the church, he seemed to me to be outraged at what he had heard."

"Look, I know enough about cloning to know the church's position is that cloning of a human is immoral, a serious sin. But for a clergyman to be outraged is a bit much."

"Worse than that, Steve. I know this sounds awful, but the priest and some others in the Catholic Church like him, and in fact, many people in other religions, don't think a clone qualifies as a human being."

"As a what?" Steve was wide-eyed. "That's absurd," he exclaimed almost in a shout. "What about identical twins that are born naturally? Twins qualify as two independent human beings. Maternal twins split from one fertilized egg. No one doubts that they each have a soul. And didn't I just hear you say we're twins— only twins that are eighteen years apart?"

"It just isn't that simple, Steve. I've spent a lot of time at the Harvard Med School library trying to understand the medical implications of this."

"Why?"

"You're my brother and you may not believe it but I do care about you. I also dug into some Catholic theology books written for the layman. I knew that some day you would find out about the cloning, probably through the church."

"What did you learn?" Steve asked, still badly shaken by the revelation.

"Frankly, Steve, there are a lot of generalities and lots of weasel wording. It poses a tough ethical question for religion. Of course, as you mentioned, the church roundly condemns cloning, but I couldn't find anything concrete relating to the ensoulment of clones."

"So, what's the conclusion?"

"If the Vatican hasn't spoken directly to the issue, a conference of bishops can consider it. Of course, their findings are subject to ratification by the Vatican. In narrowly framed cases, it comes down to an individual archbishop or cardinal to make his own decision for his diocese. And from his actions, I would say that Bishop Rhinehart, who is on his way to becoming cardinal, has come to a negative decision about clones. To put it bluntly, in the eyes of your boss Rhinehart, a human clone is a manufactured product, thus not the product of conception. There are many religious authorities, not just Catholics either, who maintain that science has gone too far in usurping God's role. They say that a clone may not have a soul. It raises the question that in the absence of a soul, is the newborn really a human being?"

"No soul? That's absurd."

"Depends on how you look at it. The tissue donor has one. The surrogate mother also, but the thing procreated? Look at it this way: what if they cloned an arm say, to be used as a replacement body part. Would God give it a soul? Take it one step further. What if they cloned a headless body, again, intended to be used as replacement body parts. Would God provide a soul for this thing? Don't you see why some religious authorities believe this whole business puts man in the position of manipulating God?"

On hearing this, Steve felt his stomach twisting itself into a painful knot. "Good grief! Right after Mother died why didn't you tell me all this?"

"First of all, dear brother, I was slightly pissed off that you couldn't even make it here on time for Mother's last few hours on earth. Not to mention all the years when you avoided contact with us. On top of that, I thought why go out of my way to tell you something that was sure to make you miserable? At the time, I thought if you never found out, what was the harm? That priest who gave Mother last rites didn't actually say he was going to do anything about it. I thought maybe nothing would come of it. I tried to keep him quiet by calling it part of her last confession. I had hoped he'd be bound by the Seal of the Confessional. He didn't seem to buy it, however, because he said he had already given her absolution. So her announcement was outside of her actual confession. I also thought there was a chance that if word got to the archdiocese, the bishop might not make a big deal out of it—considering the whopping shortage of priests. You've been a dedicated priest, and it seemed to me maybe nobody would give a damn about how you were conceived."

"They apparently do give a damn," Steve said as he got up from his chair. "Lend me a sweater or something to put over this T-shirt. I need to go for a walk."

*****

Steve Murphy the man, walked the street he had trod as a boy. He stopped in front of the church where he had served as an altar boy for so many years. The church was locked after the last Sunday Mass. Shrugging his shoulders, he walked on. A block further on, he came to the corner tavern—the place where the men gathered for a drink after Mass. It was full. He entered it for the first time in his life. Once inside, he realized his mistake. The noise was overwhelming. His hope of finding a quiet corner vanished. He bought a pack of cigarettes. He ordered a beer.

"Is that you, Jonathon?" the barkeep asked, confused in the dim light.

"No, I'm his brother, Steve."

"Ah, the priest! Forgive me, Father, but you've never been in here before, have you?"

"No. This is my first step on the way to Hell," Steve said, forcing a laugh. I was hoping to find a table where I could sit and do a little thinking."

"We have a nice quiet backroom. Sit and have your beer there, Father."

"Thanks," Steve said, bringing his beer and a bowl of chips with him. Happily, the room was empty. He sat at a corner table. He opened the pack and lit up. When his glass was empty, he was surprised to find the bar had a waitress. She brought him another beer.

He sat staring at nothing for a long time. He was still in shock and disbelief coupled with the beginning stage of self-doubt. Anger, misery, and despair would come later after the impact of Jonathon's words had sunk in to occupy a permanent spot in his brain.

Can all this crap be true? Why has my family visited this curse on me? She didn't want me—she wanted another him. And now that the word is out it screws up everything I've tried to build my life on. Now I know the reason for the transfers and why they're trying to defrock me if I won't resign. I see now that I'm an embarrassment to the church. An American Catholic priest a clone? People going to confession and receiving communion from a clone? Where does technology take us next, robot priests? Step right up, Ladies and Gentlemen, R2-D2 is going to hear your confession.

He was sick with worry about this threat to his chosen way of life, but worse than that, he was almost overcome with a feeling of unworthiness in the eyes of God. How could God love someone who was virtually an imposter—a sham not only as a priest but even as a simple member of the faith and perhaps not even a valid member of the human race?

He felt a tap on the shoulder. Jonathon had followed him to the bar. "I locked up the office. Planning to meet Marge for dinner. Care to join us?"

"No thanks. The way I feel now, I'd spoil dinner for the both of you."

"I put your jacket and shirtwaist in your car."

"Jonathon, if you've got time for a drink, I've got some more questions."

"OK," Jonathon said sliding into a chair.

"Tell me more about that doctor—the one who did the cloning."

"I don't know much more. I gather he was not a traditional surgeon— more a scientific type, an experimenter."

"What a hell of a thing to experiment on! He has created me in the image and likeness of you. I'm no more than another you."

"Not quite, Steve. Let's look at this a little closer. It's true we are a lot alike, but now that I think about it, I also see physical differences."

"Naturally, because of the difference in our ages."

"Possibly, but perhaps more than that. Steve, don't take this the wrong way, but you come across as a bit darker complected than me. The five o'clock shadow you always get, I don't get that. Then too, let's compare arms. Physically much the same but notice that you have a lot more hair on your arms. Overall, your hair is several shades darker than mine."

"That's baloney, again. As people age, their skin and hair get lighter. What you're looking at is simply the aging phenomena. Remember, you're an old man, Jonathon," Steve said, feeling a sudden urge to strike back at Jonathon.

Jonathon was at a loss to say anything that would ease the burden on his brother. He fell silent. He sipped his drink—a dry martini. Steve noticed that Jonathon's hand shook as he raised his glass spilling a little of the drink on the table. It struck Steve that although life had given him a raw deal, life had given his brother with Lou Gehrig's disease a very raw deal. He knew that Jonathon was facing a slow, terrifying death—trouble controlling muscular movements, trouble swallowing, trouble breathing, drowning in his own fluids.

Suddenly, Steve had a glimpse of the future. The horror hit him. If he was in fact a cloned twin of Jonathon, he might eventually die the same way. He believed that Lou Gehrig's disease had a genetic component; that's the way his father and grandfather had died. It might not work out that way in every case, but in his case, as an identical clone, how could he escape it? But then he had another thought. How did anyone really know how they would die if they weren't actually on the deathbed? After all, he might be hit by a train. A wry thought. It brought the trace of a smile to his face.

"I see you're smiling," Jonathon said.

"Nothing important. I just thought of something. Not even worth mentioning."

Jonathon looked at Steve. "What are your plans? Where do you go from here?"

"I'm driving up to the pond. I need to spend some time thinking things out."

"While you're thinking, pay some attention to Janet. She said she planned to join you up there next weekend. But after that, what? Forgive me for saying it, Steve, but you don't seem to have much future in the church."

"I plan," Steve said, sounding weary, "to remain a priest. I made a vow that I don't intend to break. I made it with God, not the hierarchy of the church." But even as he uttered the words, Steve wondered about the validity of his vows. His pompous pronouncements might have been little more than a cover for the fact that he did not know what else he could do, what else he wanted to do. For almost his whole life, the only role he knew how to play was that of a priest.

"How can you manage that when word gets out that you're being defrocked?"

"For one thing, Rhinehart can't do this alone. The human cloning problem is bigger than just me. And, as I understand it, defrocking has to be done by a committee of three, and even after that I have a right to appeal directly to the Vatican. Until all this takes place, I'm still a priest. You know, Jonathon, if I had done something wrong, I could understand it. But I haven't. I've devoted myself to their church, studied their theology, lived by their precepts, willingly took on whatever assignments I was given, worked hard, and believe overall I did a good job."

"I notice," Jonathon said quietly, "you're starting to refer to the church as 'their' church. You used to call it 'my' church."

*****

For a long time after his brother left, Jonathon sat in the back room of the bar sipping another martini. "They're right about the Irish," he mumbled to himself. "We drink in celebration when we're happy; we drink to soothe our misery when we're sad." Finally, he got up with a shrug, then, deep in thought, waved to the barkeep as he left, and walked slowly up Wayland's main street.

As he walked, he found he could not put aside his discussion with the priest in the hall outside the room where his mother died. For the first time in his life, he became aware of just how extraordinary the church's view of ensoulment at conception is. "As I understand it," he mumbled half-aloud as he walked, "according to the Catholic Church and perhaps all the rest of the Christian churches, the all-seeing God is present when a couple have sex. God presumably watches carefully for the moment of orgasm of the male, then following the instant of ejaculation, when a single sperm swims strongly up the birth canal outdistancing millions of his fellow sperm, to wind up fertilizing the egg, the almighty steps in to bestow the trophy—a human soul. In fact, he must do this because otherwise we would have to believe that two humans have the power to produce a supernatural essence in the absence of God. Subsequently, if the embryo splits to form an identical twin, God is still present and readily provides a second soul. I wonder: Do they really believe this? Are there really three in the bedroom during sex? Since God is God he surely is not present for reasons of voyeurism, therefore his presence must simply be to acknowledge the union and provide ensoulment to the new person being created. Does God do this for non-Catholics as well? What about atheists?"

As Jonathon crossed the street, walking by the church with a sidelong glance, he couldn't keep from chuckling. "Considering the billions of people in the world," he mumbled, "many of whom could be having sex at any hour of the day and night, a personal God would have to spend every minute around the 24 hour clock providing instant souls. Sounds almost like an industry. I can't help thinking that the whole affair sounds somewhat like the Santa Claus fantasy wherein Saint Nick delivers all the world's toys in a single night. Of course, with all due respect to God, being God, he has powers to do things like this that are beyond our comprehension. Or so they would have us believe."

As Jonathon was walking, a passerby was puzzled to hear him engrossed, talking out loud to himself about an extraordinary combination of Santa Claus and God. But Jonathon continued down the street paying the passerby no mind. "When you really think about it," he continued, head down, staring at the pavement as he walked, "I suppose you have to accept ensoulment at conception strictly as a matter of faith. The soul, being a spirit, provides no tangible evidence. From what

I've read, Saint Thomas Aquinas, one of the greatest saints in the Catholic Church held that the fetus was not fully formed, therefore not human, until roughly the end of the first trimester. And, as I understand it, St. Augustine had the same belief. But this was too vague for the church because of the implications on abortion. So, faced with a gray area, the church's black and white solution is to say the human becomes human, endowed with a soul, at conception. Thus, abortion becomes murder. Wonder what Aquinas and Augustine would have said about cloning? Normally, I wouldn't give a tinkers damn about what the church decides about human cloning except that their current position seems to be screwing up my brother's life."

21

As Steve drove up Interstate 95 from Boston in the direction of New Hampshire, his tortured brain remained fixated on what Jonathon had told him. His thoughts alternated between surging incoming waves of anger and outgoing undertows of depression. The stark revelation of the cloning, of his almost mechanical origin, cut to the heart of his being. He understood Jonathon's minimal and unwitting role but could never understand his mother's. What Jonathon did was keep the secret. It was his mother who perpetrated the crime.

Faced with what could be an unspeakable calamity, Steve now understood why the conservative forces in the church hierarchy had abruptly pulled him out of his parish and ultimately transferred him to a place where he would be coerced into resigning the priesthood. And if he resisted, as a last resort, they would have to defrock him. And frighteningly, in the case of a troublesome clone judged subhuman, perhaps something more drastic was in store for him. Despite this, Steve had to admit to himself that if the decision had been his regarding someone else, he might very well have taken the same steps. But would it have been theologically correct? Would it have been fair? Always willing to give the church the benefit of the doubt, he accepted that the church's concern did not stem simply from the embarrassment of having the product of a sinful union conducting its public ministry—it was deeper than that. It could be far more serious than that. He shuddered at the thought that over many years, hundreds of his parishioners might have thought they were receiving the sacraments from a valid priest— stepping out of the confessional wrongly thinking their sins were absolved. He could easily imagine people's long tangled history of sins which no later, valid confession, could resolve. How could people remember sins committed long ago—sins they thought were forgiven and thus forgotten? How many times did you use birth control? How many times did you masturbate? How many Holy Days of Obligation did you miss? How many lies? How many slanders? On and on...an infinity of soul-searching questions. Even if God did forgive sins confessed in a parody of real confession, how could anyone be sure? Scrupulous Catholics would find themselves in a nightmarish quandary. How many people would leave the church outright and in utter disgust, if the church said they had no choice but to submit to full confession all over again?

Thankfully, the baptisms would have been valid since it was not absolutely necessary that a priest perform baptism, but what of the wedded couples? Were the marriages valid, or were the children of these 'marriages' born out of wedlock? Hundreds, perhaps even thousands of lives and souls were at stake in answer to these questions.

But Steve was caught up by the thought that there was a piece missing here. The possibility of human cloning was an issue that had surfaced years before. And even though human cloning had been covered endlessly in the media, there was no publicized proof that it could be—had been—accomplished. But surely the theologians of the church and the pontiff must have anticipated this problem. In the continuing struggle between religion and science, why be taken unawares? But why, he asked himself, had he never received any instructions or any encyclical letters on the subject? Might Rome, in secret conclave, have already concluded that the product of cloning was nothing more than a subhuman? Or, conversely, if cloning was simply a method for producing a long delayed twin, had they concluded the twin was a valid human? If so, why no official pronouncement? But, on the other hand, why announce possibilities instead of fact? Maybe to avoid embarrassment it could have been decided to keep the issue under wraps—to be disposed of on a case by case basis. And perhaps, some in the church hierarchy might have hoped that if the problem arose, and a priest clone refused to resign, it could be resolved the way they formerly handled pedophile priests—sweeping the matter under the rug by transfer from parish to parish. Out of sight, out of mind. Maybe God would protect His true church and make the problem go away.

Bishop Rhinehart's position on the subject was quite clear: Steve was a menace to the faith. He had to be gotten out of the church by force if necessary. But what of Rome? The long history of the church gave evidence that if an issue was not considered widespread—affecting the large body of the church, or perhaps not of great theological significance, the matter was left in the hands of the local bishops. After all, each bishop was a direct descendent from one of Christ's apostles. Each ruled in his own land. So, in the absence of unequivocal statements from Rome, Rhinehart and his junior partners, Bishop Hernandez and Brother Berard, were the absolute authority—at least until they were overruled by Rome. But by the time Rome which moved at snail's pace, got involved, it would be too late for Steve.

From the depths of his feelings of unworthiness, Steve wondered if he should in fact continue to think of himself as a priest and continue his priestly functions. As he grimly gripped the steering wheel plowing along with northbound vacation traffic heading for the great outdoors of Maine and New Hampshire, he almost braked to a stop when the thought occurred to him that by acting as a priest he might be breaking church law, each act a serious sin.

As angry drivers piled up behind him—vans laden with canoes or kayaks on top, kids' bikes jouncing on rear bike racks, attempting to pass on the left and right, some giving him dirty looks, one giving him the finger, Steve knew he had to pull off the highway and think things out. He pulled into a rest stop and sat with his head on his arms, his arms resting on the steering wheel. "I need to think this out logically," he said aloud in the car. "If an unworthy human being said Mass, consecrated the Host, gave out communion, and heard confessions, each act would be a sacrilege in the eyes of God and the church. With each act, the individual would be committing the worst sin possible under Canon Law: Sacrilege—the sin so despicable that it cries out to heaven for the most severe punishment.

But on the other hand, if a subhuman—a protoplasm that had not undergone ensoulment by God, conducted these holy offices, how could he be accused of sacrilege? If a chimpanzee could be taught to say Mass, it would be a mockery, but how could that same chimpanzee be committing a sin, and even less likely a sacrilege? Animals simply do not sin." Somewhat comforted by these thoughts that tended to absolve him personally, Steve began to drive again, but before long, his mind whirled in a series of roller coaster thoughts that mimicked manic-depressive swings. Through it all, he realized he was on the brink of a momentous decision. The controlling bishopric had apparently concluded that he was merely the product of a laboratory experiment, nothing more. Something to be discarded. Possibly even to be disposed of if it would avoid embarrassment and protect the faithful from further harm. 'Put down' in the parlance of vets. In view of this, was it morally right for him to continue as a priest?

As Steve drove along the Spaulding Turnpike heading for Wakefield and the family summer home on Pine River Pond, he had a sudden horrid thought that made his hands tremble on the steering wheel: If a clone was not a valid human being, it could not be a valid priest and the priestly vows would not be valid. And for all those years in which he had consecrated the host at Mass— the essence of the Mass which involved the transubstantiation of bread and wine into the body and blood of Christ—all of that would have been a sham, make-believe. Steve remembered how as a young altar boy, answering the call to be a priest, hungry to become a priest, he used to set up a play altar at home when he was alone. A board on a set of books at either end to represent the altar, a white towel covering the 'altar', a box to represent the tabernacle, a large book to represent the missal, a wine glass filled with grape juice as the chalice and white Necco candy wafers representing the sacred host—all the accoutrements needed to make an imitation Mass. "Good grief," he said aloud in the car as he drove, were all my thousands of Masses since ordination nothing but imitations too? Has it all been just a charade?"

He thought of the Catholic women in the church who had been pressing for ordination of women—a lost cause according to the latest papal encyclical letters. He went over it in his mind: Here we have women who, unlike clones, are unequivocally one-hundred-percent human, yet who are forbidden ordination. The argument goes that they do not reflect the 'image of Christ'. Very simply, because they are not males. Aloud in the car, he blurted out: "Now...now...I understand how it is that many women feel disenfranchised by their church. And the shocking thought is that I may be far less qualified to conduct the holy offices of the church than they!"

Steve's only hope was that Bishop Rhinehart and some others in the church hierarchy were wrong or might eventually take another position, and that even as a clone, God was on his side. Would God have given him his vocation, his devotion to the Trinity and the Blessed Virgin, his competence in his performance as a priest and as a pastor over many years if he were nothing more than a lab product masquerading as a human? Would God have let him do these things? No, he was certain God would have stopped him cold.

As he approached the little town of Wakefield, New Hampshire, summer home of the Murphy family, Steve began to settle down. Feeling he had little other choice and that God was really on his side, he arrived at the notion that he should go on being a priest; that is, if he could find a place where he could practice the ministry without interference from the church hierarchy, meaning Bishop Rhinehart and Brother Berard's monks, in particular.

Regardless of the position the church might take on ensoulment of clones, Steve resolved that until the voice of God that had originally called him to the priesthood became silent, until he believed God had turned his back on him, he would continue saying Mass, hearing confessions, comforting the sick, burying the dead—in short all of the things he believed God wanted him to do. He felt his pulse quickening as a new resolve gave him an upwelling of missionary zeal. As the pines and scrub ferns lining the roadside on the turnpike whirred by, he gripped the steering wheel of the car with a new firmness. He decided that if the church hierarchy wanted to stop him, they would have to catch him first. He was distressed at the thought of being a renegade priest, labeled an outlaw in his own religion, but resolved nonetheless to continue doing what he saw as his God-given duty.

22

Steve turned off Spaulding Turnpike about a mile outside of Wakefield Center. He smiled as he pulled into the parking lot of The Wakefield Diner, its shiny metal roof glinting in the sun. As a boy, he had always thought it was a real railroad dining car that had run off its tracks, was abandoned, and later turned into a restaurant. He remembered when he was five or six, on summer mornings when they were off for a day of fishing, he had often eaten at the diner with his brother, Jonathon, who was then a young man in his twenties.

As Steve entered the crowded diner, the strong aroma of frying bacon came to him as he glanced left and right, looking for an empty booth where he could relax and maybe read a local newspaper. But finding every booth taken, he slipped onto a stool at the counter amidst the bustle as waitresses scurried in a dead run between the kitchen and the hungry customers in the booths.

Hungrily cutting into a huge stack of breakfast pancakes, Steve asked the young waitress behind the counter about St. Mary's Church. "Never heard of it," she said as she refilled his coffee cup. "Must have been before my time."

"If you mean old St. Mary's Catholic Church, it's been shut down for years. The building's still there but they haven't had any services in maybe five or six years." The voice came from an elderly man seated at the counter near Steve. The man slipped into an empty stool next to Steve. Although he couldn't be sure, Steve thought he remembered that the old man had been a neighbor of his family on Pine River Pond. Steve hadn't seen the man in years. He noted that the person who he remembered as short, stocky and vigorous was now gray-haired, bent over somewhat, and with a tremulous voice that made him appear feeble. The most noticeable and disconcerting feature of the man at the counter was the strange wide-eyed stare out of his left eye.

"It's glass," the old man said. "And if you notice, I keep swinging my head around to the left so's no one can sneak up on me from that quarter. Learned that the hard way living in South Boston. In fact, that's where some son of a bitch poked my eye out."

"Your name is Lew, isn't it?" Steve asked. "You and your wife have the place on the pond out on the end of the peninsula."

"You're part right. Came up here every summer for over fifty years with my wife, then when she died, couple years ago, I decided to retire and move up here permanent. They'll never get me back to the city. Live here year 'round now."

"You remember the Murphy's?"

"No, can't say as I do."

"What about Larkin? That was my mother's family name. Do you remember the property owned by Larkin?"

"You mean do I remember that damned seaplane they used to fly off Pine River Pond? Depending on which way the wind was blowing, they'd sometimes take off right over my house. Scare the hell out of us and come near turning over our canoe one time with the wash from the pontoons. You know that thing's gotta get up to fifty or sixty some miles an hour to clear the water. Raises hell with boats and fish I tell you. I don't mind the speedboats pulling water skiers way out in the middle of the pond. They get going pretty damn fast too, but I'll tell ya one thing—they don't fly right over my house."

Steve was a little surprised. At the mention of the Larkin name, the flood gates of the old man's memory seemed to have let loose. "I know the family you're speaking of," the man continued, "although I haven't seen anyone except the older son in some years. He comes up once in awhile and takes that airplane out. The father was all right, but the woman was a hell-raising bitch. I used to see her whacking the living be-Jesus out of the younger boy. Seems to me he was an ordinary young fella, kind of a shy boy who never did much wrong. His name was...aah...can't rightly recall. I used to take him fishing with me. The older one's named Jonathon. If I remember right, he's some twenty years older than the younger boy. Never could understand how the Larkins had two offspring twenty years apart, but maybe one was from an earlier marriage or adopted. Of course, Jonathon's gettin' on in years now and I heard the old man and his wife are dead. Jonathon sends a cleaning crew up periodic-like and then I figure he's about to spend some time up on the pond but he don't come up very often. O'course that's OK with me because if the house ain't occupied, the airplane will just sit hangared in the boathouse. Haven't heard it roaring over my house for some time now, thank God."

"I'm Jonathon's younger brother, Steve. I'm planning to spend some time up here. Might live here year 'round in fact."

At the mention of his name, Steve saw the old man's eyes get so wide that, for a moment, he was afraid the glass one would fall out and bounce on the lunch counter. "Now I'm really ashamed," the old man said. "Wish I could take back what I said about your mother. Although I'm not about to take back anything I said about that damned plane."

"There's no need for apologies, Lew. I understand."

"If you're planning to stay at the pond, I welcome you. I could use the company, but I sure hope you ain't a pilot. Tell me, if you will, I never could understand whether that family...your family, was named Larkin or Murphy. The sign said 'Larkin' but now, as I recall, some did call you Murphys."

"I can explain," Steve said. "My father was Congressman Murphy from a district west of Boston. And in order to get away for vacations from politics and the media he bought the place on the pond and put it in my mother's name: Larkin. So we sort of wanted people to think we were Larkins. By the way, are you Catholic, Lew?"

"Sure enough, what with all the Irish, isn't just about everybody Catholic up here in New England?"

"Well I hardly think so, but tell me more about the Catholics around here. What do they do about Mass and the sacraments?"

"Most of them pile in cars and travel over to Lake Winnipesaukee. There's a Catholic Church over there in Wolfeboro. It's about a half-hour drive, but in winter sometimes, you gotta go by snowmobile or not go at all. In fact, you see the parking lot here? All filled with pickups and SUVs? Well in winter it's filled with snowmobiles. They didn't have snowmobiles when you lived here I know. How the hell I wonder did we ever get around here in winter before snowmobiles? Sometimes the snow's so deep you can't even get here with four-wheel drive. O'course there's always been skis and snowshoes if you didn't mind hoofing through the snow for some miles just to get some of Miss Wakefield's hot cakes."

"I remember. But my family almost always came up here in summer. By the way, you say you're Catholic, but are you a practicing Catholic, Lew?"

"Yes," Lew answered guardedly, his suspicions raised by the question. "But what the hell, I'll be honest, I'm not too regular about it. The old joke is I'm *practising* to become a *practicing* Catholic. Since St. Mary's shut down, I get over to Mass at Lake Winnipesaukee only about once a month."

"I'm a priest, Lew and if I tried to get St. Mary's started up again could I count on you to help out?"

Lew took a long sideways glance at Steve. "I suppose so...if it don't interfere too much with my fishing. Where's your Roman collar?"

"My things are in the car."

"You mean the young fella I used to take fishing turned out to be a priest?"

"That's right."

"What do you call yourself: Father Steve? It will be nice not having to carpool over to Wolfeboro on a Sunday. Now wait a minute, are you one of them circuit riders? I hear tell there's a lot more Catholics these days and a lot less priests. Are we gonna see you once a month or maybe only once a year?"

"No, I'll be living at the pond and St. Mary's will be my fulltime ministry. Can you put me in touch with some other Catholics in Wakefield? I'll need a lot of help to get the church going again."

"What kind of help? You mean money?"

"No, money's not a problem. Mainly, spreading the word plus a bit of fixing, cleaning, stuff like that. But I won't know how much until I see the building."

Leaving the diner, Steve and Lew agreed to drive to the old church on the following Friday. Steve was happy he had found a parishioner who could be helpful. Lew was concerned that he was getting caught up in something that would keep him from fishing.

*****

After leaving the diner, Steve continued up the highway. He turned the rental car in at Ossippee and took a taxi back to Pine River Pond, site of the family's summer home. When he needed transportation he would use one of the cars stored in the garage.

Steve found the Larkin house on the pond to be in surprisingly good condition. As Lew had indicated, the cleaning crews must have come up on a regular basis he mused, as he walked through the big house that overlooked the pond. He couldn't remember how many years it had been since he had last seen the house. His second floor room as a boy had none of the memorabilia he had hoped to find. His baseball bat, his first baseman's mitt, his fishing pole, all the pictures he had plastered on the walls—all were gone. In one of her fits, Mother must have thrown it all in the trash he said to himself as he peered out a window at the rippling water on the lake that reflected golden in the bright afternoon sun.

Downstairs, he was pleasantly surprised to find the freezer in the kitchen and the pantry fully stocked. He supposed it was kept that way on the outside chance that Jonathon might want to spend a weekend up at the pond. He opened a can of peanuts as he walked around inspecting the outside of the house. In the large clapboard building they called 'the barn', everything was there: the canoe, the rowboat, the small Sunfish sailboat, two kayaks, two snowmobiles, half-a-dozen pairs of water skis and at least a dozen inflatable mattresses and rafts. Good God, he thought, how did we ever find time to use all this stuff?

The speedboat floated at the private dock. The boat was covered with a protective canvas that was sunken in the middle with a few inches of rain water. About thirty yards down the beach a small clapboard building rested partly over a narrow inlet carved from the beach. Inside, a late model Super Cub floated on pontoons. Steve climbed into the cockpit. The plane was fully equipped—radio, GPS navigation, transponder, an emergency survival kit. Regardless of Lew's complaint, Steve knew he would have to brush up with a few check flights. Climbing down, he walked back up the small private beach towards the house. Standing at the water's edge, he dipped his hand in the water stirring up a small cloud of sand. It felt like a warm bath. In the wooded area nearby, at the water's edge three tall paper birch trees made a high arch curving down to the water as if they were bending over to take a drink. The trunks of the tall pines that lined the pond were covered on the side facing the water with hairy green sphagnum moss. He pulled off a small patch and rubbing it between his fingers, held it to his nose to sniff the delicate fragrance. He saw two loons with dark green heads and dagger-like pointed bills floating on the sunlit shimmering water out near the tree-covered island about a quarter mile offshore. The loons were swimming silently. He never forgot their familiar haunting wail that usually came in the night when, as a boy, he lay in bed dreaming of the big fish he was going to catch the next morning.

As Steve stood at the water's edge, a family of brown speckled wild ducks came paddling into the sandy shallows at his feet. A truncated family of one parent and four beeping ducklings. Yes, I could learn to love it up here again, he thought, as he threw a few cracker crumbs from his pockets into the water. In a flurry, the ducklings made short work of the crumbs.

As he walked back up to the house, taking several deep breaths of pine-scented air, Steve felt his anger drifting away like a branch floating away on the pond. A feeling of exhilaration came over him. It tempted him to forget his difficulties with the church hierarchy, his renegade status. They were not likely to look for him here, because it was not common knowledge that the Murphy's of Wayland had this isolated home on a pond in a rural part of New Hampshire. Besides, since the property had always been listed in his mother's maiden name, Larkin. Just about everyone thought of the family as Larkins. He wondered if he wouldn't be safer using the name Larkin instead of Murphy, but he felt there was a limit to the amount of deception he was willing to bring to this new ministry. The only thing people had to know was that he was a priest fresh in from Arizona—which, although true, was somewhat deceptive since it was not the whole truth.

For the moment, he felt safe in familiar surroundings, but he knew the church had tentacles everywhere, and he would have to be vigilant, just in case.

23

Steve and his pond neighbor, Lew, pulled into the gravel parking lot of the small whitewashed clapboard building that had once served the Wakefield area as St. Mary's Catholic Church.

"What do you think, Father?" asked Lew, squinting out of his good eye as the pair examined the modest building with the squat open bell tower, the bell of which had long since been removed.

"Where's the bell?" Steve asked looking up at the steeple.

"It was carted off by someone from the diocese. I heard it was put in the steeple of a new church in Portsmouth."

"The building could use a coat of paint and a few roof shingles here and there, but overall it looks pretty OK," Steve said as he walked around to the rear tapping on a board here and there. "No bell up in the steeple but thank heaven, no termites down below, either."

Inside, the floors, the pews, the Stations of the Cross on the walls, and even the altar were covered with a layer of dust so thick that as the pair investigated, they had to cover their mouths and noses with handkerchiefs. Entering the sanctuary, Steve saw that the church had a small sacristy off to the right side of the altar where he would be able to don his vestments and pray briefly before beginning Mass. A closet held an array of dusty vestments. On the altar, Steve lifted the altar stone and was pleased to see that the holy relic was still in place under the episcopal seal although time had faded the name of the saint who sanctified the altar on which Christ's body and blood had been shed anew at each daily Mass. The presence of the relic told the priest this was still a consecrated church albeit one that had fallen into disuse, and perhaps all but forgotten by the diocese. "But the building and tiny lot must still be recorded on the books of the diocese," Steve mused aloud. "Wonder why the diocese hasn't sold it?"

"Probably because nobody wanted to buy it," Lew answered. "There's already three churches here in Wakefield—Episcopal, Baptist and Congregational, and since the Catholic Church couldn't spare a priest for the church here, it's just stood idle. There's no taxes to pay on church property, so they just leave it sit here."

As Steve turned about on the altar to face the dozen or so dusty pews, he saw a figure seated in the last pew. It was an elderly woman. "Can I help you, Ma'm?" he asked, voice raised but muffled through the handkerchief.

"Are you the new priest?"

"Yes, I am. I'm Father Murphy. And may I ask who you are?"

"I'm Mrs. Winters. You can call me Gladys. I live just a few doors down the street from the church. I come in and clean the church once in awhile. I always offer it up, you know, to atone for some of my past sins. Not that they were mortal sins, good heavens no, only venial sins and such. Just like at home, when I bend over, painful as it is what with my arthritis, and pick up a little piece of thread or a bit of paper on the floor, I always offer it up. I figure it's worth more to the Lord when it hurts so to do it."

Steve had a sudden uncharitable thought which he later regretted. "It's not likely" he said to himself, "that she's done anything in a long time in here to offer up. This place hasn't been cleaned, really cleaned in years. She must be blind as a bat." Out loud, he said: "But we're happy to have you here, Mrs. Winters. You know Lew, of course. He and I have been checking the building over to get it going again as a church. I plan to hold regular services here once more."

"Fine, Father, but are you really going to be here, I mean actually conducting a ministry here or are you one of those circuit riders who used to come around once or twice every six months but now don't even come around anymore."

"I plan to say daily Mass right here, Mrs. Winters. And we'll have novenas, too. A full liturgy. I live just a few miles away at Pine River Pond. Lew and I are neighbors."

"What about bingo, Father? We used to have marvelous bingo games on Wednesday nights."

Steve demurred, saying, "Well we'll have to see about that, Mrs. Winters. Perhaps in a few months."

The old lady peered through thick glasses at Steve's companion, "How are you, Lew?" she asked. "I guess we won't need you to drive us over to Wolfeboro to Sunday Mass any more. Not that you ever did it more than once a month. Seems like whenever the fish were biting, the good Lord had to hover over your pond and watch you fishing instead of praying. You better hope that on Judgment Day the Lord don't turn his back on you and just go off fishing. Leave you in the hands of the Devil he might."

Steve walked down the center aisle of the church and sat in a pew in front of the woman. Resting an arm on the back of the pew, he turned to face her. "Mrs. Winters, can you spread the word to some of the people in the old parish and have them here for nine o'clock Mass next Sunday so we can get this church going again?"

"I'll do my best, Father. You know, I can't tell what you look like with that handkerchief covering your face."

Steve pulled the handkerchief down.

"My, but aren't you a handsome young fellow. But Father, I have to tell you, there's some things going on in this town you should know about...dangerous things...heretic things."

"What do you mean? What things?"

"I may be talking out of turn, but some of the supposedly Catholic ladies in Wakefield have taken to holding their own services—without a priest."

"Well, I don't suppose there's anything wrong with that," Steve said smiling.

"What if I was to tell you they was saying Mass without a priest?"

"But that's impossible," Steve replied frowning. "Only a priest can perform transubstantiation and you can't have a real Mass without it."

"Well some of them are doing it anyway," Mrs. Winters said matter-of-factly as she labored to get to her feet. As the old lady slowly left the church hobbling along with a cane, Steve was suddenly consumed with guilt. He realized that no matter how hard Mrs. Winters might have tried and no matter that she said she was always ready to seek opportunities to offer up good works to the Lord, in her condition she had no hope of keeping up with the dust that blew into the church from chinks in the doors and windows.

"Lew, you heard Mrs. Winters. Do you know anything about some women having Mass without a priest present?"

"I heard tell of it. I do know that some of the women who used to go to Wolfeboro stopped going. I assumed they just lapsed like some Catholics do, but later I heard they were holding services."

"Where?"

"Why, in their homes o'course. Maybe when the priests stopped coming here, they thought the time had come for the women to step up and perform services."

"And there's nothing wrong with that," Steve explained, "as long as the services are non-Eucharistic like prayer meetings and bible readings. Stuff like that. Isn't that what they're doing? Mrs. Winters must have it all wrong."

"It's a bit more than that, I'm afraid. They're saying Mass and giving out communion. They take turns. One week it's in one woman's parlor, then the next week, it's someone else's."

On hearing his fears confirmed, Steve was dismayed, but decided not to say anything about it for the moment. "Lew, are the fish biting over at the pond?"

"Nope, Father. Haven't had a nibble in two weeks."

"Then maybe you and I can spend a few days cleaning this place up. What do you say?"

"Why I suppose I'll do like Mrs. Winters does—I'll just offer it up. I could use a few brownie points in heaven."

"We all could," Steve replied.

24

The water swirled, leaving behind a silent vortex as the paddler propelled the canoe—alternately on one side, then with dripping paddle, over to the other. The pond was calm with only an occasional ripple stirred up by the warm breeze. It was a sunny day and since there had been no rain, the water was a clear greenish-blue free of the pine needles and leaves that sometimes littered the surface. Closer to shore, one could see the bottom covered with small rocks but out in the middle it was too deep to see into the murky depths. Steve sat at the stern leisurely paddling. Janet reclined in the center of the canoe against a slanted board covered with a pillow. Her arm rested on the gunwale. Her fingers stirred a bubbly trail as the canoe moved through the water.

Steve couldn't take his eyes off the lovely figure in the shimmering white bathing suit, legs outstretched towards him, her pink toenails almost touching his feet. He had almost forgotten how beautiful she was.

Swimming ahead of the canoe and keeping a constant distance, was a family of loons. "Steve, one of the babies is riding on the back of what I suppose is the mother. The other baby is swimming along."

"The mother is letting the less mature one cop a ride. Do you see that tiny island? It was created by the pond association as a nesting island for the loons. It protects them from any of the land predators that can't swim this far out. The pond has several of these islands. The loons are protected because they give a distinctive character to these northern lakes. And, by the way, are you sure you can only stay up here one day? Can't you spend the night and drive the rental car back to Logan Airport tomorrow? Two hours up from Boston and two hours back is a lot of driving for one day."

"I'd love to, Steve, but we both know how risky that would be."

"Risky? I would think four hours behind the wheel in one day is dangerous. What harm can come to you here?" he asked with a broad grin on his face."

"Is that Mount Washington I see in the distance up north?" she asked, trying to change the subject.

"No, you can't see Mount Washington from here. I think what you're looking at is called Mount Chorcorua."

"You think?"

"Hey, I haven't been up here in years. I was lucky I could still find the family home on the pond. I hate to admit I even made a few wrong turns on the way through Wakefield when I came up last week. By the way, can I ask you to box up my stuff and send it up here? And about my car in Washington, I want you to keep it. It isn't worth much. Keep it as a gift. I'll send you the title."

"I can't do that. Maybe I can sell it and send you the money."

"Janet, please. I may have a lot of problems, but money isn't one of them. I came into an inheritance from my mother—a magnanimous expression of her deathbed guilt, I believe."

"Tell me about the monastery in Arizona. What did you do there—pray all day? Meditate? Work in the fields?"

"I don't want to say much about it. I'm trying to forget it. Let me just say it's a miserable place. It's run by monks—Passion Brothers who seem to want the resident priests to suffer. They're hung up on Christ's suffering on the Cross."

"What do you mean by wanting the priests to 'suffer'? You mean actual physical pain?"

"Yes, some of that, but mostly just harsh treatment. I suppose what could be called harassment or browbeating, plus hard labor in the fields. They treat priests like they were criminals. You wear a number on your robe. No names. And, if for example, you break the vow of silence, there's hardly any food on your plate at dinner. Plus other stuff. I really don't want to talk about it. I'm just happy I'm not there anymore."

"I don't understand. If priests go to the monastery for...what shall I call it, 'spiritual renewal', why are they treated so harshly?"

"Janet, the Passion Monastery is not a retreat house and the priests don't simply go there. They are sent there. I believe I mentioned it to you before I left, although maybe I didn't make myself clear. The priests sent there are three time losers—alcoholics, drug abusers, child molesters, and so forth. Some of them have broken the law, done time, and are now ex-cons. Their bishops send them there under the pretext...hope, if you will, that all other attempts to reclaim them having failed, the Passion brothers will shape them up or pressure them to resign."

"Now, I'm more confused. How could they have sent you there? Was it some kind of misunderstanding?"

"Possibly. But it's more complicated than that."

"Well, tell me this: How did you manage to leave the monastery? Bishop release you?"

"No. You may not believe this but I ran away. I'm still running. You're looking at a full blown renegade priest."

Janet was puzzled. For a moment she wondered if she had completely misjudged the man she had fallen in love with. Steve didn't seem to be the type to run away from anything no matter how bad. "Steve, you must have found out by now why they've been hounding you," she said, suddenly sitting up, anxious to hear the solution to the riddle that had bothered her for months.

Steve realized he was ashamed to tell her the story. As a priest, a man of God, an intercessor between the people and God, he had always believed, had been trained to believe, he was in a super-normal category. It wasn't ego—it was a spiritual fact. But here, in front of the woman he loved, in her eyes he would fall a long way down. Despite all, he felt he had to tell her.

"Janet, you've heard of cloning, of course."

"Sure. Microbiology is my minor at the university. What's that got to do with you?"

"I'm one of them. The church found about it when my mother was on her deathbed. Kind of a deathbed confession. There was a priest in the room who must have gone out and called Bishop Rhinehart. And I get the idea they don't like having a clone saying Mass, hearing confessions; in other words, a kind of soul-less manufactured machine developed in a lab, if you will, rather than the product of a marital union. A Frankenstein monster acting like a human being."

Janet suddenly remembered the eerie experience in the Colonial Inn when she had mistaken the older brother, Jonathon, for Steve. "My God," she exclaimed, "Could it have been Jonathon?"

"Yes, I'm afraid it was." Steve slowly recounted the story of his mother's deathbed confession. About his mother's desire to have another son just like Jonathon.

Janet's eyes filled with tears. Almost overcome, she turned her head away and gazed into the distance for a long time. When she looked back, she was so sad seeing his crestfallen face, she wanted to take him in her arms and never let go. But they were in a canoe and she didn't have any way to stand up and move to him.

Later, on shore, she let him hold her in a long embrace that was more than friendly but still not crossing the bounds of intimacy. She was beginning to melt when he suddenly stopped, gently pushed her away and turned to lead her into the house by the hand. She thought maybe he was leading her into a bedroom, but as it turned out, he wasn't. They sat curled up on the living room sofa for a long time. Although he was almost unable to control the urge in his loins, the thought that he would be taking advantage of her stopped him. He knew he didn't stop because of his vows. He stopped only because he knew she could be hurt by it. She wanted things he could never give her—a husband and probably children. She didn't need a dalliance, a romance that both of them would regret later.

They decided to have dinner at the Pine River Steak

House, just a few miles from Steve's house.

"Steve, when you compare cloning to creating a Frankenstein monster, you're making it sound worse than it really is. Clones are only twins, except that cloning of adult twins makes them many years apart. The difference of course is that the twins are lab generated rather than by natural means. A human clone has all of the attributes of a human being. Why would anyone question that?"

"I'm afraid some of the church hierarchy have questioned it."

"With what conclusion?"

"No one is quite sure. There are cardinals and bishops pro and con."

"What about the pope?"

"He hasn't yet made a definitive statement. I suppose he's waiting for the Curia to make a full blown study of the issue, which means an answer could be years away."

"By the way, if it will help your morale, did I ever tell you how handsome a machine you are?" she said playfully. "You really are, you know. Are you blushing?"

"No," he replied with a grin. I think I got a little too much sun on the lake today, that's all."

"About the church," Janet said with wrinkled brow and a slight frown. "I would think the church would accept that clones are full-fledged human beings. The only difference is that instead of sperm impregnating an egg, cells from an adult are inserted into an egg that has had its DNA removed. Then the egg is implanted in a woman for growth and nourishment. Of course, since adult cells are specialized, the trick is to reset their clock in order to produce a complete being. That's what the breakthrough was all about. There's another way to look at it—one could argue that the adult cells are already mated, and in the cloning process are just housed in an egg as an outer covering so they can be put back in a female for growth and nourishment. So I don't understand the big deal guys like Bishop Rhinehart seem to be making of it."

"It's not bishop any more. It's Archbishop Rhinehart. I hear he just got retitled and is on his way to becoming a cardinal. Maybe he already has the red hat for all I know."

"Swell," she said dryly. "Isn't he the one who's against altar girls and almost everything else where women are concerned?"

"That's the one."

As Janet returned from the salad bar, she sat down in the booth facing Steve. She looked at him levelly with a trace of worry in her eyes. "Steve, I would think the church's main concern would be whether the cloned individual was harmed by the process. That's the real moral issue, not whether a human clone is really human."

"Nobody ever said that bishops know a thing about science, especially the abstruse aspects of genetic engineering. Some of them are being stampeded by what they read or hear in the media, I suppose."

"Which brings me to the question—do you know the doctor involved? Whoever it was must have been far ahead of his time since the procedure was done about sixty years ago." She said this with a slight smile, trying to brighten the mood.

"Just hold on there a minute." Steve managed to laugh. "What's this sixty stuff? I'm not even fifty," he protested.

"It's a puzzle because Dolly was recent—about 1997, I believe. However, I did read somewhere that experiments with human cloning were performed many years ago. But no one thought they were successful."

"Apparently one of them was successful. I don't know anything really about the doctor who did it, but I aim to find out."

*****

On the drive back to Boston, Janet was still not convinced the Catholic hierarchy would have hounded Steve out of his parish and off to a monastery simply because he was a clone—an incestuous twin. In her mind he was merely a twin of Jonathon. There must have been more to it than that, she thought. But what?

*****

After Janet had gone, Steve sank into a feeling of loneliness beyond words. The euphoria he had felt when he first arrived at the house on the pond was gone. He drove to the small church, knelt alone in a pew and prayed through tears and sobs until he was exhausted. His church had abandoned him. The woman he loved was unreachable. As he looked up, he wondered if God was still there. He prayed individually to each person in the Trinity: God the Father, God the Son, and God the Holy Ghost. Then he poured his heart out to the

Blessed Virgin and finally prayed to Saint Jude, the patron of lost causes. But was anyone listening to his prayers? Because he was not the product of normal intercourse—the prerequisite so often stressed by the papacy—the union of sperm and egg in matrimonial intercourse or even in a petri dish, rather a twin conceived in a lab after a delay of almost twenty years, was he a human being in the eyes of the church? In the eyes of God? Did he have a soul? Was he really an ordained priest? Where was God now that he needed him?

In the following days, he doggedly jogged the back roads of Wakefield, past the small ancient cemeteries, the white clapboard homes—windows framed with black or dark blue shutters, past the 'moose crossing' signs, around the perimeter of the pond with laughing children diving off a raft. After his run, he would stop for a soft drink at a mom and pop store.

He ran in early morning and again at night. He ran in the exhilaration of falling rain and the serenity of cool dry mornings and evenings. As he arrived home after a morning run, he would pull off his shirt, kick off his shoes and run barefoot down across the small beach with a headlong dive into the water. He'd do a quick overhand crawl out thirty yards to a buoy and back.

And as the days went by, he steadily regained his confidence and sense of self. He wondered as he ran if the rhythmic drumbeat of feet pounding the ground and a heart pounding in his chest, had more healing power than poring his heart out in prayer.

*****

Steve's first Sunday Mass had only a dozen parishioners scattered through the pews. Mostly they came from the center of Wakefield where news of the reopening of St. Mary's had spread by word of mouth.

As Steve donned his vestments in the sacristy and glanced through the door in the direction of the altar, he was pleased to see the bouquets of flowers on the altar that had been brought by Mrs. Winters and a few of the other ladies. He made a point to thank them after the service. The white altar cloth was pressed and draped neatly over the small altar that held two newly polished brass candlesticks and the missal. The tabernacle was small, made of wood painted white with gold trim, but adequate. The nave of the church had been scrubbed bare, the wood grain on the pews reappearing after being hidden for years under layers of grime. On the outside, the front face of the church wore a new coat of traditional New England white paint. The remaining church faces were scheduled for painting in the following weeks. Although an unpretentious structure, plain and bare in every respect, the little church, a million light years from the glory of St. Peters in Rome, was to Steve a humble metaphor for the Bethlehem manger that had sheltered the newborn Christ.

Steve's sermon was brief and upbeat. He wanted to avoid laying too much on his new parishioners so he kept it light. No fire and brimstone to these good people who had responded to his call. He introduced himself as having been transferred from a diocese in Arizona. When the Mass ended, after hurriedly removing his chasuble, Steve hastened to the front door of the church where he warmly thanked the parishioners clustered outside.

As he shook hands, he overheard old Mrs. Winters, a short distance away talking to a large heavyset woman. "Now that we got a proper priest," Mrs. Winters was saying, "are you and your friends gonna keep saying Mass in the parlor?"

"Since the church doesn't allow women priests, we just might," answered the heavyset woman as she abruptly turned and walked away.

Steve walked over to Mrs. Winters. He thanked her warmly for helping round up parishioners and for the wonderful things the ladies did for the altar.

"Like I said, Father Murphy, I simply explained they weren't doing this only for the convenience of not having to drive over to Wolfeboro to Mass, but these were things that could be offered up to heaven. These things can guarantee seats closer to Jesus in the hereafter. Isn't that right?"

"Yes, of course," Steve said, suppressing a smile. Mrs. Winters apparently thought the hereafter would be held in a huge meeting hall, and she wanted a seat up front near Jesus on the stage. "By the way, did I hear you talking about parlor Masses to that woman over there?" he asked. "Who is she, by the way?"

"That's Henrietta Bergen. She's a tough one, Father. Yes, she and a few others are pretending to be priests. Since the church didn't ordain them," Mrs. Winters added sarcastically, "they must have ordained one another. Maybe they did it dancing around the Maypole."

"But the Maypole is a pagan concept."

"I know. I was just funning, Father."

"But tell me, Mrs. Winters, do these women realize they could be excommunicated for holding non-authorized Eucharistic services? Are they aware that could mean eternal damnation?"

"I can tell you Henrietta's thought of that, Father, but she says she's gonna get into heaven even if she has to knock the pearly gates down to get in."

Steve couldn't help smiling at the comment; then, taking leave of Mrs. Winters, he walked over to a group standing nearby to urge them to tell other Catholics in Wakefield about the reopened parish. Yet even as he asked the churchgoers to spread the word around the small town, he was acutely aware that there could be repercussions should the word reach all the way to the seat of the diocese. It was really just a question of time he knew; however, he also knew he had several factors working in his favor: for one thing, the shortage of priests had become acute in New Hampshire; diocesan finances had been hit hard by the falloff in collections; further, the bishop heading the Portsmouth diocese had been called away to Rome for an extended period. Certainly a priest from the diocesan seat would visit to interview him, but he was sure he could handle the meeting. His story was straightforward—he had left his parish in Maryland to renew his vows during an extended retreat at a mission house in Arizona. Pick any name but the Passion Monastery. He went on retreat because he thought his vocation was in jeopardy. His diocese had released him. Later, he had come to New Hampshire to begin anew in a small country church. He had learned the diocese could use some help. He had a substantial inheritance from his family and would make no financial demands on the diocese and, in fact, he knew that after a few months, the parish would be contributing to the diocese.

Steve was certain that Cardinal Wollman had earlier requested a review of the church's position on human cloning by the Vatican Curia. Although it was well known that the church was against human cloning, would the church's position change somewhat after it had become an accomplished fact as in the case of Reverend Stephen Murphy? Would the Curia conclude that people like Murphy—in a sense, innocent victims—were legitimate humans with God-given souls?

Steve knew that matters such as this that involved fundamental morality and theology had to be thoroughly researched. The answer would be a long time coming.

It was also extremely unlikely that Bishop Rhinehart would have widely disseminated his concern about Reverend Stephen Murphy. Not only would it have been an embarrassing revelation to fellow clergymen about one of his priests by an egocentric bishop who was bucking for cardinal, Steve also knew Rhinehart was the type who had begun a personal vendetta against him and regardless of the position that would ultimately be taken by the Curia, he would work determinedly to remove or dispose of the renegade who had become a thorn in his side. It would be done undercover—quietly and without fanfare. But Steve was buoyed by the fact that Rhinehart would have to find him first.

25

Three weeks after his inaugural Mass at St. Mary's, Steve decided the time had come to make a trip to the medical center in northern Maine where Jonathon told him he had been 'conceived'. Since he would be searching for records that went back fifty years, he didn't have much hope of finding anything, but he felt it was worth a try. For his peace of mind he had to know the full story; he had to track down whatever information might be available.

After the long drive to northern Maine on the New Brunswick border, it proved maddeningly difficult finding the remote center situated on a back road miles outside a small village. He mistakenly thought he was looking for an establishment along the lines of a hospital. What he saw instead was a small one-story central building surrounded by a conglomeration of outbuildings. It resembled the campus of a community college—a poor community college. He became aware it was not a hospital, not really a medical center—in reality a medical research lab.

Seated in the office of the director, a doctor named O'Neill, a huge, robust, red-haired woodsman of a man in a soiled white lab coat, Steve asked to see any available records concerning himself—Stephen Francis Murphy, his brother Jonathon, or his mother, Larkin-Murphy.

Doctor O'Neill raised his bushy red eyebrows in

surprise. "You're the second person in a couple of years who has asked for these records. Are you aware they date back over sixty years? I had to dig through the dusty archives in our storeroom to find them. It's pure luck they weren't just chucked out somewhere along the way."

It was Steve's turn to be surprised. "Someone else has been here checking on the Murphy family records?" he asked, but as soon as he asked, he knew it must have been someone from the church. "My parents are dead and I feel certain it wasn't my brother, so, may I ask who it was?"

"Let see now," Doctor O'Neill replied as he adjusted his glasses and pored over the visitor file with massive hands that looked more suitable for chopping down trees than handling flimsy paper files. "A priest from the Archdiocese of Washington. Name's illegible."

"The name doesn't matter. It's enough knowing it was the archdiocese making the inquiry. And the information was released?" Steve asked archly.

"Yes, the archdiocese representative said the child they were inquiring about later became a priest attached to the Washington archdiocese. He was about to be elevated to the rank of Monsignor and they were merely conducting a routine background check."

"Did they find what they were looking for?"

"Apparently, yes. My notes indicate they were allowed to make copies of some of the records. Please understand, Father Murphy, the original events took place years before my tenure began here. The record indicates that a number of attempts at artificial conception were made by a doctor attached to the center—one who is now dead, by the way."

"When you say artificial conception, are you referring to in-vitro fertilization?" Steve asked as a test, knowing that if the answer were yes, the director would be attempting to cover up the cloning.

"No," the director answered honestly. "The doctor was a researcher, perhaps one of the first to experiment with human cloning. You might say he was way ahead of his time. There is evidence that he performed a number of cloning and genetic experiments while here."

"I understand," Steve said, "but I'm really only interested in the records pertaining to me and my family. With your permission, I would like to review those."

*****

A short time later, Steve was sitting at a desk in a small study adjoining the director's office, reviewing the file that detailed numerous attempts at cloning by a scientist at the center. A file titled: Larkin-Murphy, detailed the dozen or so cloning attempts performed on Steve's mother. But the faded documents were so riddled with medical jargon and abbreviations, Steve found he understood little about the experiments. He realized how naive he had been when he thought he would simply drive up to the center, look over the information, digest its full import and return home.

After a time, Doctor O'Neill entered the study. "How are you doing?" he asked. "Getting a clear picture are you?"

"Not really," Steve replied in a tone of disgust. "In

fact I understand little of what I'm reading. These accursed documents seem more intended to obscure than reveal what happened."

"The priest who came up here had similar difficulties," the director said smiling. "I am willing to explain the protocols to you the way I had to explain them to him if you like."

"Please do," Steve replied, dropping the stack of papers on the desk, completely frustrated.

Doctor O'Neill took a seat facing Steve. "As you know, certain types of cloning have become commonplace. For example, the world now has dairy farms with high output cloned cows and cloned pigs that produce lean, very low fat cuts of pork, etc."

"Yes, I know all that," Steve said, "but what I don't really understand is why cloning was considered such a breakthrough."

"You're referring to the fairly recent adult mammal cloning like Dolly, for example. The one that was hyped in the media."

"Yes."

"Before I explain the breakthrough, let me first raise an important question that I thought you would ask. In fact, I'm surprised you haven't. As you well know, Dolly was only cloned in 1997; really not that many years ago. You are, roughly about fifty. Correct?"

"Almost fifty."

"Then how could you possibly be a clone? To explain this, let me first say that something like cloning has been known and used in botany and agriculture for many, many years. Only it wasn't referred to as cloning. The clone went under the name: variety. Completely new plants were grown from tiny sprigs. Cells also have been successfully cloned for many years. Let me ask a related question: How long ago was DNA first identified?"

"Ten years?"

"The structure of DNA was identified in 1953. Now I admit that our experimenter was far ahead of his time, but the records show he successfully cloned a few humans way back in the sixties. Although you are aware of your status—if you want to call it that, where the others are and whether they are aware of their origin is unknown."

Steve was not sure he believed what he was hearing. "So why didn't all this come to light before?"

"Quite honestly, it was considered so ethically, morally wrong, it was stopped almost immediately and covered up. And now, of course, many countries have declared that human cloning is illegal."

"Biological procedures," the director continued, "have evolved in the last few years. Embryonic stem cells, for example, are not specialized which gives them potentially wide application, but going back, concerning all the hullabaloo about Dolly—apparently the first adult animal to be cloned—let me explain that. The touted breakthrough was in the production of newborns cloned from adults. Let's get down to the basics: a fertilized human egg contains all of the genetic material needed to form a complete human being. However, as the cells multiply, they become specialized—some become muscle cells, some nerve cells, some can only produce skin tissue, others connective tissue, and so forth. Thus it was originally thought impossible to clone cells from a fully grown adult because the cells had become specialized and could not produce a complete being. The breakthrough in cloning began with a mature specialized cell from an adult which had its 'clock' reset back to the beginning, so that it was capable of producing a complete human being—arms, legs, skin, brain, liver...the works. Different techniques have been discovered to reset the clock which I won't go into now. A single adult cell can then be implanted in a woman's egg from which the genetic material has been removed. The egg is then replanted, if you will, and the woman comes to term with a cloned newborn—an identical human copy of the original."

The director stood up leading Steve to think the interview was over, but the huge lumberjack of a man began pacing the floor. He said it helped him think. "There is not much point to early-stage cloning, you understand, that is, in the production of fetal twins, but tremendous potential in cloning of adults, both human and animal. For example, if an adult animal was the last of its endangered species, a few cells could be removed and the animal cloned over and over again. If a particular cow was found to give a supernormal amount of milk, it could be cloned and a complete dairy stocked with its high-output 'offspring'. Exact copies of famous scientists and world leaders could be produced and presumably produced in quantity. You see, although there are obviously ethical objections to cloning of humans in particular, the benefits could be fantastic."

"I understand that, but there are some things about the

process as it relates to me which I don't understand."

"Such as?"

"Well, like the word 'chimera' which seems to appear here and there in these reports. What the devil is a chimera?"

"Ah yes, you have put your finger on what is most likely the real problem. As I recall, chimera seemed to be the principal concern of the Murphy cloning that most interested the priest from the archdiocese. Frankly, he seemed far more concerned about the chimerian aspects than the cloning itself. Familiar with Greek mythology? Perhaps not. Very simply, 'chimera' refers to a mixture of species. For example, a mixed breed of a human and an animal, or a mixture of several animal species. On the one hand, it might be a beast with a human head. Conversely, it could be a human with an animal head. You understand of course, that these examples are mythological, not actual. However, production of certain kinds of chimeras has been performed a number of times. Perhaps you've heard of animals like the genetically manipulated sheep-goats. They are not sheep; they are not goats. They are a new species: sheep-goats, although I feel a new name would be appropriate rather than constantly referring back to the original mix."

Steve's face was ashen. "Are you telling me that cloning experiments were conducted here mixing species, and in my case, human and animal cells?"

"Afraid so, but please remember that all of this took place some sixty years ago, or thereabouts. No one currently employed at the center is responsible. In addition, we like to feel that any combination of human and animal genetic material was very limited and was terminated almost as soon as it started. I have some records that suggest the director at the time put a stop to it as soon as he became aware of it."

"But it did happen," Steve said laconically, his white-knuckled hands gripping the edge of the desk. "And from the little that I know on this subject, if a heart valve from a pig were placed in a human, as has been done many times in surgery, it is clear that the valve implant doesn't make the person any less a human. But in a case where the cells of different species are mixed at the very beginning, will the being produced be categorized as an animal or a human? And if as you say, it is a mixed breed, how can we tell how much of this thing that results is human and how much animal?"

"We really can't," the director said solemnly. "Even if only a few cells of an animal, say a primate, were added, no one knows whether the being produced would have a proportionate response; that is, would a human egg with ninety percent human cells produce a ninety percent human? Or, might the primate cells, perhaps genetically "stronger," if you will, eventually produce a disproportionate response?"

"Meaning?" Steve asked angrily.

"Meaning..." the director responded, sympathetic but growing wary of his visitor's violent reaction and the potential for a lawsuit, "...meaning that the human so produced might become less human and more animal as it matured."

"You are admitting," Steve said, rising to his feet with hands trembling, "that animal cells were added to the 'soup' that was then implanted in my mother."

"Why yes. Remember the record is not complete but it does refer to a chimera. I can't deny that."

"What animal, for God's sake?" Steve almost shouted as he stood glaring down at the director.

"That's one question I can't answer, because the last two pages of the report on the Murphy woman have been lost. Believe me, I searched long and hard for them in the archives, but they just weren't there. We don't know what animal, and we don't know how much of the animal genetic material was mixed in. But my best guess is that he used cells from a primate like a baboon or a chimp. Baboons, as you may know, are probably the closest primate species to humans."

"Well, can you tell me this: why did the procedure have to mix in animal cells? What was the point? Merely to see what monstrosity might turn out?"

The director glared at Steve. "Please don't assume that scientists are necessarily callous. The notes tell me that your family has had a long term genetic medical condition—Lou Gehrig's disease. I suspect the scientist who did the cloning was trying to prevent the disease from occurring in the clone. Humans get Lou Gehrig's disease but the scientist may have believed that primates do not. So, you see, the scientist's intentions could have been beneficial. A genetic manipulation to benefit the human—it's done every day now."

"There is also another reason that seems to make sense," the director continued. "The doctor performing the experiments wrote that the age of a newborn adult clone was uncertain. Would it actually be a newborn— with the expectation of a long life, or might it be the age of the adult who donated the cells? This is an important issue in cloning, you understand. If, for example, you cloned an aging scientist with a life expectancy of say another ten or fifteen years, the 'newborn' clone might die in ten or fifteen years. It might not live a day longer than the original. I am uncertain of course, as I said before, but I would suspect that the original experimenter took care to use cells from a young animal as further insurance that the clone would have a full life span. Makes sense, doesn't it?"

"In some cockeyed way, yes. How long do baboons live, by the way?" Steve asked bitterly.

Seeking to end the session which had degenerated into an argument, Doctor O'Neill rose and walked back into his office. After the director left the room, Steve sat for a long time in stunned silence. He had first thought the Archdiocese of Washington was after him, intending to get him out of the priesthood when they found out he was a clone. Now he knew the problem was far more serious. Trembling, he looked down at his arms. Every hair seemed to tell some kind of story. He thought about the dark stubble on his face. If, in fact, he was a chimera, how much of him was human, how much animal? And, if so, what breed of animal? Was he unique or were there other human-animal chimeras around?

It occurred to him that some present-day basketball players in the NBA, some approaching eight feet tall, might well be chimeras. The three-hundred-and-fifty-pound pro football players might also have been produced as clones with some type of primate cells in the soup. Of course, all of that was strictly outlawed, so it couldn't be—or could it?

Certainly an Olympic swimmer cloned with webbed feet or gills, would have been recognized immediately as such and disqualified, but a somewhat taller basketball player or somewhat heavier football player—when the trend had for a long time been in the direction of taller and heavier, might not have raised suspicions, or if it did, might have been almost impossible to prove. And it was obvious that big money was at stake.

The only thing that kept Steve from total despair as he drove back to New Hampshire was the admonition he had learned years before in the seminary: uncontrolled despair was a grave sin because it negated God's love. It was an abandonment of a person's relationship with God. It renounced His mercy and the promise of everlasting life. However, in this case, he thought dourly, maybe a part-human creature has a somewhat legitimate right to despair.

26

It was early fall in New Hampshire. The summer tourists were gone; the children were all back in school. Gone from Pine River Pond were the speedboats, party boats, canoes, and jet skis. The pond was ringed with brilliant fall colors that supplanted the green of summer. Days were balmy, the nights cool, the air filled with the pine-scent of fall. Steve was finishing his fourth month at St. Mary's. Although things were going well and attendance at Mass was good, he was troubled by the continued absence of Henrietta and a number of the women in her circle.

One evening, he planned a visit to Henrietta's to coincide with the ending of her Saturday evening 'Mass'. He stood outside in the shadows on the front porch leaning against a pillar for a few minutes and finally heard voices inside growing louder as the women approached the front door. Stepping up, he tapped lightly on the door. When someone inside opened it, he saw five women standing in the entrance hall getting ready to leave. Henrietta was giving each one a hug in turn.

"Good evening, Ladies," Steve said smiling warmly as he stepped inside. "Isn't it a lovely evening? Can I count on seeing all of you at Sunday Mass tomorrow morning?" But despite his attempt at a simple pleasantry, there was no reply as the women filed past him without so much as glancing in his direction.

Steve, somewhat unnerved, decided they might be embarrassed rather than rude as he watched them walk down the street. He turned to Henrietta. "Good heavens, what have I done?" he asked smiling, trying to make light of the situation.

Henrietta was in no mood for levity. "Why are you here?" she asked with an angry glare. "And why does it happen you come precisely as we are finishing our evening service?"

"You mean your evening 'Mass', don't you?"

"Yes, it was a Mass," Henrietta said guardedly. "And I'm sure you don't approve. I hear you might be taking action to have us excommunicated."

"No, that's not true. I never said I was going to try to excommunicate anyone. That's the pope's role, not mine."

"But you are the instrument of the pope."

"That's correct, but let me put it this way—you're kidding yourselves if you think your Masses are real— if they have any real meaning. But, I'm curious. I could understand your difficulty when there was no priest available, although even then, you could always go to the church in Wolfeboro which is not very far away. So, I suspect there has been more going on here than simply the absence of a priest in Wakefield."

"You're right, Father. I'll tell you straight out. At first, when priests stopped coming around here, many of us piled into cars and drove to Wolfeboro. Then some of us began reading the encyclical letters of Pope John Paul II especially as regards the ordination of women, which he strenuously denounced claiming that women have not been created in the image of Christ.

According to the pope, only men qualify because they are males like Christ. They supposedly look like Christ, although no one in this world has any idea as to what Christ really looked like. I suspect he looked like a bearded Jewish carpenter. Show me a bearded Jewish carpenter *priest* and I'll believe he looks like Christ. And so, women have been permanently excluded from one of the sacraments—Holy Orders. And this then excludes them from being able to perform any of the other sacraments for the faithful like saying Mass, hearing confessions, administering Extreme Unction. And even being able to come in from the sidelines to attain a position of authority in the church. When you really think about it, the premise on which all of this is based adds up to pretty thin stuff. And, we believe, the product of a male-dominated church."

"Henrietta, I agree. Does that surprise you? And I can't explain why things should be this way, but the fact is...they are. If we are to be part of the Holy Roman Catholic Church we are bound to follow the dictums of the pope whether we like them or not and really whether we think they are right or not."

"Fine Father, but consider this: At the Last Supper, when Christ consecrated the bread and wine, he said, 'When two or more of you are gathered together, do this in memory of me.'" Henrietta added acidly, "Christ did not say: 'When two priests or bishops get together, or simply two men, do this in memory of me'."

"And so you ladies feel you have the right to say Mass and your Mass is supposedly valid."

"That's right. And while I'm on the subject, Father, let me say one more thing: Christ's apostles were bishops. In the beginning there were no priests. Right?"

"Yes, that's correct."

"But as the church grew in numbers, the bishops couldn't handle all of the chores, so the concept of a bishop's helper, or priest was invented. Christ ordained no priests. Priests were unknown. They came along several centuries later strictly out of administrative necessity. And all of the sacramental powers of the bishops were conveyed to them."

"That's not quite true, Henrietta. For example, only a bishop performs confirmation."

"But you get my point, Father."

"Yes, and I don't know what more I can say to convince you that what you and the ladies are doing is not real, not in accordance with church teaching." As Steve said this, he turned to leave, convinced sadly that he was getting nowhere with the woman.

"Wait a minute, Father. Let me ask you—why don't you bring the matter up with the bishop—you know in the diocesan seat. He's back from Rome, you know."

"I don't want to do that."

"Of course, you don't. I've found out you're not even attached to this diocese. You're an itinerant. What do you say to that?"

"You're right, of course. I've come here from Arizona. I'm not officially assigned here, but remember, this was the place where my family brought us every summer for many years. It's like home to me. And I learned that a priest was needed here."

"This puts you in the category of a drifter. Has the Catholic Church really come to that, Father? Priests drifting from diocese to diocese and the bishops learning about it later? Maybe I'm being a little hard on you but New Hampshire doesn't qualify as some far-flung mission. This place is not Timbuktu. Missionaries don't drift in and out of here hoping for a few converts from paganism."

Steve was dismayed at the woman's hostility. He realized sadly she was right—not about saying Mass, but right about his status. He was a drifter, a renegade priest. Not through any fault of his own, but a renegade nonetheless. He said good night and quietly closed the door behind him as he left. As he did so, he glanced back and saw Henrietta through the glass upper part of the door, arms folded, smiling as if she had just knocked down the doors of heaven.

27

There was a slight chill in the air on the lake. A soft rain had begun to fall outlining the low white buildings of Wolfeboro hazily through the mist. Steve put his arm lightly around Janet's shoulder as they leaned on the stern rail of the Mount Washington steamer that was pulling away from the dock for a cruise on Lake Winnepesaukee. The engines below throbbed frothing up a boil of white water behind the ship. Steve glanced around nervously hoping none of his parishioners were on the ship. Happily, because of the poor weather, the ship was almost empty. Janet had come up for a weekend to visit Steve and tell him more about her research on cloning. She was determined to keep the visit platonic, although his arm around her shoulder was warm and welcome. She snuggled against him even as she kept telling herself she had come to help both of them understand his predicament, rather than for any romantic reasons. But as soon as she had laid eyes on him she saw a lost soul. She saw that he was so lonely and obviously so in love, she was ready to melt in his arms. Deeply in love with him, she wanted to give him something no one else in the world, or even in heaven could give him, but she was uncertain and conflicted. Partly, it stemmed from the fact that Steve was a priest and would likely remain a priest, but also because prior to the visit to New Hampshire she was being pressured by both her and her husband's families to move back in with her husband. Neither of them was particularly anxious to make the move, but the thought of one last attempt at a normal Catholic married life complete with children seemed like the right thing to do, despite reservations about any real feelings for one another. It was the powerful primeval urge of the age-old Catholic Church that admonished the faithful to procreate and fill the earth. It was the sacrifice expected by the church—no matter how difficult or miserably unhappy the marriage, no matter the level of cruelty, in the absence of annulment, the marriage was pre-ordained to remain intact for the sake of children present or expected.

When Janet slowly explained the situation to Steve, he glumly shrugged his shoulders. "I understand. After all, I'm part of the Catholic Church. Sacrifice on earth is what guarantees rewards in the hereafter. It's a question of accepting responsibility. But more than that, any children you have will bring you untold happiness even if the marriage isn't completely satisfying."

Steve was so miserable he could hardly believe what he was saying. "Janet, on another note, I have to leave New Hampshire soon." Steve said this with resignation written all over his face as they stood leaning on the ship's railing gazing at the receding shoreline. "A few of the parishioners have been asking too many questions. One even contacted the diocesan seat to inquire about me. So, it's just a matter of time before Rhinehart and the monks from the Passion Monastery get back on my trail."

"But where will you go?"

"Somewhere far away. New Hampshire hasn't been

far enough away. I've been thinking of Alaska—the Aleutian Islands in particular."

"For how long?"

"I suppose until they locate me there, and then I'll be off to someplace else."

"But Steve, you can't spend your whole life on the run. It has to stop somewhere."

"I know. But until the hierarchy come to their senses, and I find out more about my real position with the church, I am faced with the same old two choices: resign the priesthood and ask for a dispensation of my vows, or maintain a priestly ministry in some remote corner of the world. I know this can't go on forever. I'm living day-to-day."

"Despite all the grief the church is giving you, you don't sound ready to leave the priesthood."

"I'm not. And I've just about made up my mind to go to the Aleutians. I'll write and let you know where I am; that is, if you still want to keep in touch."

"How can you say that? Of course I do." He had spoken in such a crestfallen tone, Janet instinctively reached over and slipped her arm around his waist. She shifted sideways to be closer to him.

"Steve, about the cloning, I've done some research on cloning since my last visit up here. Almost everyone thinks of clones as twins. Clones are identical twins, somewhat like natural twins, only the clone's birth is delayed by some years."

"My brother, Jonathon, has also done some research on cloning. Maybe he feels guilty, I don't know. He tried to explain the technology to me. He described it pretty much as you are now. But what about the church?

Have you read anything about the church's position? I haven't seen anything concrete. Janet, dear, it's getting chilly out here, let's go inside."

Seated in the ship's lounge, Janet took a sip of her coffee and then held a piece of pastry up to his lips. "Some people seal a relationship by exchanging blood samples," she said, trying to be lighthearted. "Let's seal ours by sharing this piece of pastry."

He smilingly accepted and they took alternate bites until it was gone. Then she licked his fingertips. "Steve, dear, I'm sure the church will come to accept all this after a time. The church's first reaction to in-vitro fertilization was to condemn it as a violation of God's laws of procreation. Conception is supposed to take place in bed not in a lab. But as you know, the hierarchy has come around. It's still not approved of, but the people born of in-vitro fertilization are not considered Frankenstein monsters by the church. Steve, it's just a question of time until the church resolves its attitude towards some of these advances in genetic engineering. I believe the church fathers will eventually acknowledge the validity of people procreated by the cloning process."

Steve rested his hand on the back of Janet's hand. "The fact that almost everyone is convinced that human cloning is immoral and, in fact, illegal, will certainly keep it from becoming widespread, and that's all well and good," he said, "but, Janet, there's something new I learned about myself. Something dreadful. I found out more information on a visit to the lab where the cloning took place. The situation is worse than I could have imagined."

"How could that be, Steve? You're a clone. So what?" Janet twisted in the seat to look into his eyes, puzzled.

"When I visited the medical center in upper Maine, I saw some notations on a report and had a long talk with the director. I'm certain a copy of the report went to Rhinehart last year and based on that, he has been adamant about getting me out of the church."

"What kind of report? I don't understand."

Steve looked away for a moment—too embarrassed to reveal the truth to someone he loved.

"Steve, I want to know. Trust me," Janet said as she ran her hand lightly through the hair on the back of his head. She looked into his eyes. "I won't think any less of you. I love you. I always will love you, no matter what."

He bit his lip. He couldn't return her gaze. He could only stare down into his coffee cup. His words came slowly, painfully. "That crackpot doctor who performed the cloning experiments using my brother and my mother, put something else in the 'soup'. I don't know what else to call it other than 'soup'. He added animal cells to the embryo mix. The director told me it was well-intentioned; the doctor probably did it to break the genetic strain of Lou Gehrig's disease that runs in my family and to improve the chances of the clone having a long life expectancy by using young primate cells. He supposedly had some concern that the life expectancy of a newborn clone might be no longer than the remaining life expectancy of a donor. In other words, even though I wouldn't look as old as my older brother—since I was born twenty years after him, in a sense, I would have the same remaining life expectancy as Jonathon."

"Steve, that's not really true. Scientists now know that cloned animals live long after the original. But if that doctor mixed in primate cells in the process, that's horrible. You could be labeled a 'chimera'—a mix of human and animal. What a dirty trick!" All she could think of as she said it was the total lack of ethics, the gross immorality of some experimenters. Some of them blindly try things regardless of the consequences. Janet gently pulled Steve's head closer to her. Leaning over, she kissed his cheek and the corner of his mouth trying to get him to turn his head towards her. But flushed with shame, he sat head down staring at the table. Her eyes flooded with tears.

She began to wonder if the worst scenario might come about. She shuddered at the thought but quickly dismissed the idea as preposterous. Steve was a human being, a man, a handsome and intelligent one at that. He had all the qualities of a good person and a good priest. Certainly there had been no ill effects so far, at least nothing she knew of. Yet, a part of her wondered whether as the years passed, as he grew older, as his immune system began to weaken, whether he might have to deal with unwanted characteristics that could come to the surface.

Steve got up and taking Janet by the hand, led her outside to the stern of the ship. They stood at the rail, staring at the trailing white foam and the gray horizon. He made an effort to snap out of his depression. He knew this was the last time they would be together for a long time, maybe forever. He knew the effect the revelation had on her. He was afraid of losing her love even though she could soon be reluctantly in the arms of another man. A man who had far more right to her and her love than he. In his desperation, he thought he might lighten things with a lame comment. "Did you know you've been hanging around an animal?"

"I love animals. One of my best friends is an animal, at least, in part."

"Want me to growl for you?" he asked, trying to smile.

"Sure, tiger. Gimme a growl," she replied, smiling through her tears.

28

Steve pushed the canoe from shore and hopped agilely into the rear, settling on the seat at the stern as he dipped the paddle into the shallow sandy water. With strong thrusts the canoe slid swiftly from the dimly lit shore into the blackness of the pond. He glanced up at the overcast moonless night sky. Although he had never before gone out on the pond at night in a canoe—dangerous because it lacked running lights, this night was different. He had to think things out. He hoped it would be alone in these dark surroundings that he could see into the depths of his soul even as he was aware that some others, including those in his church were of the opinion that he was a being not possessed of a soul. He paddled silently out in the direction of the small island that lay half-a-mile off shore. He had no plan. He wanted only to paddle for awhile, drift for awhile with the paddle across his knees and think.

Not far from shore, there was a sudden upheaval in the water below the boat that caused the canoe to rock violently from side to side. His first thought was that he had hit an underwater boulder until he quickly recalled there were no large rocks this far from shore. As he held the gunwales of the canoe trying to keep from turning over, a large thrust from below completely flipped the boat throwing him into the water. He had no idea what turned the boat over. He had seen moose and deer swimming across the pond. He wondered if the massive body of a struggling moose had bumped the boat. Since he was an excellent swimmer Steve was surprised but not particularly scared at finding himself in the water. It would be simple enough: if he couldn't manage to clamber back onboard, he could stay in the water and swim behind the canoe with a frog kick and push the boat ashore. It would be slow going because the shirt, slacks and tennis shoes he was wearing would tend to drag him back as he swam.

Suddenly something grabbed one of his lower legs and held on even as he kicked the other leg hard to free himself. Were the huge hard horns of a moose entangling his pants-legs? Something large was in the water with him. He was being pulled under the surface and realized he was gulping for air but swallowing water instead. After several dunkings, he was on the verge of panic. But knowing the overturned canoe was unsinkable, he realized he would be all right as long as he could hang onto it. Clawing the water surface, he struggled for a hold on the canoe by slinging his arms over the slippery overturned hull. It was no good, because being pulled from below, and having nothing to hang onto, he slipped off. After several tries, he gave up trying to clamber onto the overturned hull, but knew he desperately needed something on the boat to grab. It was not likely that whatever was pulling him down would be able to pull both him and the boat down. Fumbling under the boat, his hand found one of the canoe crossbars. He held on with all his strength as he continued kicking and struggling to keep from being pulled under the water. Then suddenly, whatever had entangled his leg, let loose and seemed to drift away in the dark. He was free. He felt his heart pounding in his throat as he slowly pushed the canoe ashore.

Later, sitting in the sand on his dark beach, slowly regaining his composure, he was shocked that a simple canoe ride had almost ended in disaster.

*****

The day following the incident on the pond was Sunday. In the sacristy of the church before Mass Steve went through time-honored rituals—kissing each vestment as he put it on, all the while whispering his pre-Mass prayers. But he found he couldn't put the incident of the previous night out of his mind. It was dimly possible that he had become entangled with the horns of a drowned moose or deer in the middle of the pond, but for the life of him, he couldn't tell what it was. An accidental encounter with an animal didn't answer the puzzle as to how his leg seemed to be held in the grip of something that was pulling him down.

On the altar, looking out towards the congregation, Steve was pleased to see that the congregation was growing larger every week. Almost all of the pews were full. There were even several standees in the rear. After the consecration and during the holy communion part of the service, glancing up, Steve saw two men standing in the rear of the church. He couldn't be sure, but he thought the men looked familiar. They were dressed casually after the custom in the small town where people often went hunting, fishing or boating right after Mass.

But as Steve continued to give out communion, he had a strange feeling—one that made his flesh crawl.

Could it be that Brothers Michael and John had found him? He shuddered at the thought that it could have been one, or both of the brothers on the pond the night before, trying to drown him. Why not? He knew the brothers were grimly determined to get him. They would stop at nothing either to capture him or kill him if necessary. And maybe they were more clever than he had thought. A drowning on the pond could be made to look accidental. It would likely be concluded later that he had fallen into the water and lost his way swimming in the dark.

Beads of perspiration glistened on his brow as he administered communion to the faithful lined along the railing that divided the nave and the sanctuary. To each upturned face, "The body of Christ...the body of Christ...".

He hesitated momentarily. He was shaken as he stared down at the face of Brother Michael who with half-closed eyes and tongue thrust out to receive the Host, seemed as innocent as a lamb. Could he administer communion to a man who had attempted murder? On the other hand, could he really prove it? He took a Host from the ciborium and placing it on the brother's tongue with a hand that shook slightly, he whispered, "The body of Christ." Next in line was Brother John, tongue out, also waiting to receive the Lord. Again, reluctantly, "The body of Christ."

After just a few short months establishing a ministry in Wakefield, Steve realized that the game was up. Although he hated the thought of leaving his new parish and devoted parishioners, he knew that having been found by the monks, he would have a constant struggle just to stay alive much less conduct the orderly affairs of the parish. He had to get out... fast. With a smooth gesture, Steve signaled to a deacon standing nearby in the sanctuary to take the ciborium and continue giving out the Holy Eucharist. He, the priest, hovered nearby, hands folded in prayer, forcing a slight smile, and trying to look as calm and natural as possible. Since he had often done this before as a supportive gesture to a deacon, none of the congregation thought it unusual. Steve then drifted slowly to the altar where he appeared to be busying himself with wiping his chalice and tidying up the altar as the Mass would draw to a close.

Hardly anyone noticed when the priest celebrating the Mass slipped into the sacristy. It was several minutes after the communion before any of the parishioners, heads bowed, deep in prayer after receiving the body of Christ, realized he had gone. Even then, it was easy to believe that he might have been called away to tend to someone dying or had gone home not feeling well. A few thought he had looked extremely pale during the communion part of the service. They noted that his forehead was wet with perspiration. The deacon concluded the Mass, telling the faithful: "The Lord be with you. Go in Peace."

Right after leaving the altar, Steve stripped off his vestments in the sacristy, put his chalice in its case, and rushed outside to his car. He took off, heading north on Route 153 in the direction of Pine River Pond. Through the rear view mirror, he could see brothers Michael and John in what was probably a rental car in hot pursuit. The gloves were off now. They were after him in broad daylight. As he drove towards his house on the pond, he thought he might call the police on his cell phone, but decided against it—who would believe that two Catholic monks were trying to kidnap or murder a Catholic priest?

Steve fairly roared up 153, skidding on some of the turns and bouncing over the railroad tracks. He abruptly turned left at the row of mailboxes lined up on the main road for the residents of Pine River Pond. He swerved down the winding single lane road that led to the pond. It was just lucky that no one was coming in the opposite direction. Trees flew by on both sides. He had two miles to go. Looking through the rear view mirror, he could see the monks were still behind although they had lost ground. They had been sidetracked a few times on the winding unmarked road then had to back up.

Pulling the car into the driveway to his house, Steve jumped out and started running to the beach, his black chalice case under his arm. As he ran, he almost pulled up short asking himself why the panic? Why am I trying so hard to elude two monks I had already beaten that night at the monastery? He quickly recalled however, that at the monastery he had caught them by surprise in the dark. This time he knew it would be different. The monks would be taking no chances. It was foolhardy to think they wouldn't be equipped with weapons like blackjacks or brass knuckles. And after the incident on the pond the night before, he knew they would stop at nothing to capture him, beat him to a pulp, and if it suited them, even kill him.

Brothers Michael and John smiled at one another in the following car as they approached the driveway to Steve's house. At last, they had him. He would be trapped. There would be no escape by water because earlier that morning they had slipped onto the property. Finding Steve had already gone to the church, they disabled the throttle on the speedboat. For extra insurance, they had dropped a rock into the canoe, which chopped a splintered hole in the bottom. The rowboat was cut loose and the oars thrown far out where they floated away. The inflatables were punctured.

But as their car screeched to a stop, where was the priest?

"We better search the house," Brother Michael said. "And be careful because he may have a gun in there. This is hunting country after all."

The front door was locked, but picking up a stone, Brother Michael smashed one of the small glass panes so he could reach in and unlock it. After searching the entire house and the cellar, they could find no trace of the priest; however, Brother Michael noticed a shotgun on the mantle over the fireplace. In a nearby drawer he found the shells. It was double-barreled, an old model, but he slipped a shell in each chamber and snapped the barrel in place. "Only two shots, but it only takes one to cream this bastard," he said with a grin. "Then we'll tie a rock to his body and sink him somewhere along the shore where the water's deep."

Moving out to the shoreline, they relished the fact that their prey was in a panic to get away. They decided a slow deliberate stalk was in order. There was no need for hurry now. His car was blocked in. And even if Steve decided to swim, they would simply drive around the pond and wait for him. He couldn't stay in the water forever. Walking along the small beach with an almost leisurely stroll, the monks moved down to the boathouse to corner this errant priest who had eluded them for so long.

As they approached the boathouse, they were startled by a roar and a rush of wind as the bright red and white seaplane came to life and taxied out of the boathouse. Although the monks had come upon the seaplane earlier, they had no idea Steve was a pilot and even if he were, they assumed it took fifteen minutes or more of ground checks before anyone would risk taking off. Added to that, holing a canoe and cutting loose a rowboat were minor infractions, whereas a disabled seaplane might wind up killing innocent bystanders. But as they saw Steve taxi out, if they had it to do over, they would have sunk the damn thing.

In the months that Steve lived on the pond he had kept the plane ready to go, figuring that if the monks ever got on his track, they might disable the boats but either overlook the plane stored in the boathouse or assume he wasn't capable of flying it. Happily, the engine caught quickly, the propeller spun up and the plane taxied out. Looking out from the cockpit window, Steve smiled broadly at the monks standing on the shoreline. Brother John, who ran knee-deep into the water, showed his disgust by angrily kicking a spray of water into the air. Giving his pursuers a thumbs up, Steve taxied out of the cove and down almost a mile into the larger part of the pond. Swinging around, he aimed the seaplane straight down the middle of the pond and soared into the air above a speedboat pulling a water skier. The people in the boat waved at him as he flew over. The loons went crazy at the sound of the airplane. Loud wailing echoed across the pond from the birds on the nesting islands.

In a final gesture, Steve circled over his house and dipped his wings as he made a low pass over Brother John who was still standing in the shallow water. Brother Michael was nowhere in sight. Steve had an urge to scare hell out of the monks by zooming in low and scraping their heads with the pontoons but he couldn't risk it because of the high trees that bordered the cove. Then, suddenly a shot rang out—a heavy boom from a shotgun. He briefly glimpsed Brother Michael step out from behind a tree as he fired. As the monk quickly fired a second shot and began to reload, Steve decided it was time to leave. He gunned the engine and soared up into the sky. After he leveled off, from his cockpit seat he examined what he could of the plane and rechecked the instruments. All of the controls responded correctly. The shots had luckily missed.

Although he was filled with remorse at leaving his parishioners, in the months he had spent at Wakefield, Steve knew the day might come when he would need a getaway plan. His carefully laid plan was to fly to Vermont, abandon the plane, call his brother Jonathon to retrieve it and head west on a commercial flight far away from Archbishop Rhinehart and Brothers Michael and John. As he had told Janet, he liked the idea of going to Alaska—to the Aleutian Islands in particular. The remote outer islands might need a priest. He relished the thought of an island-hopping ministry in a seaplane. He recognized that a common thread ran through all his years of flying. It hadn't dawned on him right away. It had grown on him through the years. It wasn't his kind of flying unless it was in a seaplane—skimming over the water; then lifting onto the step and soaring up into the sky over beaches, cliffs, or tree-lined shores like a giant seabird in glorious flight.

*****

As the seaplane flew over his house on the pond, Steve's neighbor, Lew, who had stayed home from church that morning complaining of a cold, heard the roar and rushed out to see the plane heading west into the blue. Since he thought Father Steve was busy saying Mass in Wakefield, Lew thought the plane had been stolen. He called the local police not so much to report the theft but mainly to complain that seaplanes were illegal on the pond and when the hell were the police going to do something about it. He also complained about someone hunting on Sunday morning. But he knew it wasn't illegal, just another pain in the neck he had to put up with when he was trying to rest easy. He later regretted his call to the police because if the plane really was stolen, it would be good riddance.

*****

Henrietta heard the next day that their new priest had vanished after a ministry of only a few short months. Calling each of her women 'parishioners' in turn, she exulted in announcing that hereafter their Masses would not be held in one another's homes—no, they would say Mass in the newly refurbished St. Mary's Catholic

Church. She asked the women to spread the word and if anyone didn't like it, he or she could just drive over to Wolfeboro. Henrietta felt she had to remind them that when winter came, it could take two hours to get there on the icy roads and two hours to get home again. And for the faithful, the long trek had to be made not just for Sunday Mass, but also for Mass on Holy Days of Obligation, baptisms, weddings, confession and novenas. Henrietta's most compelling argument however, came in announcing that a revolution was in the making. After two thousand years of male domination in the Catholic Church, women were beginning to rise from the ranks of silent observers to meaningful positions in the church: altar girls, deaconesses, administrators responsible for finances and managers of parish operations. And now they had the grand opportunity to conduct the holy offices of the priesthood. They were on the path to Rome itself! What Henrietta failed to mention however, was that the same path led to excommunication from the Holy Roman Catholic Church.

*****

Old Mrs. Winters, housebound for a week because of her arthritis, hobbled slowly and painfully into her living room leaning on her cane. Looking down she saw two tiny scraps of paper on the rug—another opportunity to be close to Christ in the next world. As she bent over in almost an agony of knee and back pain, she plucked up the scraps saying, "Jesus, remember I do this for you." Then, as she fell back heavily into an overstuffed chair and laid her head back on a white doily covering the back of the chair, she exhaled a sigh of relief. She remembered how a few weeks before she had sent the letter to the diocese thanking the bishop for finally sending them a resident priest for St. Mary's Church. In her letter, she had extolled the virtues of Father Murphy, his caring attitude, his wonderful sermons, the hard work he did to re-establish the parish and refurbish the building. As she dozed off, Mrs. Winters was happy in the knowledge that her letter would certainly move the bishop to keeping St. Mary's as an active church with Father Murphy as its pastor.

29

His excellency, Archbishop Phillip Rhinehart, successor to the recently deceased Cardinal Wollman, was livid. Never in his forty years in the church had he ever seen such gross incompetence. He found it almost inconceivable that two Passion Brothers, presumably tough, dedicated and experienced in tracking down renegades could have let Reverend Steve Murphy slip through their fingers again.

"Brothers Michael and John are here, Your Excellency. Shall I show them in?"

"Please do, Mrs. McIntyre," the archbishop said as he flopped into the executive chair formerly occupied by Cardinal Wollman and began fingering and then bending a pencil until it snapped. "And, Mrs. McIntyre, please get me another box of pencils from supply."

The brothers, dressed in their gray monastic robes lumbered into the office meekly and with a rustle of their voluminous robes slipped into seats facing the archbishop's desk. They sat upright at attention. They knew they were on the carpet.

"I did not give you permission to sit down. Get up at once."

With nervous glances at one another, the brothers stood up. Squaring his shoulders, Brother John spoke, "Your Grace, we...".

"I don't want an explanation," the archbishop snapped. "I know precisely what happened. Because of your stupidity first in Tucson and now in New Hampshire, Murphy has escaped once more. His whereabouts are unknown. God knows how long it will take to find him and stop this ministry of Satan. You do understand, I suppose, that we have not been dealing with an authentic Catholic priest."

"Brother Michael was curious. "Are you saying, Your Excellency, that Murphy is an imposter?"

Leveling a disgusted look at the brother, the archbishop barked, "Yes, only much worse. I will not give you details, but this person is a serious threat to Holy Mother Church."

"Are you saying he's a heretic? His ministry is heretical?"

"I told you, Brother Michael, I will not provide details. You have been apprised of all you need to know."

"Permit me to explain, Your Excellency," Brother Michael said at the risk of being told to shut up. "He was a celebrant at a Mass we attended in New Hampshire. We received the Holy Eucharist from him. Are you saying the transubstantiation was invalid?"

"Are you saying you were inches away from him and yet you failed to apprehend him?"

"We did have him trapped later at his lakefront house, but he is resourceful. He...."

"Brother, as I said before, I want to hear no excuses. I don't want to know what you have to do to stop him, but he must be stopped. The devil has unleashed on this earth an enemy of the church. He is using Murphy as an accomplice to harm the souls of the faithful. We must not walk away from this. I am releasing both of you temporarily so you can return to your monastery in Arizona. However, I expect you to stand ready when we locate Murphy. You will be given one more chance," the archbishop said, thinking that if there were any others in the church willing to take on the task, he would have sent the brothers packing. "Bishop Hernandez and your immediate superior, Brother Berard, have been advised of the current state of affairs and have agreed to make both of you available immediately upon my call. Do you understand? If so, you may leave."

Brothers Michael and John, somewhat relieved about being given another chance, bent forward in deep bows as they slowly backed out of the archbishop's office. Just before closing the door, they said in unison: "Your Excellency, remember the Crucified Christ."

Archbishop Rhinehart did not respond. In his anger and disgust he chose not at that moment to remember the Crucified Christ—he much preferred the image in his mind of two Passion brothers hanging upside down on crosses after the manner of St. Peter's execution by the Romans.

30

The Reeve Aleutian Airways Boeing 737 touched down at the airport serving Unalaska/Dutch Harbor on Unalaska Island. The flight from Anchorage had hopped down the Aleutian Island chain dropping off and picking up passengers at Kodiak and Unimak Islands as it worked its way west along the Aleutian archipelago that stretched from the Alaskan peninsula over towards Japan and Asia. The landing at Unalaska completed the eight-hundred mile flight for Steve. The flight had been turbulent as Steve knew flights typically were when they alternately flew across land and water. He would soon learn that the area around the outer Aleutians was known as the Cradle of Storms because it was here in these bleak treeless islands that the warmer waters from the south—the Japan current, met the cold waters of the Bering Sea to the north. The mixing of warm air and water from the south with cold in the north produces enormous amounts of rain and fog, making air travel uncertain and necessitating close attention to weather forecasts. Steve, an experienced pilot, sensed that flying in the mountainous and windswept Aleutians would be challenging and dangerous. On the other hand, the soaring snowcapped mountains and deep green valleys on the islands were a spectacular sight that filled him with awe, fully compensating for the piloting difficulties.

On the shuttle in from the Unalaska airport, Steve

noted that the tiny settlement of Dutch Harbor was no more than an enclave stretching along the shoreline with a backdrop of high rocky snow-capped mountains, one of which he was told, harbored an active volcano.

By the time he walked into the Dutch Inn, Steve was chilled to the bone. It was late in the year and the damp freezing air contained a few snowflakes— the seeds of an approaching snowstorm. The inn, one of the few public lodgings in the little seaside frontier town was actually a small well-appointed, modern hotel. After checking in, Steve sat at a table in the corner of the near-empty dining room where he had a view across the parking lot of the only supermarket in Dutch Harbor. The waitress told him the supermarket, built as part of a mini-mall, was a recent and welcome addition to the town. Before that, the inhabitants had to contend with a few small stores scattered around the island.

At dinner, he was told the current chef specialized exclusively in seafood. He had a choice of king crab, salmon or halibut, delivered fresh from a local fishery on the island. When he inquired about other menu offerings, he was informed politely but firmly that he could have steaks, chops, Chinese or Italian food—but he would have to go over to the Harbor Restaurant if he wanted anything other than the hotel's catch-of-the-day menu offerings. Glancing out the window at the snow that was beginning to fall in a steady shower, he chose the salmon.

Steve stared out the window at the swirling snow. He watched several bundled people hurrying into the supermarket opposite. He questioned why he had come to the Aleutian Islands when the islands of Hawaii would have been vastly more pleasant. On the other hand, the foggy and sometimes snowy seascape was ideal for contemplation, prayer and hopefully a ministry. And he needed someplace remote, far from Washington and Archbishop Rhinehart and the religious thugs, Brothers Michael and John. He was still perplexed that two Catholic monks living in modern times had actually tried to kidnap or kill him. If the incident had occurred during the Italian Renaissance or the years of the Spanish Inquisition he might have believed it, but hadn't the church long since abandoned such methods? He doubted the monks had been told the whole story—about his being a clone and worse than that a chimera. Archbishop Rhinehart would have kept that potential scandal a secret limited to a few of the hierarchy of the church. Steve surmised that the brothers, in their zeal to please their superiors, had been blindly following orders and if those orders meant kidnapping or even killing, so be it. The Commandment: Thou Shalt Not Kill, was not an impediment to what needed to be done. The monks knew they could be absolved of a serious sin in the confessional, but their superiors' displeasure if they failed, would remain with them for the rest of their lives.

While he was at the monastery in Arizona, Steve had tried to rationalize excuses for the brothers when they beat a number of priests which led to the death of some priests. He could understand the sheer frustration and anger they must have felt towards the derelict priests housed there. But he, Steve, had done nothing to deserve such punishment. He was aware that the brothers could be seeking revenge for that night at the monastery when he gave them a beating in a fair fight. He recognized that because he refused to quit the priesthood, the bishops could well have been playing on the brothers' need for revenge. It would suit the bishops' objective: to forcibly eliminate him from the ranks of the Catholic clergy. And if that failed, and if convinced that he was merely a subhuman chimera, to forcibly remove him from the ranks of the living.

But sitting here alone in Dutch Harbor, a thousand miles from nowhere, Steve sensed that something else was troubling him. Reared on a heavy ration of Catholic guilt, might his going to the Aleutians represent a way of helping him punish himself? Did the guilt also stem from falling in love with Janet? As he sipped his after-dinner coffee, he thought grimly that the cold Aleutian Islands would help chill that relationship. On the other hand, maybe the guilt came from his hardheaded notion that he intended to continue his ministry as a priest, defying the hierarchy of his church, when others in the same situation would have succumbed to the wishes of Holy Mother Church. One thing was certain—living in the Aleutian Islands in the middle of winter was an excellent way to do penance. Penance—the pain suffered in the name of Christ that washes away guilt and sin and opens the door to paradise.

Steve considered it likely that many Aleuts and others, isolated on a string of tiny islands, could benefit by visitations of a priest. But he wondered if there would be a welcome mat for a Catholic priest who would fly into a little village unannounced to talk to them about someone they may never have heard of: Jesus.

After dinner, he read his breviary in his room and knelt by his bedside to say evening prayers. As he lay in bed, dimly aware of the throbbing music coming from the inn's cocktail lounge, he lit a cigarette. Alone and anxious about the future, he needed the crutch it offered. He went over the outline of a plan in his head: in a few weeks, rent an apartment or a small house; lease a plane that could be equipped alternately with skis and pontoons; start hopping to nearby islands that perhaps had church facilities but no priest and begin a ministry among the Aleuts and others who were perhaps Christian or possible converts to the Catholic faith. He would discover later his plan had a few flaws that were difficult but not fatal—notably that the Roman Catholic religion came into fairly sharp conflict with Russian Orthodoxy which had been established hundreds of years before as settlers came from the Siberian mainland to the islands, a faith that was deeply entrenched in the minds and hearts of many of the locals. Then there were the remnants of shamanism, especially among the older generation, and there might have been protestant religions that had touched some of the islands. So the principal difficulty might not be in bringing religion to the island people, but rather in convincing them to convert.

*****

The next morning Steve set out in six inches of snow against a biting wind to visit Dutch Harbor's most famous landmark, the Russian Orthodox Church of the Holy Ascension that stood on a small bluff overlooking the harbor with its cold, gray churning sea. Steve wore his black suit with Roman collar. Over it he wore a newly purchased parka with fur-lined hood and calf-high rubber boots. In the reflection in a window of a store he passed, he thought he looked like an Arctic explorer. The bleak, windswept harbor, teeming with small fishing vessels, smelled of fish. He saw an American President Lines container ship docked across the bay. He couldn't tell whether it was bringing supplies to the island or loading to carry away the island's principal export: fish from the local canneries.

He had dressed as a priest because he wanted to be identified easily as such with whomever he would meet at the church. The small cemetery in the churchyard was filled with wooden white Russian crosses—easily identified by the short extra slanted bar below the horizontal cross bar. He knew that the lower bar was an added touch of Russian orthodoxy, representing Christ's foot-rest on the Cross. Implanted gravestones on some of the graves showed they were ancient, dating back to the early 1800s. As Steve walked through the cemetery, he looked up to see a dark green, cross-topped onion dome on the bell tower and another on the main body of the church, each capped with a layer of snow. From an earlier visit to Russia, he had learned the onion domes represent the flames of candles with their pointed tips soaring to heaven. A reminder perhaps that all things holy eventually rise to heaven. On mounting the front step, he read the inscription on the brass plate at the door: Church of the Holy Ascension, 1890, National Historic Landmark.

Stepping inside, he glanced around looking to bless himself until he remembered that unlike Roman

Catholic churches, the Russian churches had no holy water font. He knelt to say a few prayers on the floor of the church in front of the richly decorated iconostasis. He was alone in the church. The iconostasis, a wall of gold-framed icons, had large gold-painted scrolled doors behind which the celebrant would conduct the service. Steve gazed up at the colorful banners, golden icons of Christ, the Blessed Virgin and biblical figures that decorated the wall in front of him. The iconostasis was fronted by an elaborately carved white wooden railing. After the manner of Russian churches, there were no pews. The small, quaint wooden church—Dutch Harbor's cathedral, struck him as a far cry from the huge granite and stained glass edifices he had seen in cities like New York, Washington and Rome, but he supposed this small church was all that a frontier town needed and all it could afford.

As Steve got to his feet intending to look at the side chapels, he was startled when he literally bumped into a short stocky priest who had come into the church and remained silently standing behind him.

"Forgive me for startling you, my name is Sergius. I am the pastor here.

"My name is Steve Murphy. I'm a Catholic priest. Roman Catholic."

"Welcome to our humble church. I suppose I should tell you I took the name Sergius in the seminary—after the patron saint of Russia. Are you new in Dutch Harbor? I haven't seen you before."

"Yes, I just arrived."

"Since this is your first visit, let me show you our chapel dedicated to Saint Sergius."

Steve followed the short, stocky priest who, dressed in a black cassock had a shock of jet black hair, plopped atop a round face that held smiling black eyes—an appearance that seemed to combine Russian, Aleut and perhaps some Eskimo.

"Do you know anything about the Russian Church, Father Murphy?"

"A little. Not much really. I have visited orthodox churches in Russia."

"Our first church was built in 1826. This is the third church on this site. There are over one million Russian Orthodox in the U.S. About thirty years ago, the largest of the jurisdictions, the Russian Orthodox Church in America was given independent status by the Patriarch of Moscow. Our metropolitan who is the equivalent of say, one of your archbishops or cardinals, resides in Anchorage. So, although we are a 'Russian' church, we're not really tied to Russia any longer."

"And your parishioners?"

"Almost all Aleut."

As Steve studied the golden icon-covered wall in the side chapel devoted to Saint Sergius, he was reminded of a visit he once made to the Trinity Monastery of Blessed Sergius located in the town of Zagorsk, north of Moscow. "The body of the saint is preserved under glass in one of the churches inside the walls of the monastery," he said. Then, glancing at the Russian priest, he asked, "Ever been there?"

"No. Some day perhaps." Upon saying it, the Russian priest clasped his hands together and with a wide smile raised his eyes to heaven as if asking for the favor.

"By the way, Father Sergius, do you mind my

asking—the Roman Catholic clergy are celibate—are you in the Russian church celibate?"

"Yes. But as you know, some of the eastern rite churches permit priests to marry. Permit me a little joke I always tell: Since there are not too many women here in the Aleutians, it is not all that difficult being celibate."

"By the way, how bad does the weather get here? It started snowing soon after the plane landed at Unalaska."

"Not bad, actually. It's surprisingly mild compared to the Yukon and northern Alaska territories. I suppose it's because of the warm Japanese current. By the way, please call me Sergei."

"And you can call me Steve."

As the pair of priests stood, heads bowed, saying a few prayers in the side chapel, Steve had to think that the Russian priest's notion of mild weather was not in a category a lot of people would think of as mild. The cold, dank air and the wind had cut through him like a knife when he walked from the hotel to the church.

As they left the chapel, and walked to the outer lobby of the church, the Russian priest turned, bowed in the direction of the sanctuary and made the two-finger Russian Sign of the Cross. The two priests lingered in the lobby as Steve pulled on his boots and began to put on his parka. "By the way, Steve, where are you staying?"

"At the Dutch Inn."

"Planning a short or long visit?"

"Long. I plan to live here permanently. Make it my home. I'm planning to buy a plane and begin a ministry in the outer islands. I won't be spending a lot of time in Dutch Harbor, but I do need sort of a base of operations if you'd call it that."

"Let me insist that you stay here at the Bishop's House. It's the building over there next to the church. It's a historic building, kind of a museum, but it does have some private quarters. If you agree, I'll have a room made ready for you. You'll find it much more affordable than the hotel because the lodging is complimentary. All I ask is that you make a small contribution for the food served in the refectory. And frankly, since I am the only priest assigned here, I could use some company."

"Thanks, I appreciate the offer," Steve replied hesitantly. He wasn't sure he wanted to live in such close quarters with another priest. He was afraid of the questions that would surely arise. Where was his ministry in the lower forty-eight? Why did he come to the Aleutians? Had he been assigned here by his bishop? Was he now attached to the Roman Catholic bishopric in Anchorage?

On and on....

"I did look through the local newspaper and the bulletin board at the new mall and didn't see a single thing to rent," Steve said. "But let me ask, you call it the Bishop's House. Do you have a bishop here?"

"Oh no. Our archbishop, who as I said, we call the 'metropolitan' resides in Anchorage. As I said, I am the only one here on a permanent basis. And we have a housekeeper, of course."

"How often does the metropolitan visit?" Steve asked, unable to conceal a trace of nervousness in his voice."

Noticing his discomfort, Sergei was given to wonder but made no direct comment. "Not often. He's scared to death of volcanoes and as you know, the Aleutian chain has upwards of eighty active volcanoes. The chain is recognized as part of the Ring of Fire that extends all the way over to Japan. The metropolitan paid a visit just a few months ago after we completed renovation of the church. Since he is responsible for all of Alaska, I expect he won't be back again for a couple of years."

Steve smiled. A look of relief came over his face. The Russian priest's eyes widened. His mind raced with a dozen questions but he was too polite to say anything. He would wait until his fellow priest was ready to confide in him, if ever.

"I really do appreciate the offer," Steve said, "but let me think about it for a few weeks. I am booked for a month at the Dutch Inn. They gave me a monthly rate. I wouldn't want to let them down. They seem to be pretty empty."

"Yes, Dutch Harbor doesn't get many visitors this time of year. There are some ski parties however. The skiing is quite good on surrounding mountains, but for some reason it is not well advertised."

Steve buttoned his parka, shook hands with Sergei, and braced himself for the biting cold as he left the church.

The Russian priest walked back to a table in the lobby of the cathedral where he straightened up a stack of picture postcards of the cathedral and its inner chapels. At a dollar each, the postcards did not sell very well, although he noticed that Father Murphy had picked up a couple and had left a twenty dollar bill on the table.

Sergei couldn't put his finger on it, but there was something about Father Murphy that he liked and he welcomed the idea of having another priest living in the Bishop's House. The fact that Father Murphy was a Roman Catholic and thus a competitor, didn't bother him. Naturally, he had questions but he was not overly concerned about Father Murphy's background. It would all be sorted out in due time, he thought philosophically. All in due time.

31

"Father, let me ask you, why do you want such a big airplane? You know the Twin Otter can carry upwards of 16 passengers. You going into the air taxi or charter service? If you are, there's licenses you're gonna need. You can't just lease an airplane from us and start operating." The speaker, a very tall skinny former used-car dealer from Phoenix stood on the dock shivering and wondering why he had ever left the warm sun. He shook his head as he looked at this priest who seemed to be completely unaware of flying in Alaska, if in fact he had ever done much flying anywhere. Although the dealer's name was Henry, he had picked up the name Totem because he was a beanpole, stiff as wood, with an angular face that looked carved and a round bald head sticking partway out of the top of his parka. Although he would have been a lot warmer with a hat, he didn't like hats because they kept sliding off his shiny dome.

"Added to that, Father," Totem said, "there's already a number of air charter and air taxi outfits operating on the Alaska peninsula and out in the Aleutians. And every third guy is a bush pilot. They've been in business a long time. How do you know you'd get any business?"

"I'm not looking for business—at least not the kind you're referring to," Steve said as he stood on the dock at Juneau staring up at the DeHavilland Twin Otter 100

Series as it rocked gracefully on its floats. He liked the sleek look of the dark blue aircraft with the red and white stripe running down the length of the fuselage and the two streamlined turboprop engines. He knew the Otter was a rugged airplane that had short takeoff and landing capability. It would come in handy visiting some of the tiny villages scattered throughout the Aleutians. And most importantly, since the Aleutians comprised over 200 islands, he would be flying over a cold ocean much of the time and if one engine went out, the Otter could bring him home on the other one. In his curiosity about the plane, Steve ignored the dealer's questions.

"What cruise speed and what range will it get, Mr. Totem?"

"It ain't Mr. Totem, Father. It's just Totem. It's a nickname. In Phoenix they called me Saguaro—like the tall cactus. Here it's Totem. Well anyway, that plane will do maybe 150 to 160 miles an hour and probably 500 to 600 miles range with a full load. Empty, you can probably stretch it to 900 miles, give or take. But you didn't answer my question."

"Can you outfit it with a commercial airline type lavatory by taking some seats out in the rear of the fuselage? And can some seats be removed to make room for a bedroll?"

"It'll cost, but yes, we can do it. Of course, you'd have to pay to have the toilet taken out again and the seats replaced after the lease is up. New people may want the extra seat capacity and no toilet. But listen here, you still didn't answer my question."

"I'm not going into the charter business, Totem. I

already have a job, I'm a priest. But to answer your question—I intend to visit a number of small villages in the outer islands and if I'm out somewhere and the weather turns bad I may wind up sleeping in the plane."

"If you do, bring plenty of blankets because you'll freeze with the power off. Well if you like to fly, you came to the right place because I guess you've noticed when you get away from the big cities in Alaska there aren't many roads. And especially in the Aleutians—it ain't like the Florida Keys—these islands aren't connected by causeways." As Totem talked, he reached down and grabbed one of the heavy duty pontoon struts giving it a shake. "This is a lot of airplane, Father. Got a copilot in mind?"

Steve laughed and pointed an index finger skyward.

"I see...the man upstairs is your copilot," Totem said, trying somewhat uncertainly to join Steve in the laugh.

"But seriously," Steve said. "I have an instrument rating, 1,600 hours total flying time—most of the hours on floatplanes. I was part owner of one. Also, a current commercial license, plus 310 hours multi-engine, so other than the fact that the Otter has two turboprops rather than piston engines, I'm sure I'll be able to handle it after a couple of check rides. Now let me ask you a couple of questions. How old is the plane? It's a 100 series so they didn't manufacture it last Wednesday. And how many hours on the engines?"

"The airplane's twelve years old," Totem said, now quite a bit more impressed with the priest. "The turboprops are brand spanking new. No more than ten hours on them. The plane also comes with a pair of skiis. You may find them handy if you land on a strip covered with packed snow. You take off the pontoons and install the skis before you leave home base. Store the pontoons in brackets under the wings. But taking off the pontoons is a two-man job so you'll have to grab someone to help you. However, since you'll be hitting the islands, you'll most likely be using the pontoons landing in a bay here and there. You'll soon be able to spot where the coves are located. Unless we get a real bad winter, the water around the islands doesn't freeze up. We fitted this bird out with new heavy duty wheels and tires. So let's say you land on the water and if there's a beach, you can taxi right up onto land, as long as it ain't too steep and as long as there's not a lot of snow. You won't find many airplanes got that kind of power where they can haulass themselves right out of the goddamn water."

Climbing into the pilot's seat, Steve was happy to see the Otter had a full avionics package including GPS navigation, transponder, communications gear, and heading and altitude autopilot. "Plane can just about fly itself," he said looking at Totem with a smile.

As the pair walked into the office to sign the leasing papers, Totem took a sidelong glance at Steve. "You getting paid by the church to rent this plane?"

"No. I'm doing this on my own."

"Then you must be one helluva rich son of a bitch... forgive me Father, I keep forgetting I'm talking to a man of the cloth."

"That's OK, I've been called lots worse than that."

"And Jesus Christ, sorry, slipped again, you gotta watch that weather around the outer islands. It can be a nice sunny day and then you can get socked in in twenty minutes. The saying is...."

"Yes, I know the saying: 'If you don't like the weather, wait twenty minutes and it will change.'"

*****

Three weeks later, Steve was back in Juneau sitting in the cockpit in the right seat next to Totem. "I want to be in the pilot's seat," Steve said.

"No you don't, Father. On the first flight, I do the piloting."

Steve was impressed with the short powerful takeoff over the water and steep climbout. As Totem leveled the plane and circled, Steve looked down at the small city of Juneau nestled at the edge of the water in the inland waterway at the base of surrounding mountains. A large white cruise ship was gliding into a dock on the outskirts of the small city down near a salmon hatchery.

"You know, Father, I'm sure you're aware that Juneau's the capital of Alaska, but it's a downright curious situation, because Juneau can't be reached coming in by land. You gotta come in by water or air. It's a strange little city and how it ever got to be the capital of Alaska, beats me."

"Maybe the governor doesn't want a lot of drop-in visitors," Steve suggested. "When you consider that the governor's constituents have to fly in or come in on a ship, he can probably sit here and get a lot of paperwork done."

"The governor's a she by the way. Yeah, nice theory, Father, but the governor spends very little time here. From what I understand, the country is run from Anchorage."

*****

A few hours later, in Juneau's tourist 'Mecca', the Red Dog Saloon, made famous by the writer, Jack London, Steve and Totem had a beer while Steve marveled at the tons of colorful paraphernalia hanging from the ceiling. "I like that fake bear up near the top of that pole," He said.

"That's no fake," Totem answered. Of course, he's dead and stuffed, but he's Goddamn real...pardon me again, Father."

"Call me Steve, will you?" Steve was somewhat surprised at seeing a Washington Redskins football game on several TVs around the saloon. It made him think momentarily of Archbishop Rhinehart in Washington, but he quickly doused the thought with another beer.

After a few beers, standing outside of the Red Dog, the pair had their picture taken with a camera Totem handed to a passerby. Although Steve at six-two was not short by any means, next to his new-found friend, he felt like a kid looking up at a totem pole that towered above him.

*****

In the following days, after four check rides with Totem and a stack of paperwork, Steve had been adjudged competent to fly the aircraft and capable of paying for the lease. On the final day, Totem stood on the dock and watched Steve take off as the Otter sprayed twin white rooster tails from the pontoons and roared up into the sunshine above the surrounding mountains.

On the flight from Juneau, Steve headed west following the coastline to Seward where he put down to refuel. After a short stop, he headed southwest down the Kenai Peninsula then over the western part of the Gulf of Alaska to Kodiak Island. He flew low over Kodiak to watch the massive brown Kodiak bears fishing for salmon in the streams. Turning west, he climbed to 6,000 feet and saw in the distance across the water the Katmai National Monument with its soaring Katmai volcano and the Valley of Ten Thousand Smokes. His zig-zag route then took him southwest again along the Alaska Peninsula and finally out along the Aleutian Island chain. Crossing the islands, he flew at 5,000 feet, barely skimming the tops of several snowcapped volcanic mountains. He remembered that Father Sergius had told him that this portion of Alaska was referred to as the Ring of Fire—having as many as 80 volcanoes, almost 50 of which are still considered active. The steam coming from the cinder cones pinpointed the active volcanoes which he kept at far distance. He was aware that the amount of oxygen near these volcanoes was so low, he would risk flaming out the turbines if he flew too close.

As the plane crossed the Aleutian Island chain, Steve marveled at the spectacular islands, some shaped like huge snowcapped rocks that although treeless, were covered with reddish brown tundra in the valleys. In summer they would be green again and covered with flowers.

Over Unalaska Island under clear skies, Steve approached the airport, then changed his mind and headed to the Dutch Harbor coastline. Descending to the cold choppy sea, after two attempts, he brought the Otter in for a landing that was anything but smooth and taxied to the dock at the water's edge in front of the Russian Church. Father Sergius ran down from the church and secured a line from the aircraft to the dock as Steve hopped out. When they were satisfied the plane was properly lashed to the dock, the two priests walked back up towards the church. "Steve, you've been at the inn for almost a month and I assume you haven't been able to locate a place to rent so why not move into the Bishop's House. I have a room ready for you."

Steve, in a lighthearted mood because of a successful flight back from Juneau with his new plane, replied laughingly: "I was planning to live on the plane."

"Good heavens, how can you live on a plane?"

"Well, it's true I only have limited cooking facilities and no shower but, Sergei, it's got everything else."

"Heat?"

"No heat. Just warm blankets."

"Sorry, my friend, but I suggest you move to the Bishop's House where we can give you three hot meals and a private room with a warm bed."

*****

That same evening, Steve moved his belongings over to the Bishop's House. He was introduced to the housekeeper, a dark-eyed, olive-skinned Aleut woman named Kapa, who smiled as she bade him welcome. With traces of gray in her long black hair, she appeared to Steve to be a woman in her late forties or early fifties. As if to answer an unspoken question in his eyes, she said: "No, I'm not Russian Orthodox and I'm not in one of those other Christian religions."

"What do you believe in, if I may ask?"

The woman set down a cup of tea for Father Sergius and one for the new priest. "I believe," she said warily, "in something that Father Sergius does not approve of." As Kapa said the words, she glanced with a smirk at the young Russian priest who shrugged slightly as he sipped his tea. "She's a shamanist," he said.

"I've heard of it," Steve said, "but I don't know anything about it. Is there a shaman church in town?"

Kapa rolled her eyes toward the ceiling. Sergei gave a short mirthless laugh. "They don't worship in churches. It's a kind of magic religion, although many people don't really think of it as a religion at all. The shaman usually shows up when a believer is sick or possessed by demons from below. If they recover, he gets the credit. He is very much respected by native people but when things go sour like really bad weather or widespread disease, he takes all the blame."

"And he heals the sick," Kapa interrupted. "I have seen this done many times. Something your big city doctors don't always do even though they make you spend thousands of dollars on X-rays and pills." Kapa left the room, apparently unwilling to discuss it further.

"Steve, I don't know a lot about shamanism, but I do know it's something you'll have to contend with if you plan to visit out-of-the-way villages. It's practiced almost completely in small older settlements that haven't been exposed to anything much in the way of formal religious training or even much regular schooling. The shamanists believe that a shaman has magical powers resulting from out-of-body experiences or visions that have taken him before gods and demons. It's impressive to see a shaman performing his ritual—he'll go into a trance—a state of ecstasy as he clicks a handful of old bones."

"My God, it sounds like a kind of voodoo," Steve said in dismay.

"There are similarities," Sergei said nodding. "And incidentally, shamanism is not restricted to Alaska—there are variations of shamanism throughout the world. But it is powerful here. Some believe the penetrating cold of Alaska helps the shaman enter the state of ecstasy."

"On another subject," Steve said, "where can I say morning Mass?"

"Not in the St. Sergius chapel I'm afraid, and not in the main body of the church, but you are welcome to use a small chapel over on the left side. I'll show you where to set up in the morning. Do you have everything you'll need for a Catholic Mass? If not, I can't help you. In the centuries since the two churches split apart, the services and vestments have become completely different."

"I have everything I need," Steve said. "I'm carrying a portable altar and I found some used vestments in a shop in Juneau." While sipping his coffee, he fumbled in his pocket for a cigarette. "OK if I smoke?"

"Sorry, but there's no smoking in this old wooden building. Remember it's a National Historic building. You'll have to step outside to smoke while you live here."

Steve thought about the biting wind and dampness

coming from the sea, just a few yards from the house. It wouldn't be much fun lighting up in those conditions. He wondered if at last, now might be the time to quit.

*****

On the following morning, Steve arose early and accompanied Father Sergius to the church yard where they each said a brief prayer at the grave of canonized Saint Innocent, a Russian missionary who built the first Russian Orthodox church at Dutch Harbor shortly after arriving in 1824. The primitive original church was later succeeded by another church; still later, the third and current church had been built over a hundred years before. Steve's first Mass in a tiny side chapel may well have been the first Catholic Mass in a Russian Orthodox Church. In saying Mass there he felt he probably broke half a dozen Canon Laws, but excused himself by acknowledging that it was the only place available that he knew of. He said the Mass alone without a congregation and without a server to assist him.

After finishing Mass, Steve went to the dock to examine his new airplane. He was so engrossed and so pleased with the plane as he sat in the cockpit playing with the controls, he was able to suppress any guilt that might have stemmed from his fervor over a material object. Later, standing on one of the pontoons, he reached up and poured a small vial of sea water that he had blessed onto the nose of the fuselage. Then he stepped over to the dock and turning, made the Sign of the Cross blessing the airplane. Like a pair of newly blessed rosary beads, the plane now had been touched by the hand of God.

*****

"I assume you've heard of the Ecumenical Movement," Steve said to Sergei as they sat waiting to order dinner in the Dutch Inn. "It seems that you and I, especially you, are making more of an attempt than most to help the movement." As the thought came to mind, Steve couldn't help grinning.

"In what way?"

"Since the movement has the object of bringing the Christian religions back together again, reversing the rift that occurred centuries ago, your permitting me to say a Catholic Mass in a Russian Orthodox Church is a real step in that direction."

Sergei laughed. "Perhaps, but I still think your bishops and my metropolitan might not like our interpretation of Ecumenism. I believe they're seeking higher levels of doctrinal agreement than simply borrowing one another's churches."

"Remember Vatican Two?" Steve asked as he put down the menu and ordered the baked halibut. Sergei ordered snow-crab.

"Steve, that was quite a few years ago. I'm not old enough to remember it, but of course I've read about it."

"I was only a kid myself," Steve replied, "but I recall seeing a movie-house newsreel of hundreds of Catholic cardinals and bishops from all over the world and all races gathered in Rome, together with bishops from the Greek Orthodox and Russian Orthodox churches. It was the landmark of the century. I recall the words of John XXIII who referred to the Council as letting a little fresh air into the church."

"Yes, I read that the Russian Orthodox Metropolitans attended. They later wrote about the splendor of it all in Rome. It's a shame, it all fell apart."

"How do you mean?" Steve asked, somewhat surprised. "I believe it brought about some lasting changes in the Catholic Church."

"Well, let's say it was a real step forward for Catholics, I mean as far as updating the liturgy; for example, having the priest face the people during Mass and conducting Mass in local languages instead of Latin. But from an Ecumenical standpoint, it didn't go over so well. Don't you recall, Steve, that one objective of the Council was to urge all Christian religions to come together but, and this is a big but...under the roof of the Catholic Church. The message seemed to be: You are welcome but you will have to be subject to our pope, our papal authority. I suppose you understand that Rome's position didn't sit very well with the non-Catholic Christians."

"You're right, of course," Steve agreed with a conciliatory shrug. "And as you mentioned, the real gain that has endured after Vatican Two came in adopting the new liturgy for the Mass, even though that was an entirely unexpected result. It's strange, but if you had asked some of the bishops before the Council was held if the Mass would ever change, they would have laughed you out of the room. Then came Vatican Two."

"Face it, Steve, however well-intentioned Vatican Two was, Ecumenism has not prospered under the popes who came after John. They've been ultra-conservative. The other churches have been scared away. For instance, the popes have permitted only a token involvement of women in the church. No chance for women to attain the priesthood."

"Wait a minute, my friend," Steve said as he dug around in his baked potato. "I don't recall ever seeing a woman priest in the Russian Orthodox Church either here in America or in Russia."

"True enough, but our situation is different. We never tempted the laity into thinking things would change. Our laity, although not completely satisfied perhaps, have never expected the Russian Church to change anything, not even the simple traditions. For instance in the way we make the Sign of the Cross, which I'm sure you think is backwards. We accept longstanding tradition. The difficulty that arose with some of the more liberal Catholics is what I call the anger of rising expectations...expectations that result in frustration and anger when they're not fulfilled. Vatican Two set the stage for these expectations— supposedly opening the windows for change. But the basic dogma did not change. A divorced Catholic could still not remarry. Even some liberal Catholic theologians, tempted by Vatican Two, began openly questioning the church's position on birth control, divorce and married clergy. But the church clamped down hard in the years since Vatican Two, and today, if liberal theologians become outspoken enough, they aren't allowed to teach and may even be excommunicated. A priest can have his ministry restricted. What I'm saying is that a lot of Catholics were led down the rosy path by Vatican

Two—expecting fundamental changes, but the only changes that were allowed to stand were for the most part just window dressing."

Steve slowly ate the last bit of halibut on his plate. He recognized some truth in what Sergei was saying, but he wanted to avoid an argument with his new friend. "This is far and away the best seafood I've ever tasted," he said, trying to steer the conversation away from an argument.

"That fish you're eating was swimming in the ocean just a few hours ago," Sergei said as he finished the last of his crab. "Excellent seafood must seem to you to be one of the few redeeming features of living in this outpost of civilization. However, let me clarify— to you, it is surely an outpost, but to me it is the center of my world."

"Sergei, you speak of the frustration of liberal-thinking Catholics," Steve said, finding he was too engrossed in the subject to let it drop. "But it's more widespread than Vatican Two. American women down in the lower 48 see female rabbis, women ministers. Why not, they ask, women priests? This is not just an expectation that arose from Vatican Two. Modern women want equal rights with men."

"Do you think changes like this will ever come to the Catholic Church, Steve?"

"I doubt it, my friend. I read once about a Catholic theologian who made a comment something along these lines: A thousand years from now, the Catholic Church will still regard abortion as murder, birth control as a grave sin and married priests or women priests an abomination."

"Do you agree that this stand is right, Steve?"

"My friend, permit me to duck the question. I'm a priest and the issue for me is not whether I think these things are right or wrong. They are the pronouncements of the holy father in Rome. They represent the official position of Holy Mother Church. I accept them and am bound by my vows to preach them to all who will listen."

"Don't you think your position may be a copout?"

"No. You refer to it as my 'position'. I prefer to think of it as faith and to a large extent as obedience. Sergei, I could ask the same questions of you. Why are you grilling me?"

Sergei took a sip of wine and looked levelly into Steve's eyes. "I apologize, Steve. You're right. You could have just as easily grilled me on the same subjects. I confess to an ulterior motive. You appeared out of nowhere. Yes, you had all the accoutrements of Catholic clergy, but no formal mission, no referrals, no diocesan attachments. I was merely probing to find out whether you really are a Catholic priest."

"Well, what do you think? Do you want to see the Imprimatur stamped on my chest?" Steve laughed.

"Some other time. Let's get back to the house. You have to be up early tomorrow morning to say Mass."

32

The Otter climbed swiftly up from the smooth blue sea in the crisp morning air. Steve marveled at the weather. The day was far more like an Arizona day than one in the Aleutian Islands. His eye traced blue sky in all directions out to the horizon. Not a cloud in sight. A perfect day for flying. As he reached cruise altitude, he throttled back to cruise speed and leveled off at 7,000 feet—an altitude that would allow him to easily clear the ring of snowcapped mountains. Far below he could see the town of Unalaska and its neighbor, the teaming seaport of Dutch Harbor, and the famous landmark— the Russian Church with its onion-shaped cupolas standing near the water's edge.

He relaxed in the cockpit at the thought of a good flight to the outer islands. But a few minutes later, as he crossed the nearest mountains, the plane began pitching violently. Mountain updraft? Not likely, since he was well clear of the mountains. Clear air turbulence? Something wrong with the controls? He hadn't flown the Otter more than a few times and perhaps there was some glitch he had overlooked in the control system. The plane began to roll. He struggled to keep the wings level and cut back on power to avoid descending into a spin. Damn that used car salesman—could he be pulling some kind of deception on rented airplanes? Had the Otter really been properly maintained? Suddenly he was socked in. A dark gray menacing turbulent cloud had come out of nowhere. In a moment he was on full instrument flight. Rain droplets pinged on the windshield. He bounced around in the cockpit. Airspeed 150, altitude 3,000 feet. Couldn't be! He had dropped four thousand feet in a few seconds? What was wrong? Was the altimeter faulty or was this crate falling apart? Then the controls became heavy. He was in a dive. He struggled with all the strength in his arms to pull up. Leveling off, with airspeed dropping, he tried to apply power to keep from stalling but the throttle felt like lead. Everything was going haywire. He shouted 'Mayday' over the radio to the tower at Unalaska.

As he struggled to regain control of the airplane, Steve sensed in the near darkness of the cockpit that someone was seated in the copilot spot on his right. How could that be? Where in hell did the guy come from? Unnoticed and hidden in the back of the plane before he took off? He glanced over, it was Brother Michael. Where was Brother John? Right behind him in the cockpit, ready to clobber him? The plane went into another steep dive as Steve struggled to pull out. Brother Michael was fighting him at the controls. Every move Steve made was counteracted by the monk. Was that idiot trying to kill them? Steve felt an arm tighten around his neck. A glance over his shoulder told him it was Brother John choking him in an arm-lock from behind. The altimeter spun crazily down. The sea was a blue wall rushing towards the plane. Just before the boom, Steve had one passing wry thought: he would die but Brother Berard's thugs were going to buy the farm too.

He felt himself slamming down against something hard. He hit the floor, bed clothes in a jumbled pile on top of him. A blanket wrapped tightly around his neck. There was a loud knock on the door. "Steve, are you all right?"

He got up stiffly and stumbled groggily to the door. His pajamas, soaking wet, were twisted around him; hair tousled; eyes half-open; mouth drooping. Opening the door, he saw Sergei, wide-eyed, obviously concerned. "Steve, what's going on? This is the third time in the few weeks you've been here that I've wakened to hear you thrashing like you were in some kind of monumental struggle. Come down to the kitchen. Let me heat up some coffee. Maybe you should see a doctor, or at least, come down and let's talk about it."

In the kitchen, Steve peered out a window. It was dark outside. There was the Otter—barely visible in the light streaming from the house—floating silently at the dock. He was safe. His airplane was safe.

Sergei put down two cups of coffee. Steve munched on a cracker, still badly shaken by the dream.

"If you don't want to tell me Steve, that's OK, but I'm worried about you. About your health. Your mental health. I'm not talking about sins. This isn't confession. We've become friends in the time you've been here and I'd just like to help if I can. I'm not a doctor, but I suspect you are suffering from depression, probably stemming from some bad past experiences. I can recommend a doctor here in town who can help you."

"But what could he do—talk me into feeling better?" Steve replied with a smirk.

"He could," Sergei said, "prescribe an anti-depressant. It could make a world of difference in your mental condition. It could dampen the impact of any bad experiences you may have had. And, by the way, you don't have to, but it might help if you could tell me about what's happened to you. Lips sealed, of course."

As Steve slowly told the story, Sergei's face fell. He stared down into his coffee cup. He had a feeling of immense sorrow for his new friend. He tried not to judge in a partisan religious sense, but he began to think the Roman Catholic Church was badly overreacting in its zeal to hunt down and stop this priest. He had seen Father Murphy devoutly saying Mass every morning; reading his breviary each day as he strolled through the church yard; praying at the grave of Saint Innocent; visiting the sick in the local dispensary; taking money out of his own pocket to help a family left destitute when the father was lost in a drowning accident on a crab boat at sea. There was no insurance in that line of work. A day's wages for a hard and dangerous day of work at sea. Surely, this man sitting with him appeared to be every inch a priest. A devout priest.

In their earlier talks, Steve had told him of his years at the Vatican in Rome, his pastoral ministry back in Maryland. How he had constructed a new church. How he was at one point on the brink of being elevated to Monsignor. An unfinished story. Now, in a kitchen on a barren island half-way out along the Aleutians, he told how it had all come crashing down.

As he sat listening to Steve, Sergei wondered: Where was God in all of this? Didn't God care about this good person whose life was hanging in the balance? Sergei felt a chill creep through him when he realized they would both have to be on the lookout for Brothers Michael and John. He, Sergei, as a member of the Russian Church, had no obligation to alert Catholic authorities about one of their renegade priests. And even if he had, he knew he wouldn't take action against a friend. Surely, the Catholic Church, if it decided against Steve being a valid priest, in its vast power and resources, could eventually find a way to stop him; but hell would freeze over before he, Sergei, would lend a hand.

*****

The skipper of the ninety-two foot trawler, the Alaska Lady, eighty miles out of Dutch Harbor, had been trying since late afternoon to get back to port. There were five men on board, one of whom had gone out reluctantly with a premonition that the cold, iron-gray overhead sky boded ill. The skipper, Jake Mackey, had earlier convinced the worried fisherman that the trip would be safe and without him, they couldn't sail. The Alaska Lady, a crab boat, finally sailed out of Dutch Harbor early that morning, top-heavy with huge metal crab pots secured on deck. She was headed for an off-shore island and would crab in the waters close to the island.

By two o'clock in the afternoon, the wind had begun to howl and waves building to twenty feet were breaking over the bow. Wild salt spray and snow mixed with sleet blanketed the trawler. The wheelhouse, mast and topside crab pots were soon encased in a ghostly white coating of ice. As the afternoon wore on, Jake knew there was nowhere to put in on the small island. He had to get back to Dutch Harbor, but he found it impossible to make any real headway.

The struggle continued after darkness fell. By nine o'clock that night, after six hours at full engine power, the skipper was dismayed to realize that they had made so little headway. They were still sixty miles out of Dutch Harbor. Through it all, the Alaska Lady had buried her bow in one huge wave after another, but now she began an ominous roll that broke loose gear in the wheelhouse and below decks. With each roll, the gear slid beamwise, alternately crashing into port and starboard bulkheads. The hull began to leak. All too soon, sloshing water filled the lower decks shorting out the two electric bilge pumps. Then the engine stalled. It was too wet to restart.

When a four-story-high rogue wave came out of the night and slammed into the boat, the Alaska Lady shuddered and rolled almost ninety degrees. With the tip of her mast almost touching the sea, Jake waited for her to roll back upright. But as the trawler lay limp in the water with no sign of recovering, he knew it was all over. Another big wave and the foundering trawler would go under. In the wheelhouse, lying on his side against a bulkhead that was now under him, he screamed a frantic Mayday call: "This is the Alaska Lady—she's capsized and sinking. We're going overboard." He shouted his position. Thankfully, the Global Positioning System he had installed a few years before would give the precise location of his boat. But since his battery power was fading, he wasn't sure if the message got through. Jake also activated his

Emergency Position Indicating Radio Beacon that would send a radio signal to a satellite as soon as the boat was underwater. The problem with the EPIRB however, was that it would only give his position within a mile and in a rough sea at night, it could be difficult to pin down his exact location.

Jake and the crew began scrambling into their survival suits. With the cabin deck almost vertical, and gear beginning to float, the frantic struggle became chaotic. Finally, crawling along a side bulkhead, the men exited through the hatch. Outside, with arms locked together, they slid across the icy deck and half-jumped, half-fell into the black water. When their heads bobbed to the surface, sputtering and spitting out freezing salt water, the men watched in horror as the running lights on the Alaska Lady's mast, still lit by backup battery power, sank down under the water. The water around the submerged lights gave off an eerie glow until the lights shorted out as the capsized boat began to sink. In the blackness, Jake couldn't see it, but he knew by the suction pulling him towards the boat's location that it had gone down.

The men were now alone in the dark, struggling to stay afloat as huge waves lifted them dizzily, only to hurl them down into the troughs as the waves passed through.

The Coast Guard station on Kodiak Island received the distress call from the Alaska Lady. The trawler was almost three hundred miles from Kodiak. But Kodiak was having problems of its own. Its C-130s were snowed in; besides, although the planes could help locate the boat, they were land planes and couldn't rescue the crew. Kodiak's rescue helicopters were off far to the east assisting the Coast Guard station at Seward in a rescue of the crew of a foundering freighter that had been caught in the storm. The Coast Guard, search and rescue coordinators for the Alaska Peninsula and the Aleutian Islands, knew there was no point calling the Naval Air Station far out in the Aleutians at Adak. Although Adak was within range, it had been decommissioned several months before and the rescue helicopters were gone.

The Unalaska airport tower received the call for assistance from the Coast Guard operators at 10:15 PM. They had exhausted all other options and suggested that rescue boats be sent out. But tower personnel knew that by the time rescue boats from Dutch Harbor could reach the crew, some of the men could be dead from hypothermia in the cold water. The survival suits were probably good for four or five hours, but if any of them were torn or not fully zipped up, survival time would be a lot less. Tower operators decided there was one chance to reach the men alive. A call was placed to the Bishop's House where Sergei rousted Steve from his room and asked him to come downstairs and talk to the tower on the phone.

"I'd like to lend a hand," Steve said sleepily over the kitchen phone, "but if the trawler capsized, the sea must be rough and I could never land my plane."

The tower operator tried to reassure the priest. "The sea was rough but it isn't now. The storm was moving quickly and now has passed off to the east. The winds are down to Force 3, which means two to three foot waves. Yes, the water has been rough but it's calming down. We're in the eye of the storm."

"How do you know the trawler capsized?" Steve asked.

"We received a coded beep from the trawler's Emergency Position Indicating Radio Beacon, we call it the EPIRB. It sends out a signal to a satellite when the boat is submerged in water. We know that this boat had crab pots on deck and had a buildup of topside ice due to heavy sleeting. Then, we suppose a rogue wave came out of nowhere."

"Crab pots? How could they capsize a trawler? How many did they have forty or fifty? The crab pots in the Chesapeake Bay are pretty small and made of wood. In a rough sea they would just float, or float off the deck if they weren't lashed down. They couldn't capsize a boat."

"Father, let me explain. This boat only had eight pots on deck. But this isn't the Chesapeake Bay. The pots here are metal and as big as small houses. They weigh upwards of 700 to 800 pounds each, so the trawlers tend to be top-heavy. Father, we're wasting time. I'll send a copilot over if you will do it."

"All right, I'll do it," Steve replied, still not convinced that the sea would be smooth enough for a seaplane landing.

A few minutes later, a young man knocked on the door. He said the tower had sent him over. Sergei introduced the young man to Steve.

"They tell me you're quite experienced, Rob," Steve said studying the young man. "How much experience do you have in seaplanes?"

"None, but I have several thousand hours in

instrument flying and even in helos. You fly the plane and my job will be as navigator to locate the crew and fish the guys out of the water when we get on-scene."

"Fair enough," Steve said smiling. "I guess between us, we can pull it off."

Then, as the pilots were getting ready to leave, Sergei handed them each a thermos of hot coffee. "God go with you," he said.

*****

If there was one thing Steve abhorred it was taking off in the dark over water. No runway lights. No reference horizon. This flight would have to be on full instruments—all the way. As he taxied, gusts of wind came in alternately from several points of the compass. Barely able to see the heavy chop and the waves coming towards the beach with his landing lights, he struggled to get the plane up on the riser step of the floats. Once on the step, the drag due to the rear portion of the pontoons is decreased, allowing further acceleration for takeoff. At the point where he almost gave up because the pontoons were digging into the water and bouncing so hard he thought they would start to pop rivets, he could feel the Otter rise slightly on the step and accelerate. Then suddenly, they were up in the air. Aloft, it was calmer than Steve had expected. The Coast Guard was right. The storm had moved off. Rob directed Steve out to sea on a compass heading that would lead to the capsized trawler.

Since the position of the trawler was known by satellite GPS combined with the EPIRB signal, Steve would not have to perform a search, so he flew low, almost skimming the wave tops, pushing the Otter to max speed. Less than half-an-hour later, the Otter was circling the area where the capsized boat had gone down. They could see debris in the water. Rob's powerful handheld light illuminated five men in the water. He directed Steve away from the scene so the plane wouldn't hit anyone in the water on landing. As Steve brought the plane down, almost unnerved at attempting a landing in the open ocean at night, he was somewhat relieved to find only about two feet of chop and three to four foot waves. The tower guys, Steve thought, had been almost right but not completely because it looked to him more like Force Four rather than Three. Steve, heading into the waves, taxied slowly back to the crew. He saw that the men all had survival suits on, but if any were torn or not fully zipped up, hypothermia in the ice cold water could kill them in minutes.

Steve struggled to hold the plane in a position near one of the men. He throttled the engines back to idle and set the props in flat pitch. He didn't shut the engines down because with salt spray flying everywhere, he was afraid he might not get them started again. But he knew they didn't have much time because salt ingestion might stall the turbines. Rob stood on one of the pontoons, holding onto a strut. But the wind caused the plane to drift away. After drifting about ten to fifteen yards from the man, Steve had to turn and try to slowly ease back. Finally, Rob was able to hoist one man onto a pontoon as several other men also tried to clamber up onto the pontoon. Concerned that the plane would tilt far to one side, Rob shouted at the men to stay in the water until he got the first man aboard. Finally, after a struggle that seemed never to end, Rob hoisted the men one-by-one onto a pontoon and then into the cabin. Disoriented, teeth chattering, unable to talk, faces turned blue, some of the men were in deep hypothermia. Rob helped them strip off their soaking wet suits and piled on blankets trying to warm them up. When one of the men became unconscious in cardiac arrest, Rob performed CPR to bring him around.

With all the men secured on board, Steve took off and began the climbout. After takeoff he circled the scene on the water with his landing lights on. There was no sign of the stricken trawler. There was nothing in the water but a few pieces of debris. Then, with no time to waste, he banked to a heading that would take them back to Dutch Harbor.

The return flight to Dutch Harbor was short. Approaching the bay by the Russian church, Steve was worried that the wind had picked up because he could feel the airplane lurching in response to the gusts. The wind was blowing the chop into a chaotic froth as the sea bounced against the land. Flying low over the water, the airplane landing lights caught glimpses of whitecaps. Rob signaled to Steve he thought it was no-go for a water landing. He jerked his thumb over in the direction of the Unalaska airport. Steve nodded OK, but felt a knot in his stomach when he realized the Otter was heavily loaded and he would be making his first landing on the wheels that hung out from the bottom of the pontoons. He had no idea how much load those wheels could take.

Circling the airport, Steve saw emergency vehicles

and three ambulances poised beside the runway. The runway was lit. The airport was lit up like a church—controllers having turned on every light they had available. He came in for what he knew would be a risky landing—partly rolling, partly skidding on the pontoon wheels in a strong crosswind. Power cut back and full flaps down, he touched down. Suddenly the plane lurched to the right as a tire blew out on contact with the ground. Skidding on one pontoon and the opposite wheel, the plane almost went into a ground loop. He was dismayed to realize he had no brakes to help him slow down. Grim-faced, on the verge of catastrophy, he struggled in the cockpit to keep sliding straight for what seemed like an eternity. Finally, the plane slowed and scraped to a stop.

As the Otter came to rest, leaning at an angle with a mangled wheel and its pontoon almost ripped off, Steve made a quick Sign of the Cross. He glanced over at Rob with a sigh of relief. Although it was a chilly night, the priest was covered with sweat. He realized he would not be flying again until he could have the plane fitted with a new wheel and pontoon, but he was relieved that he and Rob had brought the men back to safety.

Hands stretched into the airplane through the side doors to help the shivering men out into the waiting ambulances. They would be taken to the Unalaska hospital where they would be warmed out of their hypothermia.

Early on the following morning, Sergei and Steve were at the hospital where they learned that Jake Mackey had died during the night. One of the crew was hospitalized with a heart attack caused by the hypothermia. The others had been treated and released. While Sergei helped the Mackey family with funeral arrangements for Jake who had been one of his parishioners, Steve spent a few minutes with the heart attack patient, then left to go to the hangar that held his plane.

He found the lead mechanic inspecting the damage. "I guess I have to try to get it back to Juneau for repair," Steve said.

"But the damage isn't too bad," the mechanic replied. "If it's OK with you, I can repair the wheel and have a new pontoon shipped in here in a couple of days. It'd be a lot better than trying to get the plane back to Juneau. I could put on the skiis but there's no convenient place to land with skiis at Juneau."

"All right by me," Steve said as he left to go to the newspaper office.

*****

"Father Murphy, I don't understand. Why are you being so modest? You participated in a daring rescue. Good God, at night at sea and with a pontoon airplane—that's big news. Those men would have been goners." The speaker was a native Alaskan named Corbet, Editor-in-Chief at the paper. He offered Steve a cigarette and a cup of coffee as Steve sat in his office.

"I really didn't do much. Yes, I flew the plane but the sea was pretty calm when we got there. No difficulty landing in the ocean. Rob, my copilot really did all the work. He was the one who yanked those guys out of the water, performed CPR on one of them. He deserves the credit."

"Nonsense, Father Murphy. You and Rob are both heroes. We're not going to play it down or let you forget it. And even if we drop your name from the story here as you suggest, what would be the point? The newspapers in Anchorage have already picked up on the story. It'll be in their late editions today."

Steve sat back in the chair. He was exhausted after only a couple of hours sleep. His hand was unsteady as he sipped his coffee. He looked at the tremor in his hand disgustedly. "Coffee's good, but I've been drinking too much of this lately."

"It's the cold weather, Father. When I was in the Navy on Arctic duty, we drank Joe all day long. Tell ya, you'll either get so's you can take it in stride or it'll kill you. Now let's head down to the maintenance shed at the airport. I want a picture of you and Rob standing next to the plane you flew to make the rescue. Rob is over there now. Father, that rescue took gumption. Just because you're a priest doesn't mean you can't take some credit for a heroic act."

"I was holding back because I had something else on my mind," Steve said, shrugging his shoulders and tagging along reluctantly behind the newsman.

*****

When news of the rescue hit the papers and TV, Steve was worried that the story would get back to the lower 48 and to Rhinehart in particular. However, rescues in the Aleutians were so common they attracted a lot of local attention, but the reports rarely went beyond Juneau and Anchorage.

After news of the rescue hit Anchorage, the metropolitan in Anchorage was on the phone to his counterpart, Bishop McPherson, the Roman Catholic Archbishop of Anchorage. "My compliments, Dear Brother. Your Father Murphy is a hero. That rescue off Dutch Harbor was a brilliant achievement."

"Yes, it was," Bishop McPherson agreed. Although he had read the news account, for the life of him, McPherson couldn't remember who Murphy was. Had he assigned him to the islands and simply forgotten about it? Was his memory getting that bad? Perhaps Murphy was a visiting priest who just happened to be at Dutch Harbor. Yes, that must be it.

"Father Murphy deserves some special consideration, Dear Brother. Why don't you visit Dutch Harbor, or better yet, call him into Anchorage for a big dinner in his honor?"

"I'd very much like to but I'm getting ready to travel to Rome. I have to leave tomorrow and won't be back for several weeks. Let me think about it. Thanks for your interest."

As Bishop McPherson hung up the phone, he felt bad about not doing something for Father Murphy, but the timing was terrible. He decided to send the priest a letter of congratulation and thanks. Since he did not know Father Murphy's address, he had the letter forwarded to the Unalaska newspaper office. Reaching into the bottom drawer of his desk, he pulled out a roster of priests serving under him in Alaska but could not find a listing for a Father Stephen Murphy. "Why can't we keep these lists up to date?" he muttered to himself. Temporarily putting the whole business out of his mind, the bishop sorted his papers for a crucial meeting at the Vatican where he would attend a meeting with the pope.

The next morning, after boarding the flight from Anchorage, the elderly bishop sat back and dozed off. As he did, he kept repeating to himself, "Murphy... Father Stephen Murphy. Where have I heard that name before? I wonder if this is the way it begins with Alzheimer's. First you lose track of things; you can't remember little things; then after awhile, you can't remember anything. I wonder if it ever gets so bad you can't remember who God is."

33

In the following months, Steve continued his visits to the outer islands. He found some of the islands virtually deserted while at others he was dismayed to find that many of the inhabitants were cool to his visits and his message. Some were even downright hostile.

Narrowing his scope, he focused on Umak Island. The people on Umak were always happy to see the blue floatplane land in the cove. As the priest taxied the airplane to shore, four or five teenagers would run out over the beach and into the shallows to tie the craft to a stout pole anchored at the water's edge. Then, shoes off and pants legs rolled up, Steve would hop out into the cold ankle-deep water where he would slosh ashore to be surrounded by smiling villagers. He always brought magazines to the isolated people on the island and cakes, candies and small toys for the children. Occasionally he brought a supply of fresh milk and bread from Unalaska. He never asked for payment and if it was offered, he always declined. Of all the islands he visited, this was his favorite. Father Sergei had been born on the island. He told Steve the people there were friendly and receptive but isolated and would benefit from spiritual and material help.

On Steve's first visit, Sergei had accompanied him to the island to introduce the priest to the village elders. He seemed not to mind that Steve would try to convert them to Catholicism because he had tried to supplant shamanism with Russian orthodoxy and had failed. Maybe Steve would be able to get through to them. Sergei believed that any version of Christianity would be better for the people than shamanism.

Warily eyeing the tall steaming mountain called Atta in the background whenever he arrived on the island, Steve always asked if there had been any noisy rumblings since his last visit that might signify an impending eruption. But even if there were, none of the islanders would admit it because they were afraid that if word got back to the authorities, they would be forcibly moved from their homes to some strange place to which none of them wanted to go. Steve suspected he was never getting a straight answer.

The villagers lived in two lines of simple homes running beside a snow covered road that served as Umak's main street. The homes were wooden and inside held reasonably comfortable furnishings. Steve noted that some of the homes had satellite dishes on the roofs. Evidently the villagers knew what was going on in the outside world. A small schoolhouse stood on the lower slope of a nearby mountain. The men supported the village with fishing and crabbing. The excess was sold to a company that ran a cannery on a neighboring island. The villagers were not well off in a material sense, but they were not poor and were content living in familiar surroundings as had their ancestors for many generations. They understood the priest's gifts were not charity, but simply meant to return the favor for the hospitality and meals he had enjoyed in their homes.

On his later visits to Umak Island, Steve received

permission from the parents to take the older children up for short airplane rides. The children, who had never been off their island and never flown in an airplane were astonished to see their village from above and were in awe of the steaming mountain that dominated the landscape as Steve flew the Otter high over the cinder cone at the top. He was careful to remain upwind of the steam and smoke.

On one visit, after landing and helping the children ashore, Steve saw a crowd gather to watch the village shaman in action. A seven year-old-boy had been out fishing with his father a few days before and had somehow gotten a fishhook embedded in the flesh of his leg. The father had promptly cut the hook free of the line and managed to get the hook out, however with quite a bit of damage to the tissues of the boy's leg. Then, two days later, the swelling began and the shaman was called to heal the boy. Shortly after Steve's arrival, the shaman, surrounded by a score of villagers, donned his tribal mask and sat cross-legged beside the boy who lay on the open ground on a blanket. Holding the bones of dead ancestors, the shaman began a ritual that filled the priest with wonder. With strange incantations, clicking of the bones, and dirty, scrawny hands held over the boy's wound, the shaman proceeded to heal the wound. There was an audible gasp from the villagers. Everyone could plainly see the swelling actually go down, although the leg did not seem completely healed.

Steve, standing with the onlookers, thought the red infected wound still looked ominous. He never believed for a moment that a miracle of healing was taking place.

The only explanation Steve could think of was that the boy had been put into a hypnotic state and his body was reacting to the swelling by power of suggestion. This did not seem too unusual to the priest because he remembered seeing a demonstration of hypnotism in which a subject was stuck on the forearm with a needle causing bleeding, after which the bleeding was stopped by means of a suggestion implanted by the hypnotist. Then, at the hypnotist's command, the bleeding was started again and then stopped again. Steve had been convinced there was no trickery in the demonstration. It clearly evidenced the power of suggestion and the power of the mind to exercise some control over the body.

During the village ritual, although he was prepared to believe there was some improvement in the boy's condition, what struck Steve as utterly ridiculous was the clicking of the old bones held by the shaman. He asked himself what possible 'power' could a few old bones hold? But suddenly he thought of the church's relics of the saints. Weren't they believed to hold some kind of power or influence with the almighty? Was the shaman doing anything the church didn't do? Were the bones of native ancestors any less influential with the almighty than the bones of saints?

Despite the intervention of the shaman, within an hour after he had left, strutting away, convinced he had cured the boy, the swelling was back, every bit as painful and nasty-looking as before. The boy lay whimpering in pain. His parents were distraught because they had relied on a remedy that had been used by their forebears over hundreds of years. However, in this case, the shaman's healing proved to be strictly temporary.

Hurrying to the floatplane, Steve grabbed a few supplies and went back to the boy. As he knelt beside the boy, it was obvious the lad was in terrible pain and a thin red line running from the wound up the leg told Steve the infection was spreading. Soon it would be too late. Steve, feeling he had no other choice, gave the boy a painkiller and waited for it to take effect. Then, after sterilizing a knife in a flame, he opened the wound, drained it, cleaned it and applied a liberal coating of antibiotic ointment. Next he bandaged the wound and told the boy's parents to let their son sleep. He said he would spend the night on the island— sleeping in the plane, and if the boy was not showing improvement by morning, he would fly the family to the hospital at Unalaska. Mention of the hospital was a mistake because the shaman had convinced the villagers that hospitals were places to go to die. Didn't everyone know, the shaman had frequently argued, that people would go into a hospital with one problem and die of something else—something bad they caught in the hospital? Wasn't it obvious that demons lived in hospitals?

After dinner in one of the villager's homes, Steve gathered some of the children around him at a campsite fire. He told them of the greatest shaman of them all— one named Jesus Christ.

The children fired questions at him: Did the greatest shaman talk to God as well as the demons? Did the greatest shaman heal the sick? Could he bring the dead back to life? Where is Jesus, the great shaman now?

Steve answered their questions by telling the story of Jesus' call to the dead Lazarus to come forth. He told them of the blind man in the tree that Jesus cured. He told the wide-eyed children how the greatest shaman fed five thousand people with the fish in just a few baskets and how he had walked on the water. The children, in frightened wonder, began scanning the sea looking for the greatest shaman to come walking to their island on the water.

One little girl raised her hand: "Father Steve, what is that thing you have hanging down in front on your chest?"

Steve smiled at the pretty girl with jet black hair cut short with bangs in front. "It's what we call a Crucifix. It has a figure of Jesus on it and the cross he died on. Now tell me, what's your name and how old are you?"

"It's Anya. I'm seven."

"Sounds like a Russian name. Do you also have an Alaskan name?"

"Yes. It's Oumam."

"My that's a pretty name," Steve replied. "And how about you, young man. What's your name?"

"My name is Pyotr and I'm a boy, not a man. After all, I'm only ten. My parents did not give me an Alaskan name."

Looking around at the group of children, Steve asked, "Are all of you from Russian backgrounds? Do you go to a Russian church?"

"Most of the families are Russian," Pyotr replied. "But we're also Americans. I guess, mostly we're Americans. We don't go to Russian church; we don't go to any church because there's no church on Umak."

"But doesn't a Russian priest visit here once in awhile?"

"Yes, Father Sergius comes maybe once a year. Why do you come here anyway?"

"I come to bring gifts and to tell you about the Lord, Jesus. As soon as Jesus was born, a bright star appeared in the sky and Three Wise Men came from the east with gifts for the baby. Many people realized he was no ordinary baby."

"Why? Was he fat? Did he weigh twenty pounds?"

"Well, no. What I mean is people believed Jesus was the Son of God."

"Do you believe that, Father Steve?" Anya asked.

"Yes, I do. In fact, from the things Jesus said and the miracles he did, millions and millions of people believe it.

"Now, Pyotr," Steve asked, "do you know where your name comes from?"

"From my parents. They gave it to me."

"What I mean, Pyotr, is the original meaning of your name. It means Peter. The rock. Jesus said to Peter, who was a fisherman: 'You are the rock and upon this rock I will build my church.' So, Pyotr, you are named after the man that Jesus picked to start his church."

"My father's a fisherman too," Pyotr offered, apparently pleased about his ties to a fisherman of old who was selected by Jesus to do important things.

As Steve stoked the fire, he told them how Jesus had allowed bad men to crucify him so he could save the world from the bad things people did. He told how Jesus had brought himself back to life, and how Jesus, the greatest shaman who ever lived had descended into

Hell where the most horrible demons dwelt and how he vanquished them and ordered them to remain in Hell for all eternity.

A little girl raised her hand. "Did Jesus smell bad like our shaman?" she asked.

"Certainly not," Steve replied with a smile. "The greatest shaman smelled like the wildflowers you have here in your valley in springtime."

Pyotr raised his hand: "You say Jesus was nailed to a cross and died. If he was such a great shaman and raised someone from the dead, why didn't he save himself?"

"Many people have asked that same question, Pyotr. The answer is that Jesus wanted to suffer and die as a sacrifice for people's sins. God the Father accepted the sacrifice of his son because people had done many bad things. Jesus' death would allow people to go to heaven to be with God."

"What if Jesus had gotten his head cut off instead of dying on the cross, what would you wear on your chest? What if he was killed with a spear? The Aleuts kill fish with a spear. Did the people who killed Jesus have spears?"

"Yes, they had spears."

"What would you hang on your chest if the people killed Jesus with a spear?"

"I'm not sure. I'd have to think about that," Steve replied, somewhat relieved that Jesus had died on the Cross.

In all, Steve spent several days on the island. He remained partly to teach the children more about Jesus but also to make sure the boy with the infected leg was recovering.

By the third day, the wound was almost completely healed. The redness had shrunken to a pinkish area no larger than a quarter. The red streak up his leg had vanished and the boy was up hobbling around, free of pain. The shaman strutted through the village taking credit for the healing, but the people began to scoff at him, saying the priest was the one who performed the miracle.

Returning from a climb part way up the steaming mountain, on the day he planned to leave the island, Steve noticed something strange about his plane. The pontoons had leaked and the plane had settled down in about eighteen inches of water. He thought it unusual that both pontoons would start leaking at the same time, although it was entirely possible if they had both been cut on the ridge of a sharp rock on the bottom. However, there were no rocks in the vicinity and he did not recall scraping on a rock as he taxied to shore several days before. On closer inspection, Steve saw that the pontoons had been cut—gashes probably made with a sharp axe. But what really concerned him were the rear sections of the pontoons that had been bent down preventing a takeoff on land. There was no way he could take off on the wheels with the pontoons scraping on the ground. He knew it must have been done in anger by the shaman—very likely while Steve was up inspecting the mountain.

The priest made inquiries, but found that no one admitted to seeing anything. He found this very hard to believe because the plane was in full view of the village houses. Even the children evaded his questions and looked away as he asked. Slowly, he realized the villagers were afraid to pin the blame on the shaman. One of the worst things that could befall a person would be to have a shaman angry at you. He could see to it that the demons possessed you forever. You would be made to writhe in torment by the demons for eons to come. Although many of the adults thought it might not be true, no one was willing to take the chance.

Steve angrily strode to the shaman's small house separated from the other houses in the village by a small hillock. As the priest pushed open the door, the stench almost overcame him. The shaman confronted the priest holding the bones between himself and the priest—either to ward off evil brought by the priest or to make sure evil befell the priest. Steve could not tell which. Pushing the bones aside, he grabbed the filthy shaman by the throat, feeling the greasy skin in his fingers. The shaman's thick black matted hair looked like it had never seen soap and water. As he forced the shaman, eyes bulging, to the ground in a vice-like grip, Steve suddenly stopped. How could he be doing this? He, a priest. What example was he setting for the children of the village?

He let the shaman stand up again. "You're going to have a busy day," Steve said in a threatening tone. "You and I are going to take the pontoons off the plane and then I'm going to try to get out of here on skis. I don't want any of your incantations. None of your stupid miracles. All I want is some hard work. Do you understand?"

The shaman gasping for breath, nodded.

*****

By late afternoon, the pontoons were off and tied inboard under the wings of the plane. The plane was sitting on a strip of hard-packed snowy road that ran down the center of the small village. As Steve revved the engines, the shaman ran back to his house; villagers scattered on either side of the priest's planned takeoff run. The airplane lurched forward, engines roaring, skis skidding in the snow. A cloud of snow blew to the rear. The craft bounced down the street on a road so rough Steve thought he'd never get up enough speed to become airborne. "Jesus, help me get this thing in the air," he cried out as he kept inching back on the wheel to test whether there was enough lift to separate the plane from the rutted and lumpy snow. At the point where he had almost given up hope and was preparing to throttle back, the snow-covered road at the edge of the village seemed smoother and the plane began to pick up speed. Finally with a Herculean pull-up, Steve managed to clear the ground only to find he was heading straight into a small mountain at the edge of town. Banking sharply to the left to head out over the water, the plane lost altitude and he saw a tiny spray as the left wingtip skimmed the wavelets on the surface of the water. If the tip dug in, he would cartwheel into the sea—end over end. Gingerly, holding his breath, applying hard right rudder, and full right ailerons, Steve was able to yaw and roll sufficiently to slide the left wingtip out of the water. Finally, he rolled the plane into level flight and, gaining altitude, started on his way back to Dutch Harbor.

During the climbout, he contacted the Unalaska

Airport tower and said he was coming in from Umak on skis and had never landed on skis before.

"Father Murphy, the runways have been plowed so you cannot... repeat cannot come in on the runways. As you approach we will guide you to a nearby snow-covered field. We'll have emergency equipment on standby just in case."

"Thanks guys. I'll say a Mass for you next Sunday." Then, more relaxed and remembering the children, Steve turned and flew back over the village dipping his wings for the benefit of the children.

One of the watching children shouted, "Jesus helped Father Steve miss Devil Mountain. Maybe Jesus really is the greatest shaman of them all."

34

Upon his return from Umak Island, Steve found a letter waiting for him in the Unalaska post office. It was from Janet, with a return address in Cambridge. He delayed opening it until he was seated alone in a booth in the coffee shop a few blocks from the Russian Church. He nervously lit a cigarette as he sat with his coffee. He had begun smoking again right after the newspaper article about the rescue of the fishermen was published. He needed the crutch. He knew his days in the Aleutians were numbered. He was almost too nervous to open Janet's letter and read it. Then, slowly and carefully he slit open the envelope.

Dear Steve,

Jonathon gave me your address. Good heavens, the Aleutian Islands! He said you wanted to get far away from...you know who, and it looks like you have. There are only two of us who know where you are. At least, I think there are only two of us. Hopefully, no one in the church has been able to track you down.

Steve, I have news. I received my Master's in Social Work last month and have received a job offer as a Social Worker with Catholic Charities of Boston. That's why the Cambridge address.

I really hate to tell you this, but since my attempted annulment failed, I have been under tremendous pressure from my family and my husband, Fred's family, to get us back together. Both sets of parents want grandchildren and Fred seems disposed to give our marriage another try. There's also the issue of religion—you know it well—'Til death do us part'. Frankly, I am confused and I feel bombarded on all sides.

You know, Steve, I love you and I always will. I wish things could be as they had been when we were at the university. Days we spent together. Days when I fell I love with you. Do people sometimes just follow the dictates of their relatives and the church even though they love someone else? Are you and I doing with our lives what God intended us to do? Say a prayer for me. I'll write again when there is more news.

   Love,
Janet

Steve read the letter three times. He slipped it into his pocket and sat staring out at the snow that had just begun to fall. Buttoning his parka and pulling the hood over his head, he left the shop and walked aimlessly back to the church. He let himself in the side door to the small chapel. He knelt at the altar. He had no prayers. How could he ask God to solve an impossible situation? He struggled to say something, anything to the Lord, but nothing would come except the image of Janet's face and a stream of tears clouding his eyes.

*****

A few days later, Steve was back in Juneau after the Unalaska mechanic had tried a patchup job on the pontoons. It was enough—possibly barely enough for a water landing. Totem's mechanic was scheduled to do some routine maintenance on the Otter. "I see the guys at Unalaska airport did some rough patching when they put the pontoons back on, but I can tell you the repairs won't last. One more water landing with those babies and you'll be swimming for shore. Let me fit you out with a new pair."

"The pity of it is that one of them was new. It was put on after my crosswind landing at Unalaska. How long will all this take?" Steve asked, worried that he might be tied up in Juneau for a week.

"I'll have the plane ready for you by tomorrow morning if that's OK."

"I suppose it will have to be," Steve answered, hoping he could find a place to stay for the night in Juneau.

After asking around, Steve managed to find a room in a small hotel out on the edge of town. Looking out the window he could see the famous Mendenhall Glacier in the distance. Then, as he took a bus back into the center of the town, he saw a string of bald eagles boldly sitting on fence posts that lined the roadside—fat and contented after gorging themselves on fish in the river.

Steve's next stop was at a Catholic Church in the center of town where he luckily found a priest who was hearing confessions before evening Mass. His confession was routine. He did not mention that he was a priest. Five Hail Mary's and a good act of contrition. Two hours later, Steve was seated in the Red Dog Saloon with Totem, the former used car salesman—currently in the airplane business. He ordered a sandwich and a beer.

"How do you like living on Unalaska? Kind of like living at the end of the world, ain't it? Careful you don't fall off," Totem laughed as he raised his beer to touch glasses with Steve's.

"It sure isn't the Garden of Eden," Steve replied. "But when I visit the villages in the outlying islands, I feel as if I'm doing something meaningful. It's become a pastoral ministry for me. Guess you'd call me a circuit rider. Or better said, a circuit flyer."

"But what do you do when you get to one of those far out islands? Can you even talk to the people? Do they speak English?"

"Oh yes, for the most part they speak English. They almost all have TVs now which helps a lot and the children are required to learn English in school. Some of the older people still speak Russian and also the native Aleut language, mostly when they don't want you to know what they're saying, but the old language is dying out."

"What islands do you visit?"

"I usually head west from Unalaska out to the islands near Adak, the former Navy base and sometimes out to the end of the chain—Attu. My favorite island is Umak. I always get a big welcome there. Friendly people. In answer to your question about what I do when I land, I sometimes take the kids up for short airplane rides. Have to be careful not to use too much gas. After that, I hold what you might call 'religion school'."

"So you're kinda like a missionary, right?"

"Yes, I suppose so."

"You mentioned Umak. I heard that island's headed

for trouble. The experts think the big steaming mountain on the island is about ready to blow. The authorities are thinking of evacuating the villagers."

"That's terrible," Steve said wincing. "Those people have worked hard to build nice homes and a small one-room schoolhouse. The men go out every day on commercial fishing boats and make a pretty decent wage. If the villagers are evacuated, they'll lose everything they've built up."

"True," Totem agreed. "But if they stay, they're likely to be dead meat."

"What's the time table for an eruption?"

"They said on the news it could happen any time."

*****

The next morning, after attending early Mass, and receiving holy communion, Steve was happy to find the Otter was ready. He took off heading for Unalaska with a fuel stop at Seward. As he approached Unalaska, word came on the radio of the evacuation of Umak Island. Some of the elders apparently refused to leave and were being warned they would be moved out forcibly, if necessary. Rescue boats were being sent to the island. "What a tragedy," he thought. "Those people must be scared and miserable."

Sergei met him at the airport. He wanted Steve to fly him to Umak. An uncle, the only remaining member of his family, was on the island.

"We can't go there, Sergei. They're evacuating the island."

"I know that. But my old uncle is a stubborn one. He'll hide out and they won't be able to find him. He's a wily one. But I think I can find him and talk him into leaving."

"If you insist," Steve said. "Let's fuel up and go."

*****

Approaching Umak Island, it became clear the island was in trouble. Huge clouds of black smoke and ash were streaming up from the cinder cone.

"Don't know if we can land. That big Coast Guard cutter is likely to wave us off. If they do and I don't fly out, they'll throw the book at me later."

"Please, Steve. My uncle's life is on the line. I think I can find him and talk him into leaving."

"Sergei, how do you know they haven't already picked him up? He could be on one of the rescue boats."

"I doubt it. If I know him, he's still somewhere on the island."

"You better find him fast," Steve warned as he brought the Otter into the cove. He noticed that the Coast Guard cutter had already turned to leave and was speeding away from the island. Apparently the officers on board thought the island had been completely evacuated. Or, perhaps, they thought they had done all they could and it was too dangerous to remain in the cove any longer. Steve also noticed that the smaller rescue boats were now miles away from the island.

When the Coast Guard cutter saw the Otter, they ordered Steve to turn back immediately. Steve decided he needed a white lie as he told the Coast Guard he was with the U.S. Geological Survey and needed to get closer in for just a few minutes to observe the volcano.

In the confusion and smoke, the Coast Guard lost

track of the plane.

By the time Steve had landed in the cove and taxied into the shallows, the windshield of the Otter was almost completely covered with ash from the volcano. He shut the engines down and drifted ashore because the turbine inlets were beginning to ingest ash. If the intakes became clogged, they'd never be able to take off again.

Sergei jumped into the shallows and ran ashore in the ankle-deep water. As he did so, he saw a man come out of a small house hidden in heavy brush and run part way up the side of the volcano.

Steve leaned out of the cockpit window and shouted to Sergei. "That's the village shaman, Sergei. Forget about him, he's crazy. Go find your uncle."

"He *is* my uncle," Sergei shouted back as he ran up the slope after the shaman.

The devil in the mountain roared. He spit fire into the sky. The end came swiftly but not mercifully as a torrent of molten lava poured down from the lip of the volcano and engulfed the two men. Steve's last image of the shaman was of the 'holy man' standing on the slope of the volcano facing the onrushing stream of lava. With mask on and rapidly clicking bones in his hands, he commanded the devil in the volcano to go back to sleep. Steve had a last view of Sergei as the Russian-Aleut priest, struggling to pull his uncle out of the path of the lava, crossed himself with the two-finger Russian Sign of the Cross and was covered by the hot glowing mass of lava which completely swallowed him and his uncle.

At the horrible sight, Steve almost became sick

in the cockpit. With one arm hanging out of the left side cockpit window, he made a hasty Sign of the Cross—blessing Sergei and the shaman who had both disappeared from sight. He had to do it with his left hand because his right hand was grappling with the throttles to rev up the turbines. He wheeled the Otter around for a quick takeoff from the cove. The windshield wipers were no use—all they did was cake up the falling ash that covered the glass. He could feel the heat radiating from the lava as it ran sizzling into the sea producing a cloud of team just a few yards from the airplane. In no time the entire airplane was covered with a thin layer of hot ash. With the props in flat pitch, Steve found he could start the engines and was relieved to see that the spinning props were throwing the ash away from the blades and the inlets, making a kind of tunnel in the air. Then he doggedly poured on every last ounce of power he could get out of the engines. The Otter began an agonizingly slow takeoff run on the water. Although it was midday, the swirling ash thrust the cove into darkness. With the windshield covered, Steve had to hang his head out of the side cockpit window to see where he was heading. Even so, he could barely make out the water surface that lay ahead. As the Otter gained speed and the pontoons went up on the step, he was able to pull up and take off. In the air, he was flying on instruments because he could barely see out of the windshield.

Ten minutes later, he brought the Otter in for a landing in the cove of another island. Standing on one of the pontoons, he doused the windshield with bucketfuls of water until he felt he would be able to see well enough to get back to Unalaska and Dutch Harbor.

*****

Because it involved a volcanic eruption, the story made the national news. TV and the newspapers told the story but at the time did not have the names of the individuals involved: The story read: *During the eruption of the volcanic mountain Atta on the Aleutian Island Umak, due to the prompt action of the Coast Guard and other rescuers, the island was evacuated; however, a clergyman died in an aborted rescue attempt of one individual who had remained on the island despite the eruption. In attempting the rescue, two clergymen had slipped by the Coast Guard in a private floatplane."*

Locally, Steve was hailed as a hero by some of the islanders for his attempted rescue of a shaman, but castigated by others for the death of Father Sergius. The Coast Guard berated him for a foolhardy failed rescue attempt which cost the life of the Russian priest.

At the inquest, a Coast Guard officer testified to the extremely hazardous situation on the island when the volcano erupted. He said he did not know that someone had been left behind on the island, and in any case, it would have jeopardized dozens of lives to remain in the cove any longer. Although he had not actually seen the seaplane land in the cove, he testified that Father Murphy later admitted making the ill-fated attempt at a rescue. The Coast Guard officer somewhat reluctantly accused Father Murphy of reckless endangerment which cost the life of the Russian priest. It did not help that father Murphy had radioed that he was with the

Geological Survey.

The hearing ended with a stern warning but no charges were brought against Steve Murphy. He believed the thing that saved him was the sympathy felt by almost everyone present stemming from his earlier rescue of the fishermen on the capsized trawler.

In the following days, going around town, Steve could tell that many people were upset about the death of Father Sergius, but he also detected some good feelings towards him after people learned that a Catholic priest had risked his life trying to save the life of a shaman.

*****

The metropolitan in Anchorage put down his newspaper and called his counterpart, Most Reverend McPherson, the Roman Catholic bishop. The metropolitan was not in a good mood. "Dear Brother," he said to the bishop, "I have lost a wonderful priest. And I feel I have to count it as the fault of one of your priests that this tragedy happened. If you recall it's the same priest who was involved in that offshore fishing boat rescue recently. But now he has gone too far. Who is this Father Murphy, anyway? Did you assign him to Unalaska? Were you aware that he flies around the islands as some kind of circuit rider taking native children up for airplane rides? Do you approve of this amusement park method for tending the flock? Let me assure you, I do not."

Bishop McPherson was contrite but confused and not at all ready to bear the brunt of the criticism coming from the Russian-American Orthodox Church.

He tried to cover up the fact that he had completely forgotten about a priest named Murphy to whom he had sent congratulations for the fishing boat rescue. He pulled out a newly revised roster of Catholic priests in Alaska and scanned it for one named Murphy. Still no listing of a Murphy. "Dear Brother," he replied, trying to sound as authoritative as possible, "this Murphy is not one of my priests. He is not on my roster. In fact, despite the news accounts, he may not be a Catholic priest at all. You know how the press and TV get things mixed up. What do you expect me to do about this?"

"At the very least, you should call Murphy in for a meeting to explain himself. Frankly, Dear Brother, if he's not on your roster, there's something fishy about this priest."

"Unfortunately, I don't have a current address for Murphy—he seems to be all over the place. And even if I did, how do I know he'd come?"

"Then send a query to your American cardinals in the lower forty-eight. Ask them if they have any information concerning a Reverend Steve Murphy in the Aleutians. Then, if they've never heard of him, he must be an imposter posing as a Catholic priest."

*****

In the chancery of the Archdiocese of Washington, Cardinal Rhinehart perused the letter of inquiry from the bishop of Anchorage. "It is just possible," he said to himself, "that the priest the notice referred to is Stephen Murphy, but I can't be sure because the name is listed as 'Robert Murphry'. Maybe the name became garbled. However, there is a way to find out."

*****

Jonathon sat at his desk in the real estate office flipping his rotary address file. He looked for Steve's P.O. Box number under M for 'Murphy,' then again under S for 'Steve.' Next, he went through every card in the file and finally concluded that the card with Steve's Unalaska address had vanished. Could he have taken it out when he sent the address to Janet and absentmindedly forgotten to refile it? No chance. He never did that.

"Marge, I can't find my brother's address. Do you have it by chance?"

"Me? No."

"Could anyone else have taken it? Anybody been going through my address file?"

"Not that I know of." Marge walked over and stood at Jonathon's desk, her arms folded with one hand curled under her chin. "Is it a real problem Jonathon? Maybe you saved an envelope from one of his letters with the return address."

"I doubt it. But it's puzzling. Has anyone been in the office... someone perhaps we don't know?"

"There was a man in here one day last week. He wasn't from around here I know. His accent sounded like somewhere south of South Ipswich, you know, down where they fought the Civil War." Marge smiled. She frequently assumed a deprecating air towards people who did not have a New England accent. "The man said he was looking to buy some property in Wayland. But when he heard the prices, he walked out in kind of a huff."

"What did he look like? How was he dressed?"

"Nothing special. He was wearing a black suit as I remember."

"Roman collar?"

"Heavens, no," Marge said in surprise. "Why would a priest be looking for land around here? The churches have already gobbled up all the available land."

"Well tell me this. Do you recall if he was ever alone in the office—even for a few minutes?"

"It's possible, Jonathon. Maybe I went in the back to get something. But look, there's nothing here anyone would want to steal. We don't keep cash here. And it's not likely he could walk out with one of our PCs, for heaven's sake."

"I suppose not. Anyway, thanks Marge. Let's just forget it, shall we?"

"That's all right by me, Jonathon."

*****

Bishop Hernandez was pacing the floor and occasionally stopping to gaze out of the window of his office in the Tucson chancery. His gaze scanned the long rows of headstones in the huge Catholic cemetery across from the chancery. But he thought not of the dead, he was worrying about problems that had begun to loom large in recent years. The court cases and huge settlements from charges of molestation brought by former altar boys against several of his priests had brought his diocese to the point of bankruptcy. Although the offenses had happened many years before, he learned there was no statute of limitations when an adult was accused of molesting a minor. Bishop Hernandez was certain the errant priests had repented hundreds of times in the ensuing years, but in the eyes of the law, it was not enough. The prison terms associated with the crimes were substantial but had no direct effect on him other than as an embarrassment. What struck him as grossly unfair were the huge financial settlements that his diocese and essentially the faithful in the diocese, had to make. These things had happened, twenty, twenty-five years before at a time when he was only a parish priest and wasn't even in Arizona. He and the Catholics in the Tucson diocese were innocent parties—unfortunately with a kind of reverse inheritance: they inherited millions in debts. He had to admit to himself that he had transferred a few priests from one parish to another, but these were done based on spurious and unconfirmed cases of inappropriate behavior. The claimants never pursued the issue at the time, so the matter was forgotten and it was part of a planned rotation that every diocese practiced.

The office intercom rang. "Your Grace, Cardinal Rhinehart is on the phone."

Bishop Hernandez suddenly remembered that Archbishop Rhinehart had recently been elevated to cardinal by the pope. He nervously picked up the phone wondering what that arrogant Rhinehart wanted now. If it was to send him another errant priest, he would have no choice but to agree and he smiled as he realized that the stipend for the priest would be accompanied by a payment. "This is Bishop Hernandez speaking...."

"How are things in Arizona?" came a voice that was trying to be pleasant, trying to smooth over old wounds. "Not too hot out there this time of year, I suppose."

"No, we're having monsoons now, Your Excellency. The problem now is flash flooding."

"Fine. By the way, Bishop, I've received information that one of our errant priests, a Father Murphy, has turned up in the Aleutian Islands. We've discussed him before, if you recall. We don't have his actual address—just a P.O. Box number in a place called Unalaska. And the name on the report isn't quite correct but can you send a couple of Brother Berard's monks up there to check it out? It would be nice if the monastery could send a different pair of brothers than those you used before."

"Your Excellency, Brothers Michael and John may have failed before but I have great confidence in Brother Berard's judgment, and he will likely find they are still the preferred monks to take on the task. I would like to notify him right away but...."

"But what?"

"But, it's going to be expensive."

"I know all that. We'll send funds to cover the airfare, hotel and all that."

"No, Your Grace. It's going to be more expensive than that."

"Why, may I ask? How much more?" Cardinal Rhinehart's attempt at a smooth pleasant tone was quickly vanishing.

"I'll be direct. I have an urgent need for fifty-thousand dollars."

"By all the saints, that's highway robbery."

"Yes, I know," Bishop Hernandez replied. The line grew silent. He thought he could hear the angry tapping of fingers on a desk coming over the phone. He thought he heard the snap of a pencil being broken.

"The check will be in the mail tomorrow morning."

"Thank you, Your Excellency."

*****

After an arduous journey that did little to improve their normally unpleasant dispositions, Brothers John and Michael landed at Unalaska airport and took a shuttle to the Dutch Inn. Inquiring at the front desk while attempting to appear as circumspect as possible, they learned the sad news that many in the town of Unalaska were in mourning. The beloved priest was dead. Killed in the volcanic eruption. A terrible tragedy.

Later, before sitting down to dinner in the dining room of the inn, Brother John placed a call to Brother Berard at the monastery outside of Tucson.

"Yes, he's dead," Brother John told his superior as he related how Murphy had died in a volcanic eruption, all the while having difficulty disguising his pleasure that the mission had been accomplished so easily.

Brother Berard, obviously pleased, said he would relay the information to Bishop Hernandez who would then call Cardinal Rhinehart with the news. Brother Berard felt sorry for Murphy and the horrible way he died, but he couldn't help thinking there was now one less thorn in the hide of the Catholic Church.

On the following day, Steve passing through the lobby of the inn, caught his breath as he got a glimpse of two monks in gray robes having lunch in the dining room. Within an hour, he had packed his few belongings and was at the Unalaska airport where he had left the Otter for cleaning, minor servicing and fueling. It wasn't that he was afraid of the monks although he knew they would try to kill him if they couldn't muscle him back to Tucson. What bothered him was the dogged perseverance of the church and its agents that would keep him from any meaningful ministry. He would be forced to spend his days looking over his shoulder. He knew they would try to sabotage his airplane, steal his vestments, possibly even attack him while he was saying Mass—in short whatever they could to carry out what they perceived as the Lord's work. He could, of course, report them to the local authorities, but they would find his complaint incredible with the end result that it would only serve to scandalize the church. It was over. He made up his mind to leave.

*****

Brothers John and Michael, who had spent the morning luxuriating in the hotel's sauna and whirlpool bath after a lavish breakfast, decided after further inquiry, that one of the priests involved in the rescue attempt was indeed Stephen Murphy. In the confusion over the death of a priest and a religious leader, they jumped to a conclusion that promised a quick easy solution to their mission. Apparently, Murphy was dead and it might be helpful to know where he was buried, and on behalf of the church, they considered laying claim to his remaining possessions. These, of course, would be turned over to Bishop Hernandez. It never occurred to them that Murphy might have a living relative who could lay claim to his belongings.

Based on their unfortunate experience in New Hampshire, they knew Murphy was a pilot. It seemed like a good idea to go to the Unalaska airport and find out if he had kept a plane hangared there. If so, when he died the plane would have been lost as well.

At the airport terminal, the brothers talked to the general aviation agent. Brother John asked if Father Murphy had a plane hangared there.

"He doesn't hangar it here," the agent said. "It's a seaplane and he usually keeps it over in Dutch Harbor at a dock right near the Russian Church. You know, the church with the young Russian-Aleut priest who was killed in that volcanic eruption."

"We learned from the hotel desk that there were two priests killed on the island." Brother Michael said.

"Not exactly," the agent said. "The Russian priest was killed but the other man was the village shaman. Father Murphy escaped. He flew out in the nick of time."

"Where is he now?" Brother Michael asked. "It's important that we find him," he said, shocked at the news that Murphy was alive.

"You see that dark blue Otter just taking off from the main runway? That's him. That's Father Murphy."

"We thought you said it was a floatplane stored in Dutch harbor."

'It has wheels. He can take off from a regular runway He just had it here for service."

"But where's he going? When is he coming back?"

"Can't answer about where he's going because since the weather's so good, he went out VFR—visual flight rules, and didn't file a flight plan. As to your second question, he told me goodbye. He said he loved the islands, but he didn't think he'd be coming back."

*****

His Excellency, Phillip Cardinal Rhinehart, Archbishop of Washington, while seated at his desk in the chancery, reread the query and a copy of a newspaper article from a paper in Anchorage. He remembered that Bishop McPherson had sent the query to all of the North American cardinals in an attempt to identify the man named Robert Murphry who may well have been impersonating a Catholic priest. Slowly, the error dawned on Rhinehart. The dead priest was the Russian-American Orthodox priest; the Catholic priest had narrowly escaped the volcanic eruption. The paper reported that after giving an explanation to the local authorities, Father Robert Murphry had apparently left Alaska, leaving no forwarding address. "Newspaper accuracy seems to be seriously lacking," he said to himself. The cardinal threw the papers on his desk. He was so angry and disgusted, jaw clenched, he almost drove his teeth further into the jawbone. "Fifty-thousand dollars, fifty-thousand dollars," he kept repeating over and over, "and for what?"

He pressed the button on his intercom. "Yes, Your Grace?"

"I'd like you to call the bank and stop payment on a check in the amount of fifty-thousand dollars made out to the Diocese of Tucson."

"I'll do it right way, Your Grace."

Ten minutes later, the intercom buzzed back. "Yes?"

"Your Grace, I'm sorry to have to tell you this, but the bank said the check has already cleared and it's too late to put a stop on it."

*****

Steve brought the Otter in for a landing at Juneau and taxied up to the dock. Totem helped tie up the plane. In the office, Steve paid the balance on the lease, had one final drink at the Red Dog Saloon with Totem and took a charter flight to Anchorage where he boarded a commercial flight to San Francisco. Wanting to leave an erratic trail that would confuse any followers, he decided to get lost in Europe. He boarded a flight to Miami, then flew to London and finally to Paris. He selected Paris because he wanted to see more of the city that he had visited years before when returning from the Gregorian University in Rome. His plan was to spend a few weeks in Paris and then go on to the Holy Land. He thought that seeing the land where Christ walked and died would be a pilgrimage to help restore his faith and especially his faith in the church. But, after that… what?

35

Steve couldn't believe the tiny elevator for two at the Royal Saint-Michel Hotel. The quaint old hotel was situated on the Boulevard St. Michel at one of the entry points to the Latin Quarter on the left bank of Paris. No room for my suitcase, Steve thought, as he squeezed into the small cylindrical tube and closed the door. I'll get it later after I check out the room. He had to laugh at the sign over his shoulder on the wall of the elevator that said in English: IN THE LIFT— ONLY TWO PEOPLE AT A TIME IN ORDER TO PREVENT BEING STUCKED. I sure don't want to get stucked, he laughed to himself. On the fifth floor he was delighted to find his room was a simply furnished but very comfortable garret with a modern bath and a balcony overlooking several intersecting streets of the Latin Quarter. He stepped onto the balcony in the bright sunshine and leaned over the railing, watching the hustling crowds of students, shoppers and tourists below. The students, he knew, were hurrying to and from classes at the world famous Sorbonne. Steve had been to Paris only once before, having stopped off on his way home from the university at the Vatican. But his earlier visit had been brief—too brief to see the wonder of the ancient city that dated back to prehistoric times.

The Royal Saint-Michel Hotel was ideally situated. From there it was a fairly short walk to the Louvre following the banks of the Seine. And best of all, it was only two blocks from Notre Dame, reached by passing over a short bridge covering one channel of the Seine to the cathedral located on the Isle de la Cite. He figured that the proximity to Notre Dame and the Louvre was the reason for the shockingly high room rate that would have discouraged anyone without a substantial income or a trust fund like he had. In fact, the concierge seemed surprised that a clergyman could afford to stay there.

Steve placed a call to his brother, Jonathon in Wayland.

Jonathon's voice was garbled, husky. "For God's sake, Steve, what's up? You're calling me at five in the morning? Where the hell are you?"

"I'm in Paris. Just arrived. I'm at the Royal Saint-Michel in the Latin Quarter. It's noon here. Sorry. I forgot about the time difference. Just wanted to let you know I had to leave the Aleutians. The brothers showed up."

"I figured as much. There was a guy who stopped in the office a few weeks ago and I think he got your address in Dutch Harbor off the rolodex in my office. The card was missing."

"Must have been one of Rhinehart's guys."

"Very likely. Well I'm sure sorry about it. It won't happen again."

"How are you feeling these days?"

"Not too good. But Marge has been wonderful. She's taking really good care of me. Is Paris going to be your new home, Steve?"

"No. Just a stop-off. After that I'm heading to Israel. I've booked a room in a boarding house right near the

Western Wall in Jerusalem. "I'll let you know my new address, but please be careful about my whereabouts. It seems as soon as I set my suitcase down somewhere, the monastery thugs show up."

"I will Steve. In fact, I've worked up a little plan to throw them off the track."

"Tell Marge I said hello and take care of yourself."

*****

Father Angelo Mazzone picked up the phone in his office located over the Saint Callistus Catacombs on the Old Appian Way just south of Rome.

"Pronto," he said in the deep sonorous voice that Steve immediately recognized.

"Angelo, it's me, Steve. I'm in Paris."

"Steve, my old roommate. "Como esta? Why are you in Paris? On my last visit to America, you were pastor of a parish in Maryland. Are you on vacation?"

"No, I've got a problem, Angelo. Since the last time I saw you my parish was taken away and I was sent to a monastery in Arizona. At the time I never knew why the cardinal sent me there. It was a hell-hole—run by a bunch of thugs, I left without permission and I hate to say it but now I'm on the run. I'll be in Rome in about a month and when I get there, I'll tell you all the details."

"Steve, old friend, I can't believe what I'm hearing. But is there anything I can do to help?"

"Yes, you may be able to help. I know you have high-level contacts at the Vatican. I'm trying to find out whether the Curia has taken any action of a case instituted by Cardinal Wollman and later taken over by Cardinal Rhinehart after Wollman died. It involves the validity of a human clone. I know the church is strenuously opposed to the cloning of humans. What I'm trying to find out is the Curia's position on a person who was born as a clone through no fault of his own. And, could the church accept a clone in the guise of a Catholic priest, complicated by the fact that he might also be a mixed-breed chimera?"

"Steve, as we used to say at the university, is this just a theological question to be pondered in endless research and discussions, or does it represent a real case?"

"It's real, Angelo, it's me, and I'm anxious because I've been waiting for over a year to pick up word. I've been constantly on the run. Cardinal Rhinehart didn't wait for an answer from the Vatican, he just moved quickly to force me out. He sent me to that monastery in Arizona. It's run like a prison by monks who call themselves 'brothers'."

"Which one? What name?"

"The Passion Monastery."

"I never heard of it."

"The American cardinals and bishops don't advertise it. It's a place where they send bad priests—ones they gave up on and are trying to get out of the church. Believe me, I haven't done anything wrong but they are saying my ordination was not valid. After I escaped they sent a couple of monks to bring me back. But there's more to the story—these guys have an old axe to grind with me and I think they are really trying to kill me. They've made an attempt so far, but I managed to escape. And recently in Alaska, they tried again but I escaped at the last moment."

"My dear friend I find that really hard to believe. How could anyone in the church deliberately commit murder? But if they have been chasing you as far as Alaska, they must be very determined to bring you back according to the cardinal's wishes. And if that place in Arizona is as bad as you say, I'll do what I can to keep them from forcing you back there. And, may I ask, are you still performing the holy sacraments?"

"Whenever I can, but it's been spotty."

"I'm surprised you haven't had your right to say Mass and administer the sacraments revoked."

"Well if my ministerial duties have been revoked, I'm not aware of it."

"Where are you staying now, Steve?"

"I'm at a small hotel—The Royal Saint-Michel in the Latin Quarter. I'll only be here for a week or two because I'm heading to Israel, to the Holy Land, to do some meditating and probably a bit of sightseeing."

"Since it's quite unlikely that I will get an answer while you're still in Paris, I'll contact you in Israel. Have you found a place to stay there?"

"Yes, I'll be at a guest house in Jerusalem run by a Jewish family, about a block from the Western Wall. I'll mail you the address and I'll get back in touch as soon as I arrive there."

"Why are you staying in a guest house? Why not stay in one of the monasteries? There are several of them in and around Jerusalem."

"Too dangerous," Steve replied. "Monasteries communicate with one another."

"Yes, I see the risk. Well, goodbye old friend. God be with you."

"And with you, Angelo. I'll need God and probably also a bit of luck."

*****

After hanging up, Steve walked over to the mirror in his room. As he studied himself in the full-length mirror, he decided to change from the black priestly garb with the roman collar into casual street clothes. He was bent on wandering through the city and mingling with the crowds unnoticed.

At Notre Dame, he said a few short prayers in a back pew. His visit was brief because he had taken the grand tour of the cathedral including the treasury containing the holy relics and had studied the famous rose stained glass window on his earlier visit. As he turned to leave, he looked up at the left side balcony and remembered that his earlier guide had said that it was the place where a sniper had hidden trying to assassinate Charles de Gaulle as he stood on the altar making a speech at the end of World War ll, just as the Germans were leaving Paris. After one missed shot, the assassin was shot by a gendarme.

After leaving Notre Dame, Steve took a cab to the Arc de Triomphe at the head of the Champs Elysees. Walking down the broad avenue and hearing the constant honking of horns of the heavy traffic, he could hear the strains of Gershwin's *American In Paris* ringing in his head. He marveled at the way Gershwin had captured the sounds of Paris in his music.

He slipped into a chair at a sidewalk brasserie for lunch and was uncertain how to order because he knew only halting French. But he had no need to worry because the waiter was an American exchange student who immediately picked up Steve's American accent. Like all the other waiters in the restaurant, he was strangely dressed in a sailor suit. Lunch consisted of Jambon de Paris, frites and espresso—to Steve it was ham, French fries and coffee. There didn't seem to be any salad on the menu although there might have been, but Steve couldn't recognize it. If I ate this way every day, he thought, I'd soon be as big as a fat overstuffed monastic friar. He had heard that many monasteries had little in the way of amenities to offer with the exception of copious amounts of food. Without that, they might have gone out of existence. Of course, the ascetic Passion Monastery in Arizona was different because being more on the order of a prison, there were few amenities.

By chance, seated nearby was an older man in black with a roman collar. A distinguished looking man with hair graying at the temples. Steve smiled in his direction at which point the clergyman walked over and took an empty seat right next to him. Good grief, Steve thought, a clergyman, undoubtedly a priest, on the prowl for converts.

"I don't want to sound rude," Steve said, "but I don't think I'm a good candidate for conversion because I'm a Catholic priest. Been there, done that, as they say." Steve smiled and chuckled, trying to keep the encounter on the light side, as he popped another French fry into his mouth.

The newcomer raised his eyebrows in surprise. "But as we used to say when I was a chaplain in the military, you're out of uniform—what we call wearing *mufti*.

How come?"

"Before I answer that," Steve replied, "I assume you're an American. Tell me, what branch of the service were you in?"

"U.S. Navy at your service," the priest answered with a mock salute. My name's Henry. And you are…?"

"Steve Murphy."

"Where do you hail from, Steve?"

"Various places," Steve answered guardedly. Then, picking the most faraway place he could think of, said, "I spent a lot of time in Alaska. Ever been there?"

"Can't say that I have. I've been stationed in Naples—headquarters of the U.S. Sixth Fleet. Seen all of the Med, but not much else. I retired as a chaplain a few years ago. Now I'm attached to a monastery just outside of Paris. Incidentally, you'd be welcome to stay there while you're in Paris."

Steve silently shuddered at the thought of staying in a monastery. The Passion Monastery had been enough for him. "Thanks, but I'm OK. I'm at the Royal Saint-Michel in the Latin Quarter."

"Don't you find that expensive? I know it's too rich for my blood."

"I managed to get a discount," Steve said, a bit disappointed in himself for the lie. "In answer to your question, Henry, I'm in mufti as you call it because I want to do some sightseeing and just blend in with the crowd."

"Well, maybe we could join forces. I know this town upside and down. We can go everywhere except the Moulin Rouge—too many bare-breasted females there, they tell me. Can't think of anything more disgusting."

Steve didn't say anything, but he thought, What's with this guy? Steve was of the opinion that women's God-given bodies were hardly disgusting, but, of course, if one gazed at them with lustful eyes, he realized they could be an occasion of sin.

Steve was reluctant to join up with another priest. There would be questions. Questions he didn't want to answer, but he finally agreed to their spending some time together. It would help having someone who knew his way around. And it was only for a few days.

*****

The pair of priests spent three full days in the Louvre. At one point, Steve remembered something that made him chuckle. "I visited the Louvre," he said, "when I was in Paris before but I was pressed for time, and I remember that I was tempted to do what the American newspaper columnist, Art Buchwald did when he visited the Louvre."

"Yes, I remember reading Buchwald's column on occasion. But what did he do at the Louvre?" Henry asked, puzzled.

"Well, Buchwald was also pressed for time, so he ran into the Louvre, saw the statue of Venus de Milo, hurried down another corridor to see the Winged Victory of Samothrace, and then to the Italian paintings gallery to see the Mona Lisa. Later, in an article he claimed it was possible to see 'the big three' in eight minutes flat."

"Not much of an art lover, I presume," Henry responded with distaste.

"Well, he did it as a gag. I suppose he was trying to

prove a point that you didn't have to spend a week at the Louvre, you could see its most famous treasures in just a few minutes."

After the days at the Louvre, Henry took Steve on almost a week of sightseeing in Paris. One day they walked through Les Invalides, formerly a hospital for wounded soldiers. "Never saw so many cannons lined up in my life," Steve commented. "Are they expecting an attack on the building?"

"No my friend. These are just ornamental. They've been brought back from the battlefields."

In Napoleon's tomb in the church called Domes Des Invalides, they leaned on the railing on the second level looking down from the large circular opening at the huge red granite sarcophagus on the lower level that held the Corsican's body.

"It's probably an overkill," Henry said, "but in order to foil grave robbers, his body lies in six coffins similar to the way the Egyptian pharaohs were entombed. The first, closest to the body is made of tin; the second mahogany; the third and fourth of lead; the fifth of ebony and the sixth of oak all inside the red granite sarcophagus. Notice the statues around the marble floor surrounding his body. They commemorate Napoleon's victories."s

"I didn't realize he had won so many wars," Steve commented.

"He didn't really." Henry answered. He won most but not all. And, of course, he was exiled, but later returned to power for awhile. He died on St. Helena in 1821 and although he had been exiled, he was considered one of the greatest of French heroes. In a way, it's similar to the attitude of many Russians towards Lenin. Although Lenin was the leader of the Communist revolution which was later repudiated, he is nevertheless still highly respected because as they say, 'He was part of our history'. And I believe the French feel that way about Napoleon. When Napoleon's body was brought back to Paris the entire city turned out for the funeral procession that went through the Arc de Triomphe and down the Champs Elyseus to his final resting place in this church."

*****

Leaving Napoleon's tomb the pair walked to the Place de la Concorde. Henry pointed out that it was the site of the former guillotine where Henry VI and Marie Antoinette were beheaded along with thousands of others during the French Revolution. "I have a surprise for you," Henry said. "Let's take a cab to the police station. It's actually police headquarters in Paris— called the Palais de Justice."

"I don't get it," Steve said. "Do they have a museum there or something?"

"You'll see."

At the guarded entrance, they walked through a metal detector. Henry had to surrender the five-inch metal crucifix tucked in his belt. It would be returned to him on the way out.

Inside the courtyard, Steve was surprised to see a beautiful chapel completely surrounded by what appeared to be a four or five story office building.

Henry, delighted by the look of surprise on Steve's face, said the hidden chapel was unknown to most tourists. He explained that this was Sainte-Chapelle built by Louis IX, located in the courtyard of his famous palace that was later taken over by the Paris Halls of Justice. "It has been preserved as a museum," he said, leading Steve inside the main entrance. Steve marveled at the chapel's two-story-high stained glass windows. "Pretty convenient, having your own private church built inside your home."

But soon after leaving the Halls of Justice, there was one happening that seemed troubling to Steve. As a young man rode by on a bicycle, Henry leaned over and whispered in Steve's ear, "Oh my, what an ass on that guy!"

Steve momentarily thought Henry was making a joke about someone with an obese rear end, but when he looked around at the bicyclist, all he could see was a young man who seemed to be quite fit. He was beginning to become convinced that his new friend was gay.

Later at Montmarte, as Steve was examining the paintings of the sidewalk artists, he saw Henry walk up to a young man and embrace him in a bear hug. The man responded by giving Henry a kiss on the cheek. In fact, a kiss on each cheek, after the French custom. But these kisses seemed to Steve to be more than just a polite greeting.

After almost ten days of trotting all around town, with frequent stops for espresso at sidewalk cafes, Henry, always jovial and full of information, was seemingly just getting warmed up, but Steve, although fascinated, was beginning to get saturated with Paris sightseeing.

One evening, the pair of priests sat at a table on a

narrow sidewalk outside a small Italian restaurant in the Latin Quarter. It was the only table available. Inside, the restaurant was full. They were a bit unnerved by automobiles that crept down the side street just inches away from their table. One car mirror almost knocked the wine glass out of Henry's hand.

"Not too good from the standpoint of air pollution," Steve commented.

"Or the restaurant's glassware," Henry responded with a laugh. "Tell me, Steve, how are things going with the church in the United States? Haven't been back there in many years and over here we only get paltry information."

"Things are not too good. And there's a strange dichotomy you may have heard about: while the number of Catholics has increased by about a third in some forty years, now approaching 70 to 75 million, the opposite has happened with the clergy. Over three thousand American parishes no longer have a resident priest."

"What in heaven do the parishioners do? How do they get the sacraments?"

"I guess many of them don't. As I understand it, in the early years after Vatican II about ten thousand priests dropped out. Many stayed in the church but as deacons, and as members of the active laity. And since then, the numbers have fallen another ten thousand. So you're talking about sixty thousand down to about forty thousand."

"How do you explain it?"

"Not sure. Some of it was due to the expectation that Vatican II under John XXIII would permit priests to marry and, of course, after he died, that never happened."

"It might have under the liberal pontiff—John Paul I," Henry commented, "but as I recall, he died only thirty-three days after being elected pontiff. One wonders if his election was not, as we might say, fully approved by the Almighty. And, an interesting historical fact: did you know that over a dozen popes died within one month after being elected to the pontificate?"

"Yes," Steve said with a shrug. "I suppose one explanation is that by the time they have acquired enough experience and influence, they're old men. And the current pontiff is over ninety, isn't he?"

"He's ninety-five but seems to be going strong," Henry replied. "But, what about you, Steve? What's your situation? Are you just on vacation? Do you mind my asking?"

"Not at all," Steve replied, trying to sound as if he meant it. But mine is a strange story and I'm not sure you'd believe it if I told you. However, it will be awhile before I go back home. I can tell you this much: I was removed from my parish by the cardinal."

"I see," Henry said with a wry grin. He was aware of the outrage in America over pedophile priests.

"No, you don't, really. Let me just say I had to get away for awhile. I was under a lot of stress running the parish and building a new church on top of that. But getting back to the American church's problems," Steve said, trying to change the subject, "the number of nuns has had a big fall-off too. In the years following Vatican II, the numbers dropped by an astonishing one-hundred thousand, now numbering about eighty thousand. That's a tough one to explain too. I suppose a lot had to do with the church not allowing women to become priests and generally keeping them as second class citizens."

"I expect America's general declining morality and materialism had a lot to do with it too. A lot of Hollywood movies and television are just filled with sex."

"You're right, of course," Steve replied, hoping to steer the conversation away from sex. "By the way, Henry, I'm about ready to shove off from Paris."

"Where to?" Henry asked as he wound the spaghetti around his fork with the aid of a large spoon. "Why are you leaving so soon? I'll really miss you, and there's lots more to see in Paris."

"I'm sure there is, but I'm heading off to see other places."

"For example?"

"I want to visit the Holy Land—you know, Bethlehem, Nazareth, Jerusalem… and I might travel to Turkey to see the house of the Virgin Mary on the mountain at Ephesus. I'm sure you know the story. The Virgin and John of the Cross escaped north after the Crucifixion to get away from Christ's enemies and, as the story goes, settled in Turkey at Ephesus. John lived in the town in the valley and Mary lived up on the mountain."

"Well, at least that's one of the stories about her," Henry commented. "Another story has her remaining in Jerusalem in hiding and after she died, as that story goes, her body was assumed into heaven. Still another story has her living in Nazareth where she was born.

In fact, the Church of the Assumption was built at the place where her body was assumed into heaven. But I'm strongly inclined to agree that she lived out her days in that house on the mountaintop while John lived in the valley below. John eventually died and is buried at Ephesus. His grave has been located. It's well documented. In fact, Pope John Paul II visited the house and blessed the waters of a spring that appeared from the side of the mountain. The water supposedly has miraculous powers. The pontiff's visit to that house gave a lot of authenticity to her living in Ephesus."

"Have you been there, Henry?"

"Oh yes. When the fleet docked at Ephesus, I took a trip up the mountain to see Mary's house. But, Steve, before you leave Paris, there's one more place we have to visit. Ever been up the Eiffel Tower?"

"Nope. They tell me there's a four-hour wait for the elevator—not to the top—just up to the observation platform. Not for me."

"Steve, I have a way of getting up there quickly."

Steve laughed. "By flying?"

"No. You'll see. Let's meet at the center under the tower at noon tomorrow."

*****

Promptly at noon, Steve was standing under the tower when he saw Henry approaching. They were both in clerical garb because Henry had said they would have lunch in a rather dressy restaurant. Steve was puzzled. He didn't see any nearby restaurants.

When Henry arrived, he took Steve by the arm and led him over to one of the legs of the tower. An attendant confirmed Henry's reservation and the pair entered a private elevator that took them up to the main observation landing. There they were greeted by a head waiter and shown to a table."

"Where are we?" Steve asked.

""You are," Henry said with a good deal of satisfaction, about to have a marvelous lunch in the Jules Verne Restaurant—somewhat expensive but excellent and with a marvelous view of Paris."

"Incidentally," Steve, said, "I'm paying for this lunch. You haven't let me pay for anything in all the time we've been sightseeing."

"No way," Henry said emphatically. "Since I am the host, my policy is that the host pays for everything."

*****

After dinner that evening, the two priests walked through the crowded streets of the Latin Quarter in the direction of Steve's hotel.

"Never been in the Saint-Michel," Henry said. I'm curious about your room. I remember that you said it's on the top floor, a garret, with a balcony. Must be a great view of the Latin Quarter all lit up at night. Maybe we could stop by there… just to take a peek."

Steve wanted to say no, but in a weak moment. He agreed.

Passing through the tiny lobby, they squeezed into the tube-like elevator that had a limit of two people. Henry started laughing at what he said must be the tiniest elevator in the world. Then, on the way up, Henry pressed himself against Steve and groped for his hand.

"Ye gods," Steve said to himself. "This guy wants to hold hands. God knows what's going to happen when we get to my room."

In the room, Henry admired the view from the balcony, took off his jacket and shoes and threw himself on Steve's bed. He lay flat-out on his back with his hands behind his head. He uttered a sigh of delight. Steve sat in a chair near the bed. Then, Henry suddenly reached out with his stocking'd foot to tickle Steve's leg.

"Please don't do that," Steve said pushing Henry's leg away. Now he was convinced about why Henry wanted to see the room. He regretted his decision to bring Henry up, but he tried to keep things as casual as possible. "Henry," he said, "now that you've seen the place I think it's time for you to leave. I'm pretty exhausted. It's been a big day. Let's meet tomorrow for lunch, and this time, I'm going to pay."

"Why? We're just getting comfy. Besides, I think I understand why your bishop in America took your parish away." He gave Steve a wink. "Look at it this way—since we're both priests we can confess to one another later and be absolved right on the spot."

"Henry, among the things that guarantee excommunication from the church is for sexual partners to absolve each other of the sin. I'm sorry if I inadvertently gave you the wrong impression, but it wasn't clear to me right off that you and I have vastly different ideas about relationships. When we first met, you said you had been a Navy chaplain. It didn't occur to me that you might be gay."

Henry put a finger to his lips. "You know the rule:

Don't ask. Don't tell." He lay on the bed, unbuckled his belt, unzipped his fly and began to slide his trousers down.

With that, Steve got up and walked to the door. He held it open. "Let me say this: you've got the wrong idea about why I was removed and, by the way, I am what they call *straight*. If the day comes when I decide to have sex it will be with a woman. Only with a woman. I'm not condemning you, Henry. Let's say, I'm just not interested. So, zip up and maybe we can get together tomorrow, perhaps in some nice café. My treat."

"That's a helluva way to treat someone who has spent the last week and a half ushering you around town paying for everything. Now you're telling me I was wasting my time and money?"

Steve picked up Henry's jacket and shoes and placed them in a neat pile on the floor in the hall.

"Goodnight, Henry!"

Henry got up from the bed and went into the hall to retrieve his jacket and shoes as Steve closed the door behind him.

*****

Jonathon fiddled with the old fashioned rolodex file on the desk in his Wayland real estate office. He inserted a new card which listed an address for his brother, Steve. "Marge, do me a favor, will you?"

Marge walked over and stood at Jonathon's desk. "What's the favor?"

"It's a bit unusual, I admit, but if a man comes in here in the next few weeks say, and I'm not here, and the man seems like he might just be nosing around—not actually interested buying real estate, sort of killing time and maybe asking a few dumb questions to cover his visit… do me a favor will you?"

"Sure, Jonathon, but I still don't get the favor. What do you want me to do?"

"Just find a way to leave the room for a few minutes."

"I don't get it. Why?"

"What I mean is: leave the room on some pretext. I'm thinking the man will go through my rolodex file trying to find my brother Steve's address."

"I still don't get it, Jonathon. If you want him to find Steve's address and the man wants to know it, why don't we just tell him?"

"It's complicated," Jonathon responded. "One of these days, I'll tell you the whole story, but for now, I want anyone who comes in trying to find Steve to be able to take a peek at the address in my file. That's all there is to it. All I'm asking you to do is find some reason, like going to the bathroom, to leave the man alone in the office for a few minutes. For Christ sake, Marge, is that so difficult?"

"Of course I'll do it. It's not difficult at all, but it seems kind of stupid."

*****

Philip Cardinal Rhinehart sat in his office in Washington and sounded unusually pleasant as he spoke into the phone with a friendly "Hello Dear Brother" to Bishop Hernandez in Tucson. For his part, the Bishop of Tucson was perplexed. He would have expected an icy greeting from the cardinal who had spent fifty thousand dollars and received nothing for it. His two monks had failed twice to capture Steve Murphy.

"My Dear Bishop," the cardinal said in a voice that seemed to transmit a smile through the phone wires, let's try again, shall we? I don't fault your monks for not apprehending Murphy in New Hampshire or the Aleutians. I understand he's a slippery eel. But now we have a new address on him, and I'd like you to send the brothers to find him. And, as before, I will be happy to cover their expenses."

"Your Eminence, do you mean another fifty thousand?" Bishop asked with a faint hope that sprang from necessity.

"Good heavens, no. I'm talking about actual documented expenses, not a major stipend for your diocese. Will you do it? Will you do it for Holy Mother Church?"

"Yes, Eminence. And let me say that after the Alaska mission failed, I know I should have returned the generous sum you sent, but I honestly didn't have it to send. So, to partially compensate, we will continue this search at the smallest possible cost to your diocese. Now please tell me, where has this Murphy gone? What is his current address?"

"He is," the cardinal said with unconcealed relish as he leaned back in his swivel chair and studied with approval a new fresco he had commissioned for the ceiling in his office, "in the Hawaiian Islands, on the island of Maui. I gather Murphy had enough of the cold weather in Alaska and decided to find a more pleasant place. We have the address of a small guest house he may be staying at. The local address was somewhat garbled so it may take awhile for your brothers to actually locate him. My secretary will forward whatever details we have."

"May I ask how you determined this, Eminence? According to my monks, Murphy left no forwarding address when he left Alaska."

"God works in mysterious way, my Dear Bishop. Truly in mysterious ways."

36

When the Greek ship Olympus out of Piraeus docked at Ashdod in Israel, Steve got into a taxi to take him to the old city of Jerusalem. Since the driver did not speak English, Steve called an old friend, Lou Lavine on his cell phone for directions. Barbara and Lou, a middle-aged Jewish couple who formerly lived in his parish had emigrated to Israel and were living in Jerusalem. Although they had not been parishioners, Steve counted them as old friends because they had participated in food drives and t-ball and softball tournaments with their kids and the kids in his parish. He had even attended their son David's Bar Mitzah and their daughter Sarah's Bas Mitzvah.

"Good to hear your voice, Father Murphy."

"Lou, the ship just docked at Ashdod. But this taxi driver doesn't speak English so what do I tell him?"

"Just say 'Jaffa Gate'. He'll understand that. The Jaffa Gate is one of the entrances to the old city which is surrounded by a wall with a number of gates. Jaffa is the western gate that leads into the city from the port. As you go through the gate just wave to the driver to keep going straight on. You'll be going along King David Street which becomes El Wad. That's our street, and when you get to a few blocks approaching the Western Wall, you'll get a glimpse of the Western Wall with the big Dome of the Rock on top set somewhat back from the wall. Then you'll be near our house. It looks like every other white stone row house around here but we'll be in the doorway waiting for you. The trip is about 40 miles so it will take about an hour to get here. You can pay the driver in dollars. He'll take dollars or euros."

"Lou, are you saying you can see the Wailing Wall from your house?"

"Yes, but we call it the Western Wall. That's the official name for it here. We can see it from the windows on the second floor. You'll be able to see it from the room we have ready for you."

*****

As the taxi approached the Western Wall, Steve had to laugh when he saw the couple standing in the doorway of their house each waving small American flags.

"First we'll eat and then we'll talk," Barbara said as they sat Steve down in their beautiful dining room surrounded with flowers and pictures of home.

Barbara and Lou looked older to Steve—they were not as plump as they had seemed when they lived in Maryland. They both appeared quite fit as they bustled about but Steve noticed that Barbara had let her hair grow out gray and he found he had to speak a bit louder when he talked. They seemed contented in their new surroundings. The thought occurred to him that much of the devout couples' apparent happiness probably came from the realization that they were finally settled in the 'promised land'.

"As you know Father Murphy, we're running a guest house here for tourists," Lou explained. "We have six rooms for guests. You are welcome to stay as long as you like and there is no charge."

"Lou, thanks for your kindness, but I plan to be in Israel about a week or two and I insist on paying your usual rate. While I was in the parish I never let anyone know that I came from a very wealthy family. And, you may be surprised to learn that I'm not in the parish any more."

"I know, you're now a bishop," Lou said with a big smile.

"Hardly that, but there have been big changes in my life."

"What happened? You were building a beautiful new church."

"It's a long, long story my friends and not a very pleasant one. Are David and Sarah here with you?"

"They were for awhile," Barbara said with a crestfallen look, "but they soon left and said they liked it better at home in Maryland."

"I hate to admit it, Father Steve," Lou cut in, "they said Israel was Okay, but they liked living conditions better in Maryland, I really believe they were both afraid of being drafted into the Israeli Army. You know, military service is compulsory for young people, male and female, in Israel. And Sarah in particular was running scared. She was in a market not far from here when a terrorist's bomb went off. She wasn't harmed but she said the horrible things she saw really scared her, and she decided to leave. Sarah and David do visit us every year and we get e-mails and telephone calls, but no more than that. And although they're both married now, there are no grandchildren yet."

"And, as I have been telling Lou," Barbara said, "grown children separating from their parents and making their own lives is a natural thing to do, although it would be nice to have them raise their children—when the days come when give us grandchildren—nearby rather than thousands of miles away."

As they sat down for a snack of warm potato knishes and coffee, Steve asked, "Where are your other roomers? I'd like to tell you some of my story but it's kind of private."

"No problem. They're all off sightseeing," Lou said. "They won't be home until dinner at six o'clock and, I might add, no one wants to miss one of Barbara's dinners."

"About my story," Steve said as he looked down staring into his coffee cup, "I was removed from my parish by the archbishop."

To their look of shocked surprise, he quickly added, "I didn't do anything wrong, please believe me, but the church came to the conclusion that I should be transferred. There was no explanation. And in the Catholic Church, a cleric is bound by a vow of obedience. If your bishop wants to tell you the reason, fine, but if not, you have no right to demand an explanation. In fact, I was transferred twice—first to a parttime teaching post at Catholic University in Washington, but then, after Cardinal Wollman died, I was transferred again to a monastery in the Arizona desert. This transfer was arranged by Bishop Rhinehart who took over after Cardinal Wollman's heart attack."

"I've heard things about Rhinehart when he was auxiliary bishop, from some Catholic friends we knew in your parish," Lou commented. "One of your former parishioners even said that if Rhinehart was alive during the French Revolution, he would have been the chief executioner."

Steve laughed. "Rhinehart is a strict tradionalist and he has a gift for making people miserable, but I think he'd stop short of executions."

"But Father Steve, you still haven't given us any clue about why they would do this to you," Barbara said puzzled.

Steve decided to tell the couple some but not all of the story.

"From what little I know," he said, "they checked into my past and said that my ordinaton to the priesthood many years before had not been completely valid." Steve was somewhat ashamed to give a more complete explanation, and on top of that, he wasn't sure they'd understand about the cloning. "I was then sent to a monastery that was more like a prison than a true monastery. Frankly, it got so bad, to keep my sanity, I escaped and have been on the run ever since."

The couple looked at Steve in disbelief. They had always believed he had a promising career in the church.

"Sounds to me," Lou commented dourly, "and pardon my 'French' but it seems to me the church really gave you the shaft."

"Not quite," Steve said defensively. "The hierarchery very likely thought they were simply following some traditional regulations."

"So, you're on the run," Lou commented. "Who's chasing you?"

"I was afraid you'd ask that, but I better tell you because they might be after me here."

"Well, they'll get no help from us," Barbara said emphatically.

"Thanks. And I may need your help. There are two burly gray-robed monks, Brothers Michael and John, who have been trying to find me and drag me back to Arizona. And I hate to admit it but they're more like thugs than brothers of the Catholic Church. If you don't mind a little white lie, if they happen to come here just tell them I was here but I left and you're not sure where I went. That should take care of it."

"By the way," Lou said. "There's something you should know. There were two men here yesterday who said they were looking for you. They were here before your ship docked at Ashdod. We told them you weren't here but you might be on your way."

"What did they look like?" Steve asked with a frown. "Did they look like the big gray-robed monks I mentioned?"

"No. They were ordinary looking young men in black suits. Nothing special. They looked like seminarians. They spoke with thick Italian accents. Do you know them?"

"Not really," Steve said puzzled. "But they might have been from the Vatican." Good grief, Steve thought, now I have two groups looking for me.

"Now, on to a more pleasant subject," Steve said. "Tell me about what I can see here in Israel. Never been here before. Of course, I've read about it but I still find it confusing. I understand you have an old city and a new Jerusalem."

"Yes, it is confusing," Lou agreed. In the old walled city, houses and streets have been built over top of crumbled remains for thousands of years. And on top of that, the mix of Jews, Christians and Muslims living near each other is hard for a newcomer to sort out. We live here in the Jewish quarter by the Western Wall, but if you walk a few blocks north from the Wall to the Via Dolorosa you'll be in the Muslim quarter. So some of the Christian sites lie in Muslim territory. If you go further north and to the west, you'll be in the area of the Church of the Holy Sepulchre which lies in the Christian quarter. One nice thing is that we all freely go from one area to the next. In fact, with the exception of a few lunatic terrorists, we all get along quite well. So, you might say there are actually three Israels here. As a Christian, you will want to see places like Bethlehem, Nazareth and the Church of the Holy Sepulchre, also the River Jordan where Jesus was baptized by John the Baptist, and Capharnum way in the north at the Sea of Gallilee where Jesus began his ministry. But there are also other places you might want to see—places from the old Testament like Abraham's tomb and David's tomb. Many visitors go up to the mountaintop, Masada, where the Jews held out for three years against a siege by the Roman army. Another popular place to visit is the Knesset which is Israel's parliament building. And, of course one of the holiest Muslim sites is the Dome of the Rock located up behind the Western Wall."

"How far is the Via Dolorosa and the Church of the Holy Sepulchre?"

"You can walk there from here," Barbara said as she brought in a platter of fruit. "Father Murphy, you have lost weight; you're too thin. You need more than coffee and a knish, so eat. While you're here I intend to put some meat on your bones."

"Thanks. After I eat, I think I'll look around at a few nearby sites, and by the way, I'd feel more comfortable if you just called me Steve. Think of me as an old friend from America. I want to blend in with the tourists. I don't want to advertise the fact that I'm a priest."

"Make sure you're back here for dinner at six o'clock." Lou said. "And in crowded places, keep an eye on your wallet and watch. In some areas, American tourists are considered fair game. And, if you want to follow an old tradition, as you approach the Western Wall, give a dollar to the first beggar you see. It's considered good luck."

*****

As Steve stood in front of the Western Wall, he remembered reading that it was frequently referred to as the Wailing Wall because so many Jews came there to cry. The wall was not part of Solomon's former temple; rather, it was part of the temple mount and apparently extended as far below the surface as above, although it has not yet been fully excavated. The section on the left was for the men; the portion on the right for the women. It was customary to place a note in a nook or cranny of the wall to ask for favors from God or to give thanks for favors received.

Steve noted that the area was heavily guarded by Israeli soldiers and police. Orthodox Jews in black suits with broad flat-rimmed black hats, and some with large drum-shaped hats ringed with fur, came to the wall to pray. It was considered the holiest place in Jewish Israel.

After leaving the Wall, Steve decided to get a closer look at the huge golden dome on the high ground behind the Western Wall. Climbing the hill to the Dome of The Rock, he was awestruck as he approached the massive Dome glistening in the late afternoon sun. Inside, he saw the rock itself—a huge flat irregular rock from which Muslims believe Mohammed leapt into heaven to talk to God. When Steve thought about it, he had to marvel at how difficult it was to believe some of the basic tenets of someone else's faith, realizing that Christianity had miraculous beliefs that non-Christians undoubtedly found equally incredible.

When Steve returned to the Lavine's house, Lou met him at the door. "While you were gone, those Italian men were here again. They wanted to rent a room, but I told them we were full up."

"Where did they go?" Steve asked.

"I sent them to a small hotel about half a mile from here."

"Did they say anything about me?"

"No, not this time. They said they just wanted a room."

*****

Dinner was a lavish affair. Among the dozen guests were four attractive young American women seated opposite Steve at the long table. They were soon into their second glass of wine. During the animated conversation about the sites they had visited, Steve felt that one of the women was coming on to him. She was a beautiful, tall, blue-eyed blonde, with the lithe figure of an Olympic athlete. He sensed that in a wrestling match she would pin him inside of a minute.

Steve was casually dressed. No Roman collar. He tried to ignore the extra attention he was receiving from the young woman who was introduced as Alice. He learned the women were all Catholics. At one point in the conversation, they started kidding about Catholic priests and how sad it was that so many handsome young men chose the priesthood.

Barbara, apologizing to Steve, said she and Lou were embarrassed. "Steve," she announced, "is a Catholic priest."

Steve laughed it off. "I should complain," he said, "when I might have been considered one of the handsome ones?"

Alice looked Steve directly in the eye, "You definitely were, Father."

A couple of the women nudged each other. "He still is," they agreed, laughing. "Better watch out, Father… you might have a nocturnal visitor in your room."

When Steve saw a couple of the young women having their third glass of wine, he decided he'd better lock his bedroom door.

*****

After breakfast the following morning, Steve walked in the direction of the Via Dolorosa. He went through a crowded narrow street that was more akin to an alley bordered with shops that had high-up rows of garments on hangers and open barrels of grains, spices and fruit in front. He breathed in the aroma of spices mixed with the odor of the jostling crowd. Confusion reigned. He wondered if anyone went into the shops since all the business seemed to be conducted out front. At one point he grabbed the wrist of a young man who had tried to reach into his pocket. He bent back the wrist producing an injury that the young man would long remember. He threaded his way through the mobs along the Via Dolorosa—the street on which Christ had carried the Cross to Mount Calvary. When he came to one of the Stations of the Cross, he remembered what Lou had said that in this region, Jews, Muslims and Christians lived literally on one another's backs. In fact, much of the Via Dolorosa, so sacred to Christians was in the Moslem quarter.

After pausing to look at the stone inscriptions marking a few of the Stations, Steve came upon a small group of tourists standing in front of the Fifth Station of the Cross. This was the place where Simon of Cyrene had helped Jesus with the Cross after Jesus had fallen under the heavy weight. Steve tried to work his way into the crowd to listen to the guide but the lecture was in German, so he stepped back and waited. Before long, another group with an English-speaking guide approached the Station. The guide was an Israeli. Steve stood at the back of the crowd of about twenty American tourists.

"This is the Fifth Station of the Via Dolorosa, known as the Way of the Cross," the guide said. "It would be very difficult to begin the tour in the first few Stations because parts of the Via Dolorosa are not accessible due to walls and other new construction. You are on the street where Jesus walked. However, if you wanted to see the actual stones he walked on you should have brought a shovel because the original street is about fifteen feet down. In two thousand years, having buildings decay and fall down, and then having new ones built on top of the rubble, some original streets are far below where they used to be. I hope you aren't too disappointed but let me assure you that the events of Jesus' life actually happened in places that you will visit in Israel, although I admit there is controversy over some of the exact locations."

As Steve listened to the guide, out of the corner of his eye he noticed two men who had been walking just behind him along the Via Dolorosa. They were young, dressed in black suits, but apparently not Jews because they wore no yomulkes, not priests because they had no Roman collars, and not ministers again because of the absence of white collars. Perhaps they were seminarians, he thought.

As the men sidled up to him at the back of the crowd, Steve edged away. One of the men who was closest to Steve suddenly grabbed his arm. Steve twisted loose, pushed the man away and broke into a brisk walk to get lost in the mob on the street. The men followed but apparently lost sight of him. The incident attracted virtually no attention from the crowds of tourists.

Who the hell were they and what did they want? He seriously doubted they could have been from the Passion Monastery because the monastery had always used Brothers Michael and John to track him. Then he remembered that Lou had said two young men had come to the house. He also said they had thick Italian accents. So they could be part of another team that could have come directly from Rome.

Steve's next stop was at the Church of the Holy Sepulchre, situated on the hilltop where Jesus was crucified. Inside the church, at Golgotha, the place of the Crucifixion, literally dozens of votive lights were suspended from the ceiling. Nearby and lower down was the stone on which Jesus' body was laid where Nicodemus prepared him for burial. Steve knelt for a moment, touched the stone and said a prayer. Moving further along in the church he came upon a cavelike room containing an altar and a stone sarcophagus. Here again, a score of votive lights were suspended from the ceiling of the small room. Although the burial chamber had originally been at the bottom of the hill of Golgotha, the inside of the church had been levelled out so that both were at approximately the same level.

On leaving the church Steve spotted the two young men who had tried to grab him lingering outside. He quickly slipped back into the dark interior. One of the men remained outside as the other walked into the entrance. In a sudden movement, Steve reached out from a dark corner, grabbed the man in a headlock and pulled him into the dark.

"Now you tell me who you are and why you're following me."

"I am not allowed," the man croaked in broken English trying to breathe as Steve held him in a stranglehold.

"You'll tell me or I'll break your neck."

"You are priest. As priest it is a sin to hurt me."

Steve put on more pressure. "A priest is allowed to defend himself and I think you guys are a threat to me."

Steve now had the man down on one knee gasping for air. "I can see you have a dagger hidden in your coat. If you make a move for it, you'll be dead before you get it out."

"I talk," the man said in a gravelly whisper. "We are from Rome. We are of the Knights of Carthage. We are told to find you and bring you back to Rome."

"Who the hell are the Knights of Carthage?"

"I can tell you no more except—we have taken the oath to protect the church."

So I really do have two groups of goons after me, Steve thought. And I wonder if these guys picked up the trail when Angelo started making inquiries at the Vatican.

Steve released his grip and pushed the young man down on his bottom in the corner. He pressed his index finger under the man's chin and dug his fingernail into the man's throat. "You sit here in this corner and count slowly to one hundred before you move, or I'll come back here and I'll really break your neck. You know what one hundred is?"

"Si, cento."

"Start counting! Ciao," Steve said as he started to walk away in the direction of the dark church interior to look for another exit. Suddenly, the young man was on his feet. He had pulled out the dagger and was rushing up behind Steve. As Steve wheeled around, he twisted the man's arm and knocked the dagger to the floor. As he picked it up, he stared at the fourteen-inch long dagger in shock. It was a crucifix—a cross with an image of Christ on the cross—and shockingly, the vertical shaft of the cross had been sharpened to a point. The crucifix had been turned into a weapon.

"This is a damned sacrilege," Steve muttered angrily to the man, "and I should break it in half, but how can I destroy a crucifix? However, I'd be a fool to give it back to you. For a minute I thought you were trying to grab me and bring me to the Vatican, but I guess if you had to, the plan was to bring me back in a box."

Looking around, Steve saw a high crevice in the stone wall—one that he could reach but the young man couldn't. He reached up and slid the crucifix into the crevice, gave the young man one final shove into a corner and hurried into the church interior to find another exit. As he glanced back, he noticed that the young man who had remained outside, came running into the church looking for his comrade.

*****

Father Angelo Mazzone picked up the phone in his office located over the Saint Callistus Catacombs in Rome. "Pronto," came through the line which Steve recognized as the sonorous voice of his friend.

"Angelo, I assume you haven't had any news about my situation otherwise you would have contacted me."

"Si, si, Steve. No word yet from the Vatican."

"Tell me, Angelo, there are two guys in black suits who have been following me and they tried to grab me today. When I got one of them alone and collared him he said he was with the Knights of Carthage. Who the hell are they?"

"As in America, you have the Knights of Colombus and in Paris at Notre Dame, there are the Knights of Malta, so too in Rome we have Knights. These are the

Knights of Carthage. But let me warn you, my friend, the Knights of Carthage are far more aggressive than the others. They believe it is their solemn duty to protect the Church. Here in Rome, they are called 'The Hounds of Rome'. They are called hounds because they are very persistent. They will hound someone until their mission is complete. They will yelp after you like dogs chasing a fox and they can be very dangerous."

"Are they sanctioned by the Vatican?"

"No. They are completely independent but they very likely have informants in the Vatican who, shall we say, let them know things the Vatican may be worried about."

"You don't have to tell me how dangerous they are—one of them tried to stab me with a sharpened crucifix."

"Si. That is their trademark. In fact, whenever the Rome police investigate a stabbing, they can be pretty sure by the unusual square-shaped wound that it was done by one of the Knights using the shaft of a crucifix. It represents the square-shaped upright shaft of Christ's Cross."

"And no one stops this?"

"No. There are two ways you can look at this— either the police are unduly deferential to the church or they are afraid of the church. You are surprised, yes? What about the situation in America where 5,000 priests have been credibly accused of sexual abuse but only one, yes, only one has wound up in jail."

"By the way, I wonder how these Knights managed to find out where I am?"

"I'm very sorry, Steve. It must be my fault. When I put your questions through channels, I was told there would be no answer unless the Church was told your location. I had to tell them or I would have gotten nothing. They said no harm would come to you. They are constantly warned not to resort to violence, but what can you do when young men get angry?"

"I understand, Angelo, but you must realize that now I have two groups of characters after me."

"Just keep your eyes open my friend. May God keep you safe."

"I'll see you in a few weeks, Angelo. God be with you."

"And with you, Steve."

*****

"Take the motorbike when you go south to Bethlehem," Lou said. "My son, David left it here when he went back to America."

"What about military checkpoints?"

"With your American passport, your driver's license, your I.D. as a priest, the registration card for the motorbike, they won't give you any trouble; in fact, you'll have them snowed with credentials. It's only about six miles south of here so you should be able to make it back for dinner."

"Great," Steve replied as he went out back to the bike and was surprised to find Alice seated on it. "Are we going to Bethlehem together?" he asked.

"Yes."

"Haven't you been there yet?"

"Yes, I've been there."

"Then why do you want to go again?"

"Simply because I get the feeling you're going to

need me. No matter what Lou told you about getting through the checkpoints, it'll be a lot faster with a blonde on the back giving the military guys a big toothy smile. You drive and I'll just hang on the back and show you the best way to get there. Okay?"

"Yes, I suppose so, but I didn't expect to have any company," Steve replied with a shrug as he mounted the bike and felt Alice's arms wind tightly around his waist.

After driving about half an hour, they fairly breezed through the checkpoint. "Do you believe me now?" Alice asked as she gripped Steve even tighter around the waist.

"I believe. I believe."

"Okay, now pull up here. This is the Church of the Nativity. Let's go inside. When we enter the cave where tradition says the Christ child lay in the manger, you'll have to stoop down because the opening was made intentionally small so no one could go in on horseback. I believe this was an idea dreamed up by the Crusaders about one thousand A.D. Much of the constuction you'll see in Israel was done by the Crusaders who were trying to rebuild the holy sites. The silver star on the floor in the cave presumably marks the exact spot where Jesus was born. And if you believe all this, you are standing in one of the holiest places in Christendom."

"Alice, you don't sound as if *you* believe all this."

"Maybe yes, maybe no. The basic church is 1700 years old. It's interesting that this site was picked almost three hundred years after Christ died. And don't forget that it was picked by Emperor Constantine's mother who was about as qualified an archeologist as the man in the moon. And this should give you a laugh, although you may know about it already—the cathedral in Cologne in Germany has three golden boxes that are supposed to contain the bodies… I should say the bones… of the Three Wise Men."

"Yes, I've heard that," Steve said with a smirk.

"How do you think the Three Wise Men were found?"

"Constantine's mother?"

"Now you're catching on. She was poking around Jerusalem, remember in three hundred A.D., and found three bodies and God told her they were the bodies of the Three Wise Men. On January sixth every year—I believe it's called the Feast of the Epiphany—pilgrims come from all over Europe to Cologne to view the remains of the Three Wise Men, and, of course, they very likely make sizeable donations to the church."

"Alice, stop," Steve said, as he looked her in the eye and lightly laid a hand on each of her shoulders. "You're undoing things the nuns taught me as unwavering truth in third grade," he said with a wide smile.

*****

Later, as Steve and Alice were standing in the church proper admiring the wall frescos, Steve was suddenly floored by a rock that hit him squarely in the back between his shoulder blades. Then, as he lay face down, Alice quickly scooped up two rocks that were the size of oranges and, swinging around, threw them at the two clerics who were standing on the far side of the church. She expertly aimed to whizz the stones close to the heads of the clergy who had assaulted Steve—intending to miss them by inches. The clergymen drew back when they realized that the young woman had a skill that reminded them of David coming up against Goliath. They quickly realized that the two additional stones that she had picked up and was aiming, could put them in the hospital or worse. In a flash, they were gone.

When Alice helped Steve to his feet, he was groggy. His back ached. Alice lifted his shirt and said although he was bruised, the skin hadn't been broken. She then went on to explain: "The Church of the Nativity had been fought over for many years with each of three religions—Greek Orthodox, Armenian and Roman Catholic claiming jurisdiction over the place where Christ was born. The church was divided into three parts and on more than one occasion when the clergy of one sect thought the other two were intruding on their turf, fights would break out. In fact, it's hard to believe but each group has piled up stones to use as weapons against the others."

"Yes, I am finding it hard to believe," Steve said, "but my sore back proves your point. What do they do when groups of tourists come?"

"Oh, then they're on their good behavior. When tourist groups arrive, it all looks like one happy family. Hell breaks out later."

"But why did they pick on me?" Steve asked wondering.

"I think when the Greeks and Armenians saw you genuflect and cross yourself, they assumed they were in the presence of a Catholic… perhaps even a Catholic priest. And, you were in the Armenian section of the church, where Catholics are not allowed, so they let you have it."

"While I was flat out on the ground, what did you do to stop them?"

"I just let them have a couple of well-placed stones. I wasn't trying to hurt them, just give them a warning to knock it off."

"Good grief," Steve said in wonder. "And all of this on hallowed ground."

"Father Steve," now you know why I wanted to tag along on your visit. One other thing, I overheard Lou and Barbara say that two guys were after you and one actually attacked you with a stilleto. I don't particularly like the idea of two against one. So I thought you might need some help."

"Alice, let's stop someplace for lunch. It seems as though I owe you one."

*****

"Do you mind my asking where you're off to tomorrow?" Alice asked as she sipped a tall cool glass of beer at a small table they had taken in a side street.

"I was thinking of heading to the river Jordan, possibly to the place where they say Jesus was baptized by John The Baptist," Steve replied as he sipped his espresso.

"I know where it is. And maybe you'll let me come along."

"I'd be glad to have you along. Bring stones in case there's trouble," he said laughing.

"I don't think this place calls for stone throwing. It's

pretty peaceful. Although, if you're thinking of seeing a river, you'll be disappointed. What with recent droughts, it's more like a creek."

*****

Early on the following morning the pair set off again on the motorbike. This time, Alice guided them east out of Old Jerusalem to the Jordan. On arriving, they found a large group of blacks from Chicago who were being baptized one-by-one with total immersion. A line of people clad in long white gowns walked slowly down a curved staircase that wound down from a high landing, where they ended in waist-deep water. Their voices were all raised in a beautiful harmonious chant. A deacon and an assistant, standing in waist-deep water, momentarily submerged each participant. Steve found himself deeply moved by the singular devotion of each baptism candidate.

The curved staircase facing the river on the right was used for descending to the water, while the one on the left was used for returning to the high ground.

"Care to join in brother? This is the way to the Lord." The words were spoken by a black man who appeared to be one of the deacons. He was a giant, almost seven feet tall and dressed in a long flowing multi-colored African robe.

"Thanks," Steve replied, "but I've already been baptized. However, if it won't disturb the ceremony, I'll just slip down the opposite staircase and wade in the shallows."

When the deacon gave him an inquiring look, Steve replied, "I just want to be able to tell the folks back home I was wading in the river Jordan."

"Amen to that, Brother. Amen to that," the deacon replied as Steve took off his shoes and socks and slowly walked down the left staircase, passing a line of soaking wet, newly baptized people. As he dipped his feet into the river, Alice leaned on a railing at the top watching him.

*****

As Alice stood on the top landing, watching Steve and keeping an eye on the motor bike, she suddenly felt a man on each side gabbing her arms. They pulled her arms behind her back and began to drag her back away from the plateau that overlooked the river. She was too surprised to resist or even yell for help. Steve, down below wading in the river, was completely unaware of what was happening. They dragged Alice to a nearby car that had a rear door open and began pushing her inside. The only thing she could think of was that they had decided to take her hostage as a way of forcing Steve to surrender.

A few minutes later, when Steve came back up the stairs getting ready to put his shoes and socks on, he noticed that Alice's jeans were torn and her hair was somewhat tousled.

"What happened to you?" he asked.

"Those two guys from Rome tried to grab me and stuff me in their car. I guess I was being taken hostage and maybe they planned to release me after you surrendered. Either that… or… ?"

"But what did you do?" Steve asked. "How did you escape?"

"Do you really want to know?"

"Of course."

"Well, this may sound a bit crude, but if you really want to know, I socked one in the jaw and he collapsed onto the seat of the car. Glass jaw as they say. I kicked the other one in his gonoids and when he bent over I kneed him right under his chin. He then staggered to the car and they drove off. Last I saw them, they were weaving down the road."

"But what about the stilletos? Did you get stabbed?"

"No. It all happened so fast they never had a chance to get their stilletos out."

"Alice, tell me, have you ever been referred to as Wonder Woman?"

"No. But you owe me a dinner in a first class restaurant."

*****

Over dinner that evening Steve asked, "Alice, do you mind if I ask you a personal question?"

"Not at all."

"I was wondering about the young women you're staying with at the Lavines."

"You seem a bit older than they, more mature."

"True. They're my students. We've been on a summer field trip. I'm an Associate Professor of History at the University of Iowa. We've been studying the Middle East—Egypt, Jordan, Israel and a few other countries that permit women to visit. Israel has been our last stop. We'll soon be heading home."

*****

In the days that followed, Alice took Steve to the Dead Sea where they floated in water so salty it was impossible to sink. Their next trip was on the cable car that took them up to Masada—the sad place where the Jews, after holding out for three years against the assaulting Roman army finally committed suicide rather than be captured. Alice also took Steve to David's tomb and the place in the same building where the Last Supper was held.

"I'll say this for you, Alice, you sure know your way around Israel, and you could hire youself out as a bodyguard."

"Well my students and I have been here for a few weeks so I've seen just about everything. By the way, if you're agreeable, let's head up north to Nazareth and Capernaum on the Sea of Gallilee. Capernaum, in particular, is an important stop because it's believed to be the place where Jesus began his ministry."

*****

At the Lavines at dinner one night, a few eyebrows were raised when Alice announced that she and Father Steve were going to travel north to Nazareth and Capernaum. Since it was a full ninety-seven miles from Jerusalem to Nazareth—a trip that would take them away for several days, Alice's students couldn't help wondering what was going on between their professor and the priest.

When one of the young women confronted her about it, Alice replied, "Please stop the rumor mill. I'm simply showing this guy the sights so he doesn't get lost.. And no, we're not falling in love."

*****

In Nazareth, Alice and Steve visited the Church of the Annunciation that was built over Mary's home, where the angel announced to Mary that she was to be the Mother of God.

"Of course," Alice said, "as you might expect, there are two stories about the Annunciation. I think it is the Greek Orthodox who don't believe it took place here. They believe the Annunciation took place at Mary's Well located just a short distance from here down in the town. But as the guides are quick to point out, all these events took place somewhere around these locations, although there is some disagreement as to the exact locations."

Later in Capernaum on the shores of the Sea of Gallilee, Alice and Steve listened to a lecture by an Israeli guide. They stood among a large group of tourists in front of the few remaining columns of what had once been a synagogue.

"It was here," the guide said, "that Jesus began his ministry. Yes, it was right here in this old synagogue. How do I know this is true?" he asked. "Simply because at that time there was only one synagogue in Capernaum. This one. And I would like to remind all of you gentiles, that Jesus was a Jewish boy!"

Later, after a short boat trip on the lake, Steve and Alice checked at the desk of a small hotel close to the seashore. They tried to book separate rooms as they had done on the previous night while traveling up to Nazareth, but the clerk said there was only one room available.

"I guess we should try another hotel," Steve said.

"You're welcome to try," the clerk said, "but this is the height of the tourist season and I doubt you'll find two rooms anywhere."

"Well, why don't we take it," Alice said. "Otherwise we might wind up sleeping on the beach."

"Does the room have twin beds?" Steve asked hopefully.

"No, just one queen size bed."

"Okay, we'll take it," he said, thinking of a solution where he would sleep in a chair or on the floor while Alice took the bed.

The candlelit dining room overlooking the lake where Jesus had walked on the water, was warm and comfortable as they shared a bottle of wine and a dinner which after a long day sightseeing, they were almost too tired to eat.

Alice showered and prepared for bed in the room's private bath while Steve went down the hall to the communal shower room. Alice, exhausted, slipped into the bed.

When he returned, Steve first tried to make a bed on a chair, then tried to use a pillow and blanket to sleep on the floor.

Alice sat up. "Steve. What on earth are you doing? This is a big bed. We're both exhausted. Come to bed. I'll take this side, you take the other side." After saying that, Alice rolled away on the other side and was asleep in two minutes.

Reluctantly, Steve slipped under the light blanket and lay with his arms folded behind his head staring at the ceiling in the dim light that came into the room from the street. He lay there for a long time, musing on the fact that he had grown to like Alice; not love certainly, but a comfortable friendship. With her knowledge of Israel he had seen things he never would have seen on his own. He chuckled when he thought of the way she had handled the clerics who had stoned him in the Church of the Nativity and he visualized what her fight must have been like with the Knights of Carthage at the Jordan River. He remembered he had asked her if she was ever called Wonder Woman.

He thought of Janet, the woman he still loved— but with whom he had lost contact. Based on her last letter that he had received in Dutch Harbor, she was probably back in her marriage and possibly raising a family. It saddened him to think of it, but considering the impossibility of any future in their relationship, he accepted it as the will of God.

Then he thought of the church—his church. It had become obvious that he was a problem that church officials would have been happy to be rid of. The shocking story—as a clone, possibly a chimera and not fully human, was he really a priest? Was he really a man? It seemed as if everything was stacked against him. If he got kicked out of the church, what future was there for him?

Steve fell asleep, thinking of Janet as he had done many nights when he was confined at the Passion Monastery. About three in the morning, still not really awake, he rolled over close to Alice. He could feel her warm body near his. Was he dreaming or was this real? Partly aroused, Alice reached her hand back and lightly placed it on Steve's thigh. Then she rolled over and snuggled up to him. He kissed her as she wrapped her arms around him.

"Relax, Father Steve," she said softly.

"But what if… what if you become pregnant?"

"Fear not—I've taken all the necessary precautions."

The warmth and the softness aroused him to a point from which there was no turning back, and they made love off and on through the night.

They slept together on the following two nights as they made their way south back to Jerusalem.

On the next day, just before departing, Alice gave him a warm smile and a deep blue-eyed stare as she gave him a light peck on the cheek. "Steve, dear," she said softly, "it was a wonderful brief encounter that I won't soon forget, but that's all it was—a brief encounter. You are committed to your church although I know there are problems with that. If you ever want to get in touch with me, just contact the university and ask for Professor Alice Devereau, and if you visit, I'll give you the fifty-cent tour of Iowa City."

Steve and the Lavine's stood at the door waving goodbye as the four women left in a cab for the airport.

On the following day, Steve packed his stuff. He knew that if he tried to pay the Lavines for his room and board, they would refuse, so he left a generous payment in an envelope in his room.

After warm goodbyes, Steve left Jerusalem headed for Lod Airport where he embarked on a flight for Rome.

*****

After Steve had gone, Barbara and Lou sat in their living room relaxing and waiting for the next group of tourists to arrive.

"Did you notice anything unusual going on while Father Murphy was here?" Barbara asked her husband.

"Unusual? What do you mean? I didn't notice anything."

"Oh you. You never do. Didn't you notice how those women took a shine to Father Murphy?"

"What's unusual? He's a handsome man."

"Didn't you notice how that woman professor kept after him and even jumped on the motorbike when he was going off sightseeing?"

"She was trying to help him find the sites. After all, she had been here for several weeks. She knew how to get everywhere. How to get past the guard posts. Stuff like that. Without her help as a tour guide, he would have been wandering around never sure of where he was or where he was going."

"Well I think there was more to it than that. Remember how he locked his bedroom door on the night he first met those women?"

"He's a priest. He doesn't want any night prowlers. Especially beautiful women."

"Well I sure noticed that when he first came he was very upset. Thrashing around in bed like he was being chased by demons."

"He explained that. He's been having some trouble with the church. They took him out of his parish. Sent him off to teach and after that, God knows what."

"But when he got back from his travels with that woman professor he seemed much calmer. No more thrashing about in bed."

"Barbara, what are you getting at? Do you think they

fell in love?"

"I know she did, but I don't know about him."

"All I can say is that for all the years I've known him, Father Murphy has been a devout priest. There has never been a hint of scandal about him. By the way, did you see all the money he left in his room? He left enough to cover two months room and board even though he was here just a couple of weeks."

"Well, I think something went on between him and that woman."

"When you think of how lonely that kind of life must be, for his sake, I hope something did."

37

The jet touched down at Rome's Leonardo da Vinci airport. Steve took a succession of three crowded buses finally reaching the pensione where he had booked a room near the foot of the Spanish Steps on a narrow street a few blocks behind the Via Condotti. After reaching the central city, he would have taken a taxi for the last leg of his journey, but as usual the cabs were on strike for the better part of the day. He loved Rome—dirty, noisy, yet endlessly fascinating. An impossible jumble of the crumbling remains of ancient Rome, modern upscale stores, noisy nightmarish automobile traffic, magnificent sculptured fountains, saucy mini-skirted women on spike heels, children begging coins, armies of black-clad clergy from the Vatican, tourists in garish plaid shirts with cameras slung over their shoulders, Italian men talking with their hands on street corners, and gypsies in long colorful dresses.

After unpacking, his first visit was to the ancient basilica of San Giovanni in Laterano—Rome's cathedral. As he knelt to pray in a rear pew, the memories flooded back to that day many years before when he had lain prostrate at the foot of the altar with seven others about to be ordained, to receive the sacrament of Holy Orders. Every nuance of the service would remain etched in his mind for the rest of his life. His emotions had run the gamut from downright disbelief that he had been chosen for this ultimate honor to the humble realization that after years of study and prayer, he was at last at the threshold of a consecrated life—one that was sanctified and devoted to the mission of saving souls for Christ. He would always vividly recall a point in the ordination ceremony: he had been almost overcome by a devotion so intense that as he pressed his face into the cloth on the altar floor beneath him, he could feel the soft touch of Jesus' hand on the back of his head and the sweet breath of the Virgin Mary as she whispered a joyful welcome in his ear.

Now, in the shadowy interior of the basilica, in surroundings of many years ago, he felt himself transported back to those early joyous years when as a young priest he was filled with the grace and zeal to spread the word of God. Now, as he knelt, his mind drifting from prayer, he relived compressed memories of his happy years at the Pontifical University in Rome followed by his years in America as a parish priest and then pastor. But too soon, as always, the evil specter spread its sinister wings over him as his mind sank into feelings that stabbed at his heart: that he was a renegade, perhaps not even a priest at all, and worse, perhaps a being that while appearing human had been deprived of a soul.

Suddenly aware that his mind had drifted, that he was not praying, he chastised himself and resumed praying to a God he wasn't sure was listening. This was his hope: returning to Rome would somehow resolve his predicament. After being hounded from one end of America to the other, and even as far as Israel, here at the seat of the Catholic Church, he hoped to rise above the narrow provincial views of some cardinals and bishops. Surely the answer was here. He hoped to prod an answer to this question that concerned not only him but very likely others like him who were not the sanctified products of normal conjugal births—instead, the products of lab experiments that manipulated synthetic life in embryonic cells. Yes, surely the answer was here. The source was here: the pontiff, Christ's Vicar on Earth, the one who entered into the inner sacred chambers where God surely dwelt. The pontiff, the one who, above all others, speaks to God. He would learn God's answer to a question that science had forced on the church.

As he knelt in prayer, Steve's attention was drawn to the high lintel on which rested two large covered urns that according to legend hold the heads of Saints Peter and Paul. If true, the heads would be no more than skulls, but since Peter and Paul were saints, saints whose bodies resist immolation, perhaps some flesh remained.

Leaving the basilica through the huge front doors, blinking in the bright sunshine, Steve walked down the broad front steps. Dressed in casual clothing much like the tourists, he stopped abruptly as two young gypsy women appeared out of nowhere blocking his way. One of the women who wore no bra, suddenly opened her blouse revealing her ample breasts. Steve glancing over, quickly put the image out of his mind as he brushed past the women. Then, a few minutes later, as he left the piazza, he found that a ten euro note he had had in his pants pocket was gone. Good old Rome, he thought. In clerical garb there would not have been a problem because the superstitious gypsies would not rob a clergyman or a nun for fear of the devil's demons coming in the night to drag them to Hell. But dressed as he was, like a tourist, he was fair game.

*****

Steve's next stop was San Pietro in Vincoli—the church of Saint Peter in Chains where in a lighted glass crypt beneath the altar can be seen the chains that held St. Peter before he was put to death by the Romans. Despite the reverence typically accorded St. Peter's chains, whenever Steve had visited the church years before he had always been amused as he was today at Michelangelo's classic life-size marble statue of Moses located against a side wall. Moses had been sculptured by Michelangelo with the horns of the Devil because it is believed that Michelangelo incorrectly interpreted the word for 'halo' in the Bible as 'horns.' As Steve knelt in a front pew at prayer, he couldn't help glancing distractedly to the right and smiling at Michelangelo's horned Moses.

*****

Saint Peter's Basilica, the largest church in the world, always filled Steve, as it did many other visitors, with awe. In the company of a line of tourists, he walked down the side aisle passing Michelangelo's Pieta. Further down the aisle, as he passed the life-size dark bronze seated statue of Peter mounted on a waist-high platform, he did what most visitors to the church usually did—he rubbed his hand on a protruding shiny bronze foot of the statue. It was an impulsive act, a lark, not intentionally disrespectful. As Steve rubbed the foot, he smiled, recalling that although the statue was original, it was now on its third set of feet.

Steve knew that when in Rome, a visit to Trevi Fountain was virtually a necessity, and although he was not superstitious, he believed lightheartedly that the coin he had thrown over his shoulder into the pale green water years before with a wish that one day he would return to Rome, had come true. Yet, on this visit, there was an ill omen: the fountain had been emptied for restoration, and Steve thought it unlikely that the wish to return could be granted by throwing a coin over his shoulder, high enough to clear the large plexiglass sheets that isolated the restoration site. He stood nearby watching in amusement as some tourists, undeterred, with their backs to the fountain, tossed their coins over the plexiglass barrier, coins that landed with dull clinks on the bare concrete floor of the fountain. Would their wish come true anyway?

With a slight smile and a shrug of his shoulders, Steve left the crowded piazza and strolled back down one of the narrow streets that led to the fountain. In one of the souvenir shops that lined the alley, he bought a postcard for his brother Jonathon.

On a sudden urge, he stopped for a slice of pizza at an open-air counter. Casually dressed in a Redskins football jacket and slacks, he leaned back against the counter holding the pizza slice high and nibbling on the cheese that hung down. Two beautiful mini-skirted Italian girls strolled by, one of whom sidled up to Steve and said in English in a low sultry voice: "Hey, handsome American, buy us something to eat." But when Steve good naturedly offered to order two more slices, the girls laughed and walked on. Until they walked away, Steve didn't realize they meant dinner at a trattoria or ristorante, not a snack at a sidewalk counter.

As the girls walked away, one of them looked back over her shoulder with a look that asked the question: Why aren't you following us? Then, shrugging their shoulders and tossing their heads, they clicked on in their spiked heels towards the fountain.

Oh to be in Rome and not be a priest! he thought. A sudden surge of guilt went through him when he remembered touring Israel with Alice.

*****

Steve found himself wandering, confused as he walked the streets of Rome. He found himself in front of a large church. Inside, he knelt to pray on a marble step beside one of the side chapels in Santa Maria Maggiore, the basilica in Rome devoted to the Blessed Virgin. The large dark church had always been a source of fascination to him partly because of the huge vaulted nave but mainly from the row of brilliantly lit side chapels each with an altar set behind tall wrought iron grillwork. While Steve prayed silently in front of a white marble statue of the Blessed Virgin that adorned a flower-covered altar in the grotto, he was distracted by the hubbub in the church. The church had become a popular stop for busloads of tourists. It seemed more like Grand Central Station in New York than a place of worship. He remembered that it hadn't always been that way. As a newly ordained priest studying in Rome, the church had been a quiet sanctuary where he was able to deepen his devotion to the Blessed Virgin. But now, Santa Maria Maggiore was crowded not only with worshipers droning in prayer, but also with a swarm of tourists bent on recording everything in the church with video and flash cameras.

Growing increasingly angry at the tourists who acted as if they were at a circus, he wondered why the church sexton didn't put a stop to it. It galled him that the house of God was being treated with utter disrespect. In a far corner behind him, tourists buzzed around a kiosk displaying racks of postcards and other mementos. He was reminded of Jesus who drove the money-changers from the temple. He suppressed an urge to do the same. Standing behind him, a teenager was noisily chomping on a piece of peanut crunch. The candy wrapper lay discarded on the floor at his feet. As Steve twisted around to admonish the boy, the teenager, noticing that Steve was a priest, slunk away into the crowd.

After a few moments telling himself to calm down, Steve resumed his prayers. His prayers became an earnest plea for help from the Blessed Virgin that his ordeal as a renegade priest might soon be ended, although he knew he hadn't the faintest notion as to how a resolution might be brought about...or even if his problem could ever be solved. It seemed as if it would take a miracle.

As he prayed, peering through the opening in the iron grate, he saw what appeared to be a glint of light coming from the face of the statue of the Virgin. At first he ignored it, but found after a few minutes that it was too obvious to ignore. Could it be that the statue was weeping? He had heard of weeping statues of the Virgin, but had always seriously doubted the incidents. He felt that until proven otherwise, the incidents were merely concocted by people, including some religious, who craved attention. But as Steve continued his prayers, the weeping became profuse. It was real. Others nearby spied the weeping statue and began to collect around Steve as he knelt in front of the wrought iron grillwork outside the chapel. One woman, recognizing that Steve had been kneeling alone in front of the chapel, shouted to those standing around, "It's the priest! The Virgin is weeping because of the priest. It's a miracle...a miracle!"

A stampede began in the direction of the chapel. Hundreds collected with those in the rear craning their necks above the crowd to witness the miracle. Black-robed clergy elbowed their way through the throng. One shouted, "I've waited a lifetime to see a miracle, and at last here is one before my very eyes!"

Then, very slowly, almost imperceptibly at first, the altar in the chapel began to move side-to-side with a slow deliberate rhythm. The crowd was transfixed in awe. Many dropped to their knees vigorously crossing themselves. Some fell back scared, ready to run. Steve was wide-eyed, stunned, as he knelt on the step in front of the iron grillwork. He couldn't believe his eyes. His first thought was that the early tremors of an earthquake were rumbling in the ground beneath, shaking the church. But as he looked around, he saw that the rest of the church was not moving—only the altar he was facing seemed to be in slow oscillation. The vibration, which at first was hardly noticeable, began to grow in intensity so that after a few minutes the movement grew almost violent. A candelabrum on the altar tipped on its base and fell over crashing to the tiled floor of the chapel. Startled, Steve saw that the statue of the Virgin on the altar began rocking on its base. His jaw dropped as he watched the statue in wobbly, erratic lurches turn to face the rear wall. The strange incident was immediately obvious to him—it was a message that his living as a renegade priest was disfavored by the Virgin. She was using the statue as a symbolic way of turning her back on him. He was filled with dread but couldn't help feeling sad and even angry at being rejected after a lifetime of devotion to Mary. Now, in the hour of his greatest need he was being left to drown without any help from his patron.

The din of the crowd in the church became an uproar as the bells of the church began a thunderous clanging. Steve was forcibly pressed against the iron grillwork by the surging crowd. A woman near him began screaming in his ear. Smoke burned his nostrils. He was so overcome, he slumped in a near faint. Was someone throwing water on him? Was he being blessed with holy water?

Steve opened his eyes and sat up groggily in bed. His pajamas were drenched. He was so disoriented, he first thought he was still in the church. As his situation came into focus, he realized the incident in Santa Maria Maggiore had all been just another bad dream. Through the window he could see that it had grown dark outside. His embarrassment was extreme as he saw half-a-dozen people gathered in the hallway just outside the open door to his room. He saw their angry, disgusted faces.

"Get up...get up!" It was the old woman who ran the pensione standing at his bedside. "Padre, get up! You have fallen asleep in bed with a lighted cigarette and have started a fire. The engines were here but I sent them away after I threw water on you and put out the fire. It was a small fire, but the bed covers are ruined. You will have to pay damages. The fresco on the ceiling was painted by my son. The smoke has damaged it. Why can't you use this room without setting fire to it? You will have to leave my pensione. Yes, tomorrow, find someplace else to stay where you can make a fire while sleeping in bed. Go there and make someone else miserable. Per favore, go." Although he apologized profusely to the woman; promised to pay damages and vowed never to do it again, it was of no use. Shaking her finger in his face, all she kept repeating was, "Padre, per favore, go! Favor me by going."

38

On the morning following the incident at the pensione, Steve packed up and lugged his bags down the stairs to check out of the room. Downstairs, he made a generous payment for the damages and asked if he could leave his bags until he could find another place to stay. He was not only dismayed about his history of strange dreams that always seemed to contain an element of violence, he was also confused about the erratic nature of their occurrences. While in Dutch Harbor the dreams were so frequent they caused some alarm to Father Sergius, but while sightseeing in Paris he had not had a single one. While in Israel at the Lavines, although he had had some initially, after the days he spent with Alice, he had not had any. It occurred to him that some element of fear surfaced occasionally that resulted in what he could only call adult nightmares. Therapy would probably help but he never seemed to be able to stay in one location long enough for a course of treatment.

Outside, in the street near the Spanish Steps, Steve learned that a taxi strike was not likely because the drivers had struck five times in the previous week, and most of their demands had been granted. He decided to take a chance on a cab. The driver took him across the city to the south of Rome where he told the driver to pull up in front of the entrance to the San Callisto Catacombs on the Old Appian Way. Entering the small rectory built above the catacomb entrance, Steve was ushered into an office where he took a seat to wait. After a few minutes, he restlessly got up and walked around leisurely examining the photographs of the catacombs on the walls.

A door opened and there stood his friend of long ago—Father Angelo, the rotund middle-aged priest with a huge nose that gave him a booming sonorous voice of which he was justly proud. Steve recalled that you could always tell when Angelo was singing in the choir at the Pontifical University chapel. His Gregorian chant could easily be heard a block away. Angelo, the ebullient, almost happy-go-lucky priest, was perhaps the only one in Rome Steve could trust to help him.

"We meet again," Steve said with a smile as he came forward to embrace his old friend.

"Steve! It is wonderful to see you. How long has it been since I visited you in Maryland… seven, eight years?"

"More like ten years, Angelo."

"I am happy you managed to elude the Knights of Carthage in Israel, and forgive me again for giving out your address. But I explained why I had no choice. Now that you're here you have to stay here with me. I'll arrange a room for you."

"In the catacombs?" Steve asked laughing.

"Good heavens, no. You'd freeze down there. Either that or the rats would nibble you to death."

*****

A rear door opened and both priests rose to their feet as Angelo introduced Steve to Lucinda, a pretty young

Italian woman who wore a big smile as she swept in with two cups of cappuccino, a tray heaped high with focaccia—lightly sprinkled with salt, fresh from the oven—and a large bowl of fagioli bianci.

After Lucinda went back to the kitchen, Angelo leaned over close to Steve and whispered, "Lucinda is our cook and housekeeper. For reasons of decorum, she is only here in the daytime. She comes here early to prepare breakfast, and lunch at midday. Then she leaves about six in the evening after preparing my dinner."

"Are we having dinner now?" Steve asked, looking at the huge pile of food. "It's only about three o'clock."

"No, no. This is only a snack."

"If I ate like this every day, Angelo, I would soon be as fat as…."

"Go ahead and say it." Every morning when I say Mass I say to Jesus, "Thank you for making me fat and happy."

Two hours later, after each had consumed three cups of cappuccino, and slices of bread which they repeatedly heaped with fagioli bianci and had relived old times at the university, Father Angelo listened attentively to all the details of Steve's story. At the end of the tale, Angelo's first reaction was that the whole business was ridiculous. "There's nothing invalid about a human clone. Yes, the church would frown on the people who were involved in the cloning—certainly a mortal sin. But," he laughed, slapping Steve's leg, "it could be removed in confession with a million Hail Mary's. The clone himself, on the other hand, would be an innocent party. Not a single Hail Mary."

"But what about the animal cells?"

"Steve, my friend," Angelo said affably as he reached over and patted his fellow priest on the shoulder, "we all have a touch of animal in us. We are animals! The only difference is that we are animals who have risen above the pack. We have learned how to build cities and churches, how to start wars, and how to make ourselves and others thoroughly miserable. Not always, but a lot of the time. So your cardinal is after you. Well, my friend, you're safe here. I don't recall ever seeing a cardinal leave the splendor of the Vatican to come to this musty underground place of the dead. And if the Knights of Carthage come looking for you, I will scare hell out of those young thugs with stories of the dangers that lie below. By the way, where have you been staying?"

"I've been staying at a pensione near the Spanish Steps."

"Ah yes, the Piazza di Spagna. Well, you must come and stay here with me. I have plenty of room."

"I'll take you up on the offer because I'm getting kicked out of the pensione. Angelo, are you still in charge of the catacombs?"

"Of course! But not all of them. Only the San Callisto Catacombs. And that is enough for one man. It is my life work. I am what you Americans refer to as the CEO. I am the Chief Executive Officer of the place where the early Christians laid their brethren to rest. You may not know this, Steve, but these catacombs are a pretty big business."

"I assume you're referring to tourist admissions."

"Yes, that brings in money, but the big money

lately has come from your cable channels in America. Several of them have made TV documentaries of the catacombs."

"You charged them for that?"

"Why not? Certainly I charged them. They paid an arm, my friend, and a leg. They can afford it. They make millions putting things like that on TV."

"From the photographs on the wall you seem to be doing restorations. That must cost some money."

"No. All that is paid for by universities. Out of their research budgets."

Father Angelo stood up laughing. He slapped Steve on the back. "When you studied in Rome did you ever tour the catacombs?"

"Yes, but briefly. I had just a quick tourist visit one day while I was jogging along the old Appian Way. I'd like to see them again." As Steve said this he had an unnerving feeling that he might need the catacombs as a safe hiding place in case Cardinal Rhinehart and the Passion brothers ever got wind that he was in Rome, not to mention the Knights of Carthage who knew he had left Israel for Rome.

"Then let me give you a real tour."

Angelo brought Steve into a large outer room. "The doors over there lead to the chapel. We can visit that later. If you decide to stay here I'll show you the rooms upstairs. The refectory is back behind the office we were just in."

"I think I forgot how you get down to the catacombs."

"There is only one real entrance. The staircase leading down is over by the wall. We bring the visitors into this room, give them a little talk, tell them to stay close behind the guide with the flashlight and not wander off by themselves. Then we take them down those stairs. There were originally a number of other entrances probably for workmen to bury bodies and seal the crypts, but the holes were kept covered... disguised. Then through the years they became completely obscured by overgrowth, and in fact, no one knew there were catacombs here until they were discovered sometime in the sixteenth century."

Angelo picked up a flashlight and motioned to Steve to follow him.

The pair descended a crudely hewn stone staircase, no more than shoulder wide. Steve ran his hands along the rough-hewn walls for support as he descended. He noticed that Angelo had difficulty negotiating the confined space. Steve shuddered slightly at the cold that seemed to be coming out of the walls enveloping him, and the dank darkness lit only by Angelo's bobbing flashlight. As they walked along a passageway, Steve noticed that another staircase led down to an even lower level. "How many levels are there in here?" he asked.

"Few people know this but in places it goes down five levels. The catacombs were ancient burial grounds, as I'm sure you know. Some historians claim they were used as places where the Christians could hide from the Romans because the Christian religion was outlawed until the time of Constantine. Others dispute this. I personally believe Christians hid here. I know this place. It is the largest of the catacombs. The intricate passageways are said to run thirteen miles—perhaps as far as fifteen miles under Rome, with scores of side passages. Who could find a better hiding place... a place where you could perform religious ceremonies without detection? And we are blessed with the fact that there is a crypt here where nine early popes were laid to rest. Now, Steve, stop me if you remember this from an earlier visit, but if not let me continue." In the back of Angelo's mind was the thought that if Steve stayed at the catacomb he might be able to help giving tours to visitors because one of Angelo's seminarian guides was off on vacation.

"Please go on, Angelo," Steve replied. The same thought had occurred to him—while living there, he might pass the time by giving tours himself. He wanted to get refreshed on the details.

"Well, in the first few centuries after Christ," Angelo continued, "religious persecution was widespread in Rome. Many Christians met death at the hands of Roman mobs or by animals in the Colisseum and Circus Maximus. They were the early martyrs for the faith. If their bodies could be recovered, they were buried here. It is believed that the Christians attended Mass and other services down here at altars built near the tombs of martyrs and saints. Here for example is an altar outside the tomb of a saint."

"Where is the body? The crypt looks empty."

"Long gone. When the catacombs were, shall we say, rediscovered, the tombs were looted for bones of the saints. It was even done by some clergy for altars in the church. As you know, each Catholic altar used to require sacred relics—the bones of a saint perhaps, or more likely, tiny pieces of bone in the small reliquary under the altar stone. Many of those relics undoubtedly came from here. Of course, as you know, since Vatican II, altar relics are no longer required. And that is good, my friend, because this place is just about empty now."

As the pair continued along the passageway, Angelo pointed to the frescoes on the walls with his flashlight. "The paintings display the message that death is not the end... for the faithful there is eternal life. This was the essential message of early Christianity. It was a powerful influence in the spread of Christianity."

"However, not unique to Christianity," Steve said. "The concept of an afterlife appears in many religions and cultures. The Egyptians are a good example."

"True, Steve. Egyptian kings and nobility were believed to have the afterlife. But Christianity brought the concept of an afterlife down to the level of the common people."

Pointing his light at the walls as the pair stepped slowly along the earthen-floored passageway, Angelo explained, "As you can see, Steve, many paintings depict beautiful gardens where the faithful would presumably spend the afterlife. Some of the artists seemed to think the afterlife would be filled with wine and perpetual dancing and merriment in beautiful gardens. It was their concept of paradise. You know, it's a shame we have had to close many of the catacomb areas to the public because of these beautiful but delicate wall paintings that could be harmed by the moisture in human breath."

Angelo stopped to take a breath after the exertion of winding through the catacombs and going up and down narrow staircases. After a minute or so, he continued his explanation. "The paintings are not only religious in nature but also give an idea of daily life in the first and second centuries after Christ." Angelo stopped abruptly. "Look down there, Steve." he said, pointing the flashlight down into the dark abyss below. "The galleries are five levels deep in this area connected by steep narrow staircases with uneven steps. You have to watch your step going down there. Further, some areas have abrupt dropoffs that go down to only God knows where. Many have never been explored."

Further along the passageway, Angelo stopped again. His flashlight made a circle of light on the dark brown wall. "These walls as you can see are carved out for resting places for the dead. The crypts are stacked— cut out one on top of another."

"Like bunk beds," Steve commented.

"Yes, bunk beds for eternal sleep. See, this wall crypt could hold six bodies from floor to ceiling in one stack of wall sepulchers."

"How many bodies to a crypt?"

"Typically only one. But some held room for a husband and wife if they died at the same time. The bodies were not embalmed. After the bodies were placed in the wall, the sepulchers were sealed after a fashion with thin slabs of stone and a type of mortar. Scratched in the mortar was the identity of the deceased. The seal was also important to block out the odor. It's moldy smelling now, but in ancient times, the odor of rotting bodies waiting to be sealed must have been overpowering."

"What's that tomb over there?" Steve asked.

"Oh that's the tomb of a wealthy person. Name unknown now. The wealthy were buried in marble sarcophagi, usually with carvings on the front."

"Was this all done with rock carvings? Must have been tough cutting all this out."

"Not as difficult as one might think. The rock under Rome is soft volcanic tufo rock—it lends itself well to carving and tunneling."

Further on, after passing through elaborately carved archways and seemingly endless rooms decorated with fading frescoes, Angelo asked, "Had enough, Steve? Let's go back upstairs."

*****

A short time later, the pair sat again in the rectory office. Father Angelo poured the wine. "Seriously, my friend. Come live here with me and I guarantee you will be safe while we wait to get word back from the Vatican through—what do you Americans call it: Ah yes, back channels. I assume the matter of cloning and chimeras has been under study at the urging of your Cardinal Rhinehart. I have an influential friend who can find out what progress is being made, but frankly, a decision could be months or years away and, of course, it is subject to the approval of the pontiff. And let me be very frank, my friend: the power structure in the Vatican these days sometimes frightens me. You probably know that the powerful cardinals at the top are ultra-conservative. This does not speak well for questions that test the limits of the faith. As you are probably aware, every pontiff who came after Vatican II tried to throw the church back a hundred...maybe even five hundred years. Take this information to heart, but don't quote me."

"Yes, I know about that," Steve said, shaking his head and frowning. "There are signs of it everywhere. If a college theology professor in the United States does not teach strictly according to Vatican dogma, he is dismissed. Nowadays in America, liberal thinkers are disciplined. And it's probably true here in Europe and the rest of the world. This latest trend troubles me. If you study the history of the church over two thousand years, you find it has not only continued painstakingly defining its dogma, but has also allowed its dogma to evolve to some extent."

"Yes, my friend. People tend to think that the church never changes but a good example of what you're saying is the doctrine of the Immaculate Conception. If you recall, the idea of Mary's Immaculate Conception first surfaced in the eighth century, and gradually grew more widespread through the centuries. And as we both know it became dogma—binding on Catholics by Pius IX in 1854. There has been a healthy evolution through past years, but in the years after Vatican II, new ideas have just about come to a standstill. It's obvious the ultra-conservatives in the church have taken over in the years following Vatican II. So my friend, Steve, I don't want to sound too pessimistic about the outcome of your case, but...well let's wait and see. Remember the old saying: 'The pendulum swings'."

Rising from his seat with some effort due to his bulk, Angelo took Steve by the arm and led him into the small chapel beside his office where the two of them knelt in prayer.

Later, at Angelo's urging, Steve agreed it would be wise to move in with his friend.

"Do you want to borrow my car to return to the pensione for your things?"

Steve was hesitant. "Honestly, Angelo, I appreciate the offer but the traffic has gotten so heavy and chaotic in Rome, I'm afraid I'd bring your car back with dented fenders."

"Then that settles it," Angelo replied with a big smile. "Take the car. You will see that the fenders are already dented. In Rome, we don't pay attention to dented fenders. Almost every car on the road has had some unrepaired damage inflicted on it—a nick here, a gouge there. Even when people get paid for the damage, many of them pocket the money and don't bother getting the car fixed. The reason is simple: why fix dents in a car that will soon be dented again?"

39

Steve found the days spent living at the catacombs peaceful and pleasant. He established a routine. After saying Mass in a small chapel in the early morning, he would be off for his morning run along the ancient Appian Way. The cobblestone road was hard on his feet and knees but the magic of running along the ancient Roman road—the former southern gateway to Rome, quickened his throbbing pulse as it uplifted his spirit. His nostrils widened to take in the clean fresh air that filled his lungs from the pines that lined the road. The joy, bordering on rapture, more than compensated for the stiffness he felt in his joints until he was warmed up. His cares were left behind like the bits of sweat that ran off his body evaporating as they hit the ground. After his run it was a cool shower and a big breakfast with Angelo.

"If I attempted to run like you, my friend," Angelo commented one morning, "I'm afraid my legs would collapse under my weight. No advice, please," Angelo added when he saw Steve's raised eyebrows and believed Steve was at the point of trying to convince him to take up running and ease up on eating. "God may have to widen the pearly gates to let me in, but I have faith He will do it."

*****

One morning, about two weeks after settling in at

the catacombs, Steve sent a postcard in an envelope to Jonathon that also included a short impersonal note to be forwarded to Janet. He found it painful writing to Janet. A bright cheery hello from Rome. He had to write as if he were no more than an acquaintance even though there were so many things he longed to say, but dared not. He wondered about her reconciled marriage. He loved her enough to want her to be happy but he almost couldn't bear the thought of her in another man's arms. Although he dared not write to any of his friends in the American clergy, he felt it was safe to tell Janet he was living in the San Callisto Catacombs, waiting for an answer from the Vatican. He never received an answer from Janet. He wasn't sure why— perhaps a return letter was lost in the overseas mail. When he communicated with Jonathon it was always by phone or e-mail because they each wondered about the reliability of overseas mail.

After a few weeks, Steve found that days spent in running, taking meals with Angelo, saying Mass and reading his Holy Office, although relaxing and rejuvenating, were not active enough. He felt he should be accomplishing something more. He decided to help out with the tourist visits to the catacombs. In black cassock, with Roman collar and flashlight, he found he could give quite satisfactory tours in English and reasonably satisfactory tours in French—the latter a language learned in college, and soon forgotten due to disuse, but which after considerable study, had begun to come back to him. Father Angelo gave occasional tours in his native Italian. Several seminarian assistants conducted the tours in German, Greek, and Spanish.

*****

Steve would not soon forget one tour in the catacombs with a group of grade school children.

Steve asked their young teacher, Maria, if she had ever been in the catacombs.

"No," she replied, "and frankly I'm scared."

"Well, there's nothing to fear. There's really nothing down there."

"Nothing except death," she said with a shudder.

"You have fourteen children with you. I'll lead the group single file along the passageways. We will make occasional stops at side vaults. You will be at the rear of the last child. Try to keep them moving along. I'll be at the front with a flashlight and I'll give you a flashlight, otherwise, when I turn a corner you would be in the dark."

As the children followed the priest along the musty path, the single flashlight bobbing in the dark ahead of the group, one boy near the rear disappeared into a side passageway. Although the teacher was positioned at the rear of the group to make sure no one was left behind, somehow, the boy had slipped away from her unseen, possibly as a prank, into a dark narrow side tunnel that led off the prescribed tour route.

After collecting the group upstairs at the end of the tour, a head count disclosed that the boy was missing. Steve, Maria and two seminarians immediately descended into the darkness to find the lost boy. They spent an hour searching side passageways—to no avail. Steve was distraught. The teacher was in a panic. Although the searchers called out, there was no answering sound. Steve was beginning to get seriously concerned at the thought that the boy might have wandered into an uncharted section of the catacombs and could have fallen down a staircase into a black abyss. The boy might have hit his head and could be lying somewhere unconscious. Then again, the boy might be nearby but simply too terrified to call out—wondering with a child's imagination whether the call would be answered by someone living or dead.

Steve recalled that he had once while walking alone in the catacombs, intentionally switched off the flashlight. He did it to feel what it was like being in the blackness far underground. For a moment, buried alive, his flesh crawled. The experience told him what the lost boy must now be going through—a prank turned into a terror.

Steve and other searchers, frantic now, began tracing their way back to the entrance. They would have to widen the search with a large search party. They stiffened as they heard the scream. The scream became a long wail that although horrifying, gave them a direction to move in. Running swiftly through a side passageway, they came upon a large dead-end alcove. It was a grotto where bodies had formerly been stacked in crypts arranged in a semi-circle. The boy was lying on the earthen floor surrounded by dogs—a pack of hungry snarling wild dogs that had begun to tear at his clothing and would soon be trying to devour him. The boy was gamely kicking at the dogs but he was in a losing battle.

Steve lunged in swinging the heavy flashlight like a weapon, the light bouncing crazily off walls, ceiling and floor. He let out a loud growl and a shout as he swept in flailing at the dogs. In the melee, some yelps told him he had hit his mark a few times. The startled animals, deprived of an easy meal, escaped and disappeared in a passageway. Steve carried the boy back to the main passageway and up the stairs.

The teacher was angry. "You said there was nothing to fear down there; nothing that is, except an occasional pack of wild animals."

"Please forgive me," Steve said contritely. I had no idea there were wild dogs down there and can't imagine how they got in."

An examination by a doctor who was called in said the boy was badly shaken but except for a few minor nips and scratches, he didn't appear to be seriously injured; however, he had to be taken to a hospital for rabies shots. Apologies were profuse. Angelo agreed to pay for the boy's torn clothes and medical costs.

"There is a risk of rabies," the doctor said. "Since we can't round up a pack of dogs to have them tested, we have to assume the worst. We can't take the chance."

*****

After the incident was over and Steve had returned from the hospital, he slumped exhausted in a chair as Angelo nervously paced the floor. "The doctors are starting to give the boy the series of rabies shots," Steve said, "and they say he'll be OK. But tell me, where did the dogs come from, Angelo? Who owns them?"

"No one knows. They are new to the catacombs. A new problem. We believe they must have entered through one of the overhead light shafts. I've seen one or two. They are narrow and steep like the walls of a chimney."

"Where do they come to the surface?"

"One comes up in the middle of a thicket over by the old Roman aqueduct. When the Christians built the catacombs, they dug a few hidden openings to the upper world at various places along the passageways. Not many, you understand, and we don't really know the purpose—perhaps to provide light or access to some areas. We can only guess. But I suspect the dogs have found a way in through one of these overhead openings."

"Can't you do anything about them? The dogs are wild; they travel in a pack and they're dangerous. They were getting ready to eat that kid alive."

"What can one do? We have searched for them but never found them. Once in a great while, like today for example, they suddenly appear. Then, in a flash, they are gone."

"What about the people who do the restorations? Do they ever encounter the dogs?"

"There have been a few comments. Not complaints really, just comments. They see an occasional curious dog but apparently the bright lights, the equipment, the noise surrounding the large crew… scares the dogs off."

"But I'm puzzled, Angelo. How do the dogs live down there? What do they eat? "

"I suspect there's a food chain: the dogs eat the rats; the rats eat the mice; but only God knows what the mice eat. Maybe bits of candy bars and cookie crumbs dropped by the tourists."

*****

On the day following the incident with the dogs, after his morning run, Steve decided to walk over to the old Roman aqueduct. He was curious about how the dogs might have gained access to the catacombs. Hidden in the center of a dense thicket of bushes covered with thorns and brambles, close to a wall of crumbling ancient brick, he came upon a small opening in the ground. It was just wide enough for a slender man or a large animal. The opening had a loose iron grate over it that had been pushed to one side. Kneeling down, he peered into the opening and decided it very likely led down into the catacombs. The walls were steep but seemed negotiable. He decided not to try climbing down. This hole, and possibly others like it, would have provided entrance for the dogs.

*****

Several days after the incident with the dogs, Steve was saying goodbye to a tour group when Angelo met him at the front entrance and asked him to come into his office. "Steve, take a seat. Here have some wine. I found out something today that you should know."

Steve didn't know whether to be happy or sad. Could this be good news from the Vatican or the end of the line for his vocation to the priesthood? He declined the proffered glass of wine and poured some espresso from a carafe on a side table. He sank into a chair in front of Angelo's desk. He noted that Angelo's face did not have an expression that would indicate good news.

"Steve, what I'm about to tell you is not about your

case but it could affect your case indirectly. Do you remember the legend about the heads of Saints Peter and Paul preserved in urns at San Giovanni Laterano—the Saint John Lateran Basilica?"

"I remember it of course, but frankly, it always sounded like a wild legend to me."

"To me too," Angelo replied. "But something has happened that relates to one of those heads. As you Americans say 'to make a long story short', there is a young man in Rome who claims to be related to Saint Peter."

"That's quite a stretch seeing as how Saint Peter died almost two thousand years ago. I'd love to see that family tree."

"He's not basing it on lineage. He claims that a tissue sample was taken from the head of Saint Peter—which by the way is believed to be no more than a skull with bits of tissue attached here and there, and probably hair from a beard. Apparently, someone stole into the church twenty-some years ago and removed a tissue sample from the head. This young man then claims that the tissue was used to clone a human— him. He maintains that he is related to Saint Peter, of course, in a kind of relationship that is difficult to define. A son perhaps? Some people are saying he is the rightful heir to the throne of the papacy."

"Even if the story is true, how does it make him an heir to the throne?"

"As you may recall, Steve, each pope sees himself not as a successor to the pope that preceded him, but as a direct descendent of Saint Peter. Presumably then, each pope is a second Peter. Some of this young man's followers say that since he is of Peter's flesh, he has more right to the papacy than a pope who is merely elected by a group of cardinals."

"Does the pontiff know of this? And the Curia?"

"Unfortunately, yes. And the way it affects you Steve is that the Curia and the pontiff have suddenly became extremely wary of human cloning. So frightened have they become of the repercussions and the threat to the status quo, their feelings about human cloning have become strongly negative. They find it hard to deal with something new when they don't know where it will lead."

"So, as a human clone, I represent a threat," Steve added dourly.

"As a human clone, not necessarily. They would probably take a live-and-let-live approach to a cloned individual, but having a clone as a Catholic priest would make them extremely nervous. The other factor is even more serious. My contact tells me the business of animal cells mixed in the cloning process has produced strongly negative reactions among members of the Curia. Frankly, on hearing of this possibility, the members of the Curia sitting around the conference table uniformly shook their heads muttering: 'No,' and words like: 'Impossible'."

"Do you mean they didn't believe it was possible to produce a chimera?"

"Oh, they believed it. Modern science has them thoroughly cowed. Centuries ago, the church fathers closed doors and windows to keep evil spirits out; now they close doors and windows to keep science out. What the Curia members meant was the impossibility of accepting that such a being could have undergone ensoulment by God. In a case like this, science is seen as having gone one step too far. Now remember, this is only tentative, an initial reaction. They haven't fully studied the issue and obviously have no formal conclusion. But it bodes ill, my friend."

"Maybe in a hundred years they could accept it," Steve said, a crestfallen expression growing on his face. Tell me more about the young man who claims to be the son of Peter. Where can I find him?"

"Preaching on street-corners of Rome to any audience that will listen to his claim. He calls himself Peter the Second. He sometimes attracts large crowds, mainly young people."

"No wonder the Vatican is upset."

"The worst part, Steve, is that people are starting to believe this young man, especially young people who feel the church has lost touch with them. They believe there are too many gray-headed bishops and cardinals running things and telling them what is right and wrong. They say Jesus sought to establish his church among the common people. Jesus was a peasant. If he was anything, he was anti-establishment. He did not intend to create a new monarchy of untold wealth and power. Added to that, Jesus was young, only thirty-three when he died. It's easy to see that today's youth might see more of a tie between the young Peter and Jesus than with the old men who have taken over the church."

Steve thought a minute, then got up and started pacing the floor. "The thing to remember, Angelo, is that if this young man is telling the truth, he may in fact be a kind of descendent of Saint Peter."

"True. But that hardly makes him qualified to act as the head of the Catholic Church. It would have the makings of a disaster for the church. This young man is nothing more than a street-corner preacher."

"If he became a real problem for the Vatican," Steve said with a smirk, "the Knights of Carthage would take care of him. By the way, Angelo, I would like to see the young Peter. I'd like to listen to what he has to say."

"That's easily done, my friend. I understand he mostly preaches at the Spanish Steps, although I don't know what days or times."

*****

Three days later, Steve parked Angelo's car in an alley a few blocks from the Spanish Steps. He was in luck. He saw a crowd on the lower steps surrounding a young man who appeared to be in his early twenties. The young man was standing on the edge of a low wall and could be seen full length over the crowd. As he glimpsed the young man from the rear of the crowd, Steve's eyes met piercing black eyes, long unkempt brown hair and a full scraggly beard. The young man was dressed in a simple coarse brown robe. On closer inspection, Steve saw that he wore open-toed sandals. His feet were dirty. My God, Steve thought, he looks like he just stepped out of the bible with the dust of Palestine still on his feet. Pressing closer, Steve heard familiar tales from the New Testament. The young man spoke in Italian, but Steve understood enough to get the gist of the message. The sermon told the stories of Jesus selecting Peter the simple fisherman as the rock upon which he would build his church; Jesus calming the storm on the Sea of Galilee; Jesus walking on the water; the miracle of the loaves and fishes; Peter held prisoner in the Mammertine Prison near the Roman Forum, and later crucified upside down where the obelisk stands in the center of Saint Peter's Square. No new revelations, just things Steve knew and had preached scores of times in his Sunday sermons at home. He waited for something new, something unique this man might have to offer.

After listening for half-an-hour to stock bible stories, somewhat disgustedly Steve turned to leave the gathering when he heard the young man refer to himself as the flesh and blood of Peter...the son of Peter. On hearing these words, there was a murmur of approval from some in the crowd. People began kneeling and crossing themselves. Steve's curiosity was aroused. As he turned back to resume listening, he realized he was intrigued by the audacity of this young man who was claiming openly to be of the flesh of the first pope. Steve wondered—what did the crowd think? Did they really accept this claim? Did they believe the young preacher was a human clone of Saint Peter? Or perhaps did they think he was a miraculous incarnation of Peter's son? Whatever they thought, it was obvious from their homage that they didn't think young Peter was a fraud.

Young Peter was now reminding the crowd of onlookers that Jesus was a peasant. As such Jesus rose up in opposition against the established religion of the day and the priests and scribes who had constructed a large wealthy organization. The young man's voice was strident and filled with emotion as he talked. "Jesus was disturbed that the wealthy and powerful had taken over the Jewish synagogues. He railed against this. And today, yes today, the same thing has happened in the Catholic Church. The church has become an all-powerful monarchy of untold wealth with a full retinue of lords and princes who are referred to as: 'Your Excellency,' and 'Your Grace' and a court that mimics the courts of the great medieval and renaissance kings of Europe. In fact, until John Paul I, popes used to be crowned with a tiara like kings. When a new pope ascended the throne, each cardinal in turn was expected to kneel at his feet and pledge absolute obedience. No room for independent thought—only absolute obedience. Yet these popes weren't chosen by God, or by Jesus as Peter was, each was elected by his fellow cardinals. Whatever the early church was at the time of Christ, it is no longer. With each passing century, the power of the papacy has become more monarchical with absolute religious power vested in its monarch. I say to you gathered here, it is time for a change."

The young Peter, arms raised, was now shouting from the steps. "If Jesus were here today, he would angrily throw these money changers from the new temple and distribute their wealth to the poor. I say to you, the time is at hand to return to the simple beginnings of Christianity. God will point the way—through me as His lowly servant."

*****

A few hours later, Steve sat in a quiet trattoria with the young Peter. After the gathering on the Spanish

Steps had begun to disperse, Steve had collared the young man and offered to buy him dinner. The offer was readily accepted for two reasons: the young Peter hadn't eaten for several days and Steve's Roman collar gave the young man an opportunity to talk directly to one he assumed represented the Vatican. Steve, concerned at first that the conversation might proceed in his halting Italian, found young Peter's English to be surprisingly good. "Where did you learn such good English?" he asked.

"I was born in Rome, but I lived for many years in America. I was studying to be a priest at Cathedral College, a prep seminary in New York. Ever hear of it?"

"Of course. Did you complete your studies?"

"No. I dropped out."

"I'm from an area further south. I was pastor of a parish for many years." Steve checked his tongue because he was on the verge of mentioning the Archdiocese of Washington; nor did the young man question the location of his parish.

"Now you are assigned to the Vatican?"

"No," Steve replied. I am just in Rome on a visit."

The waiter took a long uncertain look at the unlikely pair as he presented menus. One patron obviously a modern priest in a neatly tailored black suit with Roman collar, the other a dirty bearded tramp from the streets. He decided the priest was doing his charitable deed for the day.

Steve ordered only cafe latte, while the young Peter with an agreeable nod from the priest, ordered a small mountain of food. "You look somewhat thin," Steve commented with a concerned look on his face. "You don't seem to be getting enough to eat."

"Yes, I know."

"After your sermons, why don't you pass a collection plate around? I'm sure the people would contribute."

Young Peter sneered: "Just like a typical Catholic priest," he said. "It's always the money...always the money. You and your kind make me sick."

Steve bristled at the criticism. "It takes money," he replied caustically, "to run schools and hospitals, especially in poor areas where people need financial assistance." As he said it he was tempted to throw enough money on the table to cover the check and walk out. He resisted the urge. There were things he wanted to find out.

"Your message sounds like Communism," Steve said a few minutes later, trying to begin a dialog that would clarify what the young man was trying to accomplish. "Tear down the establishment and distribute the wealth to the common people. The difficulty as we have learned however is that the world now knows the Communist philosophy doesn't work."

"I'm not preaching Communism," the young man said, as he glanced expectantly over his shoulder in the direction of the kitchen waiting for the food to arrive. "If you must know, I'm preaching against the establishment. Any establishment. We hear first the rhetoric—idealized, glorious, full of promise; then the same old authoritarian power grab takes place and the common people are left with little or nothing, as usual."

The first course arrived. Young Peter sliced into a piece of veal and began devouring it with obvious relish. "I am not preaching Communism," he said again between mouthfuls. "You Americans are so simplistic. On the one hand you see Communism, on the other, Capitalism. Is there nothing in between?"

"There are monarchies," Steve said.

"Oh, yes, I forgot—monarchies like the Catholic Church."

Steve slowly poured a small hill of sugar on his cafe latte. He watched it sink slowly below the surface. Their talk was turning into an argument. He shrugged, thinking it best to back off...not come on too strong. After all, he suspected he was dealing with a volcanic personality and if the volcano blew, he wouldn't learn what he had come to learn. "Tell me more about yourself. You claim to be the 'son' of Saint Peter—a clone of the saint."

"You don't believe it?"

"Well, I'm not sure the average person would believe it."

"Do you believe it?"

"As a matter of fact, I am inclined to believe it. But tell me this. Do you know if you were cloned from the skull of Saint Peter which legend says is in an urn at Saint John Lateran Basilica? I wasn't aware that DNA could be extracted from bone for cloning."

"It's not a legend. The head is there. And, for your information, it's more than a skull—there are still pieces of preserved viable flesh clinging to it."

"After two thousand years? DNA from flesh? Look, I believe in the fact of human cloning, but I'm not sure I believe in the possibility of cloning the long dead."

"Surely, as a priest you have heard of Saint

Catherine Laboure. Her body is perfectly preserved behind glass under an altar in Paris. The body of Saint Bernadette lies in a glass-sided altar in Nevers, France. The church has documentation that their bodies were never embalmed or treated for preservation. And there are dozens of other saints whose bodies are wholly or partly preserved—Saint Teresa and Saint Francis Xavier, for example. Their bodies are still uncorrupted, undecayed. The flesh is supple. The DNA is intact. Going back in time to the 1200s," young Peter continued, his eyes flashing, "we come upon one of the best examples: St. Anthony of Padua. Pilgrims by the thousands visit Padua every year to see portions of his body including his tongue and jawbone. Now, since Saint Peter was the greatest of the saints, why wouldn't some of his flesh remain? And even if none remained, there is some evidence that the DNA extracted from bone marrow can be used for cloning."

Steve shrugged his shoulders. He had never really thought about the possibility of cloning the long dead, but what he was hearing sounded plausible. "May I ask who your surrogate mother was?"

"I don't know. Why all these questions?"

"I have a reason for wanting to know. You say you're a clone. I'm a clone too."

Young Peter stopped slack-jawed, with the fork halfway to his mouth.

"I was," Steve continued, "not cloned from a saint, of course. I learned a short time ago that I was cloned from my older brother with my mother as surrogate. Imagine finding that out when you're almost fifty years old."

"Are you sure it was cloning and not a bit of incest in the family?"

"I'm sure. I found the medical records. Now this may sound strange, but you are the only human clone I've ever met. What was your reaction when you found out?"

"Probably the same as yours—at first disbelief, then anger, then resignation, then...."

"Then?"

"Then, in my case, elation when I found out that I was cloned from Saint Peter. It opened a whole new world for me. Just imagine—me physically related to the first pope!"

"And I gather," Steve said as he watched the plates on young Peter's side of the table being almost licked clean, "you are on a campaign to take over as head of the church."

"I am not interested in 'taking over' as you put it. People misunderstand me. I have no desire to be pope. I have not been ordained. You're not going to see me on TV saying midnight Mass on Christmas Eve. I am merely a messenger from two thousand years ago. I bring a reminder of the original church of Christ. The original church, the original Christian religion, was in fact, comprised of numerous small isolated churches spread around the Mediterranean. The people were simple true believers in Christ's ministry on earth. Who knows the names of the early popes or even if there were popes? The pomp and circumstance, the mitered royalty came later under Constantine who decided he was not only the Roman emperor but also the head of the church. And starting with Constantine, the bureaucracy, like all bureaucracies, grew like a mushroom cloud. My goal is only to see the Vatican emptied of these pompous aristocrats and the bishops sent home to their dioceses. The treasures of the Vatican including its museums, should be sold and the money distributed to the poor."

"And the pope? What would happen to him?"

Young Peter grinned. "We're not going to shoot him, if that's what you think. Remember the current, elected pope is the Bishop of Rome. He usually delegates this to a subordinate and ignores Rome while he travels around the world. Very simply, we would give him back his diocese and make him stay home and run it. Period. It's rather strange that I should be trying to educate a priest about his own church but I suppose I must. In the early days of the Catholic Church, there were no cardinals or archbishops. There were only bishops—Jesus' apostles were simply the equivalent of today's bishops. But later came fancy titles like archbishop and cardinal—glorified titles needed to build the establishment. Each of these men is no more than a bishop—in fact, a bishop with a diocese to run. Instead of managing their dioceses, they spend a lot of time clustered around the monarch's throne in the Vatican seeking to be on high level councils and committees. They attend the king's court, always angling for power and prestige. All I'm saying is let each of them go home and run his diocese. And in later years, as the establishment grew, to fill out the ranks, they invented a lower level of clergy called 'priests,' like you. In a big establishment you need an army of low level people to do the daily work."

"This is a nice theory, but without the power of the papacy, the unified, cohesive dogma of the church would break down."

Young Peter rose to his feet adjusting his robes. "You, who supposedly have so much faith, have very little faith indeed. Are you saying that these bishops—direct descendents of Christ's Apostles—cannot be trusted to preach Christ's message?"

Almost with a sneer, young Peter offered a peremptory thanks and walked to the door of the trattoria as Steve remained behind to pay the bill. Outside in the piazza, there was a gathering crowd as people learned the young man was inside. When Steve left the trattoria, he was surrounded. He nervously tried to thread his way through. Suddenly someone shouted, "Young Peter has been with a priest from the Vatican! The Vatican is willing to talk!" On hearing this, the crowd parted to let Steve pass. It was like the parting of the Red Sea. As he walked past the people who were lined closely on left and right, he saw them smiling and applauding him.

On reaching the outer edge of the piazza, Steve looked back to see young Peter standing on one of the trattoria chairs and addressing a crowd which by now had swelled to over a thousand.

40

One evening, three weeks after Steve's meeting with young Peter, Angelo called out from the small living room of the rectory: "Steve, come quick. There's something on the television! Hurry!"

Steve rushed into the room and settled in an armchair beside Angelo. It was the six o'clock news. The scene was outside a hospital in Rome. The reporter said a young man who claimed to be physically related to Peter had been stabbed and was in the emergency room. He wasn't expected to live. It had happened right after the end of one of his sermons. A man had rushed out of the crowd, shoved a dagger into his stomach and quickly disappeared.

"Do they know who did it?" asked Steve.

"Yes and no. Steve, he was stabbed with a dagger. Some sources say the wound was square-shaped, so it was very likely done by one of the Knights of Carthage. The hypocrisy of it is if you attend High Mass on Easter Sunday, you see them all wearing their fancy uniforms sitting in the front row in Saint Peters."

"How can a religious group attempt to murder someone?"

"Usually it's only a beating, but in this case, you recall that young Peter says he is a clone. To them, I suppose killing a clone is not murder. It's more like killing an animal that is out of control."

*****

The next day, the news reported that young Peter was dead. But before he died, he said the church would never be rid of him because a clone would be made from his tissue. Thus another direct descendent of Peter would arise. And after that, another. The blood line would go on forever. When he was questioned about the viability of human cloning, he said there were other clones walking around, for example, he had met a priest from America who was now in Rome. The priest had told him he was a clone. When questioned, young Peter said he didn't know the priest's name, but he was able to give a description.

*****

Angelo was insistent. Steve had to go into hiding. No more jogging in the morning. He should give no more tours of the catacombs. For the time being, he would have to stay hidden in the catacombs.

Steve was dismayed. "Angelo, do you really think this is necessary? Aren't we overreacting? How would they know where to look for me—after all, isn't Rome filled with priests?"

Angelo had a worried look on his face. "You may have been followed back here after you met with young Peter. Some from the Vatican and others were watching him. If they saw you with him they would have wanted to know more about you."

"So you think the Knights of Carthage might have found out I'm staying here?"

"That's right. Don't underestimate their

determination my friend. You found out in Israel that they are radicals. Some of them are crazy. The police know that one of them did it. Although young Peter was stabbed in broad daylight, the killer got away. The story goes that he slipped down a side street. He was wearing a disguise so no one could identify him. And when the police gave chase, they were blocked by a jumble of strategically placed trucks and cars. They never recovered the dagger except that from the shape of the wound, they knew it was one of the Knights."

"So, if I stay here I have to hide in the catacombs like the early Christians—except that the Christians were hiding from the Romans. Now it's a Catholic priest hiding from some radical element in the Catholic Church."

"I'm afraid so."

Steve was depressed at the thought of sleeping among the ancient tombs. The cold, the rats, the dank odor...almost like being buried alive. But he knew he had little choice.

"I'll put a cot down there for you. Probably down on the third level. There is a small room hidden under the staircase. It has little more than a slit in the wall for an opening. You'll have to familiarize yourself with that area. They would have a hard time finding you down there, but if they did, you'd have to have an escape route planned."

"Escape to where?"

"Into the depths. Back into the labyrinth where they may give up the chase thinking you've fallen into a pit. You can stay up here in the daytime as long as you are vigilant, but at night, it would be better if you slept down there."

"Angelo, what happens if they interrogate you?"

"A little white lie. I'll get rid of it in confession. "If they show up here. Yes, I'll tell them you were here, but when I found out about you, I kicked you out. And if they don't believe it, they can go down and search. Don't worry about me, I can handle them."

*****

Steve rolled over on the cot. He pulled the blankets up almost covering his head. He could hear a couple of rats trying to nibble away at the metal screen that Angelo had rigged up covering the cot. He kicked at the screen. The rats squealed and ran away. But they would be back.

He was miserable. This was his third night sleeping in a pitch-black room in the catacomb. He got very little sleep. He felt as if he had been entombed alive. Half awake, he mumbled prayers. They were of some comfort—mainly because they temporarily distracted him from his misery. But after a time, they were mechanical, repetitious. Why would God want to listen to something almost akin to gibberish? He rolled over. First on one side, then on the other. He punched the pillow. He kicked the screen again. Another squeal. He wondered whether all of this was worth it. Shouldn't he just give up and make a deal to leave the priesthood? For months now he had had no ministry. Giving tours of the catacombs hardly qualified as God's work. As the weeks had gone by, growing into months, it had become less and less likely that the Vatican would resolve his case in his favor.

He thought of Janet. His one sweet memory, but a memory that had almost faded. Worse, he felt guilty even thinking of her. Another man's wife. Perhaps the mother of a child, perhaps living a reasonably happy life somewhere in Boston. Probably Cambridge. Did she still have a career in social work? Or did she spend her days tending to the baby, fixing meals, doing housework, talking over the back fence with the neighbors. When her husband came home from work and they both had dinner, did they relax on a sofa in the evening? Then later at night in bed, did they...? The thought made him miserable, but if that was her life, he was happy for her. It could be a good life, a calm, satisfying and productive life. He wondered if she ever thought of him. He thought of the few weeks spent with Alice. They were a pleasure surely, but little more than what she had referred to as a brief encounter.

It was just a faint sound. More a rustle. In a second he was up, pushed the screen away, slipped out through the opening slit in the wall, and began feeling his way along the passageway. He hoped they wouldn't find the thin slot in the wall hidden behind the staircase on the lower level leading to his so-called bedchamber. If they did, they would know he was sleeping down there. And it would not go well for Angelo or for him.

He crept along the passageway in the dark guiding himself by running his fingers along the walls on the sides. Every now and then, his fingers touched nothing. He knew the gap would be an opening to a sepulcher. Then, after six or seven feet, he would feel the wall again.

He could hear slight sounds above him. They were

on the second level, he was down on the third. Perhaps they were afraid of going too deep into the catacombs. He would have been too, if he weren't so desperate. It was dangerous. Move too fast, make one false step and down twenty or thirty feet into the abyss. A half hour passed, then an hour. It grew quiet. They, whoever they were, had probably given up for the night. But like the rats, Steve was sure they would be back.

Three nights later they were back. They were down to the third level and Steve had to move quickly to stay ahead. He could hear the muffled thud of boots in the passageway behind him. They sounded so close he almost expected to feel a hand reaching to grab him from the rear. But it occurred to him that if they were close, he would have been caught in the beam of a flashlight. Still, he forced himself to move as fast as possible. How many were there? No way to be sure but it sounded like a small army.

With more noise than he would have liked, he half stumbled down a staircase to the lowest level. He crept along a rough cut passageway that had a rocky uneven floor with a low ceiling that scraped the top of his head and walls that closed in against his shoulders. Every once in awhile one of his elbows caught on a jagged rock jutting out from the wall. He decided to stop his headlong rush. He slowed his pace. He stopped to listen. It was quiet behind him. Either they were sneaking up on him or they had given up. He twisted down into a crouch with his back against the wall. Suddenly a massive cramp seized one of his legs. It was one of those long inside thigh cramps. The pain was excruciating. Since he couldn't stand and walk it off, he lay down flat and massaged it. When the cramp subsided, he sat up on the rocky floor, legs extended along the passageway. He leaned against the sidewall. A half hour passed. Then an hour. He decided they had gone. One arm bleeding, miserable and cold, he struggled back to his cot where he slept almost until noon the next day.

Angelo told him they never found the small chamber he had been sleeping in. And during the chase they were never really sure they were chasing the priest. It could have been that they were only chasing an animal, possibly a dog or a rat. Then climbing down the staircase into the unexplored, forbidden depths of the lowest level, down where these superstitious men thought perhaps the evil spirits of hell dwelt, they had decided to turn back.

It was a day later when Angelo gave them an excuse to quit the search in the catacomb—one they readily accepted. He told them they were wasting their time looking for the priest there. He showed them a copy of an e-mail receipt from an airline showing that the priest they were looking for was flying out of Rome to America. "If you hurry you can stop him, but why bother? He will soon be gone and won't be able to cause any trouble."

Some of the Knights, apparently satisfied, left the catacombs, but a few rushed to the airport to intercept the priest or failing that, to make sure he was gone. At the gate, the airline representative would not say whether Father Stephen Murphy had left on the flight but she did say that the flight was full.

41

Phillip Cardinal Rhinehart climbed the red-carpeted steps that covered the marble staircase leading to a long corridor on the second floor of the Apostolic Palace in the Vatican. As he walked, he passed bronze busts and paintings of former popes arrayed along both sides of the corridor. He followed a young priest who had been assigned to lead him to the office of Cardinal Hartzinger—the universally feared German who headed not only the Curia but also the Congregation for the Doctrine of Faith. The Congregation, in particular, focused on disciplinary matters. Knowing this, Cardinal Rhinehart had been somewhat perplexed, not to say shaken, when the message came summoning him to Rome. He had been summoned to the Vatican before, but it had always been to attend a ceremony or conference in the company of the other American cardinals. This was different. The message was curt. "Cardinal Hartzinger desires that you come to the Vatican at once."

After greeting Cardinal Rhinehart with a stiff formal handshake and a half-hearted attempt at a thin-lipped smile, Cardinal Hartzinger ushered him into a conference room that adjoined his office. Hartzinger, the German, could have been a twin of Rhinehart—tall, trim, ramrod straight, with a graying brush haircut. In different dress, they both could have been mistaken for officers in the German army high command.

On entering the small conference room, Cardinal Rhinehart glanced admiringly at walls and ceiling that were covered with brilliantly colored frescoes depicting scenes from Christ's life. He was introduced to two other cardinals, neither of whom he had met previously, who were standing near the conference table. He shook hands with Cardinal Mbotu, a black from South Africa and Cardinal Giovanni from Sicily. Rhinehart would have liked to see an American cardinal on the panel for moral support, but it was not to be.

Relegated to seats along the back wall about a dozen bishops sat quietly waiting for the meeting to begin. They would not participate but were available to answer any questions that were referred to them. Rhinehart assumed they were part of a study group that researched matters for the cardinal.

Speaking slowly and precisely, Cardinal Hartzinger opened the meeting. He got right to the point with no introductory pleasantries: "The holy father is seriously concerned about several problems in the Archdiocese of Washington that have gained his attention and his displeasure. These pertain to the apparent proliferation of pedophile priests in the archdiocese and the manner of dealing with them; in addition, there are reports that a seminary located in Washington near the grounds of Catholic University has become almost exclusively a refuge for homosexuals. A number of seminarians have withdrawn and have filed complaints about the widespread misconduct of many of the resident seminarians.

"If I may interrupt, Eminence," Cardinal Rhinehart said, addressing his equal in a subservient manner, hoping for leniency. "Surely the pontiff is aware that the problem of pedophile priests in America is widespread—not confined to my archdiocese. Boston, for example… "

"The holy father is quite aware. The other dioceses will be attended to in due time. For the moment, however, we focus on your archdiocese because it is the seat of the apostolic delegate to the United States."

On hearing these charges, Rhinehart's face grew somber. His hands balled into fists, but to conceal his reaction, he dropped them to his lap. He wasn't aware his archdiocese was noteworthy in regard to pedophile priests, and even if it were, he resented the Vatican meddling in the internal affairs of his archdiocese. He suspected it was the overreaching power of Hartzinger that was behind it all.

"The holy father is concerned," Hartzinger said, "not only with the number of priests who have been accused, two of whom have been convicted in American courts, but also with the practice of transferring priests who have been credibly accused of pedophilia from one parish to another. These supposedly secret transfers are, thanks to the overly ambitious American media and lawsuits by those who claim to be victims, secrets no longer. Not only does this manner of handling the problem cause risk to those in other parishes, it has become a huge embarrassment to the church. We on the panel concede," Hartzinger said, nodding to left and right to acknowledge his brother prelates, "and the holy father knows that you are not alone in this." The other cardinals on the panel nodded in agreement. "Almost every diocese in America has been involved in this same practice, but as I said, we singled you out because your archdiocese has been involved in some serious abuses and is, in particular the seat of the apostolic delegate. In other words, the pontiff's ambassador to the United States.

As he listened, Cardinal Rhinehart grew increasingly angry that the Vatican had selected him as a scapegoat. He could feel the color rising on the back of his neck. He knew he had done the very best he could under difficult circumstances. He hadn't created the problem, he hadn't selected or ordained any of these priests who were for the most part middle-aged or elderly—it had been done long before his time. It was a problem that had simply been dumped on him when he was elevated to the red hat. He also resented the fact that the American church was being singled out. Surely, Cardinal Mbotu's South Africa and Cardinal Giovanni's Sicily and every other country with a Catholic population has pedophile priests. The difference was clearly attributed to the tendency of Americans to right every wrong with litigation and the scandal mongers of the American press. "You do understand that I have no control over the number of cases. These involve offenses that date back twenty, thirty, or even more years. In fact, some of the accused are dead."

"We understand, but you must defrock a number of priests and improve screening of seminarians."

"I am in the process of doing that," Cardinal Rhinehart replied matter of factly. "Those who claim they have a calling to the priesthood are now being examined closely by a battery of psychiatrists. If we detect the slightest tendencies in the direction of pedophilia, they are dismissed. We err on the side of caution, and some potentially very devout priests are lost in the process—men who have no tendencies to pedophilia, but who object to the penetrating intrusiveness of the examinations, and who are disgusted by an apparent lack of trust in them by their church. We walk a tightrope. And surely you realize that if our measures are perceived as overly stringent, they will not help to alleviate the shortage of priests in the United States."

"The steps you are taking are commendable," said Cardinal Giovanni, speaking for the first time, "and they will no doubt be of benefit. They will strengthen the church of tomorrow."

On hearing this, Cardinal Mbotu nodded in agreement. Even Hartzinger seemed to be softening. Rhinehart thought he might be coming out of the woods in the interrogation. His optimism was premature.

"Turning to the manner in which you handle errant priests today..." said Hartzinger, trailing off.

"They are given therapy," Rhinehart responded quickly. "It's true we have been transferring them to other parishes, but it is with assurances from psychiatric professionals that after completion of therapy their behavior will change."

"Apparently it has not changed in many cases," Hartzinger said, leveling a cold gaze at the American cardinal. "Which brings me to the real concern of the holy father. He believes that as soon as the question arises, as soon as you suspect a problem based on a complaint, you must conduct an intensive inquiry. We are not saying an accused priest is guilty simply based on one or more complaints, but it must not be handled surreptitiously."

"We have always acted to keep the good of the church in the forefront," Cardinal Rhinehart said. "We have acted to minimize embarrassment to the Church... to avoid scandal."

"But surely you realize that the result is widespread scandal when this is perceived as a coverup. The problem escalates from that of an errant priest to an accusation of complicity on the part of the archdiocese and possibly even the Vatican."

"Eminence, when I become convinced that a priest has not responded to therapy and continues these practices in another parish, I transfer him to a remote monastery. Priests who are deemed incorrigible are sent there from dioceses all over America."

"Yes, we are aware of one such monastery—the Passion Monastery in the Arizona desert. But are you aware that a dozen priests have died there in the past year?"

"Yes, but I understand that a few died of old age, and a few died of Aids."

"And the others? I have learned that this is not an environment for spiritual reclamation of a soul gone astray. It seems directed to elimination. Here we have the holy father traveling throughout the world preaching against human rights abuses, and word comes that priests...human beings...are being abused—even brutalized inside his own church. When word of this leaked out, the leaders of some other religions began calling the pontiff a hypocrite. Don't you understand how much harm this does... how this undercuts his message?"

"I am not familiar with the treatment given at the monastery. May I suggest that Bishop Hernandez is the one who should be called to task about a monastery under his supervision?"

"Yes, and he will be. However, we are reminded that Hernandez is merely a bishop, and a relatively new one at that, while you are one of a handful of principal leaders of the church in America. As such, you have a level of responsibility that transcends his. We in the Vatican cannot do everything. Abuses in the American church must be handled by its own leaders. It is outrageous that such matters are allowed to add to the burden of the holy father."

On hearing this, Cardinal Rhinehart's anger began to fade, replaced by a contrite feeling that he had indeed let things get out of hand. The holy father had been his benefactor and he had repaid him poorly.

"You are," Cardinal Hartzinger continued, "enjoined to investigate conditions at the monastery in the company of Bishop Hernandez, of course. Any human rights abuses must cease immediately. Please inform your brothers in America of our wishes. We do not dispute that the concept of sending errant priests to such a place rather than simply transferring them to other parishes is a correct one. Nor do we believe that traditional therapy is the answer. In the difficult surroundings of the Passion Monastery there is an outside chance of reclaiming them, but if not, the austere conditions at the monastery together with the thought that they might spend the remainder of their lives there, may convince them to resign—a voluntary step, one that allows them to remain in the faith.

Defrocking is called for in many cases, but as you surely know, it risks adverse publicity and lawsuits when these men feel they have been deprived of future salary, retirement, and health care. But let me be clear. The Passion Monastery must stop certain practices—in particular, the selection of priests for what I have heard are bloody simulated crucifixions. We have learned that some priests are subjected to scourging, the way Christ was, but worse than that, the crucifixions result in some bleeding from a crown of thorns, near asphyxiation due to hours hanging on a cross and resulting trauma. This is a form of torture that must cease."

"Which brings us to another problem," Cardinal Hartzinger continued. "You transferred a Reverend Stephen Murphy to Bishop Hernandez, apparently with an arrangement for financial support. The priest was then sent to the Passion Monastery from which he later escaped. You are aware of this, of course."

"Yes, I am familiar with the case."

"Regarding the priest, Stephen Murphy, we understand he is not a pedophile or a substance abuser, he is a clone. And there is some evidence he is most likely a chimera; that is, a hybrid."

Cardinal Mbotu spoke for the first time: "I am unfamiliar with these terms. Please explain."

Cardinal Hartzinger, recognizing that Mbotu had not been on the panel that had made an extensive review of the matter of cloning, provided details of the cloning process. He explained his and the Curia's concern about human cloning and in particular the process of mixing animal cells with human cells, thus producing a chimera.

"Can this be done? Has it been done?" asked Mbotu.

"Of course it has," replied Hartzinger. Haven't you heard of sheep-goats produced by cloning? In a word: hybrids?"

"Good heavens. What do they look like?"

"The new creatures have some of the features of both."

"And the purpose of it?"

"Merely to amuse the scientists, I suppose. If these things can be done, they feel challenged to attempt them."

Cardinal Mbotu, looking down, his elbows resting on the table, brought his hands up to cover his eyes. He slowly shook his head. "Again the curse of science," he said softly.

"Now with a human-animal chimera," Cardinal Hartzinger continued, "one winds up with a hybrid who we believe is not a complete human being in the eyes of God. Almighty God does not implant a soul in an animal. Let me explain further. A separated part of a human, like an arm or a leg, is obviously not a complete human in the eyes of the church or of God. This arm or leg does not have a soul in its own right. The soul resides in the being from whom these parts came. Similarly, a part-human formed of a mixture of human and animal cells, we conclude, has not been given a soul by God. There is one soul only, and that one soul resides in the tissue donor—the one from whom the clone was produced. The being that results is a manufactured product, a synthetic human. God alone implants souls, scientists do not."

"I am in complete agreement with what you say

about cloning," Cardinal Rhinehart interjected, "and as soon as I learned the background of Stephen Murphy, I transferred him to Arizona to, shall we say, influence him to resign the priesthood."

"You transferred him to rid yourself of a problem," Cardinal Hartzinger shot back. "And when he refused to resign and escaped, you asked Bishop Hernandez to send Passion brothers to eliminate him."

"Those were never my instructions," Cardinal Rhinehart said emphatically. "They were to apprehend him and return him to the monastery; that's all."

"But he has complained through sources that the monks have no compunctions about killing him. They have already tried to kill him in fact. Apparently, since he is a chimera, they do not believe this would be murder. But remember, the secular world sees him as human. To those outside the church it would be deemed murder."

"May I ask what you suggest I do about this?"

"Murphy is in Rome. We have information that he is living at the San Callisto Catacombs. Through sources that I will not identify he has asked for the church's position on the validity of a human clone, and in his particular case, on the validity of a chimera. We have studied this at length and our answer will be a grave disappointment to him."

"As I said, I feel the same way," Cardinal Rhinehart said. "But what can be done? We have tried to coerce him into quietly resigning the priesthood without fanfare, but he refuses. You surely understand our serious concern about the effect the disclosure of a chimera in the priesthood would have on the thousands of parishioners who have received sacraments...invalid sacraments at his hands. Publicity about this would be devastating. Can you imagine all the couples who mistakenly thought they had been married by a priest? All those who honestly thought they had been absolved of their sins in the confessional? All those who thought they were receiving the Sacred Host at Mass from someone not empowered to perform the consecration? I would have a tragedy on my hands."

A door opened. Cardinal Rhinehart was astonished to see a thin, bent figure in white standing on the threshold—the pontiff himself.

The cardinals immediately rose to their feet. Cardinal Rhinehart moved forward and bent his knee....

"No formalities, please," the pontiff said. "We welcome you, Brother. We trust your journey from South America was not too uncomfortable?"

"From North America, Holiness."

"Oh yes. Now I remember. You are from the Archdiocese of ...."

"The Archdiocese of Washington, Holiness." The rumors were true. Cardinal Rhinehart was certain that the pope, approaching ninety, and rumored to be growing senile, could not remember his name even though they had met on many occasions. Worse, in fifteen minutes the pontiff might not even remember he had been there.

"We have learned sadly, that a young man has been murdered."

"Yes, Holiness," Cardinal Hartzinger replied. "It was the young man who claimed he was a clone of St. Peter."

"By whose hand?"

"We are not sure, Holiness, but we suspect the Knights of Carthage."

"All of this killing in the world must stop," the pontiff mumbled, dejectedly shaking his head as he turned slowly to leave the room. Cardinal Hartzinger closed the door behind him. He was obviously embarrassed. "His Holiness is not feeling well."

"Why doesn't he retire?" asked Cardinal Giovanni.

"He refuses," Hartzinger said. "He wants to die—to go before God as the pontiff. If you were in his shoes, I am sure you would feel the same way."

After the brief incident, it was clear to the cardinals present who was running the Vatican. Reading their thoughts, Cardinal Hartzinger said, "I do it of necessity, my Brothers. Now let me say again: the holy father calls for honesty and openness in dealing with errant priests."

Turning to Cardinal Rhinehart, Hartzinger said tersely, "There are two things you must do concerning Reverend Murphy: first, the monks must cease their chase."

"I have no idea how to contact the monks. I will contact Bishop Hernandez and relay the message to him."

"Second, you have no choice but to formally defrock Stephen Murphy."

The two other cardinals on the panel nodded their heads in agreement with Cardinal Hartzinger, thereby making the decision unanimous. In fact, the others on any of the panels never failed to be in agreement with Cardinal Hartzinger, knowing that he spoke for the pontiff and was a demon in red when crossed.

*****

After the meeting, as Cardinal Rhinehart walked back to his room in the new Domus Sanctae Marthae residence for visiting cardinals in Vatican City. He was thankful for the air conditioning and the private bathroom—unlike previous primitive facilities in the Apostolic Palace where too many cardinals had been crammed into small rooms with beds separated by hanging blankets and not nearly enough bathroom facilities. He took a brief nap to unwind from the somewhat hostile meeting. He knew the time had come to defrock Murphy. He cared only about the bad publicity. He was not the least concerned about the effect on Murphy, the man, or chimera, or whatever he was. What had the cardinal upset were the repercussions in the archdiocese when the word got out. And rest assured, it would leak out. He thought of the impossibly tangled lives of his flock. He could have a revolt on his hands. But he had some time. The defrocking could not officially take place until he returned to Washington. His itinerary called for stops in Vienna and Paris. These were important meetings that he could not miss. Stephen Murphy would have to wait.

After his nap, Cardinal Rhinehart sat on the edge of the bed and placed a call to Bishop Hernandez in Tucson.

He had difficulty concealing the anger in his voice after the unpleasant meeting at the Vatican. "The Vatican," he said caustically, "has ordered that your monks—and I emphasize that they are *your* monks, must stop their abusive practices. Cardinal Hartzinger specifically mentioned the simulated crucifixions. He was well aware that a dozen priests died at the monastery in the past year. The cardinal also said that the monks, who are chasing Stephen Murphy, must be contacted and returned to the monastery before harm comes to Murphy."

"Eminence, I would love to oblige but Brothers Michael and John are somewhere in Rome and until they call in, I have no way of communicating with them."

The cardinal felt like ripping the phone cord and throwing the phone across the room, but he said quietly, "I'm leaving shortly for Vienna. Cardinal Hartzinger wants action not excuses. I am aware that you are not officially under my jurisdiction, but as one of the leading prelates in America, I have been tasked to see that these things are done."

"I will do my best, your Eminence."

*****

Later, strolling through the sculptured gardens of the Vatican, Cardinal Rhinehart couldn't escape the thought that if either the monks from the Passion Monastery or the Knights of Carthage in Rome, somehow managed to do away with Murphy, it would conveniently solve his problem. He had no compunctions that a chimera—a being without a God-given soul—could be eliminated without committing a serious sin. Is it any worse than euthanizing a horse with a broken leg or putting to death a dangerous animal?

42

Alitalia flight 270 from Rome landed at three in the afternoon at Dulles Airport. Steve, groggy from the long flight, retrieved his suitcase from the carousel and hopped into an airport taxi. The driver headed east on the Dulles accessway for ten miles and turned north on the Capital Beltway that surrounds Washington, DC. Steve's destination was the Regal Hotel in Germantown, Maryland, located in the heartland of companies known to be on the leading edge of research in microbiology, gene therapy and DNA testing.

As soon as he reached his room, Steve called the BioGene Company to confirm his appointment for the next morning. Yes, Dr. Richardson was expecting him.

He took off the Roman collar. He examined it. Ring around the inside of the collar. He took another from his suitcase. The black suit stretched out on the bed was not too wrinkled. It would be all right for the meeting. It could stand another wearing before cleaning and pressing. After a warm relaxing shower, Steve studied himself in the mirror. He needed a shave as usual. He wondered if electrolysis that some women used could free him from the drudgery of shaving twice a day. He remembered a Chinese friend from long ago who as a poor teenager in a small town in China was upset about shaving every day for the rest of his life. It may be that razors were scarce or nicked and painful to use. With oriental stoicism, the young man decided to pluck out every hair in his beard thinking he would never have to shave again. After his sore face recovered, his beard grew back. Steve looked in the mirror, and with a wry smile, just decided to keep on doing what he did twice a day.

He ordered a light dinner from room service. He was nervous about being in the Washington area, where all his troubles seemed to have begun. He wouldn't want to run into anyone he knew. He even planned to avoid his old parish for fear that word of his return might leak back to the Archdiocese.

At nine the next morning Steve was ushered into a small conference room in the main building of Biogene's sprawling complex of office buildings and labs. The secretary showed him to a seat in Dr. Richardson's office and offered him coffee which he accepted. A few minutes later, the doctor, tall, blonde, attractive, studious looking in wire rim glasses, professional looking in a white lab coat, walked in and sank into an executive chair behind her desk. The label over the breast pocket of her lab coat had the embroidered name 'Shelly'.

As she tidied a few papers on her desk, she studied the priest who sat in front of her. "Father Murphy, how can I help you?" she asked.

"Well, doctor...."

"Let's drop the formalities. This is not a typical doctor's office. This is a lab. Everyone calls me Shelly."

"I need an examination."

"I just told you this is a research establishment. If a physical is all you want, you've come to the wrong place. I suggest you make an appointment with a GP or an internist." With that, Shelly rose from her chair to usher the priest to the door.

"I don't mean that kind of examination. Let me tell you my problem straight out—I am a clone."

"My, my, a Catholic priest clone. Bet the Vatican loves that!" Shelly said, with a smirk as she sat down again behind the desk. "Let me ask, how do you know you're a clone?"

"I have some records. They're pretty old, hard to read."

"Considering that you are, say about...."

"I'm fifty."

"Yes. You don't look it by the way," Shelly remarked, studying the priest's dark hair, slightly gray at the temples and rugged athletic build. "You could pass for forty."

"Thanks. I'd like to leave the papers with you for a few days to give you time to look them over."

"I don't want to sound rude, but how do you know I want to look them over?"

"Please. I need help with this. My cardinal and the Vatican authorities know about my situation and there are some who'd be happy if I just disappeared or died or whatever. They've put me under pressure but I've refused to resign the priesthood and just fade away."

"They could defrock you."

"True. But that might bring out the whole story— bad publicity, scandal. They'd much prefer to keep this quiet, although, quite frankly, they may be at the point of doing it anyway."

"Look Father Murphy, it can't be that bad. So you're a human clone. A clone is really only a delayed twin.

Is that so terrible?" Shelly shook her head, convinced the priest was overly concerned about his situation. Although she had never met one, there were strong rumors of the existence of other human clones. "The early furor has died down. People now seem to be taking it in stride."

"It's worse than that, I'm afraid," Steve said, deciding to drop the bomb. "I suspect I may be a chimera; that is, a human-animal hybrid."

Shelly suddenly leaned forward in her chair. She stared at him over the rim of her reading glasses. "Now you have my attention, Father Murphy. This is straight out of Greek mythology. Tell me more."

Steve recounted the story of his mother and Jonathon and the medical center in northern Maine.

"I'm beginning to get the picture," Shelly said, "but what was the point of experimenting with a chimera? Sounds unethical. And, by the way, what animal are we talking about?"

"Don't know. The cloning records are fairly complete, but the chimera experiments offer a sketchy explanation. Marginal notes are about all there are to go on concerning the aspects relating to producing a chimera. And several pages of the report have been lost. About a year or so ago, I went up to the center and talked to the director. He said he thought the doctor who did the cloning might have mixed in animal cells to stop the genetic transfer of Lou Gehrig's disease. My brother has it by the way and is dying of it. It's been prevalent in our family for many generations. It's the only reason that makes sense."

"That might explain it," Shelly commented. "The

experimenter could have been trying to stem the course of the disease—sort of an early attempt at something roughly akin to gene therapy but at the level of the cell."

"Well that's the miserable story," Steve said glumly. "Can you study these old records and run DNA tests and do whatever else is needed to get to the bottom of this? Call it a research project. I'd be happy to pay whatever it costs. Frankly, it's driving me crazy. I was pastor of a church for years and now I don't even know if I'm a valid priest or even a valid human being."

Shelly studied the priest, her interest growing. "Tell me, Father Murphy, have you tried to compare yourself with other men? What I mean is...do you think you have any characteristics—physical or mental—that would distinguish you from other men? Let me put it this way: characteristics that you think may not be completely human?"

"I can run like the wind. And I'm stronger than most men...in my age category, of course. I'm not bragging. Since you asked, I'm just telling you what I've observed about myself."

"I'm not doubting your abilities, but I can understand why, believing you are a chimera, you started thinking you might be part deer, part large primate and part human."

"When you say 'primate,' what animal are you referring to?"

Looking him straight in the eye and with a slight smile, Shelly said, "a gorilla."

Steve winced.

Seeing his pain, Shelly quickly added, "I'm not really

serious, I just wanted to see your reaction. The animal characteristics that you think you observed may just be a fantasy that grew in your mind after you saw the medical records. You may be a fast runner and strong and not be a chimera at all. By the way, is that medical center in northern Maine still in existence?"

"Yes, but their current operation strikes me as completely legitimate. The human cloning business is no more than ancient history at the center."

"Father Murphy, let me explain the reason for my interest in this case. I am a researcher as I said before. If tests show that you are a living, breathing chimera, and if I can have your permission to document this case in a research paper, there would be no charge for the testing. You would not be identified in the paper. I would make some reference to the subject being a cleric, but no denomination would be mentioned. However, considering that the cloning was done years ago, the chances are slim that a successful chimera was produced. So, in a way, there is little for you to worry about. If there is no evidence of a chimera, I couldn't prepare a research paper and I would have to ask you to pay some nominal charges for the testing and preparation of a report. Is that OK with you?"

"Fair enough," Steve answered, somewhat relieved to hear the comment about the unlikelihood that human cloning in the early days could produce a chimera.

Shelly picked up the phone. "This is Doctor Richardson of BioGene speaking. I want to schedule a subject for a full body MRI, blood chemistry, DNA sampling and hair analysis. Today is Monday. I would like the testing complete by Friday." Cradling the phone on her shoulder, she asked Steve, "They can begin on Thursday and have results by the weekend. Is that OK?"

"Yes, of course. It will give me a couple of days to do a few other things."

Shelly stood up and walked around the desk. Standing next to Steve, she knew she was tall, but he was several inches taller. He was handsome, no doubt about that. Why were so many priests so good looking? What a waste! As she walked him to the door of her office, she said, "As I mentioned before, we are a research lab. The tests will be conducted at the medical center about a block from here. You will report there at nine on Thursday; nothing to eat after mid-night on Wednesday."

As Steve left, Shelly wondered, what if he is part animal? The thought gave her a fleeting erotic thrill that she couldn't explain.

*****

On the morning following his visit to BioGene, Steve rented a car and drove up the interstate from Rockville, bypassing Frederick, Maryland and then headed west to the little town of Brunswick located on the Potomac River near historic Harpers Ferry. He was searching for the sister of Father Elmer Gustafson, his former inmate at the Passion Monastery.

"Never heard of Elmer Gustafson," the post office clerk said, "but there is an Anna Gustafson living in town. Four houses down to the left."

At Anna Gustafson's house, Steve learned from a housekeeper that Ms Anna was at work. "She's a teller at The Farmers and Mechanics Bank in Frederick."

So, back I go to Frederick, Steve thought with a shrug.

Finally, locating the bank, Steve introduced himself to a woman who had a strong resemblance to his former friend, although she seemed about ten years younger. "I'm inquiring about your brother, Elmer," he said. "He and I were friends at the Passion Monastery in Arizona."

"Yes, I know about that place," Anna commented. "That's where the church sends the bad apples."

From the sour look on the woman's face Steve picked up vibes that Anna Gustafson immediately concluded that Steve, like Elmer, was one of the 'bad apples'.

It took some coaxing to get her to agree to lunch at a nearby restaurant.

Over lunch, he described the months he had spent with Elmer at the monastery. He noticed that Anna was extremely reticent about making any comments concerning her brother. Steve knew the problem. Elmer had acknowledged that he was a three-time-loser alcoholic and his sister had become completely fed up with him.

"Ms Gustafson, I spent a lot of time with Elmer and I feel we became close friends. Under difficult circumstances, I might add. I know he had a drinking problem. Not at the monastery, of course, but from earlier times. He was completely sober at the monastery and in therapy. Please believe that I'm here to see you as a friend of Elmer's, not as a representative of the church."

"Why were you at the monastery?" Anna asked

bluntly. "And how did you get out? I notice you're still dressed as a priest."

"My situation is complicated and I could try to explain that I was sent there through no fault of my own, but I doubt you'd believe me."

"You're right. I wouldn't believe you," Anna commented as she poured dressing on her salad and then looked up at Steve with obvious distaste in her eyes. "Again, Father, how did you get out?"

"I escaped. I ran away. In fact, I'm still running."

"Ran away from helpful therapy?"

"I wasn't in therapy. Please, can't we just talk about Elmer?"

"I have strong mixed feelings when I think about Elmer. The way he screwed up his life—it's too difficult to talk about. The church transferred him all over the place until he became such an embarrassment they sent him to that monastery."

"I know it's unlikely that he could have gotten a letter out to you, but in case you have heard from him, I'd like to know how he's doing."

Anna stared head down at the plate in front of her. A full minute passed. Then she looked up: "Elmer's dead."

"What? How?" Steve asked in shock.

"They said it was an accident."

"Don't you have any other information about how he died?"

"No. All I have is a death certificate that came with his body for burial here in Maryland. The death certificate says he died from the trauma of an accident. That's all. We buried him at a cemetery not far from here."

*****

An hour later, Steve knelt in the grass at his friend, Elmer's grave. The small headstone read: Elmer Gustafson. Rest in Peace. The emptiness, the utter simplicity of the stone brought tears to Steve's eyes. No memorial, not even any dates listed. All that was left of a friend: a small stone, a name and a few words. He prayed for the repose of Elmer's soul. He hoped someone had given him last rites before he died from 'the accident'.

Steve stood up. He wiped the grass from his knees. He made the sign of the cross over the grave. Reaching into a small paper bag, he pulled out a single red rose that he had stopped to buy as he and Anna were driving to the cemetery. He laid it in front of the stone.

Anna was standing under the trees a dozen yards away. Their cars were parked beside the lane along which she had guided him to the gravesite. As Steve walked back to her, she saw the tears in his eyes. "Thanks for coming," she said. "I appreciate it. Elmer would appreciate it… if he knew. I hope you have a better future than Elmer did. Now I have to hurry back to work."

After a polite handshake, Steve watched her walk quickly to her car and drive off.

*****

Steve would never remember what he did for the rest of that day. He drove through miles of Maryland countryside in a mental fog. In the evening he stopped for dinner in a place that would remain nameless in his memory. Later in the evening, back at the hotel, he slipped into casual clothes and went into the cocktail lounge for a drink. He was smoking again. He despised the habit, but still when traumatic events came along, the first thing he did was reach for a cigarette. There was one thing he wanted to find out but knew he never could: Where were Brothers Michael and John when Elmer had his 'accident'? What a convenient way to dispose of someone who was troublesome—an accident in a remote place. And what authorities would question the word of the monastery—the word of the Catholic Church?

*****

The next morning, Steve was up early. After breakfast, he drove into Washington to the National Zoo. He had no intelligent idea as to why he went there. He was on autopilot. It was in answer to a compulsive need to see the animals. He drifted around finally winding up in the building that housed the primates. He stood looking first at the gorillas, then the chimps, then the monkeys. He studied them closely. He watched fascinated at their movements— the way they picked up tiny pieces of something or other and nibbled on it. Reaching down, he pulled up a sleeve. He looked at his arm. He compared it to the hairy forearms of the chimps.

Maybe I'm looking for a relative, he thought wryly, miserably. I can't tell by studying them but perhaps they can by studying me. If I get as close as possible to the cages would any of them pick up a faint smell? Would they approach me out of curiosity?

Steve suddenly walked swiftly out of the building and left the zoo. This is madness, he thought. Why am I trying so hard to make myself miserable? After the tests are run, and I see Dr. Richardson; that is, Shelly, maybe she'll have an answer for me.

On the following Thursday and Friday, Steve underwent a battery of tests that began at nine A.M. and lasted until six. Each day as he left the medical center, he was dizzy from the whirlwind of testing and the tiny amount of food he had been allowed. He spent part of the weekend visiting the National Shrine of the Immaculate Conception and also, dressed as a tourist, he took a look at the church he had been building until he had been removed from the parish. It was to him a magnificent building.

At the National Shrine, he had a cup of coffee and a sandwich in the cafeteria where he had spent so many pleasant lunch hours with Janet. Too many memories came flooding back. He decided to leave quickly. Happily, he did not run into anyone who recognized him.

*****

On Monday morning, Steve Murphy was again sitting in Dr. Shelly Richardson's office sipping coffee supplied by the secretary, waiting for the doctor to appear. Now he knew how potential cancer patients must feel when waiting for the verdict. He could feel his heart pounding in his chest.

When Shelly entered the office, she was smiling.

"Good news, Father Murphy. The MRIs and X-rays are anatomically human. Your blood chemistry is well within the normal range for humans. Healthy humans at that. The hair analysis shows some nutritional irregularities, for example, a somewhat high mercury level, but nothing to worry about. Besides, hair analysis is at best an uncertain tool. We do it just to cover the waterfront. The DNA tests show no evidence of animal DNA. Remember, however, DNA results are probabilistic. For example, if we are looking for a DNA match, we might say the odds are one in ten million, or one in fifty million. Our answers are always given in terms of probability. But based on all of the tests we have done so far, you appear to be as human as anybody else."

"So that's it," Steve said rising to shake hands with Shelly, thank her, and be on his way. "I'll tell you where to send the bill and can you send me a written report? I might be able to use it to convince a cardinal or two in Rome."

"That's not quite it, Father Murphy. We're not finished yet. I think we should also give you a hands-on physical exam."

"Is that necessary?"

"I wouldn't feel completely confident in preparing a written report without it. Think of it this way: it may give you extra peace of mind. Now, please go into the examining room next door and take off your clothes. You can leave your shorts on."

"Who's giving the exam?"

"I am," Shelly said with a slight grin.

"But you're a researcher. Isn't this a bit out of your

line?"

"Yes, I am a PhD, but I'm also an M.D. I'm licensed to practice medicine in Maryland but I prefer research as I said before. Now be a good priest and go in and take your clothes off." Shelly was amused that this big rugged-looking man seemed scared to death to be seen by a woman in his shorts.

*****

Twenty minutes later, lying on the examining table wearing nothing but his briefs, Steve felt a chill. He looked for some kind of cover on the table but there was nothing he could put over him.

Shelly entered the room. She went to the sink to wash her hands. She saw the scared look on his face. "My, my, pink underwear."

"I mixed colored and white clothes in the laundromat and these came out pink."

"If you would feel more comfortable having a man here in the room while I examine you, just say so."

"No, just go ahead," Steve said. He was never so mortified in his life. His doctors had always been men and even then, like most men, he had always felt uncomfortable at being examined. It was especially troublesome being a priest. As he lay on the table, he decided this whole thing had been a terrible mistake. He began to realize that although the tests might be negative, there would be no absolute certainty. And letting this woman's eyes pore over his body was most likely a grievous sin. At the very least, the church would label it an occasion of sin.

"Please turn over on your stomach."

Her soft touch felt warm and friendly as her hands moved over his back and down his legs. He began to feel relaxed. Her hands tapped, glided, pressed and almost seemed to knead parts of his body. He imagined it was very much like a gentle massage although he had never had one.

"Now please turn over on your back." For a few moments, lying stretched out with his eyes closed, he imagined Janet was running her hands over him. As Janet's hands explored his body, he almost couldn't resist the urge to pull her to him and embrace her. He opened his eyes. It wasn't Janet.

"Pull down your shorts."

"Is that really necessary?"

"I know you're embarrassed but you shouldn't be. This is completely impersonal as far as I'm concerned. What I'm doing is necessary because I'm searching for any traces of unusual skin, hair growth, or animal musculature you may have—the kinds of things that don't show up on the other tests."

Fifteen of the hardest minutes Steve had ever experienced in his life passed in slow motion. This surely was a mortal sin, but he recognized that the worst, the most sinful part, sprang from the arousal he felt. It was something he couldn't control. Shelly noticed it but said nothing. Finished with the exam, she stepped away from the table and made some notes on a pad. "You can put your clothes on. Then, when you're ready, come back to my office and let's talk."

*****

A short time later, Steve sat in Shelly's office as she

pored over her notepad. Then, looking up with a smile, she said, "Now that didn't hurt did it Father Murphy?"

Steve shrugged and managed to smile back.

"My conclusion is that there is absolutely no evidence any animal characteristics are present, or that any animal cells survived in the cloning process. We now have negatives from several different protocols to confirm this. It may sound a bit redundant saying this, but there is no evidence you are anything but a man—a complete man, nothing more, nothing less. So I don't get a research paper, but you get good news. And, of course, you get the bill."

"I have a question," Steve said. "What were you looking for in the physical exam? You know, that business on the table."

"Let me explain that. You've heard of hybrids like cloned sheep-goats and sheep-cows, I presume. A sheep-cow, for example, may look like a sheep but have the markings of a cow—sometimes brown and white blotches or black and white blotches. Today, numerous hybrids—mixed breeds of various types have been produced by cloning. In each case, each successful case that is, there are characteristics present from each of the species. The resulting animal has some physical properties of each. Without evidence of that, the hybrid doesn't exist."

"You're saying I have human skin with no traces of gorilla hair?" Steve asked, trying to be lighthearted about it all. He could afford to be lighthearted now on hearing the good news.

"You have dark hair on your arms and chest but it's all human." Collecting the papers concerning Steve into a neat pile on the center of her desk, she added, "We can give you a complete report if you like. It may persuade some of your church authorities. Of course, they may not believe us, but we can't do anything about that. By the way, I also studied the papers you brought with you—the ones from the center that did the cloning. From what I can deduce about the protocols used, although the cloning was successful, there was almost no chance the animal cells would survive. I would suggest that for your own well being, you ought to forget about the chimera business. There's no evidence of it. It didn't take."

"Can I give you an address in Rome to send the report to?"

"Of course. We can mail it in about a week."

"Please send it to: Reverend Stephen Murphy, care of Father Angelo, San Callisto Catacombs, Via Appia Antica, Rome Italy."

"You're living in the catacombs?" Shelly asked in surprise.

"Yes. I've been living like an animal in hiding, but maybe it's about time I came out into the open."

43

Steve peered through the storefront window of Jonathon's real estate office. In the interior he saw Marge on the telephone. Jonathon was nowhere in sight. Marge smiled, waved to Steve and motioned him to come in.

Steve took a seat beside Marge's desk. While she was talking on the phone, he glanced around at the office. There didn't seem to be anyone else there. Jonathon was probably out closing on a house or something. Marge, in her middle fifties, was letting her hair grow gray. She looked thin to Steve. She looked tired. Hanging up the phone, Marge reached over to shake Steve's hand. "How are things in Rome?" she asked.

"Rotten. How are things here in Wayland? And by the way, where's my brother?"

"Things are not too good here. Jonathon's out with a client."

"How's his health?"

"I'll level with you, Steve. Some months ago, the only symptoms were hoarseness and difficulty writing. But lately he has had trouble swallowing and sometimes difficulty getting words out. Eventually Lou Gehrig's disease will affect everything he does—dressing himself, eating, walking—even breathing."

"I don't know much about it," Steve said. "Guess I should read up on it. I do know there's no cure." He looked at Marge. He saw a glint of tears in her eyes.

Good old Marge—plain looking, a spinster. A loyal fixture in the office for almost twenty years.

"We've been living together, Steve. Seeing as how you're a priest, does that shock you?"

"Not really. It would be better if you were married, but I'm happy he has someone."

"He wants me to marry him."

"Are you going to?"

"I might. Right now, in addition to a housekeeper, we've hired a live-in nurse...I guess I should say he's hired the nurse."

"All in the Murphy mansion?" Steve asked, thinking the old mausoleum might be coming alive with three women looking after things. He smiled at the thought of stuffy old Jonathon with a cadre of women bustling around him.

"How long will you be in Rome?"

"Not much longer. The church is giving me a hard time."

"I know all about it—the cloning, I mean. Jonathon told me the story. It's really lousing up your life isn't it?"

"I'd say so," Steve replied as he looked around and stood up to greet Jonathon who had just come into the office.

"This is a surprise, Steve." Jonathon spoke slowly with a measured effort to make each word clear. "Why didn't you let us know you were coming?"

"Just a spur of the moment visit. A stop-off on my way back to Rome. I visited DNA specialists in Maryland to get a reading on my genetics."

"And?"

"It turned out OK. Better than I would have expected. They're forwarding a report to me at San Callisto. It might be helpful in convincing Vatican authorities, but in any case, it's helped me a lot psychologically."

"I suppose the church authorities know by now that you've been staying in Rome. When you left the Aleutian Islands the church sent a man here snooping around. We tried to decoy him into thinking you had gone to the Hawaiian Islands."

"Thanks, it helped throw them off the trail for awhile. But they will find me and unless something has changed, those goons from the monastery are still after me. Even if the church called them off, I'm not sure they'd obey. They seem to have a personal vendetta going."

When Marge went to the restroom, Steve asked Jonathon if he had heard from Janet.

"Not a word, Steve. Some time ago I heard she was living in Cambridge with her husband."

"Any children?"

"Don't know. Why don't you call her and see how she's doing?"

"No, I'd better leave well enough alone. I did send her a postcard with my address after I arrived in Rome, but I never received an answer. And tell me, how are you doing, Jonathon? How are you feeling?"

"I feel OK. My problem doesn't involve physical pain. But simple things— things people take for granted—like eating and talking can be difficult at times. And there's the worry, the fear, the knowledge that this illness gets worse over time. There's no cure."

"I pray for you Jonathon."

"Thanks. But my dear kid brother, does it do any good? Will it change anything?"

"You never know. It might. Marge said you proposed to her."

"Yes. After all these years I finally realized how much I care for her. By the way, when I'm gone, I'm leaving the real estate business to her. I have a potential buyer who's interested in the accounting and tax preparation business. And Marge will inherit the house and surrounding estate. You will both share fifty-fifty in the financial settlement. Is that all right with you?"

"As I've said many times," Steve chuckled, "I have zero interest in real estate and less, if possible, in accounting and tax work. And as for the rest, having to put up with you—you moody old dog—for twenty years, Marge deserves the property and half of any remainder."

Marge came back into the room. She leaned back against the edge of her desk. "Ever coming back to America, Steve?"

"Maybe sooner than anyone thinks. If the church doesn't accept the BioGene report, I may have to resign. But don't start worrying that I'll meddle in this business. If I do anything, I'll try for a university teaching job. Then when I'm off in the summer I can spend time up at Pine River Pond driving everyone crazy with my takeoffs and landings."

Marge laughed. Jonathon tried to laugh but wound up with a fit of coughing and gurgling. He struggled to breathe. For a moment he looked like he was turning blue. Marge put her arms around him to steady him. He recovered slowly, embarrassed that Steve was there to see how the disease was beginning to take hold.

Pulling himself together, Jonathon tried to make light of the episode. He invited Steve to have dinner with Marge and him. He promised a great meal followed by a show at a theater in Boston.

Steve declined the invitation. As he was leaving, he put his arms around Marge, pulled her close and whispered in her ear: "Take care of him, Marge. You're the best thing that's ever happened to him. And as the disease progresses, you won't be able to provide 24/7 care so we will see that you have power of attorney. You will then be able to purchase whatever assistance is needed. And if you are called on to make any decisions that you aren't sure of, we'll keep in touch, but rest assured that I won't countermand any decisions you make even if they aren't strictly in accordance with the rules of the church. Besides since Jonathon isn't a Catholic any more, there's no reason why the church should even be involved."

"Thanks Steve. I'll do my best."

44

Angelo was upset. With his hands clasped behind him, his voluminous black cassock billowing as he walked, he paced the floor in his office above the catacombs. Steve sat in a stuffed leather chair in a corner watching Angelo fume.

"Why are you doing it, Steve? I don't understand it. We have word that the Vatican has rejected your claim and you are about to be defrocked. Of course, it doesn't happen here, it will be done by Cardinal Rhinehart back in America. This is a tragedy, but what I don't understand is why you want to keep sleeping down in the catacombs. They've won. You're being kicked out. Of course, you remain a Catholic and you can serve as a deacon in a parish of your choice in America. But the battle is over, the war is lost. I say have faith in God and try to make the best of it. I did enjoy having you here, you were a big help with the tours, and your companionship was welcome."

"I appreciate your saying that, Angelo."

"But now my friend, it's time for you to go back to America. It's safe for you to go back to America."

For a moment, Steve thought Angelo was afraid of reprisals for harboring him at San Callisto.

Angelo read his mind. "I'm thinking of you, Steve... your well-being. Please don't think I'm worried about the Vatican because I'm not. There's another thing that puzzles me, Steve. You've been taking food down there—a lot of food I might add, for over a week now. What do you do with it? Are you compensating for the loss of the priesthood by eating yourself to death?"

Steve sat watching Angelo pace back and forth. "Angelo, bear with me," he said quietly. "You may think the danger is past, but I don't. It's true the Knights of Carthage have probably given up, but there's been no word about the Passion Monastery monks. I know these guys. They have a personal grudge against me. Even if their bishop told them to stop chasing me, I doubt they would. Try to put up with me for just a few more weeks and then I'll clear out."

Angelo exhaled an impatient sigh as he walked to his desk and sat down behind it. "OK, Steve. But hear this: until you leave, you can pray all day in our chapel if you like, but I would advise against saying Mass since the decision has been made and the defrocking is imminent. God might not appreciate it."

"I understand," Steve answered glumly. "I have a question."

"What?"

"Can I borrow your car?"

*****

Steve drove north through the city in Angelo's car to Saint John Lateran Cathedral. Walking down the aisle in the dark interior of the church, he looked up at the urns resting high above. He thought of young Peter who had said he was cloned from the tissue fragments in one of the urns. Young Peter, murdered. He wondered whether other clones might be produced either from the remains of the original Saint Peter or perhaps from the body of young Peter.

Steve knelt in the first pew. He didn't pray. He had come to sort things out in his mind while God listened in—if God cared to listen in. He was angry at being tossed out of the church. So they will let me remain as a Catholic parishioner, he thought bitterly. Perhaps I could be a deacon—like a dismissed surgeon in a hospital being told he could stay on as a medical technician or an orderly.

Their decision was unfair, but there was no way he could convince the church authorities of that fact. They had taken the BioGene results with a grain of salt. They wanted him out. It resolved a dilemma for them. He thought of the parishioners he had counseled through the years—people who had lost loved ones, lost jobs, lost hope. People who had been treated unfairly by events or by other people. He would tell them life was like that. You learned to live with it after a time. You learned to make the best of it. You held onto the belief that God had a purpose in mind. The unfairness would be straightened out—if not in this life, then certainly in the next. It was faith that would triumph over the unfairness. Faith was the key. All you needed was faith in God and faith in yourself.

As he knelt, he was aware that the messages he had given through the years in counseling parishioners, were messages that he now sorely needed to take to heart. Like so many people who had lost homes and all their belongings in tornadoes, floods or earthquakes, you couldn't let yourself go off the deep end he told himself. You had to rebuild. You had to learn to turn away from the past, and simply press on. Through all the calamity, you had to trust your faith in God's goodness.

His anger faded. He began to pray. He began to trust.

*****

Steve Murphy walked back up the aisle to the front entrance of the Saint John Lateran Cathedral. He paused briefly, turning to look back at the altar, then walked out into the bright Roman sunshine.

*****

Steve opened his eyes, although in the blackness, he wasn't really sure they were open. He groped for the flashlight but something told him not to switch it on. It was a soft sound. He had been asleep on the cot in the small alcove that lay behind the narrow slit in the wall on the third level down. At first, half awake, he thought the noise that wakened him was made by rats searching for a way under or through the metal cage that covered his cot. He kicked at the cage. These past nights spent trying to sleep in the catacomb were the same old misery he had had to put up with weeks before when the Knights of Carthage were after him. Many nights were filled with prayer because sleep was elusive. He often lay on his back with his arms folded behind his head for hours, wondering what he would do with the rest of his life after the priesthood. But on this night, he was so exhausted, he had finally fallen asleep.

Was it the rats? He knew that if he simply left the rats alone, they might gnaw through the wire mesh of his cage. He kicked again, careful to keep the sound as muffled as possible.

After a few minutes in the silence, he decided the rats must have given up. Then he heard a whispering voice. He knew it couldn't be Angelo because when Angelo's head hit the pillow in the upstairs bedroom of the rectory, even a strong earthquake was not likely to wake him.

The whispering grew louder. Someone was creeping down the steps to the lower level. He was whispering to someone else. Was it the monks?

Steve lay frozen in his cot. He could see a glint from a flashlight that reflected momentarily on the wall just outside of the alcove. It told him that his pursuers, whispering to one another, were dangerously close. He held his breath and lay motionless on the cot. His only hope: that they wouldn't see the narrow slit in the wall that led to his sleeping chamber. He strained to listen. The soft footsteps passed by the opening to his alcove. The whispering began to fade in the distance. They had missed his opening. He began to relax. Fifteen minutes passed. Then he heard the sounds growing louder. They were coming back. He distinctly heard the voice of Brother Michael. He could afford to wait no longer. If they found the opening, he would be trapped in the dead-end alcove.

Pushing off the screen, he bolted to his feet and ran out into the main corridor. He had forgotten the flashlight, but there was no time to return for it. They heard him and started running after him. With hands touching lightly on both sidewalls as he ran in the dark, he knew they weren't far behind because the light from their flashlights flickered crazily on the crudely carved tufa rock ceiling and bounced on the earthen floor. He turned a corner into a side passageway and slid into an empty open crypt in the wall and laid flat. He had seen it before. Carved deeply into the wall, it was one of the few crypts that had been carved deeply enough to hold two bodies side by side. He pressed as far back as he could hoping not to be seen by his pursuers.

He could feel the rush of wind as the brothers ran by with flapping robes and sandals crunching into the soft earth. He figured they hadn't seen him as they continued down the passageway.

As Steve pressed against the back earthen wall, he found the crypt not long enough for his body. His knees pressed against the roof of the crypt. Crumbles of dirt fell on him. Then the roof fell in. Something large landed on his chest. In the blackness, he had no idea what it was. Was it a large chunk of cemented earth from the crypt above? He tried to shake it off. In the confined space, he tried to push it away. His hands explored it. He shuddered in disgust. It was a body from a long-sealed crypt above. More than a skeleton, it seemed to have pieces of flesh attached. Groping, he felt a shoulder and a bony arm. The skull was pressed face down on his neck. The kiss of the dead. He decided the ancient must have been buried face down although he had no idea why. He tried to calm himself by remembering that if flesh remained after two thousand years, it was probably the body of a saint. "Whoever you are, pray for me," he whispered as he climbed out of the crypt and tried to run in a direction opposite to the one the monks had taken. But something in the crypt kept dragging him back. A skeletal arm with long bony fingers had caught in his clothes. As he grabbed the arm it separated from the hand. He had to pull off bony fingers that seemed to be grasping on to him in a death grip. Wrestling himself free, he took off.

Hearing the noise of the falling debris of the crypt, the brothers turned around and started running back. Glancing to the rear as he ran, Steve saw the glint of a knife in the light from one of the flashlights. He gritted his teeth in a flash of anger. He remembered Elmer and what they had called an 'accident'. He thought of Saint Peter who had denied Christ three times on the night before the Crucifixion, while he, Steve, had cast off his anger in front of God in the Lateran Cathedral only to have it come surging back. The weakness of the flesh.

Surely the monks had been told he was about to be defrocked—that he was no longer a problem for the church. He was certain now that they would never give up pursuing him even after he left the priesthood. They had made up their minds to kill him. It would be easily done in the catacombs and easy to cover up. They'd simply dump his body into an unexplored crevasse.

Thudding feet. They were close behind. They had an advantage: they were running with flashlights to light their path, he was running in the dark. He took a turn into a side passageway just as he heard one of the brothers shout, "There he is. We got that shithead now."

After turning the corner Steve halted abruptly. He fumbled with the latch on a wrought iron gate in the sidewall that led into an alcove. He swung open the gate but didn't go into the alcove. Instead, he squeezed by the open gate and ran along the passageway. The decoy saved him a little time as the monks, seeing the open gate, searched the alcove. Cursing, they were soon after him again. Now, the pursuers and the quarry were deep into the catacomb.

As the monks closed in on him again, Steve stopped to fumble with the latch on the gate of another alcove. This time the monks knew the game. This time they would not be decoyed into searching another alcove where he might be hiding.

As Steve tried to squeeze around the open gate one of the monks came up behind him and, reaching out, slashed him on the shoulder with his knife. Steve felt a surge of pain and felt blood running down his left arm, but at this point, nothing was going to stop him. He took off running again. As he ran he quickly glanced back. He mumbled under his breath: "This is for Elmer." Then he heard the yelps begin—at first just a few, then a clamor. Then the sound of scrambling, yelping dogs fighting their way out of the alcove and crowding into the passageway. The pack of dogs he had been daily feeding small portions of meat in the alcove were still hungry enough to want more. The gate had been locked, now it was open. As the dogs charged, moving back, trying to escape, Brother John fell in the narrow passageway. Brother Michael fell on top on him. As the dogs piled on, the monks slashed frantically with their knives. Blood spurted on the walls and ceiling. The yelps turned into growls as the dogs bit into the monks' faces, necks and hands, and chewed away their habits. The monks' yelling turned into screams. Steve debated whether to turn back to help but although he had fed the dogs, he had not befriended them. With no weapon in hand, there was nothing he could do to help. His plan had been to use the dogs, if necessary, only to scare off the monks, but the dogs had gone into a frenzy of attack when the monks slashed at them with their knives. After a few minutes, the screams stopped and the only sound now was from the growling, gnarling dogs tearing at the flesh of their victims.

For Steve, the pursuit from Arizona to New Hampshire to the Aleutian Islands, to Paris, Israel, and finally to Rome, was ended.

*****

Steve shakily climbed the steps to the rectory. He tore off his clothes and wrapped a crude bandage on his upper arm and shoulder. He struggled into a cassock. It was one of Angelo's. He felt like he was wrapping himself in a tent. After a few minutes spent trying to catch his breath and calm down, he poured himself a glass of wine. His hand shook so badly, he had to refill the glass. He slumped into a chair. But he found he couldn't just sit there knowing what had happened down below. A sudden thought: maybe the monks were still alive. He jumped up and called for an ambulance and the police. A few minutes later, the police arrived accompanied by two ambulances. Hearing the sirens, Angelo came running in from the chapel.

"Steve, what in heaven is going on? The carabinieri are here."

"I called them Angelo. I had a struggle with those two Arizona monks down below. I also told them to bring two ambulances because the monks are badly wounded. In fact, I hate to say it but they may be dead."

*****

Half a dozen carabinieri rushed into the rectory. Angelo recognized the inspector—an old friend. They shook hands as Angelo directed the other policemen and the medical team to the stairs that led down to the catacomb.

The police fired shots to scare off the dogs; then, after witnessing the aftermath of the carnage—three dead dogs, blood everywhere, and two partially eaten men, the medical team called for the coroner.

*****

An hour later, the police inspector and the priests were gathered in Angelo's office. The police inspector was puzzled. "Tell me, Father Angelo, you didn't hear anything at all?"

"I was asleep in my room upstairs. I heard nothing."

Addressing Steve, he asked: "What about you, Father?"

Steve, who had slipped into a cassock after he had taken off his torn clothes, tried to appear only mildly disturbed by the event. "I couldn't sleep and as I was sitting here having a late night glass of wine, I heard screaming. It was very faint. Must have been coming from deep down in the catacomb. That's when I called you and the medics."

It was a trap he had set. One he hoped he wouldn't have to use. But it was the only way he could think of to stop a pursuit that could only end in his death.

He thought sardonically: As the old saying goes, 'better them than me'. He realized that he might have complained to the police, but as in the case of New Hampshire and again in the Aleutian Islands, who would believe that two Catholic monks were trying to kill a Catholic priest?

The police inspector, an old friend of Father Angelo, had other questions—unspoken questions: Why had a cot been set up in a tiny, almost hidden alcove near the bottom of the stairs that led down to the third level? Who would want to sleep in the cold, damp, blackness of an underground cemetery? And if, in fact, someone had been sleeping down there, why hadn't the dogs attacked that person?

The inspector was no fool. He knew that the priest, Murphy, who claimed to be innocently sitting in the priesthouse drinking wine in the middle of the night, was surely covering something up. The dust on his shoes and what appeared to be a few drops of blood on the floor below his cassock were the tipoffs. Although the priest must have been down there and knew what had happened, there wasn't any way the inspector could link him to the deaths because the monks had clearly been killed by the wild dogs. He could grill Murphy of course, but what was the point? Besides, if his old friend, Father Angelo, seemed to have accepted the matter calmly, the inspector was content to let it remain a mystery.

"Father Angelo, what should we tell the press? Surely news of the deaths will be reported to the media."

Father Angelo leaned forward and gave the inspector a penetrating look and a pat on the shoulder. The inspector offered a convenient solution: "Let's just say that two American monks were curious about the catacomb and perhaps were looking for a religious relic to take back to a church in America. The affair, unfortunately, resulted in an accidental death."

As the inspector got up to leave, Angelo gave him a grateful bear hug.

*****

The story appeared in the newspapers and on TV the next day. Two American monks, looking for relics, had apparently slipped into the San Callisto Catacomb unobserved. They were attacked and killed by a pack of wild dogs. The police reported that the passageway was awash in the blood of dead dogs and men. There were several unanswered questions: Why were the monks in the catacomb late at night? And why were they carrying knives? Could it be because they knew there could be wild dogs down at the deepest levels? The monks had apparently gone down to the fifth level which was as yet not completely explored. Nothing like this had ever happened in the San Callisto Catacomb which was generally considered safe; however, since many areas and the deepest levels were as yet unexplored, there could be hidden dangers. Visitors were urged to be escorted by an official guide who would lead them only to areas considered safe.

45

Several days after the incident, Steve was off for his morning jog on the Old Appian Way. When he returned, he had taken his shower and was seated at breakfast with Angelo. He saw a puzzled Angelo staring at him. "There was a phone call for you, Steve. It came while you were out running. It was a young woman. She said her name was Janet."

"Did she leave a phone number?"

"No. She said she's attending to some business this morning and can't be reached. Did I mention that she's here in Rome? She said that if you can make it, she will meet you for lunch at noon at the Santa Lucia Trattoria right across from the Colosseum."

*****

She was seated alone at one of the sidewalk tables of the trattoria. The huge Colosseum was framed behind her. She wore a mini-skirt after the fashion of many young Italian women. They revealed a pair of crossed legs that several men at a nearby table were openly admiring. When Steve arrived, the men turned back to their wine glasses and conversation. As Steve looked at her, the noise of the roaring traffic that flooded the area surrounding the Colosseum virtually disappeared. He was almost breathless at her stunning beauty. He had forgotten! His memories of her face had long been out of focus, dimmed by time. But now, her soft blue eyes and flowing chestnut brown hair brought the faded memories back to stunning reality.

As he approached, she smiled. Her smile lit up her face. She extended her hand. He was disappointed, hoping for something more. Her hand felt unbelievably soft and comforting. Since he was casually dressed in a light jacket and slacks, none of the other diners paid any attention. But if he had come in his black suit and Roman collar, there would have been looks from those around them questioning why a priest was having lunch with a beautiful young woman.

For almost a minute, neither of them spoke. He sat, gazing into her eyes, studying her face. Wisps of her hair danced in the breeze.

She was the first to speak. "Before I came to Rome, I went to see your brother. Jonathon told me you're about to be defrocked. You must feel terrible about it. I'm so sorry for you, deeply sorry. Do you plan to appeal it?"

"No. I've come to terms with it," he said quietly. "I will always have my private devotion. They can't take that away from me."

"Jonathon said the tests at BioGene were all negative. You must be happy about that."

"I am, but the church authorities don't really believe it. You know the Catholic Church—everything tends to be either black or white. There is no in-between. Since the BioGene results are probabilistic rather than one hundred percent absolute, the church authorities are playing it safe. And it's more than that. They're still not convinced that a clone is just a twin, even though it is a delayed twin with laboratory involvement. By the way, Janet why are you in Rome? I can't believe you came all this way just to see me." His face showed traces of a smirk.

"You're right," she said, noticing the look on his face. "I came for two reasons—an annulment, and I did hope to see some of the sites of Rome. The committee in Boston turned me down even though there were no children and the marriage was very brief and conducted between two teenagers who didn't know what they were getting themselves into."

"But you went back for a second attempt."

"Yes, under pressure. And that second attempt lasted all of two days."

"I see you're still wearing your wedding ring."

"That's only to keep the wolves away."

Steve was doubtful about the possibility of an annulment. "I know the Vatican has become concerned about the proliferation of annulments in America. That's probably why you were turned down—just another case in the midst of hundreds or possibly thousands of others, even though your case seems to be more worthy than many others I've read about. What will you do if you don't get the annulment? You know you'll never be able to marry in the church."

"Oh, I'm pretty sure I'll get it," she said with a trace of a smile. "In fact, my new Italian lawyer here in Rome says it's in the bag. He has contacts at the Vatican and says they owe him some favors."

Janet ran her fingers lightly through her hair. She took a sip of wine. Since Steve hadn't been served, she put the wine glass to his lips. He sipped without taking his eyes off her.

She sat back and smiled. Then she leaned forward, reached across the table and gently held his hand. He remembered the first time she had done that on their first dinner date in Washington. He remembered how it had electrified him. It still electrified him. From the look on her face, Steve couldn't really tell what was on her mind. Did she still love him or was she just happy to be in Italy and on the way to getting her freedom?

She suddenly stood up and pulled her chair around the table so that now she was sitting right beside him. She leaned close to him; her lips an inch away from his ear as if to whisper a confidence. "Sure and 'tis happy I am to be seeing you again Father Murphy," she whispered playfully, with the touch of a brogue that made him laugh. He remembered the months they had spent at the university when they laughed through lunches with happy banter and imitation brogues.

"But now that I am in Rome at last, there are things I want to see while I'm waiting for the annulment, and I thought you'd be an excellent tour guide. I also want to meet your friend Father Angelo at the catacombs."

"How long have you been here?"

"Three days."

"Three days and you just called me today?"

"I had to spend a lot of time with the attorney. He needed to hear the whole story from the beginning and go through a pile of paperwork from my previous annulment claims. Then yesterday, I sat on the Spanish Steps in the glorious Roman sunshine reading a book of poems by John Keats."

"I suppose you know that he died in the house beside the Spanish Steps. The apartment he lived in is now a museum."

"Why here? Did he love Rome?"

"Not sure. He came here for his health. In the 1800s, some of the British moved to Italy for their health. Keats was one of them. He had TB. I understand the doctors didn't help because they bled him which hastened his death."

"Maybe it was a blessing in disguise."

"Possibly. At the end, Keats' friend Percy Bysshe Shelley visited him just as the landlady was piling all of Keats' furniture in the street to be burned. But as the story goes, Shelley locked the door to Keats' study where his manuscripts were stored. He told the landlady the room was empty. That's how Keats' original manuscripts were saved. When I take you on tour we'll visit the house and you'll be able to read the originals of some of his poems. What else do you want to see?"

"The Colosseum."

"That's easy. It's just down the block."

"Also Trevi Fountain. I want to throw a coin over my shoulder so I'll return to Rome."

"You've come at a good time because they've taken down the plexiglas walls that surrounded it and filled the fountain with water again."

"So, I won't have to stand with my back to the plexiglas and throw a coin high in the air over my shoulder and listen to it clunk in the empty fountain?"

"Make sure it's a euro. They don't use lira any more. And what else do you want to see?"

"Oh, Saint Peters, the Vatican Museum, the Sistine Chapel, the Forum, the Baths of Caracalla, the catacombs, the Appian Way…"

"At this rate," Steve said with a laugh, "we'll be here a month."

Steve had hardly responded when two young men in black suits who appeared to be seminarians came up to the table and stood glaring down at him. He stood up, towering over them. "I remember you guys from Israel," he said. "Have you recovered from that kick in the gut?" he asked the one who seemed to be older.

"This is not the woman who did it," the older one said." Then, glaring at Steve, he muttered, "Your friend, Angelo, of San Callisto, told us you were gone—back to America."

"Angelo told the truth, but you see I've come back and if you think of pulling out that unholy crucifix dagger, I'm going to ram it down your throat."

Oh hearing this, Janet jumped up in horror and stepped away from the table.

"All we want to do is warn you. Since you are not to be a priest by order of the Vatican, do not pose as one. Do not try to say Mass or perform any of the sacraments."

"I will not dishonor the pontiff."

"Now we leave you. We know you were responsible for the killing of the two American monks, but they were disobedient and deserved to die."

Then as the men were walking away, Steve fired a parting shot. "I know that one of you, or one of your guys, stabbed young Peter. And you got away with it. But make sure you go to confession and I hope you get a whole year's penance."

"What was that all about?" Janet said trembling.

"I'll tell you the whole story one of these days," Steve said disgustedly.

"But who were they?"

"They are members of The Knights of Carthage. They supposedly protect the faith—by force, if necessary. They are commonly known as *The Hounds of Rome*."

"They said you killed two American monks."

"I didn't. Ever since I left that monastery in Arizona there were two monks who followed me wherever I went. They were supposedly trying to drag me back but it was a bit more sinister than that. It's true they were killed but as I said, I didn't do it. I will admit that I did some things to protect myself and they paid the price, that's all. I'm sorry if I sound cold-blooded, but as the saying goes, desperate situations call for desperate measures."

*****

Angelo greeted them with open arms and a bear hug for each. "Steve, you didn't tell me you had a beautiful American friend. If I wasn't a priest I would be on bended knee proposing. I'm sure she will want to see the catacombs and since you are one of my official tour guides, I will leave it to you."

After two cups of espresso and nibbles on a mountain of food, Janet was anxious to take the tour.

Steve led her down the narrow staircase to the first level. "Stay close behind," he said as he aimed the flashlight along the passageway describing the crypts they passed.

"Don't worry about that," Janet said. "I'm holding onto the back of your jacket."

Steve stopped, turned, and switched off the flashlight as Janet shuddered in the darkness and pressed up against him. He held her in a tight embrace.

"That was a sneaky way to get me into your arms," she said.

"I know. I love you. I want to be close to you forever."

"Is that a proposal?"

"Yes. When you're free will you marry me?"

"You picked a strange place to propose."

"But, will you?"

In the pitch-blackness of the catacomb Steve waited for what seemed like an eternity.

"Bend over and turn your head so I can give you my answer in your ear."

Standing on tiptoe, she whispered, "Yes."

That one word made up for all the pain and grief he had gone through for the past few years.

*****

Later, they were walking arm-in-arm on the cobblestones of the ancient Appian Way in the warm Roman sunshine that filtered down through the overhanging trees.

"Now to the actual planning," Janet said with a mock voice that sounded like an executive at a corporate board meeting. "We'll be married in Concord. OK?"

"Of course."

"I want to get married in that small Catholic Church in Monument Square just across from the Colonial Inn. We can have the reception at the inn."

"Whatever you say."

"It will be a small wedding—families only. No

ushers or bridesmaids."

"Of course."

"The same for the reception—small. Families only."

"The only way."

"I must say, Steve, you're beginning to sound like a real husband. Next on the list, do we have to live in your family mansion in Wayland?"

"Absolutely not. It has too many unpleasant memories for me. Besides, Jonathon lives there with Marge, a housekeeper and a live-in nurse. Too crowded. We'll find a place in Concord."

"That fits in nicely," she said, "since my new job is at a social service agency in Concord. But what will you do all day? Real estate? Tax work with your brother?"

"No way! I have prospects. I have a friend at Harvard who has offered me a position as an Assistant Professor."

"Good heavens," she said with a laugh. "Don't tell me you're going to teach Latin by total immersion. If you recall, that didn't go over so well at Catholic U."

"You'd be surprised," he replied, raising his head, jutting out his chin and trying to manage a supercilious look even though he wasn't sure it was effective. "I'll have you know," he said with mock haughtiness, "My friend wants me to teach World Religions. And I want you to know that I have become much more tolerant of other religions and I know I can do the job splendidly."

"I'm sure you can," she said apologetically. "I was only kidding about your early days in the classroom."

"Well, I've changed. I've become much more sympathetic to students. And, after we get settled, in the summers when school is out, and when you can take a break from helping your patients get their lives back on track; in summer, I know of a place on a lake in New Hampshire that my brother has turned over to me. This lake has loons that call in the night, and there's this red and white seaplane…"

They stopped in the middle of the road. She was in his arms. She stood on tiptoe and kissed him full on the lips. Her lips were soft, parting and yielding. "You mean a *pond*," she whispered.

CPSIA information can be obtained at www.ICGtesting.com
Printed in the USA
BVOW07s2222081213

338431BV00005B/48/P